# NOTHING HAPPENS IN CARMINCROSS

## BENEDICT KIELY

DAVID R. GODINE · PUBLISHER
BOSTON

First U.S. edition published in 1985 by
David R. Godine, Publisher, Inc.
306 Dartmouth Street, Boston, Massachusetts 02116

Library of Congress Cataloging in Publication Data

Kiely, Benedict.
Nothing happens in Carmincross.

I. Title.
P R6021.I24N6   1985   823'.914   85-70139
I S B N 0-87923-585-3


FIRST EDITION

Printed in the United States of America

*for*
*Emer and Barry*
*in Canada, and for*
*Niall, Alison and Conor John.*

# Contents

# NOTHING HAPPENS
# IN CARMINCROSS

# *Reveille*

History is a nightmare from which I am trying to awake.

We had fed the heart on fantasies,
The heart's grown brutal from the fare.

> —*Extravagant statements by
> two well-known Irishmen.*

I look toward a land both old and young—old in its Christianity, young in its promise of the future: a nation which received grace before the Saxon came to Britain and which has never questioned it; a Church which comprehends in its history the rise and fall of Canterbury and York, which Augustine and Paulinus found, and Pole and Fisher left behind them. I contemplate a people which has had a long night, and will have an inevitable day. I am turning my eye toward a hundred years to come, and I dimly see the Ireland I am gazing on become the road of passage and union between the two hemispheres, and the centre of the world. I see its inhabitants rival Belgium in populousness, France in vigour, and Spain in enthusiasm.

> —*A quite crazy statement
> by a well-known nineteenth-century
> Englishman.*

3

The Ireland which we have dreamed of would be the home of a people who valued material wealth only as a basis of a right living, of a people who were satisfied with frugal comfort and devoted their leisure to things of the spirit; a land whose countryside would be bright with cosy homesteads, whose fields and villages would be joyous with sounds of industry, with the romping of sturdy children, the contests of athletic youths, the laughter of comely maidens; whose firesides would be forums for the wisdom of old age. It would, in a word, be the home of a people living the life that God desires men should live.

*—An euphoric or idiotic statement*
*by a well-known twentieth-century*
*Irishman of Spanish and Irish origins.*

# ONE
## *The Landing*

TEN MINUTES OUT from Kennedy Airport he discovers that the man sitting beside him has no legs. The takeoff is effortlessly accomplished on the seven brandy alexanders he has taken in the El Quixote on Twenty-third Street, and the three taken in the airport to reinforce the seven and for luck, one for the Father, one for the Son, and one for the Holy Ghost: and to keep the kindly, courageous glow from dying inside him. Not till the fire is dying on the hearth, seek we our consolation in the stars. If he had been a glutton and/or if he had had a little more leisure he could have filled his belly and, with twenty brandy alexanders or brandies alexander, he could have flown the Atlantic without benefit of aeroplane. He is a big bald man, but that is still a lot of brandy. Who in hell anyway was Alexander? Which Alexander? The man from Macedon? A good title for a new musical with Julie Andrews double-roling as the lovely Thais and as St. Cecilia, sharp violins proclaim. Or the Alexander from Ulster who did all the generalship for which Montgomery, another man from Ulster, claimed the credit? Once on a road in Donegal he had seen Montgomery's mother stopping people, and handing them Bibles. Or was it the Alexander who owned the ragtime band? Or Alexander Korda, or Alexander Knox who, in a movie, pretended to be President Wilson? Or Alexander Pope?

He sits right in the front of the plane, in the Vippery, in the best seats.

In the tin sheds that were cinemas in his boyhood the best seats were at the back. You went there to Saturday matinees in the fond, seldom or never realised, hope of groping Loreto girls sometimes sprung for the afternoon from the penitentiary of the convent boarding school: the holy house of Loreto carried by angels over land and sea. He unfastens his safety-belt when the girl tells him he is free to do so. A command or permission so worded would, long ago in the dark cinema, have provoked outrageous hilarity: Unfasten your safety-belts, young ladies of Loreto.

The girl in the plane also gives him a large brandy, no alexander, paid for by the airline because he is up front and a VIP, God help us: and little does the girl know and he already awash like the ocean below him. Brandy to brandy, dust to dust, and bugger the broad Atlantic.

In all honesty his safety-belt hasn't been all that exactly fastened. His stomach is too ample, nor is the man beside him a slim boy and, even though the seats in the Vippery are wide like the Brenny plains in old Padraic Colum's poem, the contiguity is embarrassing. Now as he struggles to push the unfastened belt out of the way, he upsets the rug on his neighbour's knees (he is about to think) and sees that his neighbour has no legs and consequently no knees. As well as which, his neighbour clutches in his left hand one of those white enamelled vessels, shaped like a carafe gone askew, oddly called bottles, into which bedridden patients piss. Out of fellow feeling he looks the other way.

A second girl, hostess, stewardess, Irish and lovely, readjusts the rug, removes the bottle, delicately covered with a green cloth, a priestess bearing away a veiled sacrament. The first girl brings him another brandy. The second girl comes back with a fresh bottle or the same bottle emptied, rinsed, sterilised, as good as new. When this act of removal and renewal happens for the third time in thirty or less minutes he follows the girl up to the door of the sanctuary where the bottles are emptied. He says: Look, excuse me, but I spent a year or so in hospital once myself and perhaps I could look after my neighbour's little needs. It might save you a spot of trouble.

They love him, big and bald as he is. There are three of them. Perhaps they love him all the more because of his baldness, fatherliness, grandfatherliness. Also: they hadn't bargained on so many bottles. He goes back to his seat. He empties and cleanses bottles at intervals of about twenty minutes, slowing up somewhat as they sweep eastward, on and on, high up with the sun, toward Europe. Sam Weller said about Job Trotter, who could command instant tears, that 'e 'as a tap in 'is 'ead as is always turned on. His legless neighbour is a perpetual pisser, 'as a tap somewheres else. Every time, almost, he empties a bottle one of the grateful girls gives him another brandy. He eats well when his food comes. As a volunteer bottle emptier he has a larger ration of Beaujolais than any VIP among the Vippers. He could achieve drunkenness but he has a big stomach and a hard bald head: and he is there when he is needed and carries the bottle as if it holds elixir or ichor itself. He remembers the lovely young nurses who had carried bottles, and worse, from his hospital bed. In those enthusiastic days, when the touch of a hand on a knee could result in a horn, it was scarcely possible to insert oneself into the enamelled orifice of the bottle, feeling it carefully first for chips, abrasions, cutting edges, without allowing the mind to toy tenderly with the thought of the fair hands that had rinsed and sterilised it: Pale hands I loved, and all that, beside the Shalimar. The thoughts of youth are long long thoughts, said Longfellow, and a good man too.

—Peoria, Illinois, his neighbour says.

Then a long time afterwards: It was a rail accident, both legs destroyed, the bladder too.

Then much later: Compensation big but what hell good is compensation?

Finally: Relatives in the County Carlow. Haven't seen them in generations. They'll be at the airport. It'll be good to see Ireland again. The last Sunday before I left home there was snow on the ground. A light skiff of snow. The brother and myself coming from Mass. Tracks of a hare in the snow. We followed it over seven fields. Often wondered when I was in the hospital after the accident did the hare realise he had written his death warrant with his own legs.

The only story he can think of to cap that one is vulgar, trivial, and most inappropriate in view of the relationship the fates have set up between himself and his neighbour.

In this rural place a penurious young bank clerk has established good relations with the daughter of a rich farmer. One night when there is snow on the ground he leaves her home from a dance. Next time he calls, the father has him thrown out. So, somewhat shaken, he asks for an explanation.

FARMER: You left my daughter home that snowy night?
YOUNG MAN: I did. So what?
FARMER: You stopped to talk under the chestnut by the avenue gate?
YOUNG MAN: We did.
FARMER: You peed on the snow and wrote your name in pee?
YOUNG MAN: What if I did?
FARMER: It was my daughter's handwriting.

No, under the circumstances and since he has not gauged the delicacy of his neighbour's humor, that story will not do: all the brandy in France wouldn't make it apt. So they don't talk much. So many stories and bons mots seem ipso facto barred. You can't even say the hostesses have lovely legs. He pours out piss and rinses the bottle and drinks free brandy. He pisses now and again himself so as to be in the swim, and watches with mellow eyes the second-hand brandy go the way of all water. He tells his neighbour that he is going north when he gets to Shannon, to the wedding of a niece in a place called Carmincross: also to see his aged mother and, between one thing and another and going to Guatemala once and Mexico and Alaska at other times, and even though it is a swift business to cross the Atlantic nowadays, he hasn't been home for four or five years.

Once he dozes for a full five minutes, but comes coldly awake for that he is the slave of the lamp, the djinn out of the bottle, and has no liberty to sleep. Thereafter his catnaps are briefer, a minute or two at a time, never taking him quite away from the naked sun outside the plane, from the jet-drone that could be a sound in his own body. He nods and starts up again, nods and starts up again, in and out of the same continuous, vinous dream: to be able to do that is a gift he has. He is a young sailor on the deck of a windjammer sailing east for Ireland. The white sails fill, the deck sways like all adventure. The long green-and-purple headlands of Cork and Kerry, the mariner's first glimpse of Europe, reach out over the water to touch and welcome him: Green, green was the shore though the year was near done, high and haughty the capes the white surf dashed upon. A grey ruined convent was down by the strand and the sheep fed afar on the hills of the land. White surf dashed upon, white surf dashed upon.

He is awake again and emptying another bottle.

In hospital long ago the man in the bed beside him, a modest poor bastard, had suffered hell in pain and humiliation every time a nurse gave him the catheter. Then one day, for one happy moment, it seemed that the waters, stirred by an angel, were about to flow of their own accord: but just when the sufferer was ready to shout his joy to the ward, in came his maiden aunt or something, all flowers and fruit and lucozade and chocolates, and talked and talked nonstop for an hour, and the man was too polite to beg for the bottle while she was there: and the fountain, frustrated, sank back into the earth. When she left, backside bobbing and bouncing, smiling aleft and aright even at the guy in the corner by the door who had had all the skin burned off his back and sides and was having himself resurfaced at a square inch a week, when she finally left, her nephew had to call for the catheter in a voice cracked with agony and shame. There is a tide in the affairs of men. It must at least be less painful to be a perpetual pisser.

—Not long now, he says to his legless neighbour. Two hours to Shannon.

Delicately he nibbles or nipples at a new brandy and is back again on the windjammer but not, this time, as the young sailor. He is old, feeble, and thin for Christ's sake, his arm around the young sailor's shoulders, his boy's voice that had long ago learned the poem from a schoolbook he can see, open and dog-eared, on the little table beside the brandy, his boy's voice coming out of the aged body and asking the sailor to hold him up so that he may after all these years see Ireland: As a starveling might stare at the sight of a feast. Forty years work a change: when I first crossed the sea, there were few on the deck who could grapple

with me: but my youth and my pride in Ohio went by and I've
come back to see the old land e'er I die. He sank by the hour and
his pulse 'gan to fail as we swept by the headland of storied Kinsale. . . .

Kinsale, Kinsale, and he is wide awake, grasping his brandy
with expert cunning, muttering to himself, sensing the sweet
South that breathes upon a bank of violets, stealing and giving
odour. It is the perfume of the first girl. She is bending over him.
She is smiling. She says: Do you come from Kinsale?

There has been something in his brief dream about his father's
funeral. But that could not have been taking place on the deck of
a windjammer. There has been something, also, about an old
black Virginian mama or great-grandmama who had once asked
him were there black servants in Ireland: all over the world, she
thought, privileged white people had black servants. Dreams cast
a wide net.

—No, he says, much further north is my place. But I do like
Kinsale. The history, the headlands, the long twisting inlets, the
sunset on the Bandon River.

—It's a swinging place now. You'd hardly know it with tourists, and yachts and expensive cabin cruisers. New shops, all
artsy-craftsy.

He agrees that he mightn't know it. She has a Cork accent. He
hasn't been in Cork or Kinsale, in West Cork, for fifteen years.
She wears an engagement ring. She will be married next spring.
He tells her that he is going north to the wedding of a niece, his
favourite niece, one of five sisters: Once I was in London with her,
he says. We met an old friend of mine who said with a leer that he
supposed this would be my favourite niece. And she said: It so
happens that I am his favourite niece.

They laugh at that and the man with no legs laughs with them.
It isn't really noticeable yet but he knows they are going down,
paying the first nodding respects to the earth that has nourished
them: crowded talkative Cork, fertile Carlow and the great Barrow River, far Fermanagh, a filigree pattern of lake and water-
meadow hooked on at the west to the lonely Cuilcha mountains.
He empties another bottle. He says to himself: This must be my
last brandy.

For he has promised to wheel the neighbour out to meet the

waiting relatives, and to be drunk in charge of a wheelchair is bad news. He has no catnaps now, no dreams good or bad, just gentle freewheeling memories, a boy on a bicycle again, as the plane slackens speed, tightens reins so that you can feel it, as if it wanted to go back to the smells and confusion of New York. Down there below the clouds the Shannonside air will still be clean and breathable: he'll be able to pump the gasolene and whatnot from his lungs.

Down we go to Ireland, spokes spinning and humming: never when I was young did I dream I'd freewheel down a hill thirty thousand feet high: six Scotch firs, humpbacked, bald patches on their heads, gesticulating in the wind in a gossiping huddle at the top of the hill: a winding river in the valley below and a white creamery with red-rimmed windows and a high shiny cylindrical chimney ejecting puffs of steam: thirty-three years ago, writing a fragment of doggerel verse in my head as three of us, school friends, reunited, scorch down that hill: All day long our whirring wheels sing their song, and there steals on the air every scent of the spring. Oh, the tingle of wind in the hair as we speed without need down the hills: and the rush and the race and the push and the pace, and three friends parted long, met again in the spring: and the laugh and the chaff and the song never end . . .

And do you remember an inn, Miranda, and so on and so forth. . . .

The second girl goes up the plane saying: Fasten your safety-belts.

God knew it hadn't been much of a poem but it was still a golden memory.

He knew a funny fellow once who said he always had a horn when he freewheeled. But although now, sinking to Shannon, he considers that that is a fairly comic idea, it is hardly the class of a joke he can pass on to his deprived neighbour. Christ alone knows what the sufferer lost when he lost his legs.

That day, thirty-three years ago, they were cycling to visit an old man who thirty-three years further back had been a fervent language teacher, a timthire, a messenger, a courier, an angel bringing on a bicycle good news from the Gaelic League: giving to such Irishmen as wanted it the gift of their own language, or the language of the forefathers of some of them. *Gan teanga, gan tír,* without a language, without a motherland, Ireland Gaelic, Ireland free, and more besides. That was when fighting for Ireland had been a clean business, the handful of brave men with muskets and rosary beads standing up to privilege and the might of empire. Patrick Pearse surrendered in 1916 to prevent further slaughter of the civilians of Dublin: the heroes of the Seventies aren't so choosy. John O'Leary, the Fenian whose nobility had affected the poet Yeats, said that there were things a man might not do, not even to save his country: he meant telling lies, being dishonourable, not being a gentleman. Blessed are the gentlemen for they shall make no mark in urban guerrilla warfare.

The old man they cycled to see had, as a boy, herded his father's cattle, found a sheltered corner behind a dry-stone wall and under a hawthorn hedge, pure pastoral, cars or car-bombs unheard of, studied there the language out of a tattered grammar, so that later for the joy and glory of it he could cycle the roads, passing on his knowledge, saving his country by syntax and sweet sound, folk wisdom, songs, folktales lopped off from sagas. Cent per cent, the old man kept saying, *fuair mé cent per cent in achan sgrudú a dtearn mé ariamh:* I got cent per cent in every exam I ever did.

Dear glorious St. Patrick, a happy memory, a simple vision. The object of terrorism is to terrorise. Kill or maim the people so as to make them free. The naked sun is gone. They are floundering in cloud.

—Cent per cent, he says to his neighbour or to nobody in particular.

Where, in the name of Christ crucified and the water that flowed from his side, does the piss come from? Is the man simply dissolving? He drinks little or nothing, one small brandy, two cups of coffee, a glass of water.

On the bridge by the creamery in that lost valley the three of us danced a reel, right in the middle of the road. The river laughed away from us. The Scotch firs on the skyline danced with us. The puffs of white steam shot metronomically up from the creamery's silver cylinder and faded into blue. Richness of grass and cattle. No traffic on the road to disturb us. The traffic congestion that year was in France, in the neighbourhood of Dunkirk.

—Cent per cent, he says again.

And thinks of the journey he will make from Shannon up through the beloved west, and finds himself humming the tune that goes with the words of an old patriotic ballad: Forget not the boys of the heather where marshalled our bravest and best. When Ireland was broken and bleeding, she looked for revenge to the West.

Broken and bleeding, like the man in Peoria when the train rolled over him.

Forget not the boys of the heather, the shadowy folk heroes who live forever just a little inch away from the margins of the pages of history: Rody McCorley who went to die at the Bridge of Toome, on a day one hundred and seventy-five years ago: the men of the West who marched with Humbert's French to a brutal end at Ballinamuck: the reaper of Glanree by the Camlin waters brown in the county of Longford: Kelly the boy from Killane in rebel Wexford: the boys who beat the Black and Tans, the boys from the County Cork.

To honour the patriot dead there is in a square in Dublin city a spendid symbolic statue of the children of Lír casting off their enchanted swan-shapes, awaking from centuries of dream to decrepit old age and death: ironic symbol for an old-new nation. Nowadays the heroes, escaped from the heather, blow the legs off girls in city cafés. Were the bladders of the victims also affected? The ballads may have to be rewritten. Another sculptor in coming times may remember the maimed: Laocoon and his sons and the writhing sea serpent, tortured limbs straining, jagged mutilations showing, blood flowing like his neighbour's perpetual piss: they lost their legs that Ireland might be free.

The plane shudders, shakes him out of the brandy torpor, and Ireland is there below him, flat and marked in fields, green and brown, bog and marsh by the silver estuary. One small cloud, cast out by the herd, limps and melts away toward the northeast. He says to his neighbour: Lindbergh had a better view.

He is leaving the man forever and is now madly anxious to say something to him by which he will be remembered. He can hardly ask the poor devil to keep in touch: Write and tell me if your legs grow again, if the ever-springing fount of Helicon dries up. So he talks of Charles Lindbergh who had a better view of

Ireland than they have now because Lindbergh flew in low, as good as or better than coming in by sea: green green were the shores though the year was near done: and in that movie they made about the Spirit of St. Louis, Lindbergh and people in cinemas all over the world could see the details of fences and green fields, and the sheep who fed afar on the hills of the land breaking and running in terror before the sound of his low-flying plane. Nowadays the sheep down there by Shannon wouldn't bloody well bother to lift their heads.

On the night that Lindbergh made it to Orly he had stood for hours outside the window of a greengrocer's shop where the latest news was posted as it came in on the greengrocer's radio. Radios weren't all that plentiful then. Similar waiting groups in thousands of little towns in Europe and the States, and thousands of shouts for the lone flyer: it had seemed a wonderful thing at the time. . . .

And so on: as they circle into Shannon and the sun is shining and he can see on the grass the shadow of the plane. His neighbour isn't responding, isn't listening much, which momentarily annoys him. But, dear God, the man or what's left of him must be a bundle of nerves: looking fearfully ahead to the horror of moving or being moved, meeting relatives, wondering will he wet himself before he gets out of the airport. At home does he have a tube attached, all day long Maryanne?

When they land he waits until the poor hoor is fitted into the wheelchair, then, with a ground hostess walking beside him, he wheels the chair to the relatives from the fertile land of Carlow. Clean air and the acts of standing up and walking make him aware of the brandy. Madly he wants to sing as he pushes and the wheels turn: Curse and swear, Lord Kildare, Féach will do what Féach will dare, now Fitzwilliam have a care, fallen is your star low. Up with halberd out with sword, on we go, for by the Lord, Féach McHugh has given the word: Follow me up to Carlow.

He restrains himself. The watchful son of Hugh of the Byrnes in the wild Wicklow mountains descends like God, in Glenmalure, on the soldiers of the first Elizabeth and Earl Grey and the poet, Edmund Spenser, casting his cold eye on, as two other poets said, the rough rugheaded kerne which live like venome where no venome else, but only they, have privilege to live. Meaning us, the bloody Irish, reptiles in an island, our own, out of which our patron saint has driven the more conventional reptiles. What would the lovely hostess walking by his side make out of this line: Do not let a Saxon cock crow out upon an Irish rock?

For every cock there must be sometime, somewhere, a bottle or other container.

Oh would, said that great Elizabeth when she looked around her and at the courtier, Essex, bogged down to his arse, as the pitiful end of empire is at this moment, in the quagmires of Tyrone, oh would, said she, that I were crusted not cleft.

That woman, now, could speak English.

If he explains all that to the hostess he'll be arrested and rightly so: for here he is, a big bald man in his middle fifties, home to see his aged mother and to attend the wedding of a favourite niece, and just now performing an act of charity, wheeling a maimed man to meet those Carlovian relatives who do not seem to be impressed by him or his charitable act. There seems to be a woeful conglomeration of them. But then his eyes are warm and weepy and he may be seeing double, or triple. All the women are solemn and dressed in black mourning clothes. For two legs left in far Peoria? Or for some other deceased relative? In some families somebody is always dying. He speaks a few words. They seem to respond. The ground hostess is cheerful and talkative. He shakes several hands. Being Irish country-cute they are well aware that he's boozed.

Then he is alone, conscious of his size and suddenly of his false teeth, swaying slightly in that crowded place. The Empire State Building has to give a little at the top. If it didn't it would collapse. A loudspeaker, as always in airports, is shouting unintelligible words. He kisses the three girls from the plane as they walk past. They are lovely: and grateful, not for the kisses but for the gallons of urine emptied into some bottomless pit in the airliner. He watches the Carlow contingent diminish, fade into mist, led by the ground hostess. A gaunt, gigantic, black-gowned woman wheels away the remnant of a man. What hell good is compensation? What all else went when the sad man's legs were sheared away? All that liquid has to come from somewhere. But by what conduit?

Half-ashamed of such unneighbourly speculations he goes into the bar, orders a long cold lager, nibbles peanuts, listens to somebody's transistor saying that three British paratroopers have been blown up and killed near Crossmaglen in the County Armagh. One of them has been identified as Warrant Officer Peter Jones, aged thirty-six, of the second battalion, the parachute regiment: a group of men who have not succeeded in endearing themselves to the political and religious minority in the six counties of the northeast. Peter was married and came from Aldershot, Hampshire, to be blown up at Crossmaglen, Armagh. The innocent young thooleramawn in the ballad went guilelessly to the fair and encountered the crooked horse dealers from Crossmaglen: It wasn't the lads from Shercock nor the boys from Ballybay, but the dalin' men from Crossmaglen put whiskey in me tay. The smallest drop I only took when up the ructions rose: I stood up like a hero and slaughtered friends and foes.

Also the transistor says that the first man to escape from the British internment-without-trial camp at Long Kesh near Belfast has come south of the border, as in down Mexico way, and married a beauty queen in Dundalk. As the bride, formerly queen of a maytime festival, arrived outside the cathedral, some onlookers greeted her with shouts of: Up the Provisional I.R.A.

A Republican leader was among the guests and posed with the bride for photographers. Recently released from the Irish internment camp on the Curragh of Kildare, famous for horses, short grass, sheep, soldiers, and internees, he said he was feeling better after a holiday in Connemara. Asked where they would spend their honeymoon the bride smilingly said: It is a secret.

The reception was held in the Imperial Hotel. . . .

Doubtless when Ireland will be free from the centre to the sea the name of the hotel will be altered.

The bride, unlike another bride recently blown up in a Belfast restaurant, had the benefit of her legs. . . .

And by beating Leeds, the favourites, Sunderland, have won the English Cup. . . .

When he makes to pay for his lager he discovers that he has no money on his person, English, Irish, or American. He no longer knowns anybody in the airport as he did five years ago. But he is at home again in Ireland of the Welcomes; warrant officers going up with a bang: Maytime beauties smiling off to secrecy with escaped internees.

Isn't he, anyway, the head bottle washer from the Vippery?

—No sweat sir, says the barman. I'll ring Mr. Burns for you myself. As a matter of fact he was in here last night on the way back from a hoteliers' conference in Dublin.

Robinson Crusoe is back on his island. The first thing to do is to find a roof to cover him, a bed to rest on. The barman says: Mr. Burns can't come himself. He has the house full of Americans. But the hotel car is on the way. He says to say you're welcome back and all is well.

—Except for the widow Jones, in Hampshire.

—Yes, sir.

—The paratrooper's widow. She must have loved him.

—Bloody awful business, sir. Where will it end? They're astray in the head, up there.

—I only took the smallest drop then up the ructions rose.

—Yes sir. Build a wall around the Six Counties, I often say, let them settle it among themselves.

—And slaughtered friends and foes. A last lager. And then a long sleep.

—Yes sir.

From the door of the bar the three girls from the plane, which will now fly on to Dublin, wave a final farewell. How long will it be again before a passenger needs the bottle? He thinks: And slaughtered friends and foes, and friends and foes.

From the coloured collage pasted on a square of cardboard, three feet by four, and spread out on the bed, Mr. Burns reads: Is there a plot to overthrow British gin? Help free America of stuffy noses. Eighty-six proof, it helps prevent diaper rash, no rot, no warp, no sag, no burn, no termites. Do you have to taste all 208 to find the one Scotch that's smoothest? So you think water is a moisturiser. Come where the flavour is. Happy St. Patrick's day to the Jolly Green Giant.

—Big and fat and bald and Irish and cheerful. That's why those good young women call me the Jolly Green Giant.

—I can see that, says Mr. Burns who has known him for a long time and in many moods.

—After that TV ad, you know. Peas and beans and cauli-
flowers. Vegetables.

—Oh, very apt. Sprouts, too, I suppose. And cucumbers. Symbolic.

They laugh. They are old friends. Mr. Burns, who doesn't
drink, has allowed him one nightcap. It is exactly six o'clock in
the morning. On the collage, which is unrolled and extended on
one of the two beds in the hotel bedroom, the Jolly Green Giant
sits on a stool and tosses six green balls into the air. The six green
balls make a sort of inverted rainbow linking an exhortation to
Mervyn, to live it up: and two juxtaposed magazine clippings
that say: Danger, Teenagers, and, By Golly, I love them.

Mervyn is his given name.

—A young woman from Nashville put it together as a joke for
St. Patrick's Day. They also put an alligator in my bed.

—A whatilater?

—A very little alligator.

—Nevertheless. He did, I hope, no permanent damage. We old
chaps must hold on to the little we have left. You will find no
reptiles in the bed in this hotel unless you bring them along with
you: and only with my permission. I own the fishing rights. If
fishing is what you do for reptiles. Shooting, more likely. Rough
shooting.

The bay is blinding with reflected morning sunshine so that his
watery eyes cannot see the sickle-shaped strand. But from the
block of headland beyond the bay, Andy More's tower rises up
out of morning mist and the dazzle of light and sea-spray. It
seems to be quite close to them and moving: an oblong, headless,
armless, sable giant, one great eye in his chest where sunlight
flows through an aperture designed, or created by decay, in the
stone. He says: The tower's moving.

—Air tiredness, Mr. Burns says. And a bellyfull of brandy.

—A swim and a walk on the sand would be the thing.

—Dear God, Mervyn, do you know what time it is? Six in the
morning.

—I've just descended from a world without time. Inhabited by
legless people who pissed all the time. An eternity of piss.

—God pity him, Mr. Burns says. And a lot like him up north
now. There was one yesterday. A British soldier. Booby-trapped

in a house in Derry at the corner of Foyle Road and Brooke Street. Searching for explosives and the explosives found them, three of them. Lost both legs, Warrant Officer Robert Johnson, age thirty-four; from Gateshead, Durham, a wife and two children.

—And half a husband. All for Ireland.

—No end to it. Not that the army are acting the gentleman. But.

—Our own crowd.

—Exactly. We were misled to expect better. The heroic past and all that. Everything you were reared to believe in misled you to expect better.

—Car-bombs. What do you drive? Slaughter friends and foes.

Mr. Burns is five years older and long ago, at school, was a sort of elder brother. The years close the gap but the memory remains. He has red hair, closely cropped to diminish the creeping greys and whites. He has the routine dark jacket and striped pants of his guild, trade, craft, or profession. He is suave, as you or his clients might expect him to be. He is also scholarly: which is not compulsory in hotel management yet not uncommon: they meet a lot of people, have odd moments at which books can be read, and good chairs to sit on. He says: Sleep now for six hours. Pray to your guardian angel. As my mother used to say.

He draws the curtains against the blinding bay, the morning, the moving tower. He says: I'll take this with me. Not Solomon in all his glory had your luck. A thousand young women between the ages of eighteen and twenty-two.

This, a large-format book, is the illustrated yearbook of a women's college in the semi-Deep South. By way of New York and some misery he has come from a never-never land of dogwood and forsythia and chipmunks and young people, and is going by way of the province of Connacht to the mountainy peace of Carmincross. He knots the cord of his pyjamas and goes backwards and downwards with a groan and a crash. The light in the room is the colour of peaches in syrup. By way of New York and misery, he thinks: and Mr. Burns at the door, broad yearbook in hand, and with the empathy of the days when they shared the same lodgings above a pub in a sidestreet in a provincial town, turns and says: Where is she now?

—New York.

—Have you got the money?

—Sure.

—Then let her cool her backside for a bit.

—She won't find it easy. She's living with that sailor.

—That should keep her quiet.

—He's not exactly a sailor. He's not a bad guy.

—Worse luck for him.

—He's no fool.

—He'll find her out all the sooner, so.

—He goes down to some hellhole in the Caribbean where the tankers rest up between voyages. Temperatures of a hundred and something. They go down into the bellies of the tankers. Swab and scour them out and slick the ocean. Big money.

—They'd need it.

—It breaks a man by the time he's forty. Or sooner. He's thirty-two. He aims to make a stack and get out in three years.

He is talking to a door that has closed quietly. Drowning in peaches and syrup and brandy he sleeps for five and a half hours.


A pleasant plump lady I know says that if you've been drinking you should not lie down level on the bed. That way you only get drunker because the booze goes like a torrent to the brain. You should, instead, prop or tie yourself into a sitting position. There's a theory also that in drink you don't dream. Which is why, when the drink is dying along the veins, the weird dreams come tripping over each other. All that could or could not be true.

It is true, though, that Sunderland have won the English Cup.

He lies lazily for an hour, soaking in the coloured light, his eyes half-open, casually remembering past loves, which after a certain age can be as entertaining as the expectations of the young: seeing simultaneously on the ceiling a changing mathematical pattern, the precise moves of a soccer game. In the lodgings over the public-house in the sidestreet Mr. Burns, not then Mr. Burns but a schoolboy, had kept in a huge heavily stoppered glass jar a substance called ale-plant or bees-wine. There was a fungus that you fed with hot water and sugar, and treacle or syrup. The end product, as the management people say, was a drink that tasted like whiskey. One day, to the scientific delight of all, the jar burst like a bomb. Fermentation? Gas? They were playing soccer that day for a team they called Corinthians. At school they played Gaelic football. But Corinthians, above politics and national or sectarian prejudice, played against the Protestant Academy or, in the Soldiers' Holm, against teams of British soldiers who mostly seemed to come from Wexford.

The decent natives of New Guinea had all sorts of variant ideas about the design and colouring of the stripes, patches, and spots they painted on their faces and elsewhere. In a pub in Dublin Brendan Behan roared at a man he, clearly, didn't like: You're banned by the Gaelic Athletic Association. Masturbation's a foreign game.

If people couldn't get together about the way to paint a face or kick a football, it was unlikely that they'd get together about anything else.

Sunderland, anyway, have won the English cup and it's time for me to get up and go out and look at Ireland.

Never knew exactly what ale-plant or bees-wine was but, as Burns brewed or concocted or distilled it, it tasted like the best whiskey, and that day long ago the thick glass jar burst like a bomb, and Sunderland have won the English Cup, and a sixteen-year-old boy, Tommy Kinsella, an apprentice gardener from Cork city, has blown himself to bits on the Border while laying mines for Ireland. Strange seed, strange fruit, let me lay you a mine for Ireland, lord, and you're nearer God's heart in a garden than anywhere else on earth. His colleagues in patriotic bombery say that the cause of his death was a premature explosion, you might call it an early spring: and the old sow still eats her farrow. A Protestant farmer called Frank Kedoo, a member of the Ulster Defense Regiment, has been shot dead while leaving creamery cans at the end of the boreen.

He switches off the radio, inset to the table between the two beds on one of which the jolly green giant still juggles his balls. The radio has given him two pastoral scenes on which he can meditate while shaving. He lathers and hums: Day's work, week's work as I go up and down, there are many gardens all about the town.

A witless boy will no longer grow begonia or sweetpea in Cork city on the steep slopes above the banks of my own lovely Lee.

Down the boreen or lane to the main road, to the rough wooden platform where the milk is left for collection by the milk-factory trucks, comes the honest farmer, silvery jingling splashing cans on a trailer or, perhaps, a horsecart. His murderers crouch behind the hedge.

Razor poised, he stops and sees the scenes in the mirror.

From the never-never land of dogwood and young women glistening by the blue pool, he is returning to his idyllic native Irish fields.

Wasn't there an old crazy comic movie in which the fall guy from the audience clambers right into the screen, into the action. The cameras cut, dissolve, pan, make montage, do all the things that cameras and film editors do. The scene changes again and again. The clown from the real world is there all the time, falling over himself, miraculously dodging disaster, nobody seeming to be aware of his existence.

Patting a shaving lotion on his shaven jowl and bald head he smirks at himself in the mirror and remembers how, as a boy, he had once called his father Baldy and how that kindly man had knocked him down with one well-directed blow. Every man has his sensitivity. He turns on the radio again and roots for a clean shirt. A voice says in Irish that *Adriano agus a chuid,* the magic accordions of Adriano, will play that it's springtime again and violets are blooming. Also, a U.S. diplomat has been kidnapped in Mexico.

Alone in a corner of the lounge Mr. Burns is having his after-lunch coffee and feasting his eyes and imagination on a thousand women. Yet, as a good hotel manager should be, he is also unostentatiously watching everything that goes on around him: the people coming and going and who and what they are, the girls in reception and in the gift and curio shop, the porters, the short-skirted waitresses orbiting with coffee and booze. He is famous for his ability to pick presentable waitresses. His corner is strategically placed. Through a wide doorway and a glass wall or partition he can also see, if he wants to, a good third of the dining room. That sharp, blue eye, the unhurried precise voice, the smooth-shaven, highly coloured face, the unshakeable good-humoured politeness are, together, more effective than the roar of a sergeant-major. He says: Deborah would like to see you. She married since you went away. But it didn't stick. So I took her back. This here was a wonderful stable you had.

He rubs his hand over two glossy pages of the yearbook. The college belle of the year has just been photographed as queen of the May court. She is tall, blonde, and southern and, all in white, gloves to the elbows, splendid gown, hair piled high, stands with her back to a wall-size mirror. In the shadow of the mirror can be seen glimmering shoulders and a great white bow over her buttocks. Facing her from the opposite page are three of her maids of honour or ladies in waiting, Ellen and Eden and Susan, and, as Mr. Burns lingeringly turns the pages, there are Ginny and Mary and Gail, Marian, Isabel, Carol, Liz, Ray and Jackie, Alice, Betsey and Suzanne, Susan, Grier, and Brooks, Katie and Candy. The sun is bright on southern lawns and gardens. Black servants in white jackets stand by the trestles of soft cool drinks. Snapshots are taken by enthusiastic fathers. His jest that the ceremony should conclude with the ritual deflowering of the queen by the chaplain, who is a celibate Baptist, could perhaps have been better chosen. But then he is Irish, and acceptably odd. The chaplain laughs bravely: he is a man of the world and open-ended toward any religion, race, or nation. He has been known to say quite frequently to the young women: Cannot we know God?

—That's a lot of women, Mr. Burns says.

He closes the book, balances it on the palm of his hand as if he were weighing the entire thousand: I'd take any one of them on the staff. What happens to them all, year after year?

—They grow older. Two million Americans get divorced every year.

—So what? There's a lot of Americans and divorce is available. Keeps the stuff circulating, old boy. Will you eat now?

—I'll see Deborah first.

—Eat then in half an hour. And I might walk the strand with you. For health, old boy. Deborah's checking up in the public bar.

Something at the reception desk has attracted his attention

and Mr. Burns is away, easy perfect acceleration, no fumes, revving noises, or backfiring. Smoothly and quietly across the deep carpet.

*Newsweek,* purchased at the magazine stand in the centre of the lounge, tells me that: The young, the old, the weak, the strong, Protestants and Catholics alike, all have felt the cruel sting of the violence in Ulster. Since riots in Belfast and Londonderry touched off the current sectarian strife four years ago, the fighting has taken an awesome toll: 841 people dead – including 189 British soldiers – 10,000 wounded and 101 million dollars already paid out for property damage.

The picture beside the news story shows a young father carrying his baby's white coffin out of a church.

For Ulster read the six counties of the northeast of Ireland: that's the way I was reared to look at it. My Ulster was always the Nine Counties. The little details we bother about.

Wounded is a mild word. Count among the wounded: people blinded by rubber bullets, people beaten, degraded, and tortured by troops and special branch police, those who were kneecapped by gunmen: or those girls who, while one of them was shopping for her trousseau, had their legs blown off in the Abercorn restaurant in Belfast. Or a postman on his rounds, blinded by a letter-bomb intended for the mother of a Royal Ulster constable.

Adding dead and wounded the grand total is 10,841. Multiply that by ten since, on a moderate average, each happening may affect at least ten lives. Total comes to 108,410 cases of varying degrees of human suffering, strife, strain, misery. And what of the men who did the deeds? Will they remember them in time to come? And how?

Now, may we say that all action should be judged by its consequences in human happiness or misery? Did Jesus know what he was talking about when he said he came not to send peace but a sword? To send fire upon the earth? Dangerous talk. Mahomet took him at his word. A sunstruck Jew. A Koreishite from a more killing climate. Was the revolutionary love of Jesus to give his life for others? Not to kill the present for the sake of an improbable future? Except the grain falling into the ground die. Oh bullshit!

Christ stopped at Eboli and was never next or near the Abercorn restaurant. And Deborah is checking up in the old public bar.

But the bar, the one part of the house that has not yet been touched by tourism or modernisation, is in an advanced state of bedlam. To get to it from the lounge he goes by a long corridor. Lush vegetation of wall-to-wall carpet thins out to blue, antiseptic linoleum, then to stone steps descending, then to a black-flagged curving corridor, stone-walled, whitewashed, glimmer of bottles in caves to either hand. The black flagstones have been chiselled from the back slopes of the great cliffs of Moher. Another stone stairway ascends to noise and singing. An easier but less intimate way to get there is to walk in through the doorway from the street.

Deborah is hard at work and three barmen to aid her. But busy as she is, she sees and knows him. She should. But, all the same, he is gratified. As adroitly as a stout man may he works his way to the counter. She leans to him and, holding on to a beer handle for leverage, kisses him welcome. The crowd cheers. She has his drink ready for him, the usual she says, a ball of malt and a cold Coke, a lethal and/or medicinal, unethical, international mixture, only to be taken on a bad morning nor, perhaps, even then. She tells him it's a crazy party: and when it's over and all quiet they'll have time to talk: and that he's looking lovely and has lost weight. His teeth are hurting him as always when he hears nice things and knows they can't be true. He grasps what Deborah has called the usual – although he knows he shouldn't and Mr. Burns would disapprove – and eases away from the counter into mid-current. Two of the party, faces flaming with merriment, ask him what he's having. He says that he's working well at the moment but that he'll join them for the company: What is this? What are you all at? Is it a funeral?

Deborah apart, there isn't a woman in the bar. The walls are all zany, tessellated reflections caught living in long, lettered mirrors, antiques and curios now, advertising whiskeys and ales long gone off any market. Forty men or so are enjoying themselves and making a lot of noise.

—No, 'tisn't a funeral. Though, mind you, I've been at funerals

that were every bit as merry. But they were exceptionally successful funerals.

So much from a tall lean-faced man with bushy eyebrows. He
is in morning dress. So are six or seven others. The rest are in dark
lounge suits, a large number of waistcoats and watch chains:
strong farmers, well-established merchants from small towns,
their sons and nephews and sons-in-law.

—A wedding then?

—No, 'tisn't a wedding. Although it might be, in a class of a
way.

That from a young broad-shouldered fellow with sleek black
hair. A glass of mineral water in his fist. By the cut of him a
county footballer or hurler.

—Then if it's not a funeral nor a wedding, what is it? It's not a
football match.

—At this time of the day? Yerra man, where do you come
from?

—An airplane from America.

—There it is, you see. He don't know day from night.

A dozen faces are round him, friendly and laughing: but pro-
vocative.

—Guess, they say, and all the drinks are on us.

—A christening?

—There hasn't been a child born in these parts these twenty-
five years. There does be a blight on the husbands.

For what then, he asks himself, do his Christian countrymen
normally make holiday: for births, marriages, deaths, for football
or hurling games, cattle fairs, gatherings of folk musicians, commemorations of patriots who are gone, boys, gone: and, in parts
of the preaching North, in honour of William of Orange, or something. In his mind he runs his way through the list, tries out a few
guesses for fun, is shouted down with great laughter and, finally,
put out of pain by the tall, bushy-browed, lean-faced man: 'Tis
an ordination. This blessed day we manufactured a priest.

—A class of a wedding I told you, says the footballer. He married the Church the way nuns are the bride of Christ.

From somewhere outside the circle somebody shouts: He must
have a high time with the reverend mothers.

—Respect for the cloth, says somebody else.

But the laughter rattles the bottles behind the bar. He finishes his drink and, as if by radar, another is fitted into his fist. He is beginning to like the company: Where is he now? The ordinand, I mean.

—The what is it?

—The young priest.

—Oh, we left him in a private room with the women. Blessing all before him.

—Wouldn't you bring him in for a drink?

—Well you see, the way it is now there's a new rule from Rome since Pope John, the aisy-going fellow died. The clergy aren't allowed to drink until they're in full charge of a parish and can pay for their round. Unless, of course, they have private means. Or their fathers will pay for them. And Himself here is very tight-fisted.

He has been so long away from a Catholic church, in Ireland or anywhere else, that the thought of an ordination has not occurred to him. He knows now, for the first time since the disorientation of flying, that he is really back at home in Ireland: the fleering abrasive talk is only a sort of mask for a half-ashamed reverence. As a stranger in that particular place he is careful not to join in the mockery: by saying, for instance, that he thought they'd given up making priests altogether these days, not only in Ireland but in Rome itself, that the ones they made now seemed to suffer from planned obsolescence. His new merry friends might not assault him, but the fun might fade or the topic change.

—Jokes aside, says Himself. But after this I'll have every reason for being tightfisted. This caper today will cost me a thouand pounds.

He's a quieter man than the rest of them, either by nature or by the thought that he's paying the bill. He stands a little apart. Now and again he glances, under his eyelids, at his reflection in one of the more translucent, uncluttered pools by one of the long, lettered mirrors: a handsome, solidly built man with neat moustache and healthy, well-filled cheeks. He wears black-rimmed, executive spectacles, and drinks a very good Scotch. When he takes off the spectacles and, in spite of the financial distress of sanctifying a son, smiles pleasantly, there is something familiar about his face.

—Begod Bill, says the footballer, you'd marry a daughter for less.

—And, says Bushy Eyebrows, you wouldn't have to finance her for the foreign missions. And you'd get some return for your outlay: in the way of grandchildren. And a hearth to warm your feet at in your declining years.

—He's a smart young man all the same, a comforter says. You've reason to be proud.

A tubby red-faced man comes forward: He won't be long smart then. Didn't he grovel on his belly before the altar the day before yesterday and take a vow to remain ignorant for the rest of his natural life.

The devil can assume the oddest shapes. There's a lull in the jollification. A cold wind blows into the mirrored barroom, even if the sun is visibly rejoicing in the street outside. He thanks the god of wanderers that he, a stranger, hasn't made that remark or anything like it. His glass is empty. The footballer, looking as if he has just taken a boot in the navel or worse, says that old Jeremiah is at it again. Bushy Brows, looking extremely serious, says that it's a case of Jeremiah by name and Jeremiah by nature.

—Would you like to meet him, says Himself. My son, I mean. And don't take Jeremiah too seriously. He's my brother-in-law.

—He may be a brother-in-law of mine, Jeremiah says. But I'm no brother-in-law of his.

This remark, crude seemingly, seems also to be familiar to all: and is accepted with a return to laughter.

Jeremiah to his right and Himself to his left, he is escorted back along the cellar passageway to the main body of the hotel. To Deborah he waves a temporary farewell. She will do or, for old time's sake, be done, later.

—Those were all my wife's relatives, says Himself. Solid farming people. All except Jeremiah here who's a multiple renegade. Good Catholics all who would drink Loch Lomond dry. I live in Dublin myself. Come to see me when you get there.

—In a new suburbia, Jeremiah says. American style. Two cars. Three bathrooms, so that when he throws a party three of his guests can pee at the same time.

—Five, Jeremiah. There's a closet off the entrance hall and another off the garage.

—And in rural places in the days of our devoted forefathers it could have been forty or four hundred: the high sky over them, the green grass before them, the high hedges all around them: and their arses not six inches away from the nettles.

—I'm on the way to a wedding myself, he explains. A niece. Away up North. I never had any children myself.

None, anyway, that I knew of. Or were registered in the stud-book. Or unless I'm having one now by proxy by a sailor in the saddle on a wilful woman in New York. Not exactly a sailor but a strong young man making big money swabbing out the intestines of tankers. In the lounge Mr. Burns is nowhere to be seen. Even he may be resting, or, perhaps, from some secret place he is observing.

The private room where the young fellow is blessing all before him is spacious, deep-carpeted, wide-windowed. It is on the first floor and ten tourist campaigns away from the old public bar. The angle of the sun being, inevitably, altered, the bay is now clearly visible, the early morning glitter gone. There are bathers, mostly children, on the strand. But the tower on the headland is unchanged, tall, dark with all the menace of the past, that cyclopean eye glittering balefully. There is a silence in the room. All the women are talking. But, because of virgin priesthood and hands still wet with holy oil, it is not the customary gabble. Two members of the staff, one male, one female, are on their knees to be blessed. He is introduced. And kneels. It is the custom of the country: and a blessing from anybody, from here to Tibet and home again the other way round, never did anybody any harm. Then he sits for a while sipping tea, the whispering talk drifting like smoke around him. It's a long way back to the tumult of New York, even to the drone of the plane beating in his body and to the legless man with the bottomless bottle: even to the noisy camaraderie of the public bar.

He is on his way from the dogwood and forsythia garden of the young women, and sits here among women whispering around and kneeling before a priest. He will go on to see his niece, his flesh in a sort of way, given in marriage, a priest being witness: out of which marriage a son may come who may be a priest, if by that time there are any priests. From a pile of leaflets on a side table the matron who sits nearest to him takes a leaflet, prayer-book size. She hands it to him, her lips moving silently so that he doesn't know whether she's talking to him or to her divine redeemer. He reads the name of the young priest, the time and place of ordination: then, not knowing what else to do, smiles his thanks and sits looking foolishly at the leaflet. She turns the leaflet over so that he may read the other side. He does so.

A priest: To live in the midst of the world without wishing its pleasures; to be a member of each family, yet belonging to none; to share all sufferings; to penetrate all secrets; to heal all wounds; to go from men to God and offer Him their prayers; to return from God to men to bring pardon and hope; to have a heart of fire for charity and a heart of bronze for chastity; to teach and to pardon, console and bless always. My God, what a life! And it is yours, O priest of Jesus Christ.

My God, what a life indeed, a secret agent, a superman, a superstar! Now who wrote all that? It could be anyone from John Henry Newman to Pope John, more likely Cardinal Manning, who did write a book about eternal priesthood. Looking at the young fellow there, seated like Christ by the side of his mother and circumnavigated by handmaidens, he wonders will he ever measure up to the job. Staring at the print on the leaflet until the letters dance before his eyes, he goes into one of those trances that are the product of a mind disordered by odd information and aimless interests and reading.

Seventy-eight years ago on an Irish hillside a man and his friends, in all a party of thirteen, burned the man's wife to death and buried her charred body in a nearby marsh. Some people who don't know much about it call it a case of suspected witchcraft. But it wasn't anything of the sort. One or more members of the sad thirteen thought that the woman was not the real woman but a changeling: that the fairies (a fatally corrupt word nowadays) or the Good People (as country folk in fear of their vengeance used politely to call them) had come out from their dwelling place under the ancient earth-mound or rath, close to the hillside farmhouse, and taken the real woman with them and left one of their own in her place.

Why did they think she was a changeling? Once, from reading the records of the court case, I thought it was because she was pale and wasting away with consumption. But a learned man who came from the place and knew the local lore told me it was because she was a somnambulist. To simple country people sleepwalking could be a very strange thing.

One of the ways to detect and banish a changeling, and bring the true person back from the other world, is to swing the suspected changeling back and forward over a fire, while repeating three times: Are you so-and-so in the name of God?

In this case the unfortunate woman's name was Brigid Cleary.

A subsidiary part of the treatment is to sprinkle the changeling with a holy oil compounded of human urine and the excrement of hens.

While all this was going on, and it went on for some time before the final disaster, the husband asked one of the priests of the parish to say Mass in the house for the health of the woman. The priest did so. Not knowing what was in the air all around him. To be a member of each family yet belong to none. Christ moves here among the matrons, young and old and middle-aged. On that black hillside he stood among strange gods, older than himself. On an Irish hillside, seventy-eight years ago.

What puzzled me for a long time was why they burned the woman to death. That same learned man was able to tell me that at that time the country people in the really boondock places were little aware of the inflammable qualities of paraffin oil. One night the husband in a fit of temper threw a can of oil over the woman as she lay in bed: at the trial there was a hint that he may have been jealous of his wife with some travelling salesman or eggman or packman or peddler. Then the following day when the court of psychical enquiry took her out of bed and swung her over the fire, the nightdress went ablaze and that was that. They buried her, all charred and crumpled up, in that nearby marsh.

But after death the resurrection. One of the thirteen seems to have been a sort of herbalist or wise man or witch doctor: it may have been his imagination and inventiveness that was mostly responsible for the strange tragedy. He had great influence over the mind of the deluded and/or jealous husband: and what does he do now but foretell that on the next night of full moon the real true wife will come back from the other world. She will come naked and riding on a white horse, her feet bound under the horse's belly. They are to wait for her above there on the old rath or fairy fort. The husband will step forward and cut the rope that binds her feet. His own wife will step down into his arms: and so strong are faith and hope that they did wait for her, up on the ancient mound by moonlight, brambles and branches twisting in the wind, in a place where some of the first people who ever reached this island may have lived. She didn't come. The police came instead from the town of Clonmel: and the horrified neighbours, and the stricken priest who had carried Christ into strange places. The woman did not arise again. Yet what a symbol of glorious resurrection that mountainy witch doctor was offering to his people: a naked woman by moonlight on a white horse, cut the rope and open her legs and set her free. So much better than to pray the enchantment away from swans and turn them into geriatrics, and when he gets to Dublin after the wedding in Carmincross he'll search out the sculptor who made that statue and tell him and tell him. . . .

His head jerks up suddenly. He has been nodding. The room is warm. The voices low and soothing. The matron who has given him the leaflet is now offering him a cup of tea.

—Excuse me. I'm absent-minded.

—You're tired after your long journey.

A group of them gather around him.

—Are you glad to be back in Ireland?

—Will President Nixon resign?

—Those dreadful murders in California. Twenty-seven young boys.

—Tell us now what it was like when you left New York. My husband and I are flying to Florida next week for a holiday.

So he tells them: just enough to be polite and to keep the talk and the tea going.

The children are shouting together and racing along the sands.

From a mind mouldy with overmuch reading, he tells Mr. Burns, every experience takes the form of a quotation. Mr. Burns argues, though, that every experience is a quotation and that every quotation is a renewed experience, a light switched on again in a darkened room to reveal familiar objects. Mervyn recalls that Marx said that history repeats itself, the second time as farce. Marx was too kind. History is farce the first time. God only knows what it is the next time round.

Mr. Burns says that he didn't come out into God's good air on the Atlantic shore to talk about Marx. He prances on the strand as long ago he danced on the bridge by the creamery. He prances in a pair of costly calf shoes so casual that, with the white pants and broad belt and bright striped shirt and silk scarf that go with them, they transform casualness into a Byzantine ritual. To the surf on the left and the wind in the bent grass on the dunes to the right he recites: The walrus and the carpenter were walking on the strand.

Then he roars, raising his voice as he never does when on deck in his hotel: The walrus and the carpenter. Which is which, as Jack Jones said. Do you remember Jack Jones and which is which? That's the mood I'm in. It's good to see you again. Race you to the river, boy.

The hotel staff would be astounded. He's off like a rocket, white sand spurting like vapour from his casual heels. The big bald man flounders along behind him, the distance between them widening until Mr. Burns, a good fifty yards ahead, stops and turns around and gives the victory sign. The little coloured town, dancing up and down on the clifftop, seems suddenly at a great distance. There are no bathers here, no sound but the gulls or a lonely sandpiper, and the wind in the bent grass and, inevitably, the wash of the sea. The river and the rocks and the pasture land beyond are still half a mile ahead. He plods on: across Nevada after gold or silver or the path to the virgin West, bleached bones of men and beasts as milestones on the desert road, one weary vulture sucking the last of the marrow from a fallen mule. Even Mr. Burns is puffed although his smiling casualness will not admit it. Some years have passed since the dance on the bridge. They walk on toward the tower on the headland.

Jack Jones was a one-handed war veteran in the town they went to school in. The missing hand was at Mons. His father and Jack Jones had been friends: because of something sib in their dispositions. Also because his father was another old soldier. Jack had a red plethoric face, walked stiffly and slowly and as if there was something wrong with his back, was generally a civil obliging fellow but a roaring dangerous demon when he had the drink taken. More dangerous than most: because instead of the missing hand he had a sort of iron hook meant to help him in his work which was mostly lifting cases of poultry onto lorries. That hook was a wicked weapon in a fight.

—It was on a St. Patrick's Day, he says, that Jack forfeited his hook.

He is twelve years of age at the time. His father and himself, in the town for the market day, are turning the Dublin Road corner into the main street. There's a crowd round the mouth of an entryway that goes in by the side door of a pub. A man, hatless, in a navy-blue suit, bursts out of the crowd and shouts to his father: Michael, for God's sake, Jack Jones is down there murdering Joe Brunt from Corraheskin. With the hook. Stop him, Michael. He'll listen to you.

Calm as a machine his father goes through the crowd down the entryway to the scuffling men and tells Jack to stop. Jack stops. A constable in black-green uniform follows at a safe distance. Then his father persuades Jack to walk to the barracks and face the music. Jack to his right, his father to his left, the twelve-year-old leads the parade. The cautious constable comes six paces behind, and, after him, the more curious of the crowd, hoping that the fun isn't all over. Jack is charged and later tried, and any amount of solid citizens, including his father, testify to Jack's husbandly and other virtues, with special stress on the hand left behind at Mons in the service of King and country: not even his own country. The latter appeal has particular pungency because the magistrate was once officer in command of Jack's regiment and the only penalty imposed on him is that, for his own and the general good, he is not to wear the hook except when actually at work. Found wearing it at any other time he goes to jail.

—Which is which, as Jack Jones says, Mr. Burns says. It became a proverb. The most respectable used it and didn't know what it meant.

For Jack one night, away from work and from his hook, had a tramp woman against the wall for a knee-trembler in a dark corner. He grunted and pushed and fumbled in the customary fashion, but was overheard to mutter hopelessly again and again: Would somebody tell me which is which.

The guns of Mons were far behind him, the ground manured with men and bits of men: the worst thing of all was to see a fellow you were friendly with vanishing, shlupp-shlupp, into the mud and not to be able to do anything about it. He had once heard Jack Jones say that, quietly remembering: the hookless, red and purple, scarred stump protruding from his sleeve. Which was which?

How many *mutilés* now in the world in this moon-conquering year of 1973? How many in Ireland? Only a few of them might, like Jack Jones's stump, be matter for any sort of comedy.

—Your father was a solid man, Mr. Burns says, a calm man in a crisis.

There are wide brown steppingstones across the river. Upstream, little trout are playing. Beyond the steppingstones a rough, sandy cart track follows the shore, rising toward gentle headlands and good pasture land going down to low cliffs. The long half-ruined building over there to the right can only be an old coast guard station: another melancholy monument, like a crumbling castle or a huge silent eighteenth-century mill, to a way of life that will never be again. They are walking upward and backward into history.

The path curves to the west and their vision is caught and held by the tower on the headland. From this angle the cyclopean eye is not visible. A cloud has come over the sun.

The MacDonnells of the Isles, the Hebridean gallowglasses, *na gallóglaigh,* the foreign warriors came as far south as this: mercenary men carrying monstrous, doubleheaded axes. They built a tower, too, but not the one on the headland. Their tower was right here, close to the water and the narrow rock-walled haven where they disembarked. The stump of the ruin is still to be seen.

The brown rocks by the shore here are carved and moulded much as the rocks are out on Black Head, the gloomy nose of the Burren of Clare. Forearm might be better than nose. Great round boulders are tossed here and there as if some Hebridean giants had abandoned a game of snooker and gone away forever. Kelp, saved from the sea for the making of iodine, is neatly stacked by the wayside. Cattle are plentiful on the daisied grass.

—Oh be my lady, he sings, and in Limerick laces your delicate ways shall airily pass, with quiet feet in your blue pampooties and guinea hens on the daisied grass.

No guinea hens are here to be seen, but a Dalmatian dog, every bit as alien and exotic, comes running, barking at them, but friendly. Men, paying no heed either to the walkers or the dog, haul a boat up from the water's edge.

—Be your lady, indeed, says Mr. Burns. A romantic to the bitter end.

—Beyond the end.

—Was it all the young women in that place that finished her?

—She was never near that place but twice. Anyway one didn't tamper with the young women. At least not until they graduated. One was in loco parentis. On your honour.

—On your arse.

The Dalmatian, his barking duty done, goes trotting back to the men hauling the boat.

—It would seem to me old man, says Mr. Burns, that you all were passing up a heaven-sent opportunity.

—Oh, some didn't. A bit of it went on.

—I'm relieved to hear it. I abominate waste.

Laughing in the conspiracy of youth remembered they follow the climbing path, dry-stone walls now to right and left. There's a farmhouse with China roses, red and a richer red that is almost a regal purple, showing their outrageous regency heads over a garden wall. A man and woman come meditatively out through a gateway, iron buckets in hands. They have been feeding calves. Oh, Mr. Burns and his friend are welcome and more than welcome and no need even to ask or to mention it, to walk their land and look at the tower. They walk along the track that has now turned green.

—By God, he says, what a heavenly place to live. Even in winter it could be dry and snug.

Mr. Burns is doubtful. Not so long ago he has walked alone, he walks a lot for his health, over a mountainy place to the north, coming down from rocks and heather and stopping at a house to ask the way. A woman leaning over a halfdoor, which is something that will soon be as rare as a donkey or a cowslip, gives him the information he needs, then says: You'd be from Dublin.

—I've lived there.

—A busy place. I was there one day on an excursion. You must like walking. You must like mountains.

—I hate them, she says with sudden venom. I hate mountains.

Like the woman who lived in John Synge's shadow of the glen, young, discontented, shackled to misery and an old or an aging husband, the mountains looking in the door at her, she longing for a young sailor or a wandering man.

—Deborah, says Mr. Burns, made a sad mistake with that husband of hers.

—How so?

—She'll tell you herself, no doubt.

—No doubt.

They clamber over a rough sort of stile set into a stone wall. To the left there's another farmhouse but the street before the house is grass-grown, the windows shuttered, the people gone to God knows where. Perhaps they had come to hate the headland, the tower, the fertile coastal plain, the sea and the Galway mountains far beyond it, the eternal struggle that only lasts a lifetime but that's as much of eternity as any of us can expect: to hate the dark sculptured rocks, the cattle grazing. As they are now, all around myself and Mr. Burns, and advancing toward us with the stumbling curiosity of cattle that can nowadays frighten young people, out from the city, who have grown up totally apart from the ordinary ways of the earth.

—Eight hundred dead, says Mr. Burns, would only be forty thousand if there were as many people in Ireland as there are in the States.

—Only.

—It's not all that many in modern terms. One night of love in Dresden.

—So we don't want to be out of the pattern of the world we live in. Ourselves and the Arabs.

—And the Jews. And the Americans over Vietnam.

—This is no place for such talk.

Behind them the semicircle of sand and surf reaches out to the coloured train of houses switchbacking on the edge of shelving sandy cliffs. Before them the coast rises to higher cliffs, black and austere. Seabirds, halfway down to the water, seem motionless.

—But this tower, says Mr. Burns, was built for fighting. To

keep the neighbours out when they came gatecrashing with hatchets. Listen to the echoes. Iron on iron.

Mr. Burns is right as he so often is, even on matters that have nothing to do with hotel management. Short of the heart of Greenland or the summit of Everest is there a place in the world unafflicted by such echoes? Send all our madmen, Orange and Green, to the Greenland ice cap where, doing no harm to decent people, they can gelignite the bejasus out of each other.

Taking the air they walk among the friendly curious cattle. But on that day they hear no echoes: even though there were people here, long before the man and woman feeding the calves, long before the Norman men who built the tower, before the Hebridean hatchetmen who came in to fight for pay. For the tower stands in the dead centre of a grassy ringfort of enormous circumference. Three thousand years are all around them. The tower is elaborately ornamented and faced with false, needless fortifications: embrasures, battlements, crenellations, added long after its death by some nineteenth-century fantasist. Did the Normans who built it, did the man who seven hundred years later tarted it up, realise that they were treading so heavily on the remote past?

—One generation, he tells Mr. Burns, abandons the enterprises of another like stranded vessels.

—How very profound of you, dear boy.

—Nor are our skeletons probably to be distinguished from those of our ancestors.

But Mr. Burns also has read Thoreau, who is neither a usual nor an appropriate author for hotel managers. He says that Andy More Maguire was the man who really made his mark and wrote his name in this place, that nobody knows who the others were but that Andy More must still be alive and laughing, like the blackguard he was, in the wind around them. That wind strikes at them around the corner of the tower. They struggle against it. Unexpectedly, they hear the cries of the birds drifting halfway between the breakers, too far down to be heard, and the frilled and puckered edge of the black cliffs. The sea is totally empty. A westward-bound jet has left its mark on the sky. For the hundredth time they read the inscription on the plaque, fastened to the tower by the fantasy man who added the decorations: This plaque was placed here to honour the eightieth birthday of Andrew Maguire, father to his people, friend to the poor, protector of the widow and orphan, true servant of his native land.

—The wind, says Mr. Burns, is laughing at us. Old Andy is laughing at us. He wrote his name with his prick. It's a sort of writing that lasts.

—Not if the snow melts.

They laugh. They listen. The cattle no longer regard them. This hilltop could be possessed by the randy old villain of a land-lord who made the additions to the tower to please himself, who placed the plaque there to honour himself the day, it was said, his hundredth bastard was born: true father to his people, marrying the mothers off to his tenantry or shipping them to his gentlemen friends in London if they were too restless or ashamed to settle at home. But always taking good care of his bastards.

How many worlds have lived and died in this place?

—That was a good day, Mr. Burns says, when we had the singsong in Andy's memory. The old whoremaster.

It is a pet of an autumn day all of fifteen years ago. The hundredth anniversary of the last lord of this headland. There are eight or nine of them, a picnic party from the hotel, white cloths on the sunlit grass, the food the best, the wine plentiful. In memory of that carefree day Mr. Burns sings. He has a fine tenor voice. He sings that young Donal sat on his gallant grey like a king on his royal seat and that the heart of the girl who sings the song leaps up at his regal way to worship at his feet. For had he come in England's red to make her England's queen she'd have roamed the high green hills instead for the sake of the jackets green.

—Deborah, says Mr. Burns, was in great voice that day.

—It's a death song. Death and vengeance, bejasus. For grief will come to our heartless foes and their thrones in the dust be seen: and Irish maids love none but those who wear the jackets green. And I cry: make way for the soldier's bride in your halls of death, sad queen: but I buried my heart in the grave below for his and for Ireland's sake. A cheerful fucking crowd, our Irish patriots: death and dying and now, by Jesus, the madmen, Orange and Green, bombers by day and sectarian assassins by night, the U.S.A. by day and the R.A.F. by night when they were doing Dresden, have come up against the blank brick wall in the blind alley, freedom fighters all for Ireland's sake, scattering broadcast the liberty to die, kill anybody, burn and blow up everything.

—But what about the bloody British army. You've been away too long from your native place.

—A professional army sent in by politicians to do police duties when government and justice have failed can only act up to its nature or the nature of the situation. Or down. What they do leaves me unmoved.

—It mightn't if they had you leaning against a wall, arms up, legs out, for twenty-four hours. Or running barefoot on broken glass. In Hollywood barracks. Brigadier Kitson would be the man for you. He dined with the Queen. What small talk had they? The Duke of Wellington had none.

—What my Orange fellow countrymen do I can try to understand. I grew up with them.

—So did I, boy. They didn't make sense.

—The most backward people in Western Europe. Their bosses kept them that way. Their god, in a fierce Scots accent, told them they were saved and superior. Anything that ever made this country civilised they never had anything to do with. Comic apes.

—Honest men. Courageous. Dangerous.

—No literature. With one or two exceptions even their ballads are bad. Thinking always they were part of an imperishable empire. On their banners Queen Victoria handing a Bible to a kneeling negress is still the secret of England's greatness. Now it's all over. England would be glad to get rid of them. And the shit's frightened out of them.

—More dangerous than ever. You really need to go home to the North to see for yourself.

—When were you last there?

—At the funeral of the people murdered by the paratroopers on Bloody Sunday. I met that young priest you saw on the TV, trying to save people, waving a white handkerchief, crouching under bullets. No southern belles reading St. Exupery. No magnolia blossoms in the Bogside. A young boy led me from spot to spot to show me exactly where each one of the thirteen had been murdered. The ground still sodden with blood. I sat in one of the houses and smelled poverty. Not accidental poverty. Not poverty brought on by booze or improvidence. But poverty forced on people by neglect and bad government. No government. For generations.

—Dogwood and forsythia. You're jealous of myself and the southern belles.

—Jealous about what, old boy? Since you say you didn't. Jealous about a thousand passed-up opportunities?

—But what is done in the name of the free united Ireland, that the heroes once dreamed of, cuts me to the quick. The young woman who wanted only to be wrapped in his coat of green might lose her legs if she went into a restaurant for a cup of coffee at the wrong time. Bury my heart at Wounded Knee. But I have no knees. Bury my arse in the grave below. Or bury what's left of my royal loyal patriotic Irish arse. The old songs have been polluted. Blood and vengeance and death and bigotry. Vengeance and blood.

Mr. Burns says that they were always with us: Not all our fault, old boy. We had pushing neighbours who wouldn't stay at home.

—We were murdering each other before they ever got here.

—So were they. Murdering each other. Most men are murderers. Even by the sword shall the unwholesome boughs first be pruned and the foulness cleansed and scraped away before the tree bring forth good fruit.

—Nowadays even the gardeners blow themselves up. Andy More at least was all for life. Fuck 'em all and feed the bastards.

—Sing your own song. Honour old Andy.

—Ireland's prime prick.

—You're on your way to a wedding, for God's sake.

So hopping and prancing like fools, or Red Indians, on the southward side of the great fosse, the coastal plain below them and the daisied grass, the exotic Dalmatian, the deep-bosomed roses, they chant: Haste to the wedding and haste to the wedding, no more I'll sit sobbing and sighing alone, for old Andy More is above on the headland and I've got a man with a prick like a bone.

The men who were hauling the net have gone and the dog with them. Yet the whole place seems populous. Andy More and many others sing with them. Did the women weep when they left for London?

They walk eastward to a crossroads where Mr. Burns has arranged for a car to meet them. The words that run in Mervyn's head are the words of a song some unknown countryman made long ago to praise a girl he met in the place to which Mervyn is going: Attention pay, Fermanagh men, I have a song to sing. It's all about a rural lass is fit to wed a king. Oh, some men strive and some men strain for profit or for loss. But I sing about a lovely maid one June in Carmincross.

They are driven home, or back to the hotel, by way of the holy well and the shining white ruined abbey. The well is in a natural grotto, a place of flowering bushes and water spurting musically from carelessly piled rocks. Over the centuries pilgrims have left here their odd offerings to the saint of the well: crutches no longer needed, rosary beads that one might have thought would have been, pious lithographs, prayerbooks, statues of assorted saints, old hats, even a crimson waistcoat with brass buttons. What had the grateful suppliant suffered from? And into the trunk and crooked branches of a tree, of some soft wood, copper and silver coins have been hammered edgewise. The metal rims glisten and wink at the light of the candles burning in the grotto on a brass candelabrum as arrogant as a cinema organ. Mr. Burns remembers sadly a girl who worked some years since on his kitchen staff and who was up here forever lighting candles for something or other, and who drowned herself off the cliffs and was washed up on the strand below, right in the middle of the playing children.

—She was so mad to light candles that if she had no money and if anybody was looking she'd drop holy medals into the paybox to make a rattle.

—God was not mocked. He can spot a dud coin. Whatever she prayed for he didn't grant.

—Unless she prayed for a happy and quiet death.

—Or a short journey by water.

—Or to have children around her.

—Even the children love Maryanne down by the seaside sifting sand.

The candles burn quietly in the holy windless corner. The grotesque red waistcoat grins at them through the palisade of crutches. The walls of the old abbey ruin shine white on the velvet setting of grass. From the waist up, the mountains around it shine white over green valleys. Walking alone in this empty place a man might imagine that the scattered stones at a distance move like animals: and, once, an arrangement of rings of stones by the roadside turns out, indeed, to be not stones but wild goats resting, chewing, studying the world. The wind blows toward them and from the goats.

—They stink a bit, says Mr. Burns.

—So do we all.

—As our emotions rise so does our underarm odour.

—It's an ordered society. No bomb throwers there. Nor religious murderers. The goats have it all worked out.

—They fight, though. They fight like bejesus.

—Only over women.

—And social position. And power. Just like ourselves.

—They have no guns. Or bombs. They know their place when the fight is over.

The goats make no sound. The air is rancid. The great buck sits in the dead centre of everything: his court and his women in a circle around him, and around that circle the lesser bucks with their lesser circles. Through the air above them fly, according to the legend, the enchanted dishes of venison from the table of the king's gluttonous courtiers. The dishes are carried by angels to bring one day of holy feasting to a group of anchorites in the white rocks. The courtiers run furiously after the flying dishes, following the route that brings Mr. Burns and myself back to the hotel. The date of the original flight is uncertain. Around the holy well the water plays tunes among the fuchsia bushes. The goats like gurus and their devotees sit in circles and meditate. Nor does the stink of one goat seem to annoy another goat. What's left of the ancient abbey shines like a jewel in the evening. Savoury dishes fly west carried by unseen angels. Gluttonous courtiers run hopelessly after them, shouting and waving fists, falling over each other like Keystone cops. In a square, in Dublin, swans are unenchanted into geriatrics in honour of the risen people. It occurs to me that it is an odd thing to have a dreamland to come home to. Or a madhouse. A drowned girl lights a million candles. Deborah will tell me all about the short straw her husband was. Carmin-cross is quiet, above in the moorland, by the swift river and below the glistening lakes.

Mr. Burns tells him that the honeymoon couple in the dining room come from close to Pomona, California: from a place of orange groves still surviving to the south of Los Angeles, the maze without a centre. Or a plan. Which should a maze have?

He has been once in Los Angeles.

President Nixon in his time thought that tangles of streets were better than groves of oranges and avocados. At any rate he said so. But perhaps he did not mean it that way. It could be that he merely meant that houses are a good idea. And so they are. Where would young married couples be without them?

The dining room is crowded. There is nothing for him to do but share a table with the pair from Pomona. The girl is olive-complexioned. Or between honey and olive. Mexican or Spanish-Jewish origin. Dark hair parted and pulled back hard. They are, as is the custom, very much absorbed in each other, hand clasping, lip brushing, glances audibly meeting. Beyond a polite smile they pay no attention to him. For which he is just as glad. Because for a moment the sight of the girl has brought back to him visions of dogwood and forsythia, of young women naked, as good as, by a blue pool.

The stout lady who is professor of physical culture has set her heart on two things. To bring him back to the Catholic church, to get him into the pool: to make him live a holier and healthier life. Skillfully he resists. But he has been known to dodge behind bushes or buildings when he sees her coming. She tells him that he must not be shy, that she will ensure that none of the young women are in the pool when he gets there. So he tells her that he wouldn't dream of getting into the pool unless it was crawling with young women, unclad in multicoloured bikinis. He laughs to himself at the memory. Then all the way from New York the woman's voice cuts with a rasp through his moment of comic contentment. She is saying: Don't expect me to go to that place with you. The smell of sanitary towels would suffocate me.

—They don't use them any more.

—Did they tell you so? Or did you find out? Research? Do they still bring their slaves to school with them?

—Only horses now.

—Off to the boondocks with you so. Look for me if you're ever back this way.

The petals fall from the dogwood. Delicate and transient as daffodils. The forsythia fades. The first sip of wine is bitter to his palate but he knows that he can't blame Mr. Burns for that. Mr. Burns, as is well known, keeps one of the best carafes in Ireland. Then he hears the bridegroom, tall, fair-headed, smooth spoken, say: Carmincross.

The bride says: It's a lovely name.

He doesn't mean to intrude: not with that sour taste in his mouth. But the name is too much for him. He says: That's where I'm bound for. Carmincross.

The bride says: Well, how about that?

The groom says: My great-grandfather came from there. And we're going to see it. But you're the first person I ever met who knew it was there.

—It's a quiet place. There's a lovely village. An old eighteenth-century church. Rooks and doves. There always seem to be a few snow-white doves walking the streets. Strolling past collie dogs sleeping in the sun. And a rough mountain river coming down from a pear-shaped lake. Nothing much ever happens in Carmincross. I'm going there to a wedding.

The bride says: Weddings happen.

They all laugh merrily.

—And births and deaths.

—Neither to be referred to, he says, for some time yet.

More laughter.

—Carmincross, he says, only appeared once in literature. Oral literature at that. The story was never written down.

—Tell us, they say.

To be as young and handsome as that. To have such ripe olive beauty at one's disposal. The birds are nesting in the cliffs. The surf is shining in the darkness. Do the wild goats sleep sitting in circles?

—It's a story my mother tells.

—Tells?

—She's still alive. Ninety-two. Still able to sing and tell stories.

—Tell us the story.

So he tells them. That, anyway, was what he was leading up to. He can't help himself telling stories.

—It was a story about a thrawn old Presbyterian farmer called Alexander who one day in the market in the neighbouring big town had a theological and political disputation with three brothers called Breen. They parted in wrath. Toward evening the old man is driving home. Rope reins slack on the horse's rump, Alexander's feet trailing close to the ground and he sitting on the edge of the flat cart. His pipe going. Standing outside a pub are the three Breen brothers, arms folded, eyes grim. We'll get you, Alexander, they say, when you're going by Carmincross. So he halts the horse and takes the pipe out of his mouth and says: But, boys, I'm nae gaen by Carmincross.

—And the Breens saw the logic of it and laughed, and shook hands, and all four went into the pub to cement or liquefy their restored friendship.

The groom says: Henry Kissinger.

The bride says: Kissinger's a hawk not a dove.

—You read that in *New York* magazine, darling. Your story is a good story, sir. It makes a point.

—It's the only story ever about Carmincross. There's a ballad too.

—We'll sing along with you.

—Mr. Burns mightn't like it.

The three of them are suddenly a happy family party. From a distance Mr. Burns with a wave and a smile approves.

—If you're in Carmincross at the time you must come to the wedding.

—We'd be pleased. But it might be an intrusion.

—No. My niece, she's my favourite niece, empowered me to ask any seven or nine people I cared to ask.

—Why seven or nine?

—Mystic numbers. So far I've asked nobody.

He had asked one person but she had refused.

—We'll come then, they say, if we're there.

The timing of their itinerary is uncertain. They have the world before them.

Later, when the lovely couple have gone aloft to their pleasures, Mr. Burns joins him over his brandied coffee and cigar.
The memory of the airliner and the legless man is fading. He's in
Carlow by now and happy among his people: all counting compensation.

—Do you think now, says Mr. Burns, would that pair be at the
beginning of the road to divorce.

—Honeymoons, Mervyn says, used to be lovely things.

—They still could be, my boy. Should I have exercised my
rough shooting rights there? Droit de seigneur. I'd say there's fire
in that one. Mexican fire.


Deborah says: We have a lot to talk over.

—Tarry with us, Deborah, for already it is late and a perverted
world seeks to blot thee out of sight by the darkness of its denials.

—Blot who out of sight? That's an odd welcome to give a girl
after years of separation. What does all that malarkey mean?

—It's part of a prayer my mother used to say, consecrating the
household to the Sacred Heart of Jesus. On the road to Emmaus,
Jesus the travelling man meets the two disciples.

—I was never in that place. The travel agents don't mention it
in the brochures.

—And they knew him in the breaking of the bread. Tarry with
us for already it is late.

—That's what I came for. To tarry with you. It's a dinky name
for you know what. And to talk. Mr. Burns won't mind. We're
old friends. We have a lot to talk over.

—Whatever demented parish priest wrote that prayer I often
thought that he had the elements of literary style.

—About that sort of style I wouldn't know. You're aware that I
never read a book in my life. That's a lovely thing he put on your
bedside table.

—Mr. Burns.

—Who else? You don't think I did it. I couldn't be so indeli-
cate. Anyway I know you have one of your own. I prefer them
that way. Natural and white. And with a man and so on attached
to the other end.

—What is it?

—Innocent you are. Course I keep forgetting you were roving

in foreign parts. It's a rubber bullet. Isn't it the spitting image of a black man's thing.

—Spitting?

—Funny you are. Not that I ever saw one. To make the comparison, I mean. They've become all the rage now. As souvenirs and mantelpiece ornaments. Rubber bullets, I mean. In among the stopped clocks and China dogs and shepherdesses.

He fingers the dildo meditatively: All praise to Priapus I don't yet need one of these things.

—All praise to whoever he was but I can guess he wasn't hail glorious St. Patrick.

—These things could hurt if they came out of a gun.

—Tell that to the unfortunates in the North. A woman was blinded by one of them the other day in her own front garden. Those paras are a pack of bastards. A deaf-mute in Strabane went around waving one of them things. As if it was his own thing. All for the fun of it like. A soldier thought it was a gun and shot him dead. So the soldier says he thought it was a gun. It doesn't look like a gun to me.

Deborah has entered his room from the left, by way of the bathroom door. She has been here waiting for him while he was still at dinner. Her hair, which was blonde when he first met her, and that was some time ago, is now more blonde than ever. The shaded light by his bedside is much less bright than the light in the bathroom, which glows through, and enhaloes, her blonde hair. Her face is in shadows. Her comfortable body is silhouetted. She crosses the room and sits on the spare bed from which she removes, without looking at it, the collage of the jolly green giant. Printed matter, even pictures, and apart from the racing pages in the newspapers, has seldom had any interest for her. He crosses the floor to the bathroom. He switches off the bathroom light then sits on the other bed facing her. She has brought with her a bottle of Niersteiner and two long slender glasses. Niersteiner is her only drink. He gently feels her double chin and kisses her twice. She is fifty years of age but she still tastes like a spring morning. The room is shadowy and warm and companionable. They sip the Niersteiner. She is in a pink dressing gown frilled with white ecru lace. She is not unlike something large, bland, and quivery from the after-dinner trolley. But very comforting:

and perhaps just what a man needs after a long journey and a life, like every other, more or less wasted. He draws the curtain on dogwood visions of slim girls like white fish in a blue pool: on the thought of a young class of a film star fellow wrestling under this very roof with a brown Mexican or Spanish-Jewish wildcat. Dip your buckets where you are.

—You're home for a wedding, I hear. Only for that I suppose we'd never see you.

—Come to the wedding. Be my guest.

—It's not your wedding. I should hope.

—I have permission to ask seven or nine people. It's my favourite niece.

—How many nieces have you?

—Five. All in one family. And no brothers.

—How do you pick a favourite niece out of five sisters? It's a bad thing to show favouritism among young people.

—Hard to say. Something about her when she was younger. Carnaptiousness. Unbiddableness.

—Did she read books at school?

—Can't say for certain.

—I never did.

—Not after school?

—I never could see anything in books. I never listened to a teacher either. They'd talk and talk and I might as well have been out in a field picking daisies. But I had my dreams all the same, love and all that. It must have been you I was dreaming about. It couldn't have been that husband.

—Why not?

—My best dream was always about living in a big house. You see I grew up in a small house and not too rich at that. On the fringes of Dublin southside. But a lot of the old mansions were still standing with their walled gardens around them. I always wanted to live in a mansion.

—Aren't you? Now?

—By courtesy of Mr. Burns. I also found out what it takes to run a mansion. Money, staff, overheads, hard work, and value-added tax. So much for dreams. And books are nothing but dreams.

—Would you read a book of mine if I gave it to you?

—Read a history book? That's what you write, isn't it? Whatever for? I know my history. Get the English out of Ireland, I say,
and there'd be no history. Anyway, I know what you say. I know
what you do. It isn't that I don't like what you do and say. Especially do. But why strain my eyes and melt my brain to find out
what I know already.

—You like what I say?

He fondles her chins: somewhere between two and a half and
three of them. She is the picture of pink purring content and her
grey eyes are moist. But he is aware that they can take on a dry
stony colour: and that her decided nose, nothing retroussé about
that, and her primary chin can seem to slant downward in parallel lines. She is a businesswoman. If she hadn't been, Mr. Burns
would not have asked her back.

—I like what you do, too. I like how you look. Old and fat and
bald and all.

—And false teeth.

—Your fabulous face. It's like a sunset seen from the clifftops.
If you had stuck around I'd never have married. There's comfort
in you.

—There's comfort in bed. And husbandry in heaven.

—That's the place to keep it. And husbands. Far away and
long ago in never never land.

He switches off one of the bedside lights. He resists the impulse
to clear up the misunderstanding about the word: husbandry.
Suiting their actions to the mood of the moment and the mellow-
ing effect of the wine they go through the motions of undressing.
They are a little too old and too used to it to bother helping to
unharness each other. They roll into one of the beds. They fill it
almost to overflowing.

—Tell me, he says, do you still drink nothing but Niersteiner?

—Mere alcohol, she sings, doesn't thrill me at all. So tell me
why should it be true that I get a kick out of you.

—More prick than kick.

—Your fabulous face, sings she.

She has a husky voice. She remembers Ethel Merman. Under
the bedclothes she renews old acquaintance, going through a
comic pretence of shaking hands. She no longer refers to rubber
bullets. She says: Welcome home.

He remembers the first time she had so grasped him was in a cinema at a showing of the movie about Frankenstein meeting the Wolfman. Alarmed by the howls and the horror she had reached out for something solid to hold on to. She now says: Put that where it should be.

He obliges to the best of his ability. She has put on flesh, she tells him later, after she left her husband: through overeating, not by no means because of fretting as is often supposed to be the case with bereft women. But with relief.

He is at this moment vividly aware of that increase in flesh. So he says: Find the right wrinkle in Egypt's dark sea.

Since that is a parody on a line in a poem it doesn't mean anything to her. Her verbal responses are now mostly monosyllabic and not worth writing down. Any average novel nowadays will tell you the sort of thing that happens from there on in. Or perhaps your own memories of such occasions. By and large it is a satisfactory, if exhausting, night. Once in a lull before dawn she makes what is almost a speech. She says: No need for the ring any more. You used to say that it stubbed your toes. I'm safer now than all the pills in Peoria could make me. There must be some advantages to growing old.

He thinks it very odd that she should mention Peoria. Telepathy? For he has not told her about the pisser on the plane. Perhaps Mr. Burns has, and the name has imbedded itself in her memory. The morning comes amber-coloured through the drawn curtains. She is asleep. In the morning silence he can hear the gulls and the sea. He switches off the other bedside lamp. In the shadowy corner beyond the bathroom door a deaf-mute squats, an aborigine defecating or warming himself at a fire, and slowly, rhythmically waves a rubber bullet, a conductor's baton. Two fat people over fifty have been making fun of love: sleep upon a golden bed that first morn in Helen's arms, and an earnest elegant honeymoon couple are awaking dew-wet to continue their journey to Carmincross where nothing ever happens. His eyes are burning with weariness. The pleasures of an aging man are different and may exist mostly in the memory.

So he remembers that Gráinne had said to young Diarmuid, before they fled around Ireland pursued by the outraged and cuckolded Fionn, that she had sat in her bower with the clear view, with the blue windows of glass, and looked out on Diarmuid, and turned the light of her eyes on the sight of him: and never, from that time to this, gave her love to any other man: nor ever would.

Awaking now in Carmincross his niece also may feel that way.

The deaf-mute has gone from the corner, taking the shadows with him. When he awakes again Deborah has gone, leaving the rubber bullet on the pillow where her blond head has been.

Mr. Burns says: You may remember McGivern who went to school with us. He joined the Royal Ulster Constabulary. Rose to some considerable rank. But he had the good luck to get out before all this trouble began. Went into business in Belfast as an insurance consultant. Then moved to Dublin.

—Is there anything left in Belfast to insure?

—There's always a future, my dear man. They say the Japanese are buying up the city so as to get a toehold in the Common Market.

—The Japanese have seen worse wrecks than Belfast.

—And they recovered from it, Mervyn. Prospering like bees in a hive and just as crowded. Except that Tokyo smells of shit. I was over there at a tourist conference. One man told me it's because they manure the gardens with human excrement. But I couldn't see any gardens.

—A man told me it was because the sewage system couldn't cope with the crowd.

—Dublin may soon be as bad. With a million people as expected in twenty years. That's at least a million shits every morning. Your poet friend Abbot Smith, who swims all the year round, leaped into the Forty Foot in Dublin Bay on a Christmas morning and got a turd between the teeth. As an appetiser for his turkey. He wrote a poem about it. And about ecology. And called it "Lines Written in Dejection." The printer printed Defection.

Laughter. While I rasp my chin with the razor.

Sitting on the beside Mr. Burns tosses the rubber bullet into the air, spinning. And catches it as it descends.

—It was decent of you to leave that object by my couch.

—Dear boy, I thought you might need it. Not so much for use as for encouragement. Like the boy who owned the bantams and put the turkey egg on the pedestal before their nests: Keep your eyes on this and do your best.

—I am happy to report it wasn't needed.

Mr. Burns draws back the curtains. The morning light from the sea is something to sit up and blink at.

—Killoran that you were talking to in the bar yesterday says he's going on a trip. If you care to join him you're welcome.

—Might do. His son blessed me, bless him. What was that about McGivern?

—Who? Oh, McGivern. Oh, nothing about him. Only he was on the phone from Belfast saying it wasn't the man they were after at all, not the senator, but the woman, and the man, unfortunately for him, happened to be there.

—Being there is a bad idea in Belfast. What did they want the woman for?

—Because, being a Protestant, she spoke civilly to Catholics.

—Most untheological.

—She was handsome. Twenty-nine. A famous ballroom dancer. His only place in politics was doing good works. Free or subsidised busfares for old-age pensioners. That sort of thing.

—He didn't live himself to travel free.

—Thirty stab wounds and his throat cut. She a mere twenty times, as *Time* magazine might say. A Captain Black of the Ulster Freedom Fighters phoned a Protestant newspaper to say that the deed was done because the I.R.A. murdered a retarded Protestant boy.

—There was a Captain Black in an old Orange ballad.

Mr. Burns recites: Captain Black like a stout Orange hero came riding by on his white steed. He asked us what number we carried and where did we mean to proceed. Right boldly we stood up and answered him: Our number's three ninety and two. For we are the Aghalee heroes, and we did the rebels subdue.

Mervyn nicks himself shaving. There's a permanent sensitive spot below his right jawbone.

—Both dead in their blood, Mr. Burns says. On the edge of a lonely quarry on the Hightown Road. I'll tell Killoran to wait for you.

He soaks for twenty minutes in a warm blue sudsy bath. After last night's exertions his old bones need relaxation. The rough towel used recklessly has drawn multiple pinpoints of blood from the sensitive area on his throat: seventy stabs in the scurrying, cursing, grunting, screaming dark: blood dripping over the edge of a quarry, all in a golden-and-white setting of dogwood and forsythia. On the radio the voice of a political opponent says that the butchered senator was one of the most human and good-natured of men. The senator's political leader says that the dead man was a devoted lifelong democrat, that he believed utterly in progress by peaceful political means, that it is imperative that we should all try to be calm, that young misguided people might be tempted into taking some form of retaliatory action, that he says in God's name don't, that there has been enough and more than enough of killing.

Golden opinions that good man won: and a dirty death. Over the phone his murderers have said that after the murder of the retarded boy they decided no longer to put up with those animals, the I.R.A. So they butcher a good man and a lovely woman who have nothing to do with the I.R.A. And the Reverend Dr. Paisley says that the murderers were I.R.A. pretending to be Protestants. And the I.R.A. say that the murderers were the British army who murdered the senator so as to get votes in the forthcoming elections for moderates and capitalists.

For light relief and common sense the radio tells him that in Lake Kavasu city, Arizona, a baseball player has been struck dead by lightning.

The media does so much for us. Beatle-beat music, whining androgynous voices lull him as he half-slumbers in the bath. Every morning before breakfast the news gives us an appetiser, a turd between the teeth. So many people you never heard of become part of your life, sit at table with you, walk to work with you, come in the evening between you and the book you read. You are the zany fall guy clambering into the moving picture. Diarrhoea of song rushes forth like an arrow: but the radio is too far away to be switched off without swamping the floor and disrupting his pleasant lethargy. So, to neutralise it, he meditates on Deborah.

She was delighted to see me and to be beside me last night, or under or above me, not bad for her age, the seasoned branch crackling and rejoicing in the flame, no spluttering and weeping of green wood. Yet if I had never turned up she would never have missed me.

If I had been gone when she woke up in the morning she would have been puzzled. But once she knew I was somewhere and alive and safe she would have been, if anything, amused. Such relationships, if there are many or any such others, may be preferable to the clingings, the rendings, the tempests. What any more have I to do with the grand passions?

Deborah is the convenient symbol of the casual. The best things in life may be uninvolved. Once she told me that her first real womanly pleasure was when she discarded her first lover. Liberation? She was exactly nineteen when she met him. She was cycling with another girl in Glencullen in the Dublin mountains. She punctured her back tyre. He came along in rucksack and big boots and fixed the puncture: stopped a hole she says merrily, he was good at that, cracked the icing, had the first bite at the bun. They went about together for four years. Their favourite walk was along the banks of the River Dodder by the Dartry dyeworks, the high skyline above them, old mansions standing up out of the trees. Always autumn, as she remembers it, and his big boots, always big boots, kicking the crisp, dead leaves. She loved him dearly right up to the moment on her twenty-third birthday when she decided that, although she still loved him, she was weary looking at and listening to him. Nothing, she says, should last longer than four years. My survival in her affections may be accounted for by her never having seen me for more than a week at a time: which also suits me fine.

Dried, refreshed, talcumed he lies flat on the bed that wasn't used last night, relaxes to ready himself for Killoran's trip. The *Irish Times* that Mr. Burns has left on the bedside tells him that a young white woman, just arrived in Boston to take up a new job, has been forced by six black youths to soak herself in gasolene. Then they set her on fire. She had been carrying a can of gasolene for her car: for want of a nail the shoe was lost: which she had left a few streets away, when it had run dry: for want of a shoe the horse was lost, for want of a horse the man was lost. The youths set fire to the gasolene. They didn't actually compel her to strike the matches. She rolled on the ground to try to quench the flames, then went into a shop to ask for help. One of the shop assistants said: Her face was black. It was amazing she could even talk. Her clothes were smouldering. Her skin was peeling. She walked in and said: Will you please call an ambulance? Then she turned around and walked out, just like nothing had happened.

Her face was black.

Mislike me not for my complexion, the shadowed livery of the burnished sun.

With sulphur from the pit and oil from the Arabs, six sporty black cats whose ancestors were snared and sold by Arabs, bought and transported by whites in the barracoons when Boston was ruled by Puritans whose ancestors sailed, for their souls' sakes, from the town of St. Botolph on the Wash in England, six sporty black cats have painted a white girl their own colour: black is beautiful. And thus the whole round earth is every way bound by gold chains about the feet of God.

It is time for breakfast. And Killoran's trip.

The newspaper also tells him that the people who enjoyed themselves at the parties run by Janie Jones, great queen of London's daughters, were BBC disc jockeys, television people, millionaires, peers, and Arabs. That's something to discuss with Mr. Burns who, as a hotel manager, will be most interested in the order of precedence.

Deborah takes a day off and comes with them. Killoran drives a station wagon. They cross the Shannon by the ferry from Killimor in Clare to Tarbert in Kerry and drive on deep into the mountains of the southwest. Jeremiah sits beside the driver. Mervyn sits behind with Deborah. At intervals he palms her crotch as if his palm were itchy. It is a gentlemanly gesture, nonchalantly made under a hot morning sun. The station wagon is a coral island. At intervals she nips his thigh with thumb and forefinger. She is a girl again, kicking dead leaves by the Dodder. It is a relaxing, restful drive.

They leave a winding road by a wide, much-islanded bay, turn right over a humpy three-arched stone bridge: a river easing out into deep trout pools and white sandbars beyond. Then up a mountain road until they come to a place where the crags seem to hang against the sky. So Deborah says. But Jeremiah says they do not seem to hang, they do hang.

On the journey and over a good lunch in a hotel in Killarney, Mervyn has found out that Jeremiah is no lamenter, like the prophet he's called after. He is a sour comic as, perhaps, the prophet at moments was. He is a higher civil servant in Dublin. It is good for a man, he says, when he hath borne the yoke from his youth. He is blocky in build and low to the ground: with a tonsure of hair of no particular colour, a ruddy, pear-shaped face with the plump end of the pear to the top, billiard-ball eyes, and a slow sinister smile. He is quite cynical about the small amount of work he does in relation to the large amount of money he draws. His cynicism, though, has a special quality. It takes its strength from watching even more important people than himself, government ministers included, who are doing even worse than he is and who are still wearing the mask of virtue: who would not be heard pronouncing the word cynicism in case some avenging angel or echo might apply it to themselves. He talks of a minister for education, of all things, who once said: I don't reason with the young, I tell them.

And of a measure for augmenting the salaries of ministers in relation to the needs of a minister who rides to hounds: You have to be properly accoutred to ride with the Kildares.

The wine at lunch sets him off on these subjects. But the mountains, and this valley in particular, have for the moment silenced him. He does, he says, still reverence the mountains. Men are another matter.

Below them is the sweep of the valley, widening from nothing in the grey-brown mountains down to deep-green pastureland. The river winds in the most approved style. The farmhouses are square and white and solid. No poverty in this part of the world.

Never in my life nor in my nightmares have I heard so many sheep. Heard rather than seen. Thousands of them. Say a million, for the sake of easy accountancy. Their mouth-noises, after a while, seem to disturb the primeval peace more than the noise of engines. Bleats and meh-meh-mehs by the million while, in the sky, the larks still gaily singing fly, scarce heard amid the sheep below.

They park the car, sit on the roadside, meditate on the price and succulence of mutton: and on the obvious advantages of being a sheepfarmer in a wild beautiful valley. Deborah asks them to think of what they'd pay for a plate of that in the Hibernian or the Shelbourne, or in Simpson's on the Strand.

—Not to talk, says Killoran, of the price of wool. They're secure in this valley.

—Listening to the bleats of the bloody things, says Jeremiah, might be the hardest part of it.

For a full five minutes they listen to the bleats. The sound is a continuing pattern or a line on a graph, rising and falling but never breaking. There is never a moment when twenty or more sheep are not simultaneously speaking. Killoran says: That's his house, the long one, where the river makes the double bend. He was one of the world's greatest guerrillas, this man we're going to see.

—Of course I've heard of him, Deborah says. He fought for Ireland.

Jeremiah bleats back at the sheep. Then: But tell me, madam, what has he done since then?

—You tell me, smartass.

She likes Jeremiah.

—Easy in the telling. Talk. That's what he's done. Talk. We've come all this way to listen to him. Old hero in the inglenook. Oisín after the Fenians. Killoran loves it. Killoran worships him. How many men had the British here? How many men had the British there? And we shot them in pairs coming up the stairs in the valley of Knockanure.

Jeremiah sings that sentence in Galli-Gurchi bel canto. And: What Michael Collins said to him the time he met Collins in the snug of a pub in Gardiner Street. What Tom Barry, the greatest guerrilla, said to him two days before or after the ambush at Crossbarry. The number of commemorations and unveilings he has attended since 1922. We're great at the commemorating. We commemorate Wolfe Tone, father of the republic, that blue baby, the mongoloid child, four times on the one day by four opposing groups. Under the clay at Bodenstown in Kildare the poor bastard must be as confused as Jesus. And Jesus, they say, had the wit and ability to get out of the grave and up and away.

Deborah says: Are you an Irishman at all?

Yet it is still obvious that she likes Jeremiah. Possibly because he makes a vocation of not being taken in. Killoran pays little attention to his brother-in-law. He must have heard it all before. From the car he takes a massive pair of Japanese binoculars, then walks to a low wall at the roadside and surveys the valley. He says: I see him. He is up the slope two fields away from the house. Walking like a young fellow. Crossing a stile. God, he's a wonder for his age. Come and have a look.

Deborah is given the first chance. She wrestles with the focussing. She can see nothing but the sky above, which is darkening for rain. Jeremiah deliberately puts the wrong end to his eyes, because that, he says, is the way he prefers to see Ireland. Mervyn slowly focuses: and surveys, first, the empyrean. Rain is coming and heavy rain. Then: the ridge of the mountains, smooth in places, jagged in others: then the higher slopes where even sheep are few and where dry gullies gape for torrents: then down through the bleating thousands to the oblong, well-kept fields, the fine farmhouses, the winding river. In a field above the house at the river's double bend a tall man is standing quite still. He is wearing corduroy knee breeches, white woollen stockings, a green zipper jacket. His hair is white and copious. He shades his eyes with his left hand and looks up toward them. From the binoculars he may catch reflected the last glimpse of the smothering sun. Old Hawkeye himself. Scanning the horizon for Britannia's Huns with their tanks and their long-range guns.

Mervyn feels himself outstared. He waits almost for the man to talk to him, right into his ear. Then, disconcerted, he hands the binoculars back to Jeremiah. Who, this time, gets them right way round and sweeps the valley as if he were a field marshal. Killoran is back at the station wagon, holding the door for Deborah. Jeremiah shouts: She's a beauty, that's what she is, a beauty.

—Not you, Deborah, he says as they go down toward the house of the hero. Although that's true, too. But I saw a sheep there and I never saw the like of her before.

—Are you fond of mutton?

—No, it's not that. But a fellow I know was a secret agent or something in Greece told me never have a sheep. He did once, he says, in Crete, nothing else being available, and the silly thing, he says, got so fond of him she used to follow him around.

Then, after a pause while they manage a steep tricky series of descending bends: This valley must be a paradise for the bucolic bachelor man.

Killoran makes no comment. The larks are above them, the bleating choirs of sheep all around them. They are on the floor of the valley.

When they come to the house the old man is no longer standing in the field. He has quite clearly seen them and has gone to his throne room to receive them in proper style. It is a large, square, low-raftered room, down two steps to the left of an oval entrance hall. The steps and the floor are of grey flagstones. There is a wide, open hearth with a whitewashed brace ornamented with the Stars and Stripes and the green, white, and orange of the Irish Republic. In spite of the summer outside there's a blazing turf fire. To the right of the fire, his back to a closed latticed window, the old man sits, his left elbow on a long oaken table, his right hand holding a book. They are led into the room by a tall, middle-aged, grey-headed woman: one of the two daughters the hero lives with: and they are down the steps and well into the room before he takes his eyes from the book and acknowledges their presence. He doesn't close the book. He says: You're welcome, Killoran, you and your friends. Margaret, the other girl, got your message below in the post office. We wouldn't have a telephone in the house. We value our peace. We fought hard for it.

He holds up the book. He says: The young fellow who wrote this is either ignorant or a damned liar. He says there were only thirty-five British military lorries at the Killeen ambush. Ergo: Only three-fifty British troops. When every hog, dog, goat, and divil knows there were at least thirteen hundred, at most sixteen hundred.

—Next Tuesday, says Killoran, there'll be a debate about it on the radio.

Softly, Jeremiah hums about shooting them in pairs coming up the stairs, but nobody pays any attention to him. Mervyn says to the old man that his valley is very beautiful. He has his doubts about heroes but, unlike Jeremiah, he has no intention of farting in the cave of the oracle.

—Beautiful it is, the old man says. And Irish it is. And the Irish is still spoken here from the bridge below to the highest house on the mountain. And the fuchsia, *na deora Dé,* the tears of God, scarlet for blood, purple for kingliness, do you see the way it grows? The fuchsia and the Irish language, all the way from Dingle to Donegal, go together.

—As in Japan, says Jeremiah.

Mervyn is alarmed. But the old man is only amused and he is quite pleasant when he laughs, dentures dancing and shining, great oblong face corrugated with what seems to be genuine kindliness, eyes a bright blue: Jeremiah Gilsenan will have his little joke. Up in Dublin they pay him well for it.

Jeremiah says he is not complaining.

—The bottle, Polsh, the old man says. And glasses for Killoran and his good friends and the lady with them. 'Tis an historic valley moreover. Didn't the great O'Sullivan, chieftain of Beare, lead his people through this valley in the end of the wars with Elizabeth of England, Wilmot waiting for him there, Carew pursuing him here. That was after the heroic defense and tragic fall of the fort of Dunboy on Bantry Bay. And Carew's men after the seige ran their swords to the hilt through the babe and mother and paraded before their comrades with children writhing and convulsed on their spears and the survivors of the gallant garrison they threw over the cliffs and showered on them shot and stones.

The walls of the house must be thick like the walls of a fortress. In the square room the bleating of the sheep cannot be heard. The old man broods. Jeremiah for the moment leaves well enough alone. Killoran says: It was the end of the sixteenth century. Wars were rough.

—War is hell, the old man says. Sherman said. But sometimes there's no way but war. Some authorities say that O'Sullivan Beare went up the Pass of Kimaneigh to the northeast to pray at the shrine of St. Finbar in Gougane Barra. But I know he came up this valley. The old people said so. And over the point you were all standing on a while ago.

He had seen them then. He had stared Mervyn in the eyes.

It is winter in the valley three hundred and seventy years ago. Crooked Domhnall O'Sullivan, one shoulder lower than the other, and Latin and English and Spanish and Irish easy on his tongue, leads the remnants of his broken people on that marathon northward march to O'Rourke's country: not all that far from Carmincross.

Jeremiah breaks the spell: Thisaway, thataway, all we know is that he never came back.

—But his spirit, Jeremiah Gilsenan, still lives on in the men of today. Ireland is Ireland through joy and through tears, hope never dies through the long weary years.

—A lot of other people die, says Jeremiah. Kill now, live later.

Rising wind shakes the fuchsia bushes outside the latticed bay window. The first heavy drops of rain strike separately, sullenly on the panes. The whiskey bottle circulates, or Jeremiah does, carrying the bottle and a glass water jug, a coloured handkerchief draped like a waiter's napkin over one elbow, bowing and scraping and covering up for the sourness of his last remark, finally giving himself a triple helping, unwatered, and relaxing into a low couch beside the tall stiff daughter.

—Show them the albums, Polsh. Show the strangers the albums.

Then the storm is around them, darkening the room, battering at the windows, leaping over the high ridges, rushing into and swamping the valleys. The tall woman rises, lights two oil lamps that hang from the low brown ceiling and have tall flower-patterned globes. By the warm mellow light she brings for examination two huge old-fashioned photograph albums that she takes reverently from the lower portion of a mahogany bookcase. The hero says: If my memory ever fails me it's all there, caught by the camera.

—Your memory will never fail you, father.

That seems to be the first time the daughter has spoken. She sits down again beside Jeremiah. She smiles at her hands locked together in her lap. Her faded brown hair is pulled back in a bun. Jeremiah cups his hands around his whiskey, looks into its depths as if he is seeing the sunken towers of the past in the waters of the great lake in the heart of Ulster. But, as he afterwards tells Mervyn, he is sharply conscious of the clean hotpress odour of the woman, of her fine long thighs, not as young as they once were but, Lord God, have they ever been parted in fun, escaping from the surveillance of that eagle father into an unsanctified hedge-row or an hotel bedroom in city or seaside resort? For her black clothes mourn not a husband but a mother. Or has she all her life done nothing but look after Fionn MacCumhaill here: and listen to his hero-talk about scuffles on Munster roads with British soldiers, the gutters of London as he keeps saying. These photographs and the commentary that goes with them, over and over again, shouldered his crutch and showed how fields were won, only he needs no crutch, and without looking at either album he can tell which photograph is being, at any moment, inspected. Behind him the wind threatens to uproot the fuchsia bushes. He raises his voice to conquer the storm. For emphasis he hammers his left fist into his right palm. He has the look of a man who, when not otherwise engaged, has been making that gesture all his life.

—That there's Tom Barry himself, the prince of them all, a natural soldier. He went with the British to the big war not to uphold the empire but to get a gun in his fist, to see other countries and to feel like a grown man. Those there are the officers of the fourth and fifth battalions of the third Tipperary brigade in training camp in 1921, the good old days. That's an enlargement there on the wall beside the printed declaration of the Irish Republic, Irishmen and Irishwomen in the name of God and of the dead generations, nobler words were never spoken, not even by Lincoln at Gettysburg.

Four young men tailor-squat, four more kneel behind them, seven more stand in the back row, all clutching rifles, wearing big boots and leggings, knee breeches, trenchcoats, peaked cloth caps worn back to front, and stare into the room over the heads of Jeremiah and the tall woman: and through a space in time of more than fifty years. They seem pleased with themselves and their regalia. Some of them are even happily smiling. Jeremiah hums: Forget not the boys of the heather where marshalled our bravest and best, when Ireland lay broken and bleeding. . . .

—That's the crowd there outside Mountjoy jail in Dublin the night before Tom Trainor was hanged and he the father of a large family. But we held District Inspector Potter hostage and when the British hanged Trainor we shot Potter.

—Oh, fair play all round, says Jeremiah. Hang one, potshot

another. Was Trainor hanged for being the father of a large family? Did Potter have any little potters?

—It was war and an eye for an eye, Gilsenan. Not just sitting on your arse in the civil service.

—Father, Polsh says. Language.

—Sit on your arse for fifty years, says Jeremiah, and hang my hat on a pension. As the poet says.

—In a land, says the hero, made safe for you by the blood and sacrifice of the heroic dead. The dead generations.

—If we were all here at the same time, Jeremiah says, there wouldn't be room.

The hero seems peeved. Killoran polishes the fingernails of his right hand on the lapel of his jacket, then studies them as if they were interesting and, surprisingly, smiles: and now I know where I've seen him before, in Madame Tussaud's, that well-dressed, amiable, charming, smiling English businessman, John George Haigh, who used to chat up aging ladies in private hotels, bring them along to inspect his plant, tap them on the head and put them asleep in baths of acid. Did he smile above the Lethean pools? In wax he smiles forever.

Deborah walks to the bay window and looks out at the storm. Mervyn studies his album and wishes he were somewhere else. The old man rises out of his chair and stands behind Mervyn. The album rests on the table. The wind is easing. The movement of the fuchsias is now only a coloured summer dance. The two lamps are irrelevant. The crowd around that jail fifty-odd years ago is, young and old, a most decorous crowd. Killoran comments on that, in an effort to make the peace. The hero agrees: None of the dirty long-haired louts you see today on television throwing stones at the Garda Siochána, the natural guardians of the people.

Jeremiah is also peeved: Behold I come to thee that dwellest in a valley upon a rock above a plain: who shall strike us, who shall enter into our houses?

Nobody bothers to ask him what he's mumbling about.

The two albums do add up to an elaborate picture gallery. Mervyn is reminded of a photograph album he once saw in an English country house, a record of shoots made by parties at country houses all over these islands, pictures of elegant long-skirted women and powerful hairy-faced men, glosses giving extravagant statistics of slaughtered wildfowl, the air stifling with feathers. Jeremiah grumbles: We must have had the most photographed small army in the world. Our memories and military records are superb.

The hero says nothing. Mervyn, feeling his tenseness behind him and above him, turns the pages slowly so as to simulate an interest he scarcely feels. Deborah stands beside the hero. Her odour comfortingly reminds Mervyn of other matters.

Dan Breen, a happy warrior who stole the first move in a war by shooting two policemen at Soloheadbeg, smiles at them from one page. He wears breeches and kneeboots, a Sam Browne and an enormous holster, a cigarette and a wide-brimmed hat. He digs, for the fun of it to judge by his smile, and for the sake of the picture, in a Tipperary field. The year is 1921. At the time of the taking of the picture the British, who over the centuries have done their share of dirty shooting, are offering ten thousand pounds, a lot of money in 1921, for this Tipperary farmboy whom they describe so villainously on the reward notice that he has only to smile and not even Sherlock Holmes would recognise him.

Here on another page and by way of contrast (to put it mildly), is Field Marshal Lord French, spurred feet steady on the ground, riding crop in hands, survivor of all the attempts the patriots made to shoot him. Once, it is rumoured, they came close to decimating his female entourage: he had a marquee tent full of the old hoohah at the western front. There, by his side, but in another photograph, stands a thin ascetic boy who was eliminated while trying to eliminate Lord French and preserve the purity of nations.

Here, backs to the wall, is a round dozen of Black and Tans vainglorious enough to pose for a photograph, and somewhere in the County Limerick where Black and Tans were not the social success of that season. The camera then was still a bit of a novelty. The thugs who bodyguard film actors had not yet started knocking down photographers. Criminals leaving courthouses had not yet taken to hiding their heads in bags. A vain and flattered world smiled back at the camera: watch the little birdie. Yet that photograph had fallen into patriot hands and some of the dozen were X-marked for identification and elimination.

Here's a slew of Tipperary fighters overflowing a charabanc: and here's a crowd in a Dublin street around the dead body of the guerrilla Sean Tracy: and here's a governmental murder gang all in caps and mufflers and looking murderous, and X-marked and numbered on the picture so that they, the murder gang, may the better be murdered. Here's the crowd outside the gate of the ancient fortress of Dublin castle waiting to hear that the truce has been declared between Great Britain and Ireland: and here's the corpse of the hero, General Liam Lynch, after the treaty has been signed and the Irish have gone on murdering each other for the principle of the thing: and here is the house that Jack built.

So Mervyn thinks. And says nothing. Jeremiah says: It's a wonder to Jasus none of them were photographed after exhumation.

This will end bad.

The old man is back in his chair, knitting his fingers until the knuckles crack. Behind him the window is bright, like stage lighting, with sunshine on the glistening rain. He is in the pulpit and ready to preach. He says: It was well said by a good man that the highest expression of our nationhood was the flying column of the army of the people.

—The man that said it, says Jeremiah, was running a flying column.

—Irish towns, villages, factories, creameries, and homes had been burned out or blown up by the high explosives of the British.

—Home industry can do it all nowadays. Sinn Féin Abú or Up Ourselves and blow up the lot of us.

—National institutions were banned or declared illegal. Farm implements and the wheels of carts were taken by the enemy so that the land could not be worked. The use of motorcars and pedal cycles was not allowed except under permit. In the town of Bandon you were not allowed to walk with your hands in your pockets.

—So that you couldn't, says Jeremiah, even scratch yourself in comfort.

—But begod we fought fire with fire.

Fionn, the hero, and Conan the Bald, the mocker of heroes, are off like two galloping horses. Killoran, respectable in dark pin-striped suit, is struck dumb. Mervyn curses Mr. Burns who is happy and safe and faraway. Deborah makes the gestures and twittering noises that can mean only one thing, and is led away by the tall daughter.

—But tell us, says Jeremiah, about the Auxiliaries, Britain's fighting best. Daddio, it always blows my mind to hear about the Auxiliaries. Come tell us all about the war and what they fought each other for.

God bugger Burns that walked me into this embarrassment.

—Then Gilsenan you'll hear begod: that other times may hear and know. The worst flesh and blood that ever walked on Ireland's ground. Officer class they called themselves. Looters, murderers, and maltreaters of men, women, and children. Each man with two revolvers and a rifle, and two bombs hanging from his belt.

—Ready to fight, sings Jeremiah gurgling into his glass. Ready to die for motherland.

—They took a village prisoner once, parish priest and all. And stripped the men naked, and bate them black and blue before the women.

—Rest is pleasant after toil as hard as ours beneath a wild and stranger sun.

—These things happened, Killoran says.

—Oh Killoran, dear brother-in-law, so did the Fomorians, each man with one eye, one leg, and one tooth. So did Genghis Khan. Today we have other problems.

—It's a poor day, Killoran, that I should be mocked in my own house by a relation of yours.

—He's not a blood relation. His sister's a good woman. He may be a relation of mine but there are times when I'm no relation of his.

Killoran, Mervyn realises, is a man to be reckoned with. His smiling composure soothes the old man for a moment, gives Jeremiah a chance to steady himself, to slither soft-footedly across the room, to tinkle at a grand piano that supports yet another gallery of portraits, family and patriotic, men in uniform, men and women in graduation gowns. He is a glib pianist. He hammers out a patriotic marching tune: An outlawed man in a land forlorn, he scorned to turn and fly, but kept the flag of freedom safe upon the mountains high.

—It's a rousing tune, the old man says. And Gilsenan, bad as you are, you play it well. We marched to it in our youth.

Killoran sings, surprisingly, for the slow, self-possessed smile of Mr. Haigh putting the ladies to sleep in the acid baths does not go with enthusiastic patriotic song: Oh leave your cruel kin and come when the lark is in the sky, and it's with my gun I'll guard you on the mountain of Pomeroy.

—Pomeroy, Killoran. A magic name. That's in the fighting North. If I wasn't so old I'd make the journey up there to see how the boys are doing in O'Neill's Tyrone.

Jeremiah has stopped playing. Pray Jesus he keeps his drunken mouth shut. Mervyn says: I'm heading north myself. To a wedding. That's why I came home from the States.

The old man says: It's good to be home. Even in troubled times. There's no place like Ireland. The exile's bundle is a heavy one to carry. Four years myself, after the so-called treaty, I spent in Chicago. There was no welcome in Ireland for the likes of me in those days. But this time, please God, we may see the end of the struggle with the hereditary enemy, the fulfillment of the hopes of the dead generations.

—The dead have no hopes.

That was Jeremiah speaking. But as he continues to play the piano nobody pays much attention to him. He tinkles and hums. His singing voice has no harshness: Come back to Erin, mavourneen, mavourneen, come back, aroon, to the land of thy birth.

The room is suddenly amber with sentiment. The old man wipes an eye with a stiff hand. The tall woman and Deborah have returned, chatting and laughing down the steps from the hallway, then falling silent and listening and standing close to Jeremiah. He turns and rises and slithers towards them and the door. He says: Polsh, sound the loud timbrel in my stead. I go away to meditate.

As he passes he hums to Deborah: Bless you for being an angel.

Her blonde wrinkles are soft and curved with good humour: You're no angel. Heaven is not for you.

He stands on top of the three steps and raises his arms for the curtain speech: Meletus says I am an inventor of gods. And it is precisely because I invent new gods and I do not acknowledge the old ones that he has brought this action against me.

Polsh sits and plays fragments of old operas, the heart bowed down and marble halls and the moon hath raised her lamp above. Jeremiah does not return. Killoran goes looking for him but comes back, smiling over the sulphurous pool, hands deprecatingly extended: We'll find him in the pub at the crossroads. He had the sense and decency not to take the car.

—You'll read my book, the old man is saying to Mervyn. You'll see what I mean. Gilsenan is a bitter man.

—Bitter with booze, Killoran says. We shouldn't have brought him in the state he's in.

—A sad day, Killoran, that I should have to turn on one of your friends. And that a servant of the state should have so little respect for the four glorious years that have made us what we are. Certain things are sacred. Through joy and through tears.

He stands up, it seems with effort. He gives to Mervyn a copy of a paperbacked book. His hand is shaking. Holding his daughter's arm he walks with them to the door. In the bright evening the floor of the valley is sparkling green, beyond comprehension. The sound of the river is twice as loud as it was. The calling of a million sheep comes from a real world that has nothing to do with old men's dreams. Mervyn knows that he is very hungry. All that mutton around him he supposes and the drop of hospitable whiskey. The old man wishes him luck on the journey to the North. After the rain the birds are as loud and plentiful as the sheep. To assuage the hero Mervyn reminds him that the birds do whistle and sweetly sing, changing their notes from tree to tree, and the song they sing is old Ireland free.

Jeremiah is waiting for them in the pub at the crossroads.

Or not exactly waiting. Just there. And singing, But not like the birds.

What he is singing is: Just a lad of fourteen summers, but there's no one can deny that in Belfast one sunny morning he shot a policeman in the eye.

The wisp of a girl behind the counter wipes glasses and pretends not to hear him. Killoran says, quietly and still smiling: Jeremiah, you are the most unmerciful drunken lunatic. Every man and woman in these mountains is, as you know, a good republican. Do you want to get us all slaughtered?

—Oh Killoran who art not a rebel in thyself but merely the friend of rebels in case they might some day come to power, who also begot a priest on my sister, tell me, pray, what is a good republican? Merlin the wizard, all the way from America, tell me what are we supposed to call a fourteen-year-old boy who shoots a policeman? Answer me, Merlin, or you're no wizard. A national hero, of course. Didn't the bloody Brits in 1920 torture and hang the boy, Kevin Barry, for merely shooting a policeman? Not only a boy but a Belvedere boy. Like James Joyce. In Ireland there's precedent for everything. Except common sense.

He sings again: At Scullabogue as the Prods were burning on the bright May meadows of Shelmalier.

He says: I'm revising the patriotic ballads of Ireland and calling the book Gilsenan's Irish Minstrelsy and dedicating it to the smiling Killoran who tells me it isn't sporting to criticise the gallant Provos because thereby we may encourage the Baddies, meaning the Brits and the Orangemen . . .

—It may be the Provos are humane, Killoran says. They want to get the bloodshed over quickly.

But Merlin the wizard, sitting on a window seat and rubbing his bald head as if (Deborah says) it were a magic bottle, thinks, but is too weary to say it: As humane as Lenin. And bloodshed is never over quickly.

—Kill now, live later, says Jeremiah. And Killoran has a son, a priest who every day and night prays to Jesus and what, in the name of the Jesus he prays to, are the Provos: angels of mercy leading Bernadette's feet where flows the deterrent Our Lady too-hoo greet. . . ?

He is singing again, hymns this time. Deborah, who hasn't come further than the threshold but who is rather smiling than anything else, says: What will we do with him?

In the hotel business she has seen a weary lot of boozed men. Killoran says: Give him more drink. Knock him out.

—He'll smother.

—That could be a good thing. But not a smother. He'll sleep.

Behind that smile of Mr. Haigh of the acid baths standing in on the children's hour, Killoran might well be a callous guy. He orders the round and Mervyn pays for it and Jeremiah, because he says he has had enough Irish for one day, has a double Scotch and soda. In the bar there are, fortunately, none of the valley's good republicans. For Jeremiah, no longer singing but still talking loudly enough to be overheard, says: The only thing that kept Fionn MacCumhaill from belting me was that the true Irish patriot, Orange or Green, never hears anything except the noises that go on between the ears.

Deborah says that it wasn't good manners to annoy an old man but it was funny in a way. She asks if Jeremiah hasn't in him somewhere a single spark of Irish patriotism.

—No, now that I think of it, says Jeremiah, it wasn't Fionn MacCumhaill. It was Conor MacNessa was the man. Who or what was Fionn MacCumhaill but a gigantic cuckold?

Jeremiah sounds almost rational. The Scotch has had a sobering effect on him. Mervyn, who is good at such things (after all they gave him money for it in the U.S.A.), can provide the relevant text: 'Twas a day full of sorrow for Ulster when Conor MacNessa went forth to punish the clansmen of Connacht who dared to take spoil from the North. For his men brought him back from the battle, scarce better than one that was dead: with the brain ball of Mesgedra buried two-thirds of its depth in his head. His royal physician bent o'er him: great Fingan who, often before, staunched the war-battered bodies of heroes and built them for battle once more. And he looked on the wounds of the monarch, and hark! to his low-breathed sigh: On the day when this brain ball is loosened, King Conor MacNessa shall die.

—On such bullshit were we reared, says Jeremiah. No wonder we are the way we are.

Killoran, content on a couch in the corner, fingers his gold watch chain and says that that was a poem of the heroic ages.

Mervyn suggests that all Europe, all the world, was reared on something similar. Look at the Lusiads, slaughter from start to finish and all in the name of a Christ as proud as a Portugee.

Deborah tells him that if he wrote a book called Look at the Lusiads she might go so far as to read it. To find out who the Lusiads were. A pop group?

—But the hat we must humbly lift, says Jeremiah, to our remote ancestors. If what we hear about them is true. They killed a bloke. They cut off his head. They made balls out of his brains or vice versa. They threw the balls at other blokes. MacNessa staggers home with a ball imbedded in his brain and is recommended a rest cure. But one day thunder and lightning flatten the forest and he asks his druid what it's all about, and the druid tells him about the crucifixion going on over thataway and about this decent bloke being done in. So he flies in a fit of fury against whoever's doing it and grabs his sword and rushes through the forest lopping the branches off the trees, and out pops the brain ball and down goes he. The true first Christian martyr, and he was Irish, died in a wax when he heard how they done in Jesus. You Irish constantly amuse me.

Deborah says that as well as having no patriotism he has no religion. But she doesn't seem excessively worried.

—That old man, says Killoran, once had the power of life and death.

—Who gave it to him, Killoran?

—He was then part of the military arm of the elected government of the Irish people.

—He is Conor MacNessa sitting up there with the past buried like a brain ball in his head. Up in the North the lads with the bombs instead of brain balls don't give a continental bugger who they throw them at. And King Conor goes on ranting forever about the glorious dead. Commemorations. Commemorations. In 1920 forty Irish Volunteers disarmed fourteen members of the R.I.C. who were idiotic enough to venture into this valley. So commemorate the forty heroes with a Celtic cross. You can see it over the road there.

But when Deborah and Mervyn stand by a window to look across the road the most notable thing they see is that the sunshine has gone again and large unseasonal hailstones are falling, bouncing off the road and off each other: like people, says Deborah, and tells him that she had seen her husband at a distance in a hotel in Killarney: He follows me about a bit, like Mandrake the Magician, sitting in a corner at a safe distance in a black suit waiting for me to leap back into his arms.

—I run, I run, I am gathered to thine arms.

—I do in your big hind end. Why did I ever do it? I mean marry him.

The shower has passed and the road is crusted with half-melted hailstones: People, she says, when the bouncing is all over. In the car Killoran says that the old man will have a big funeral and Jeremiah rouses himself to say: We were always good at funerals. Everything in Ireland begins at a funeral.

The sun is out again. Their road out of the glen repasses the hero's house. In the glass porch, a miniature conservatory, he is standing between two tall women, one of them dressed in green slacks and a red pullover, the daughter they have not met. Killoran hoots the horn. The old man salutes.

—Le rouge et le noir, Deborah says.

Mervyn is surprised: until it dawns on him that she means gambling and not French novels. Killoran says that the red-and-green one is a widow: She doesn't meet people much. She's a dipso.

Relentless Jeremiah says that she was driven to it, listening to that drivel day in and day out: and her husband dead and she with nowhere to go: and the whole country clean crazy listening to the like of that for centuries.

—Oh God, says Killoran, give it a miss. We've had our share for one day.

South of the highest mountains they drive through magic, sunslit drifting mist. But over the ridge the southwest wind is behind them, the mist dispersed, the evening sun glorious over the plains of Limerick, the Galtee mountains clear in the distance. An animal's body, shining silver in the sun in the middle of the road, halts them: a dead badger struck down by a passing car. With an ashplant torn from the hedgerow Mervyn, for the sake of safety, pokes the corpse: telling Deborah that in Baton Rouge, Louisiana, a man walking on a riverbank saw a recumbent alligator on the grass and, thinking it was dead, kicked it, and the alligator wasn't dead. But this badger is dead, blood still oozing from his snout, blood spattered on his fine fur. So Mervyn lifts him by the brush and lays him to rest on the grass margin: knowing nobody who would stuff him for immortality or skin him for the sake of his coat.

They drive on and leave him. The sunlight fades. Jeremiah sulks and sleeps all the way home. Deborah rests a hand on Mervyn's left thigh: No bounce left in you, old boy. Melting hailstones.

She is speaking the truth, for he has been overtaken by an intolerable weariness: advancing age and air travel and all the talk, and the abrasive memory of the wilful woman and the tanker-man back in New York, and the drink, and all the talk and all the talk, and Ireland and Ireland and Ireland, and the drink, and all the talk: but Deborah is wise and well-rounded, even if she is pursued by a black shadow of a husband: and he looks forward to the night and a pleasant pneumatic onset when he has had, as a preparation, a good dinner and wine and a little recuperative sleep.

Later, after dinner, he watches her, fresh and lively on her feet, go from bar to lounge bar to restaurant, checking the day's takings in the cash registers: a great woman at her job. Mr. Burns has a treasure in her and knows it. She wears a cream blouse and a long wine-coloured skirt held up by crossed military-style belts. She whispers to him as she passes that she has put Jeremiah to bed and that she will come with him on his journey and all the way to the wedding. Mr. Burns is agreeable, and, anyway, she's due some holidays and she hasn't been at a wedding since she was mad enough to marry Mandrake. Killoran is nowhere to be seen. Nor Mr. Burns. She doesn't come to him that night: and he sleeps like a dead man, and comes back to life with the sun burning on the drawn curtains.

Over coffee and toast in bed he flicks through the patriot's book: and gets from it the feeling of a lost time, even of a lost chivalry. Old melancholy songs become alive to him again. Perhaps the drunken rancour of Jeremiah has inclined him to give the old man's book a more sympathetic reading. Perhaps Jeremiah's cynical bitterness has shown him an ugly caricature of himself. After all there may be something to be said for the actions of young men who have inherited a sorry history, and hoarded hatreds. But myself when young had the same inheritance. Why then was I never out robbing banks, shooting neighbours, bombing pubs, or tarring-and-feathering teenage girls: and all for Ireland? Nor even, like my brother-in-law at Eastertime, tying green-white-and-orange flags to the tops of trees?

He closes his ears to all questions, and sees and hears the valley of a million sheep, and listens to the old man.

* * *

Some men you have to kill anywhere and one of the most dangerous enemies we had was a sergeant, an intelligence officer of the
R.I.C. He knew we wanted him so badly that he seldom came out
of the barracks except to go to Mass. Seventy steps went up to the
church porch and the only place we could safely shoot him was
on those steps and he fell dead into the church porch. That was in
1920. We acted under the orders of Tom Barry who describes the
whole thing in his book.

In the town of Bandon the British stripped two prisoners naked
and set at them with pincers and pliers, pulling out hair and
crushing nails. One was left unconscious: the other insane, until
ten years later he died in a home.

If we'd shot Major Percival that time we tried, we'd have done
a good day's work for Britain. Didn't he go on to surrender Sin-
gapore and 90,000 men?

The bravest man of all in guerrilla war is the man who can
carry a mine across an open space on a bright night and place it
against an enemy post. But we did not, in 1921, know a lot about
explosives. Sometimes the mines didn't go off. Sometimes they
went off too soon. Any boy, they tell me, can make a bomb
nowadays. There's an American expert who says that, very soon
and very simply, people with a bit of chemistry will be able to
make atom bombs in their own backyards.

And this time we were ready to shoot a certain judge when he
appeared at a lighted hotel window. But a woman appeared
instead and, by God's own grace, we were able to stop in
time. We'd never have slept easy again if we had shot an innocent
person.

And the priest came along the night before the ambush and
asked were the boys going to attack the Sassenach and he said:
God keep you all, and kneel for my blessing . . . and he rode away
on his bicycle into the darkness of the night . . . and Flor Begley
marched up and down playing his bagpipes as the British bullets
flew past . . . there is a man in Listowel wrote a good song about
that: A health to brave Flor Begley, boys, who raised the chant of
war, who strode among the fighting men while his bagpipes
droned afar, for the music of his warlike songs, it cowed the
enemy, 'twas the piper of Crossbarry, boys, who piped old Ireland
free.

* * *

To the music of the pipes, then, on a West Cork hillside fifty-odd years ago, and carrying the mail and the morning papers, Deborah comes into the room. She is dressed in green: slacks and a jacket. He says: Commandants all for Ireland's sake honour be theirs and fame.

She says: Wassthat?

He says: In the I.R.A. in the old days when they used to kill only soldiers and policemen, they had nothing lower than the rank of commandant.

—We always had big notions. If you don't think well of yourself nobody else will.

—Think like a vice-president. That's what a television ad says in the United States.

She tells him that Jeremiah has departed to catch the morning train for Limerick: He says the nation needs him. He left a note for you.

He opens the folded slip of paper and reads: Dear Merlin, My eyes have failed with weeping, my bowels are troubled, my liver is poured out upon the earth, for the destruction of the daughter of my people, when the children and the sucklings fainted away in the streets of the city. See you at the wedding in Carmincross. What and where would, and why should, a wedding be without a wizard and a prophet?

—He must, Mervyn says, know the book by heart.

She reads the note: Very appropriate. What book?

—The Lamentations. The Bible.

—I've read bits of the Bible. There's a copy in every room. Just there: in the drawer under the telephone. He could be right about his liver and bowels.

She removes her green slacks.

—Mr. Burns, she says, is off to Limerick for the day. And to see Jeremiah safely aboard for Dublin. You should be fine and fit this morning. Bouncing hailstones.

For corroboration she feels and fingers. They make what used to be called love. The papers, the mail, the patriot's book are scattered on the floor. Later when he's leaving he forgets to pack the book and never again, or never since, has he caught up with it. His mail is three postcards to welcome him back, one from the third cyclist who, long ago, had danced on the bridge by the creamery. In minuscule handwriting it says: Come with the shamrock and springtime, mavourneen, and it's Killarney, shall ring with our mirth. See you at the wedding in Carmincross.

There is also an airmail letter from New York. It contains only a coloured picture, a clipping from a publicity sheet sent out by a magazine to boost a book about the origins of man. In a field of deep grass men, women, and children, semi-ape and naked except for the hair, wander about looking cheerless and lost and lewd. A handwriting that he easily recognises says: Having a lovely time. Wish you were here.

He is only sorry that he hasn't studied it before and not after his onset with Deborah. Fornication is as good a way as any for working venom out of the system. Some seed may be venom, some lives may begin and continue and end in venom. Even the mildest man grows tense with some sort of violence. Fornication, it is said, is also a sure specific for hangovers but not as easy to come by satisfactorily as the hair of the dog: it calls for a nubile maiden as a sacrifice to the god or, failing that, a strange woman: and Deborah is neither strange to him nor is she a nubile maiden. But dip your buckets where you are. As a strange woman she would have qualified to cure the bowels and liver of Jeremiah and set him safely on the road to Dublin and the needs of the nation. Perhaps last night: but dear God don't tell me that I'm jealous of Deborah, peeping on her, like Mandrake, through the rough high grass of some prehistoric meadow. That woman in New York has my mind polluted.

He tears to tiny pieces the picture of the half-animals, half-human beings, morosely lewd in the long grass, and flushes the pieces down the jakes: and use his blood to daub a jakes: a word he much prefers to the American euphemism, john: and projects his seven curses to the woman and his sympathy, he supposes, to the man who scours tankers. He fixes himself to face the world, and picks up the newspapers, and goes out.

From the back porch of the hotel a gravelled path crosses a lawn, passes a swimming pool. Nobody yet in the pool but splashing children in the shallows, some happy and shouting, two or three nervous. Three young matrons, brown bellies and bikinis, sure cures for hangovers, eyes drowned in black tarns of sunglasses, lie back in abandon in deckchairs: offering breasts and mounds of love (just about covered) and navels like dimples to the sun and Mervyn's sour eyes. They all bid him a good morning. Aloud, he returns it to them. In silence, he wishes them as many good nights as life may afford them. The path leaves the lawn and cuts through a spur of the dunes. Concrete steps lead down to a sheltered corner where he can sit and sleep or read as he pleases and soak up the sun. He never much liked the sun and knows that the sun never liked him. He has neither breasts nor humps of love with which to propitiate the flaming god. The only offering he could make might be misunderstood by the sun, by passing people, by the police. He reads the papers. He falls asleep in his deckchair and in bright sunlight has nightmares: the news is mostly nightmares.

In a pulpit in Belfast a broth of a boy of a free Presbyterian minister is roaring to rapt thousands that the prophet Samuel told the Israelites that they must turn away from false gods: he would ask the people of Ulster to go and do likewise. By false gods he means ecumenism, whatever that may be, and Christian unity, or something. Meanwhile in another part of the jungle eleven women between the ages of sixteen and fifty are in the dock for beating to death another woman, aged thirty-one, who died of oedema of the brain associated with fractures of the skull due to blows on the head. She had fallen foul of the Protestant militant organisation to which she belonged: so her sisters in the Lord chastised her. The reverend mother and director of operations was forty-one years of age and in ten of the forty-one had built up a record for smuggling, forgery, assault, drunkenness, and brothel keeping. Three unemployed female teenagers do most of the chastising because they have been threatened by men and women of the organisation, who recently gave to one of the three a broken hand, and shaved the head of another and washed her not with hyssop but with tar and feathers.

What would the prophet Samuel say to that?

They bring the victim, the sacrificial lamb, to a place jocosely called a romper-room. She goes obediently, even abjectly, leading by the hand her daughter, Charlene, aged five, of whom she is very fond. Loaded with wood for the holocaustal fire Isaac ascends the mountain: how dumb can you get? Abraham follows with fire and sword. One of the three chosen priestesses, teenagers, gives a silver tenpenny piece to Charlene and sends her out to buy sweets. Then the three, led by a fourth who is a little older, and all wearing white masks, go into the room in which the lamb has already been blindfolded with a tea towel; and a dark brown bag has been tied over her head. They push and kick the lamb until Broken Hand and Shaven Head panic and try to stop the ceremony. But one of the other two beats with a brick at the brown bag, beats and beats with a brick as hard as she can. The victim is now prostrate. They stop for a smoke. Their breath ascends in the sight of the God of Abraham who has found a ram in the thicket and slit its throat and incinerated it in the place of his son. They continue to beat and batter at the brown bag. Outside the locked door little Charlene nibbles at a chocolate biscuit, and hears the thumps and thuds, and cries out that she wants her mammy: who stops twitching on the floor and gurgles in the brown bag and dies. A ram of a man emerges from a thicket and takes the body away and dumps it on the edge of a motorway. The two priestesses who had persevered to the end take off their white masks and dance at a disco. And Sarah lived a hundred and twenty-seven years. And the children of Heth answered and said to Abraham: Thou art a prince of God among us. Bury thy dead in our principal sepulchres: and no man shall have power to hinder thee from burying thy dead in his sepulchre. And the prophet Samuel said: When lovely woman stoops to slaughter. And come back to Erin, mavourneen, mavourneen, come back aroon to the land of thy birth, come with the shamrock and springtime, mavourneen, and it's Killarney shall ring with our mirth. And the papers slip from the fingers of Merlin, the magician, and he awakes in his deckchair and remembers his nightmares in the presence of the bright sun before whose glorious rays our heathen fathers bent the knee.

In the afternoon the sky darkens and breaks in thunder and downpour, and by midnight a gale follows. In the morning it is still blowing. There is crushed salt on the windowpanes and the strand is spume and rolling surf. The tower and the headland have vanished. One lone holiday-maker makes the best of it and in sou'wester, yellow tarpaulin, and kneeboots strides along the drenched promenade.

Mr. Burns does not come down to breakfast. He has returned very late from Dublin the night before. But Deborah and Killoran and Merlin visit him in his bachelor bedroom, and Deborah and Merlin, for the fun of it, kneel with joined hands at his bedside while he, in blue-and-white striped pyjamas, pronounces them man and wife: and Killoran records the moment with his camera.

Jeremiah is on the way to his desk in Dublin and they are all happy.

Later, as a gesture, Deborah and Merlin struggle with Killoran through the gale and the rain to the parish church, where, at the side altar dedicated to the Mother of God, the young priest is saying Mass. A dozen drenched people make up the congregation and when the Mass has been read they are all specially blessed. The radio says that by midday the gale will have blown itself out.

It has, too: but it has left its mark all along the fifty miles they travel to the house of the religious order to which the young priest belongs. Trees are down in roadside woods and here and there they come to detours and danger signs, and men working with machine-saws to clear the road. Deborah travels with Killoran and Merlin drives the young priest. Merlin and the young fellow haven't a lot in common. They talk a bit about the troubles in the North and the young man says that if Ireland had been united and free all this could never have happened. His neck is too thin for his high Roman collar, a duck looking over a whitewashed wall we used to say, a collar out of date, Merlin would have thought, in times when so many young priests are going about in turtlenecked sweaters, sailors on shore leave. But this young man, son of Haigh-Killoran, is no ecclesiastical subversive. The real evil, he says, in Ireland has always been the British presence and, indeed, in that he may have some part of the truth. Yet it is not exactly an original remark. Merlin, to say something, mentions that a psychiatrist and a police inspector in the case of the women who battered the woman to death said that although those people were rough types from the gutters of Belfast, they would never have gone so far if it had not been for the surroundings of political violence.

The young man is much concerned about clerical celibacy and contraception. Naturally enough, not clerical contraception. He tells Merlin that an internationally known Irish theologian who teaches at a university in Wisconsin has recently left the Church and given as one of his reasons for doing so that the church had tied the priesthood to celibacy. This worries the young man.

He tells Merlin that the cardinal in Armagh, a great churchman, has condemned contraception because it strikes at the special quality of Irish life. Merlin wonders about the special quality of Irish life. The young man, as if he were quoting from something, says that legislation to legalise in Ireland what is euphemistically called family planning, what a farce! A more correct name for the measure would be a bill to relieve restraint on the open practice of libidinousness.

A fine word and one not too often used nowadays, Merlin thinks, and pulls up suddenly to prevent himself driving into a fallen tree, unmarked by any sign. He hoots the horn to warn Killoran who is bringing up the rear. They are on a side road and in mountainy country. They back out carefully and the young man guides them by an even narrower road: a little child shall lead them. He says that he doubts if the politicians in Leinster House can act in the best interests of the people on the contraceptive issue, that a fundamental of our great traditional way of life is threatened. Bombs on the streets, thinks Merlin, and kneecapping, the bullet in the back, and general savagery: but contraceptive issue is a fine concept and could, also, easily be misprinted as contraceptive tissue.

That very morning Mr. Burns has told him that as he walked, in Dublin, past Leinster House a voice, an old woman's voice, called him by name. Mother Ireland, Merlin suggested. Kildare Street was very quiet at the time. Mr. Burns looked high and low and all around and could see nothing or nobody except two civic guards and a soldier at the gate through which the representatives of the people enter and exit. But there was a poster leaning against the high iron railings. The writing on the poster said: Contraception offends the Mother of God. Contraception will destroy the Irish. Human life is sacred, the Hierarchy says.

The poster also had two feet and an old lady's head, two hands with forearms attached. The hands were knitting. It was an old lady he knew, from Kilcar in County Donegal, seventy-five if she was a day and picketing against the Pill. Only one pill in Ireland. They talked about people they knew in Kilcar and Mr. Burns went on his way wondering.

Meanwhile Killoran is telling Deborah how he was, once in a pub in Dublin, mistaken by an old lady for Jack Doyle the singing boxer. He is, fair enough, about the same shape if not the same size nor colouring, and there is some slight facial resemblance: except that Jack Doyle never wore a moustache. Killoran tells the story well and is not, Deborah decides, a bad fellow to be alone with, and last night if he hadn't been so drunk, she might have done her best to console Jeremiah who was willing but helpless and not half as nasty as he makes himself sound: although for the moment Merlin the Magician is her man, an old friend, but new and born again because of long absence and, for his age, as good as any girl could hope for.

High above the trees, in a gentle watered valley, between two steep mountains that had protected the woods from the havoc of the wind, they see the towers of the castle inhabited by the religious order: nineteenth-century Gothic and once the residence of a British general. In a hall big enough for a battle, with antlered heads and the head of one sad tiger still on the panelled wall, they sit and have high tea, cold ham and beef but plenty of it: and in the company of five of the fathers and the young priest. One of the five is the superior, a stout, bald, twinkling-eyed, happy man who is worth watching for his methodical way of spreading honey on thick, brown, buttered bread. Later they sit in another, smaller room where on colour television the internationally known Irish theologian from Wisconsin is explaining to Ireland why he got married. The news, also in colour, follows to tell them that near Banbridge town in the County Down (and those words are the beginning of a famous love song) the Miami showband on the way from Banbridge back to base in Dublin have been ambushed by members of the Ulster Volunteer Force (Protestant). Three of the young men who make music and sing of love have been murdered. In the process two of the Protestant Volunteers (for what had they volunteered?) have blown themselves up, and an arm with U.V.F. tattooed on it has been found by the road-side.

Quae cum ita sint or sunt, the U.V.F. claim credit for the operation.

Also, near Banbridge town, men with automatic rifles and machine-guns have opened fire on a minibusful of papist pensioners returning home from a bingo session: killing one male octogenarian and wounding six other people. So far no autographed and severed arms have been found on the roadside.

The other crowd, as Mr. Burns says, will want their turn, fair is fair: and a young Protestant man has been taken, by his co-religionists, from the home of his brother-in-law, a Roman Catholic, and shot through both thighs: high. That should contracept him from marrying Roman Catholics. Do the Roman Catholic clergy still preach sermons about the dangers of mixed marriages?

Deborah and Merlin say goodbye to all, sit back into their own car and wait until Killoran, who was once mistaken for Jack Doyle, the singing boxer, says a father-to-son farewell to the young priest who is mortally concerned about celibacy and contraception. Then Killoran drives after them, down a winding avenue that had once resounded to the carriage wheels of a British general who had fought in the Ashanti wars and, in the wake of General Gordon, on burning sands along the Nile.

They stop at a crossroads pub for a farewell drink. Up the valley the towers of the holy house are still visible. In the shadow of the timbered mountains it is dusk, and in the pub an oil-lamp is lighted and a fire burning against the damp. One other lone customer, a gaunt, bearded, mountainy man, sits by the fire drinking a pint and at his knees a bitch fox or vixen muzzled and on a lead. He tells them that a fox will mount a bitch dog or a dog mount a vixen but when the deed is done the male will as likely as not tear the female to pieces. Or is it the other way round?

—Breeds and creeds, he says, never mix.

He accepts another pint.

Outside, a great sycamore sweeps up out of a circular surround of clay and flowers contained by granite blocks: one of the four roads goes to Dublin and another to Carmincross. They shake hands. Killoran, in Deborah's eyes, is the image of Jack Doyle, and to Merlin he is the twin of that smiling Mr. Haigh who used to hit the ladies on the head and dunk them in the acid. Then Deborah, the prophetess, and Merlin, the wizard, are on the road together and heading, more or less, north: Her hair it was the raven, her breath was honeydew. The words she whispered in my ear I will not tell to you. The heather it was purple all along the Moorlough Moss, the day she said to me, we'll wed next June in Carmincross.

# TWO

## *The Honeymoon*

HASTE TO THE WEDDING, and haste to the wedding, no more I'll sit sobbing and sighing alone: and a journey like this should, legitimate or otherwise, be a sort of second honeymoon, a freedom, a discovery of something new and, by spitting at the years, young. Where at this moment are the burning Mexican beauty, in my memory she is now nothing but Mexican, and the tall young man whose people came from Carmincross? The sun, the green and brown and purple land, the little mountain wind. Looking down now into a garden before the first hotel and out over a misty forested glen. The morning of the first full day. Neither the three cats nor the man in the garden can have been out all night; they seem too dry and rested. Two of the cats squat. The third prowls round and round the base of a grey stone sundial. Prowling for birds who are plentiful but high up on the boughs or in the air. Over the high mountains across the glen the sun is doing his damndest to burst the mist and touch the dial. Outlines of mountains emerge: one, a pure pyramid: another, a round-shouldered, hunchbacked giant, head still invisible. The man makes no contact with the three cats. He stands by a narrow, white, iron-barred gate that opens from the garden to a roadway on which a car is parked, engine running, a red car.

She says: My red baby. It did everything for me I wanted it to do.

He sees no baby.

—The car. The red car. I left it behind me. I was in such a hurry to get away. What ever persuaded me?

—You mean?

—My husband. He hangs around. Peeping. I told you. Just peeping. He'll go away after a while.

—Well, I'll be.

—You'll be anyway. If there's such a thing as damnation. That miserable wart will go to heaven. If there's a heaven it's for people like him. What ever persuaded me? Pay no attention.

She goes to the bathroom. He watches the man and listens, not deliberately, to the trickle of water, then the flushing torrent's roar. She returns. The man is going out through the gateway. He wears a dark grey suit. His black oiled hair is parted up the middle and when he turns he flashes a bald spot. He has a pale face and a long nose and black-rimmed spectacles. Deborah's breath is warm on my neck.

—Because he was gentle I pitied him. The lost mother in me. How was I to know that he was a pious miser and dead in the bed? All my principles I broke by marrying him. As you well know. Four years is long enough for anything. He had bankbooks hidden under the carpet. He has a face like de Valera. He was afraid of me because he thought I was a bad woman.

—So?

—You should talk. But at least you're not creepy, gentle, mournful nor a miser.

The red car is driven away. There goes her red baby. She could reclaim it if she wanted to. But that would mean admitting that the man, the pursuing shadow, exists. Across the glen, the hunchbacked, round-shouldered giant shows his glistening head. After the rains, white rills and cataracts pour down his flanks and shoulders. *Tá sé in a lá*. Or: so here hath been dawning another blue day.

—A young gentleman in the city of Dublin dreamed one night that his sister, who was lately married and living at a small distance, had been murdered. This gave him some uneasiness . . .

—It certainly should have done. I swear by dreams.

— ... but feeling it was only a dream he went to sleep again, when the same dream was repeated ...

—Twice last night I dreamt that I was married to that man again. Dreams. Nightmares. Hell and high water. Death walks in dreams.

— ... He then arose, went to another apartment and told his dream with great agitation of mind. He was laughed at for this and bid go to bed again. He did so, fell asleep, and dreamed the third time that his sister was murdered. He again arose, dressed himself with all speed and hastened to his sister's house, where he found her cut and mangled in barbarous manner.

She sings: But you can't stop me from dreaming.

She slips out from between rumpled sheets and dances, tiptoes through the tulips, naked, to the dressing table. He finishes his reading; She lived to speak a few words to her brother and then expired, having been murdered by her husband. The villain was apprehended, tried and hanged for the crime.

—And ruddy rightly so, Merlin the magician. That's a superb old green book, dreams and death, death and dreams. I'd almost read it myself if you weren't here to read it for me.

—George Meredith got money for reading out aloud to a rich old lady.

—Never knew him. Was he anything to Maggie Rob-the-Children Meredith who had the sweetie shop in Gardiner Street? Anyway, who wants a rich old lady? And they only want young fellows. I'll pay you in kind. What I have to give is more than gold.

She sets the words to music and sings them as she wriggles into a blue dressing gown. It is six o'clock in the morning. Deborah and he are not sharing a room except when contiguity is absolutely essential. She is well known in the hotel business and Ireland is too small. Besides: a little love, she says, or a lotta love, as much as we feel fit for, and then a decent night's sleep in a single bed.

He is young enough at heart to pretend to protest although he knows well that what a man of his age needs is less love than the persiflage of love.

\*   \*   \*

After breakfast, and while he is packing his bag, the telephone rings. He asks it what the time is in New York. The sun, bright over the glen, is on the way there. What he really means is how in hell did you find me here in the middle of mountainy peace. She tells him that she didn't make a transatlantic call just to tell him the time of day. That Mr. Burns had told her where he might be: and blast Mr. Burns, he thinks, but then he supposes that she had badgered Burns until he had to say something, probably kept calling and calling and calling, and she says that it's a matter of money, that his check (cheque) is late: and oil, he says, I smell oil, dip your buckets where you are, there's money in oil, offshore oil.

She says that she'd need any money she could lay her hands on, that he was clever enough to get into New York and out of it again before she could swear out a warrant against him: and your cheque (check) is in the post, he says, spend it wisely, buy him a drink when he wakes up, what between his hot work and his hot play he may need it: and she calls him a bastard: so he tells her that the phone call must be costing her a mint and asks her doesn't she know that she can't reverse charges to Ireland. She calls him a double-dyed bastard: and he asks her to give his regards to Broadway, to remember him to Herald Square, and to tell her manly boyfriend that all the drags on Forty-second Street expect that he will soon be there. He is almost singing. Just now he feels that he is more than a match for her. But the line goes dead: most likely she has slammed down the phone with a crash audible over a large area of Manhattan in the early morning-oh. Mid pleasures and palaces, he hums, though we may roam, and remembers that the eminent author of that sweet song had once toured in the southwest of Ireland and, even in the company of Daniel O'Connell, the Liberator who incarnated a people (Balzac), no mean feat, visited Killarney's lakes and fells, emerald isles and winding bays, blow bugle blow: and that, also, in a house still standing in the state of Georgia, the songwriter had once been imprisoned in the basement for being a friend of the Cherokees, doomed to the trail of tears: and haste to the wedding and haste to the wedding: and although the phone call has not left him unamused, war to the knife, he feels a little weariness as he gets ready for the road. Last night the lovemaking with Deborah while it lasted had been fast and furious: small showers last long but sudden storms are short, he tires betimes that spurs too fast betimes: and the mind of a reading man cursed with a plastic memory, who also goes to the movies, and watches television, is a jumble sale, a lumber-room, a noisy carnival: no still pools, no quiet corners there.

Banana Ben with shillings ten will call on you today: and the phone rings again before he leaves the valley: and this is the third man on the telephonic communication, *an tríur fear ar an ghuthán,* as young and lively as he was when he danced with you and Burns on the bridge by Shaneragh creamery: and glad to hear you're coming North for the niece's wedding, how the years pass, and the young grow up and older like the rest of us: and we haven't seen you for a long time while you've lived in Paradise with bright girls and hummingbirds and white dogwood blossom, and where all the crimes are solved by Kojak the Bald or Columbo or Joe Mannix. But up here now we accept murder with the morning cereal: there's a guy here in my town who goes about in a poncho and carries a pistol and belongs not at all to any murder gang, Orange or Green, Protestant or Catholic, and never uses the pistol but it will (sure as God) be someday the cause of his demise: and at a street corner in Belfast two teenage girls (I saw) fighting for the possession of a pump-action shotgun so that one of them could take a crack (not the sort you're thinking of) at a soldier. In the town of Coalisland when all this began the young fellows went off to a riot as if they were going to a football match (in Britain today there isn't much in the difference), and one middle-aged man here, a complete political amateur, carries a catapult and ball bearings, all for the fun of it, very quiet, unassuming, and effective: and in the Creggan, high over the Bogside in Derry city, old ladies on good evenings used to take their armchairs out of doors, so that they could sit in comfort and, from their grandstand seats, look down on all the lovely rioting: in the beginning was the fun and everybody wanted a bit of riot and civil rights: but with nail-bombs and petrol-bombs nous avons changé tout cela, and God be with that dawn in which it was bliss to be alive, with marines, seven feet high, chasing children seven years old, mostly, but not all, boys who were throwing stones and shouting filth, which can break no bones nor decapitate bodies, at men trained to drop behind the lines and break necks and split skulls and cut throats: and when they'd catch the children they could do nothing with them except hand them back to their mothers who would join in the abuse: but the children now have armelite rifles: we progress: and they cry their nursery rhymes, throw well, throw Shell: and in Derry city a big nigger soldier (I saw) chasing the children, apparently to impress some observing officers, and from a safe distance the children shouting, Watch out, Sambo, the officers will melt you down for rubber bullets.

—A moment, a moment.

It would be good to be back again dancing on the bridge.

—There's somebody knocking.

It is Deborah at the door to say she is ready for the road out of the deep glen.

—The third man is on the phone. You'll meet him at the wedding.

She stands close beside him, breathing like a young girl. It is a lovely morning over the glen. She is with a man she likes to love with. She is going to a wedding that is not to be her own. She speaks to the third man: then, mouth close to the mouth of the man she loves to lie with, she also listens while the phone says that people don't notice bomb effects in their houses for weeks, then ceilings fall, walls crack, mysterious draughts plague them: and the third man must remember to ring Alex McConnell re disastrous incendiary bomb at his shoe shop: must also remember to ring Billy Westhouse about his fish-and-chip shop, it got a five-hundred pounder, it was just beside the Ulster Defence Regiment Unit: we're all businessmen together, Orange and Green, Catholic and Protestant, you can get shot nowadays, or kidnapped, just for being a businessman, so as to prove to Colonel Khadafi, who gives them money, that the Provisionals have a proper political motivation: and the third man must call again at the house whose son was murdered in the mountains by the British army: I saw his blood, not upon the rose, but clotted on the meadowgrass. During that week British soldiers go on a rampage in the Pomeroy countryside, they visit a red-haired twenty-three-year-old boy as he is cutting hay on a small mountain farm, they come back that way at six o'clock as he is taking his tea with his mother, take him down to a meadow, march him into the middle of it, order him to stand there on his own land where he has often swung the scythe and disturbed corncrakes: then they go back to the roadway, one shot rings out, Dan McElhone falls dead in his own meadow, his seventy-year-old father watching from the road, crying, Why did you kill my son: and hearing, If you don't get into the house you'll get the fucking same. So last Sunday I thought I should visit the parents: near the top of a hill in Gort na Sgraheen: and I went on past the house to the scene of the murder: the spot is now marked by a stone circle the way the first men who ever came into these mountains marked things, except that they made the mark for the sun and for life. Or was it for death and blood sacrifice? His blood is clotted in the grass, about twenty people there looking down at it, then at the spot from which the soldier marksman fired the shot from behind a rough fence of stone and clay: and some of the people looked at the house and everyone talked in hushed voices and they looked at you as if it were a cause of wonder that you and they were alive: and daily living here now is dicy and dangerous but we are not going to be scared into rabbit warrens: accepting a tolerable level of violence, Jesus eff Christ what a phrase for a so-called civilised statesman to use, is difficult, but the eleven-plus group have been brought up on it and are getting used to it: and three motoring girls were halted by a group of youths on the road at night, they should have known better than to be out at night, between Coalisland and Dungannon: But, fuck it, they're only slips of cutties, says the ringleader to his crew and two of the crew say, Shoot them anyway, they're Catholic cutties, what hell matter whether they're cubs or cutties.

Her breath is whistling into his vacant ear. She is fiercely gripping his right forearm: Did they shoot them?

He cups the phone in his hand: He doesn't say.

—They can't have shot them, I suppose. They wouldn't be there to tell the tale. Don't they go in for rape, at all?

—They're good Protestants. Although there was a sombre case in Belfast.

As indeed there was. The spaltering comic or clown climbs again out of the audience and into the screen. On a chair in the corner of a humble room in a mean abode, but not on the Shankill

Road, sits a widow woman knitting a pullover for her son who is asleep in the next room. You can't see him. He's not on the screen. He's fourteen years of age and mentally retarded. The spaltering clown stands in another corner: he has entered, head first and wriggling, through a hole in the wall, his face is a mask of white paint, his nose a red snooker ball, he weareth a conical hat, white with a red tassel. He faces a door of the room (there are two), which at that moment is broken open. Enter four men. One wears a balaclava helmet and a mask of black cloth. Two wear cushion covers over their heads: the woman's cushion covers. It's a mummery, a masquerade, a Hallowe'en party, bite the swinging or the floating apple. The third wears only his own face: and his clothes, workman's clothes. In one hand he has a pistol, in the other a bottle of wine: we did recruit our venery with wine. He holds the pistol to the woman's head. You hear no words. It is a silent film. The clown mimes and points and looks at you and mocks and mows. The woman is forced across the room to a creaking sagging sofa, and the mummers, the Hallowe'en heroes, Devil Dare, Martin Luther, Cruel King Herod, Dirty Harry Eight, close in around her. The camera discreetly retreats. The cinematic treatment is from the time when the silver screen did not show all. Then the camera retreats still further: and steadies to show the mean abode in all its entirety, a lighted upstairs window, then advances to show the interior of the lighted room, a man, the lodger, pacing up and down in frenzy, rushing to the door to open it and descend, retreating again, then standing still, alone, weeping, shaking with grief and fear and anger. It is a silent film and you cannot hear the sobs. Nor the screams, nor the grunts and groans. Camera retreats. Advances. There are technical terms for all this. The living room, repeat living room, again, the woman, the four men, the gesturing clown. One man stands in the second doorway, which leads into a bedroom. You are not told so, but it is obviously his intention to shoot the boy in the bed who is fourteen and mentally retarded. The woman rushes in to prevent him. He shoots her three times. Exit the Four Just Men. The woman crawls in her blood on the floor. The clown crawls like a worm out of camera through the hole in the wall by which he has entered and is next seen sitting on and clinging to a crude chandelier in a courtroom in which the Four Just Men, heroes of Ulster, stand in the dock being judged. On behalf of the Queen a learned counsel speaks and you cannot hear him because it is a silent film, but then, helpfully, a golden legend on a silver screen gives you his words: The ostensible motive, melud, is that the Healeys, mother and son, were Fenians and had arms in the house, their lodger was a Protestant and that they had allowed firing from the house. They, the accused, also stole eighty pounds. The woman did not die. The boy has died: and Lord Grey, the governor of Northern Ireland, has said that there should be imaginative expenditure of public funds on opportunities for recreation. The last bit is in golden words in a golden-rimmed balloon that comes like a comet out of the head of the dangling clown.

Fadeout.

—Never before in what we call history has it been so possible for everybody to become part of the action everywhere. So that the world can go mad all together and for the same reasons. In another age or aeon, forty to fifty years ago, a humorous Irish-American uncle of mine used to console himself with the thought that we didn't all go mad the one way. But now some unseen diabolical craftsman is working us into one universal pattern. Perhaps he was always there, but now we can see on the instant the result of his work. Our spasms and convulsions are no longer isolated or parochial. All the world for the first time is my neighbour, and everybody sits with everybody else in every house, and the absurd comic climbs in and out of the screen and is aware of but never quite part of the action.

She tells him that he isn't so comic but that he has frequently been part of the action.

She is the picture of pink purring content and her eyes are moist. But he is aware that they can take on a dry stony colour and that her nose, nothing retroussé about it, and her primary chin can slope down in parallel lines.

—Haste to the wedding, she sings as she drives.

She is a bad driver. But his eyes like his false teeth hurt him at times. And, also, while she drives he is free, fond if not dirty old man, to fondle foolishly, and close tired eyelids upon tired eyes, and dream of three youths dancing on a bridge: or dream of a Mexican spitfire and her tall young man on the road to Carmincross, and haste to the wedding and haste to the wedding. My journey is across a map every contour of which is cut in colour in my memory: meeting people I have known for so long I can no longer understand them. What, under God, can I make of the mind, if it is a mind, of the nitwit who writes here in this shabby little illiterate newspaper (Newspaper? What else is new?) an elaborate study (study?) of British spies in Ireland? Who, what, in the name of Blessed Oliver Plunkett, who was a spy himself, are they spying on? Or what can I make of a hypnotised teenager who murders a judge at his doorway in the morning, and in the presence of his eight-year-old daughter, because somebody has told the teenager that the judge, known to be a just and humane man, is part of the British war machine? If the Brits, an ended empire, wish, by snooping about the boozers of Derry or Belfast or Dublin or Crossmaglen, to find out who is liable to have planted a bomb that murdered women and children on a crowded day in the Tower of London where the Brits, in their time, but more quietly, murdered a few, then the best of British luck to them: and haste to the wedding: and she says she's tired driving with a deaf-mute beside her, and that now would be the time to halt and open the hamper and take the sun and eat the chicken and drink the white wine.

Ahead of them, and beyond an arm of lake that glimmers through young forest, is a long line of low mountains.

He says that there will be mist on the Curlew mountains.

—What mist? On a clear day? You're rambling. Or was that a piece of a poem?

—Talking to myself. Remembering a winter's night in a town that we'll be passing through on the road to Carmincross. Two of us long ago, I was a young fellow, on a job for the radio station. Talent scouting. And due that night in a bigger town on the other side of the mountain. But my mate, my senior, won't leave the hotel bar. He keeps muttering: No night for travelling. Mist on the Curlew mountains.

The arm of the lake widens out to a shining islanded body as she drives upward out of the shadow of young trees. The cloth for meat and fruit and bread and wine is spread on a high heathery embankment. They take the sun and listen to the skylarks and recruit their venery with cool Niersteiner, a ninety-ninth honey-moon, the day she said to me we'll wed next June in Carmincross. She is dressed for the mountain on a summer morning: tight green pants, rope-soled sandals, orange sweater: orange for the North, she says, green for the South, and the white of peace and a united Ireland in between them: but she has little regard for hon-eymoons, she has been on one too many, in the Canaries where else, where I found out that he was a pious miser and, although he was afraid to say it out straight, thought that I should right away go back to work so that he could save, somebody should have warned me about him: and less regard she has for Mexican spitfires, Carmen Mirandas, or young men, handsome or other-wise. She beats them off, in her business, at the rate of a dozen a day: They think I'm fast, they think I'm easy, they think, by God and his holy mother, that I ought to be grateful. And where any-way could you go with a young man that people wouldn't make jokes about you behind your back? And I always did like older men, older songs, Simon and Garfunkel, they may not be really old but they sound as old as a nice banshee, Bing Crosby, older men understand better, more to offer in every way, fixing punc-tures and all, greater staying power, they all seem to understand me, some day I'll tell you a real story.

—Old men grow older quicker. No mist today on the Curlew mountains.

A red car passes, going east the road: but it isn't her red baby.

—Move out of the hotel bar in that town my senior in talent scouting would not. Mist on the Curlew mountains, he said. And we missed the date in the next town, and there, and back in Dublin in the radio station there was bloody murder, and in the morning I found out by accident that he had slept with the re-ceptionist. It was a lesson to me. And in the morning, too, when we crossed the Curlews you couldn't, with the mist, see your nose before your face.

The meal is over. The larks still gaily singing fly. Suddenly there are three white sails inching out from behind an island.

They walk up a twisting boreen, open, and close behind them, a creaking, rusty, five-barred gate. Far ahead up the slope of rug-ged heather and small stone-walled fields there is a white house. A woman wheeling a bicycle comes down the boreen and wishes them a happy holiday. When she has reached the main road and gone spinning down the way they have come, they find the stillest place in all that quietness, below what seems to be an ancient stone circle half-smothered in fern and hazel. Green pants folded tidily on green grass. Young love they make in the corner of a field: I begin through the grass once again to be bound to the Lord: beds aren't any better she says, and beds, he thinks, now remind him only of sleep and illness and death: advancing incontinence of an old man, excretory nightmares, performing the simplest, most natural of bodily functions in the most impossibly public and unclean locations: sleep can be a fearsome place. Will some such nightmare be the last memory I carry with me into eternity? Is an aging man making love merely writhing and grovelling in the pit into which with hopeless resignation he has been lowered: and where are the songs of spring, ah, where are they? That very morning, red in the face with alcoholic constipation, he has considered devoutly that St. Anthony, the hermit and not the Paduan who is the restorer of lost property, blushed when he had to eat or perform any other bodily function. But bugger all that and enjoy yourself: and thank the sun and the green grass that you still have the knack, and somewhere hidden in the hazels a goat calls out to him, cor ad cor loquitur, and oh boy, that in our embers is something that doth live.

Relaxing, eyes weary with sleep and sun, they doze for a while, the wine still working: and open their eyes to look at three curious cows who have advanced to look at them. Cows suffer more than cats from curiosity: and in Forkhill, in County Armagh, there was, the day before yesterday, a cow that was so goddamned inquisitive that she led her herd, a little boy of seven, to his death. At Forkhill where once I saw, skimming low over the water like a sharp bright stone falling from the sun, the loveliest kingfisher I have ever seen. But there at Silverbridge, what a happy name, three armed and masked men hijacked a car and in it placed two cylinder bombs. Then they ordered the driver to drive the car into Forkhill and park it in front of the police station. But an army bomb-squad towed the car out again into the countryside and set fire to it. Driving three cows, the little boy approaches. The soldiers shout to him to stay back. But one of the cows forges on to see what all the fuss is about, and the boy runs after it: the cow is valuable and, perhaps, a beloved cow, and no boy would wish to go home to admit that he lost a cow: and boom go the bombs and up goes the boy, and up goes the cow but not over the moon.

That could go down in history as the battle of Forkhill: and now the heroes who put the bombs in the car and forced another man to carry the cargo can blame the bloody British army for: not leaving the car where it was meant to blow up outside the police station: if the soldiers had not moved the car the boy would have got safely back to bed and the cow to the byre. Item: for not taking strict precautions against cows and little boys wandering into danger zones. Item: for little boys being devoted to duty and for cows being curious.

—And Merlin the magician, that's a hell of a thing to think or talk about and you still puffed and panting from making love to me in the corner of a field and, no thank you, I'm quite capable of finding my way back into my own pants, and shoo cow don't bother me, get away, old man, get away.

But she isn't really angry. She holds his hand and dances by his side and sings like a girl as they walk back to the road: and, sure as God, from the top of a slope fifty yards from where they have parked and picnicked they see and hear a red car starting suddenly: and see also all the wide silent beauty of the lake. The three sails have vanished.

—Does it annoy you? Being pursued?

—Do you know I could look at that man and not see him even if he was dancing there starkers, I could forget that he ever existed. Does it annoy you?

—What do you mean?

—We're both pursued. Me by land, in my own red baby. You by air, by telephone.

Very true, he thinks: and says that everybody is pursued by somebody or something, and sometimes even simply by themselves: and asks her does she know Fionn MacCumhaill.

—Never did actually meet him. Never had the chance to give him the four years ration of love. But I do know who you mean. I'm not all that ignorant.

In a faraway Munster glen Fionn, the hero, sits and broods

over pictures of the past, Conor MacNessa sits with the brain ball of Mesgedra buried and buzzing and beating in his head like a bomb in a creamery can: and two tall women, speaking little, move about the hero's house. By pictures and memories, and even by smells and tastes the Frenchman said, and by Christ knows what else, we are all pursued: and she is almost all that ignorant, for all she knows of Fionn, the ancient hero, is something that was read to her out of a child's book and, naturally, when she was a child: but she can still see the book even if she never actually read it: a wide, green book, mostly pictures inside, black-and-white pictures of comic fat giants, men and women, the women had long skirts and no beards, that was how you knew them, the men had beards and miniskirts. The rest of the book was a poem about Fann MacCool, not the way you say it, a giant with a short skirt and a beard who lived in the County Antrim in the northeast of Ireland and up among the Orangemen: and that across the sea in Scotland was a greater giant whose name was Cad MaCullach, the biggest of them all: and Cad heard about Fann and decided to come over and see was he as big as he was boasted to be, and to fight him if that were feasible. Over he came across the Giant's Causeway, which then linked the two islands, and Fann, frightened, got into the bed and pretended to be his own baby: which Mrs. Fann told Cad was, in truth, the case, and Cad said it was a braw bonny bairn and put his thumb in to test the infant's teeth and lost the thumb in one swift snap, and fled in terror, and kicked down the Causeway in case Fann the father might follow, for if the bairn could bite like that what might not the father do? That's why, to this day, there are only two bits of the Causeway left, one on either side of the water.

—That, Deborah, wasn't the Fionn I was thinking of.

—And in Dublin, Merlin, when I was young and if a baby was crying and the mother hadn't the time or a dummytit, comforter I mean, in the house, she would give the baby a bit of fat to suck on and, in the slums of Dublin, they called that a Fann McCool: the thumb, you see.

—No. Fionn sucked on his thumb because he burned it when he tasted the first pinch of the salmon of wisdom, caught in the Boyne and grilled on the river bank on a day as hot and bright as today.

—Was you there, Schnozzle? A wise salmon would never be caught.

—That pinch and taste made him the wisest man in the world of his time.

The wide estuary spreads before them. They sit on a grassy bank, a Norman keep behind them. The salmon, pursued by the dolphin, run in the shallows around the rocks and far out the blue-nosed dolphin dance: sleek warm-blooded bodies, weighing up to a thousand pounds, leaping straight up twenty feet into the air, curious creatures, susceptible to music and the human voice.

—But not all his wisdom kept Fionn from making a roaring bollicks of himself when he was growing old and without a woman and thought to marry Gráinne, the golden, the beautiful, and the daughter of the high king of Ireland.

—Buckteeth and all I can see her, big backside.

—Diorraing the druid said she was the woman of the best make and shape and speech of all the women of the world.

—Sophia Loren. Liz Taylor. A druid was a class of a priest. It wasn't his business to know.

—She looked at grey-headed Fionn and said, He is older than my father. She looked at Diarmuid and his cap fell off and revealed the lovespot that a faery-woman had left on his forehead.

—The what spot?

—The love spot.

—That spot shows up somewhere else, lower down.

—You're no lady. Diarmuid had this lovespot and if any woman in the world saw it she fell in love with him. So he wore his cap low to keep it covered.

—That was decent of him. I've met a lot like that. No spots on your old shiny skull. Except rust or blue-mould.

—But his cap fell off when he was separating fighting hounds and Gráinne saw the spot and that was that, and she slipped Mickey Finns to Fionn and all his men, and fled. Putting Diarmuid under spells to go with her. But wherever he went he left behind him unbroken bread to tell Fionn, his old friend and leader, that he had not betrayed him by getting between Gráinne's thighs.

—Unbroken bread, Merlin, a lovely idea. He was a considerate young fellow. A bit of pork I should leave here, half-chewed, plus rat poison for my following Fionn. He was partial to pork.

Then after a silence: Who baked the bread?

Startled by some deep-down electric shock of danger from the dolphins the salmon shatter the surface. Far out the sea is quiet.

—Around and around Ireland Fionn followed them.

—Mandrake driving my red baby. Following.

An angry voice on a transatlantic telephone, he thinks.

But up now and on to Carmincross where the heather it was purple all along the Moorlough moss, the day she said to me we'll wed next June in Carmincross.

—And Aengus, the god of love, who walked with singing birds flying around his head, warned Diarmuid that while he was flying before the fury of Fionn he should by no means go into a tree that had only one trunk, nor into a cave that had only one door, nor onto an island that had only one harbour. And wherever he cooked his food he wasn't to eat it there, and wherever he ate his food he wasn't to sleep there, and wherever he lay down to sleep he wasn't to wake up there in the morning.

—A likely story, Merlin, a likely story.

—What he meant was: Keep moving, the man's after you, the spear is at your back.


—Along this road, Merlin, there's a house I want to see.

—Your wish is my command.

—It's close to a tower and an old Protestant church.

—I'll drive. You watch.

—There's a town, too, a small town.

—That should be easier to see.

She has no sense of direction, no memory for the names of small towns.

—What made you marry an American?

—Money.

She doesn't, though, believe him. But she laughs when he says that he did it for the pleasure of running around automobiles, opening doors and closing them again: American women, some of them, certainly southern ladies, certainly his wife, would stand all day waiting for the man to open the door of the automobile and tuck them safely in. The problem was made more poignant because, coming from the island of the right-hand drive, he never knew which side of the car was which: which is which as Jack Jones said.

She searches for the town and the tower and the church. He tells her the painful story of the dilemma of Jack Jones: the horns of. . . .

—She smothered you at first, I'd say. A woman can smother a man: American women do, I've heard, bossy, especially the ones with money. She was too beautiful and too much in love with something different from what she was used to, better or worse, how should I know, never had an American, don't believe in tourists. Then you betrayed her, changed her into another person, you were afraid of beauty.

—How do you know?

—From what you half told me. You talk an awful lot but never really about yourself. But once you showed me her picture. Or, honest, once I took a peek at it in your wallet. Big Baldy still carries his scars about with him. That's my theory: and a woman can kill a man with kindness. There was a woman I knew in Dublin, a quiet woman, always had his slippers ready for him in the evening. And everything else, for God's sake, hot and steaming: then one evening, after twenty-one years of peace and quiet, he upped and said he was leaving, just like that.

—He had a young one.

—What else?

—Who killed whom?

—Who killed Cock Robin? Whom did Cock Robin kill? She took to drink. A wreck now.

—Your wits are wandering again. That wasn't me. That wasn't her.

—I'm not saying it was. You or her. It's only a story.

She is the ultimate in the denial of all logic. Dead leaves blown along a road always remind her of love. But here is the little town, and she recognises it: she never forgets a face and that's a useful gift to have in the catering and hotel business: one long wide straight street, fine stone houses, grey and modest, and a few gaudy modern commercial intruders, a new hotel with a timber and glass sun-porch. That main street or one street is a cul-de-sac ending at a semicircular stone gateway to a demesne.

—We used to play in the grounds inside the demesne wall.

—You and who else? You grew up in Dublin.

—Summer holidays, Merlin the Wise. Any fool can have relations in the country. It's lovely inside.

But the iron gates are closed against them and a white-painted notice on the blackboard says that there is no admission except on business.

—Of all the cheek, Merlin. Germans, I suppose. They're buying up everything. They're worse than the English. But not half as cunning.

It is the hour of the midday meal. The broad street behind them is deserted. The sun beats down. The storm of the day before yesterday may by now be troubling Norway.

—We're going in, as Eisenhower said. Before any Germans were here, I was here, in all my girlish innocence, dreaming my dreams: and what have I in the end? You by my side, Merlin, and Mandrake on my trail. The old colonel and his wife who lived in the mansion then, they never minded children playing about the place, even welcomed them.

Leaves from last autumn, the storm must have shaken them from their tombs, stir before them in spirals of faery wind as they ignore the warning notice and drive on. Dead leaves blown along a road always remind her of love, but what she says is: The most that ever happened to me in that little town is that I was nearly raped, age of fourteen, by the father of my best friend, big farmers, my best holiday friend I mean. Lost contact with her when those holiday years were over. Big farmers, rich but rough, they owned a big garage, too, filling station to you. There was this party, her elder sister's wedding, another wedding I remember, we were two out of four train bearers, little virgins all in white and wreaths of flowers, booze like where the Shannon river meets the sea, even the little white virgins giggling and sipping, enough to send me asleep in a bedroom, clothes on and stretched out on the coverlet, any bedroom, the first I tottered into . . .

He watches for another minatory notice to attempt to halt them, or listens for an angry roar or a growl, or a blast flying high from a shotgun: the poor man's garden the open countryside: but there's nothing to be heard, nobody to be seen, and the long avenue winds on between high trees and shrubbery and undergrowth struggling back toward the jungle: nothing German about any of this.

—. . . and I woke up with a jump and there's my best friend's daddy, daddio indeed, standing by the bed, the gate open and the animal on show: two of his pals in the room: one with my white dress hoisted and in the most gentlemanly manner removing my pants, knickers we called them–

—So I've heard.

—. . . knickers was a word I always hated and the third man was–

—Gloating? Licking his lips?

—. . . trying to stick in a finger as broad as a baton and as rough as sandpaper, I can feel it still and I've felt a lot since, coming and going. So I kicked and screamed and jumped and left my pants, reefed, behind me for a souvenir that I'd say none of them ever boasted over, and they ran falling over each other like bullocks, or bulls, more likely, the party was still on and their wives were there: a girl has many escapes.

She hums: There's nothing left for me of days that used to be, there's just a memory among my souvenirs.

—Merlin, there's the church.

—And there's the steeple.

—Walk inside and see the people. There's Johnny Minister running upstairs and here he is saying his prayers.

There are no people at that time in the small cold interior: but people have been here, leaving behind them, for the coming harvest-thanksgiving, cases of apples, mounds of potatoes and turnips, well-washed and colourful cabbages. An apple she picks and bites and chews, a sleek, sweet, hard, green apple: at fourteen she must have been something like that apple, sleek and green and sweet, but hard and well able to hold on to what she didn't wish to give away.

—Tell me Merlin, granddaddio, what do the proddywoddies do with all this stuff, eat it all at one sitting, spuds and cabbage and apples to follow . . .

—Windy feeding.

—. . . and singing hymns all the time? The Arcees never had it so good. Do you know that when long ago I met you for the first time in Waterford I thought you were a Protestant, not that that would make any difference to me . . .

—A man's a man for a' that. There was a Protestant with me, an old friend, dead now.

—. . . and I also thought you were a photographer . . .

—That Protestant was a news photographer.

—. . . because most of the time you seemed to be carrying a camera . . .

—The Protestant photographer or Photographer protestant had strained a shoulder and I was helping out.

—. . . all that, I know, you told me then. Never did know what they did with all this stuff, cabbages, apples and all . . .

—Burn it as a sacrifice before Jehovah.

—. . . Protestant and Catholic all the same to me, not like up in the place we're going to, but I draw a line at Shakes or Sheeks as they used to be called and, that first day we met, you had a Shake with you . . .

—An Indian doctor, a most respected graduate of Trinity College, Dublin.

—. . . anybody, for God's sake, anybody, even Catholics, can go to Trinity nowadays: and having a Sheek with you made me suspicious of the whole lot of you: a flighty young one I may have been, but I had read all about Shakes or Sheeks in the magazines and Sunday papers . . .

—Read?

—. . . had heard about them from other girls who read about them in the magazines and Sunday papers: and not for me, I said, and firmly resolved I was that never never would I be the twenty-seventh mistress of an oil-well. . . .

My chosen part, he thinks, to be with a girl and alone with her secret and her gift. That's something he has read somewhere when he was young, and felt that way: an idea that would lift a young fellow up, as the Lord himself was lifted, into clouds and the wildest dreams. And here in a little church, cold and damp, stone walls indifferent to the sun outside, I am now quite happy listening to the rattlings of an ample woman who has known of many comings and goings, alone with her secret if she has one left, and her gift of accepted experience. Can you give and give and give and still have something left to give?

The church stands deep in a V-shaped cleft, tall trees on the slopes, the rooks savage at being disturbed. The rooks seem to know that these two strangers have nothing to do with the family that held this Norman land for centuries, and kept with them, even into the days of Victoria Regina, the old faith and the Gaelic poets: and one lord of the place was, because of his easy ways with women, cursed in Gaelic by the priest: and the lord's poet in the same language cursed back at the priest: right here in this hollow: and it could well be that the scolding rooks have caught the echoes.

On low ledges in a side porch there are boxes and boxes of planted garden flowers, the air is sleepy with their odour: and those Gaelic poets once walked the rich ground on which this church and the tower, if there is a tower, now stand, and had their own dreams about the secret and the gift, dreams now in the mind of a young man alone with a Mexican spitfire on the road to Carmincross, or in the mind of a young man somewhere up there, bombs and burnings all around him, and ready to marry my favourite niece: How delighted I was when there appeared, all alone, a gentle fair lady delightful of form: truly I thought that Venus or Isis or limewhite Deirdre was approaching me. Her brows stretched like a single hair over her glancing eyes, calm and gentle was her forehead, delicate her mouth, her throat and fair body like the swan on the flood, and in her cheek the red of the rose strove against gleaming whiteness. Shining, brilliant, long in curling tresses, her dark locks descended to her ankles, and all perfection she was to the white tips of her toes.

Pale, positively pallid, girls they dreamed of, those wandering poets who never saw anything except rural wenches, brown from and smelling of peatsmoke, utterly unacquainted with bathtubs: and Deirdre abroad with the three sons of Uisneach in the wild woods of Alban must have been as tough as an unpeeled hazel: and Merlin, she says, you're in a daydream, and there's the tower, and all we have to find now is the house where the old colonel and his lady lived when I was young and almost raped: a lovely house it was and, as you know, I always liked to look at mansions.

\*   \*   \*

The tower is a normal Norman, stone, square tower, one of them in every fifth field in certain parts of this island. It stands on a white rock that comes up just like yesterday out of a half-sphere of meadow. A river, still full after the storm, rims the meadow. They bypass the tower, leaving it for later: first she must find the mansion she remembers. Faraway, he tells her, in sunny California there is a mansion whose middle name is Hell: a corner of hell in the middle of the Garden of Eden: two thousand four hundred men, some black, some white, Protestant or Catholic doesn't make any difference there, no more than it does in hell itself, all sweating and stinking together in a cauldron of a prisonhouse. Hate like most things grows better in a hothouse. Was there ever a civil war among the Eskimos? In twenty-six years in that hothouse in the Garden of Eden eighteen of the prisoners have been slaughtered by other prisoners. Reason? Some are black, some are white, common chains, common suffering do not unite them, weasels fighting in a hole, the poet said, any more than the common lot of living unites people in the world outside the walls. The prisoners call the prison the school for gladiators. Is there a classical scholar among them? No, but somebody has seen the movie about Spartacus the slave in which is shown how in the school of gladiators in the days of ancient Rome, the lowest of the low, if they were tough enough, were trained to kill each other for the amusement of their betters: onion sellers to emperors. She wonders if it would do any good to the gangs in the North if they were trained in one special place to kill each other and leave quiet people alone, would that keep them happy? But he pays no attention to her and goes on to tell how Jesus came singing to the men in the corner of hell in the middle of the Garden of Eden. Jesus was a black man and he sang: Take me back, take me back, dear Lord, to the place I first received you, I need your help just to make it home.

That black Jesus had eight disciples, four white, four black, and on a chain around his neck Jesus wore the glittering golden Star of David, for he said that Jesus the First was a Jew, as had been his own grandfather. He broke bread with the men in hell. He also broke the unwritten law of hate that separated black from white, and black and white from Chicanos. With dignity and ease he passed from one group to another, saying: I come in the name of Jesus, wash me in your precious blood as I open the door of my heart, and receive me as your lord and saviour.

And singing: I've had many tears and sorrows, I've had questions for tomorrow, there've been times I didn't know right from wrong, but in every situation God gave blessed consolation, that my trials come to only make me strong.

—Not much of a song, she says.

—But the grace of Jesus was in the black man's voice, in the notes of the prison's battered piano: and as the glow of the gospel music touched on the audience of dishevelled, jean-clad and self-segregated men (blacks seated on the left, whites on the right, Chicanos in front), they began to thaw. Black prisoners started to sway, clap their hands rhythmically and shout an occasional hallelujah. One white inmate drummed his tatooed fingers and pulled at a diamond ornamentally imbedded in his earlobe.

—Fancy boy, she says. But did the transport last? And where is Jesus now . . .

—Fresh home again from the harrowing of hell.

—. . . and how long will they remember him, and what difference would it have made to me if I had been gang-raped when I was fourteen: and there's the house now but, dear God, it's not a mansion any more.

Lone stands the house now and ravished the woodland and what, from this out, shall we do without timber, the last of the woods are down? What trees are left close in and drip eternal damp over the rutted way. Another notice has warned them that they are to beware of tree felling: and yet another notice has warned them that they are not to reverse while driving through electrified barrier which is two quivering antennae almost touching over a cowgate: they crash boldy through and all is well. Nothing can stop her now from getting to the house: and yet another notice bids them to beware of cross dogs, and they see a small horseshoe-shaped lake set among hillocks, and then a ragged orchard, trees dead or dying or diseased, and a silent Alsatian, very dark in colour, loping toward them over the orchard's tangled grass: and she tells him that never in her life was she afraid of any dog, and

proves it by stepping out of the car and walking toward the steep
narrow twisting steps that lead up through a shattered rockery to
the door of what had once been a white three-storeyed house, roof
tapering as if it had been made in Japan, but the walls now all
streaked and stained with drippings, and the high narrow windows are curtainless and blind. Shamed into courage he follows.
He dislikes dogs and he knows they don't like him. The dog, still
silent, studies them from a distance.

She pulls a sagging bell handle but there is no sound. Six more
dogs, all silent and of varying breeds, have joined the first dog: if
the door doesn't open we are savaged and eaten, a damned sight
worse than rape.

She says: I'll ask if Colonel Dobbs still lives here. He never did.
It was a colonel of another name. That was a game we played as
chisellers around the mansions near Dartry in Dublin. You'd ask
at one house for some grandee that you knew very well lived in
another house. It was great fun. It kept them guessing.

—Ask the dogs. Keep them guessing. I am naked and cold.

—All as bald as your hoary head.

She hammers with her fist. He helps her, that door must open
before the dogs advance: and from where they stand at the top of
the steps they can look into a grass-grown farmyard incredibly
furnished with at least a dozen goats, a flock of geese, half a dozen
donkeys: then the door opens with a gulp and they are looking
at a stocky, square-shouldered young fellow, shabby, dirty, un-
shaven, in whipcord breeches and kneeboots and blue high-
necked sweater.

—No, Colonel Dobbs does not live here he never did, Colonel
Dutton did but they're both dead and gone for years, we bought
the place to sell the timber and fodder cattle: and whoever you
are it doesn't matter but come in or the dogs will eat you.

An oval hallway quite bare of furniture, coloured oblongs and
ovals on the walls where pictures, mirrors, furniture had once
protected the wallpaper from the light. Smell of must. Hollow
echo of the floorboards under six trampling feet. Beyond the
hallway what might once have been a drawing room, now collapsed, not converted, into a kitchen and cookhouse and eating,
not dining, room. Dirty dishes piled high and threatening to
slide to the floor. Dirty utensils already littering the floor. Smell

of dogs. Smell of stale food. A sullen bitch and a litter of squeaking pups in a lidless trunk in one corner. A narrow, bare passage beyond and two shotguns, shining, bright, and clean and held on the wall on hooks: the only cared-for objects to be seen in the house. A voice from a room at the end of the passage: Edward, who's with you, the curse of the Almighty God on that Californian pine, half-dead but hard as teak . . .

—That's my father, the hard man. Two strangers, da, looking for Dobbs.

—They'll find him in hell. Or in the churchyard with the rooks singing his requiem. And Dutton to keep him company.

—My father near lost his leg to a chainsaw, rooting out the remains of a Californian pine. Hard as granite I told him but hell to the heed he'd pay and now he knows, he always will have his own way.

On a rumpled coverlet on a creaking bed, a florid-faced giant of a man, fully dressed in strong tweeds as rumpled as the coverlet: one foot in a plaster: asks them are they relatives of Dobbs or Dutton, both deceased: decent men in their own way and day, but their day is done.

—Not relatives. Just acquaintances.

—Both their places fell to me. The gentry are gone and good riddance in a way, I don't live here, don't think it, but I have to come here, leg or no leg, to see that the work goes on, clear the timber, we'll have a housing estate here to go with the new factory, Dutton was daft, mad dogs, goats, geese, and donkeys, a sanctuary as he called it for senior citizens, I've got rid of most of them, put them down, but that son there of mine likes the creatures, there's a bit of the gent in him, maybe, shooting and fishing and dogs and fine breeches and no work, should be keeper in a zoo.

—Da, the gentry weren't the worst.

—Nobody knows, lady and gentleman and Edward my son, who was the worst. My father was a blacksmith, shod horses and cartwheels and lived by the gentry, the hunters, and looked up to them, he had to if he wanted to see them, they were in the saddle and he was on the ground and stooped moreover, paring the toenails of their horses. Dutton that was here was a gentleman, a decent one, old stock, and Dobbs was another and a bit of a blackguard with the women but which of us isn't. It was said of him that he rode every woman of his own class within a fifty-mile radius, Dutton's wife included and more besides, but he didn't keep a tally on the wives of shopkeepers, small farmers, or labouring men: and one day Dobbs, who had very big feet, and Dutton were shooting on the mountain, climbing a loose stone wall, on the mountain you leave on the left as you come from Dublin, if you came from Dublin: and Dutton's gun went off, both barrels, and Dobbs with the feet like canal barges was wounded in the left foot and Dutton in the stomach and never overed it, some vital organ, and died a month later. Nobody ever knew exactly what happened: for Dutton didn't go shooting but once in a blue moon and only then for the good of the species: and I heard two of my own garage hands saying one to the other, Jim, wasn't it too bad about Colonel Dutton and wasn't Dobbs lucky, the big feet saved him. And the other says: Dobbs will be able now to ride Mrs. Dutton again without undue fear of interruption, his vital organ wasn't even scratched: three miles from where I'm here like a cripple, and the roaring curse of Christ on chainsaws, Dobbs's dining room's a piggery, more eating done in it now than ever was in the days of Dobbs, and they ate well in their time and were there since the days of Oliver Cromwell: and when the big war and the Irish rebels broke Britain, and the gentry and the horses went and the motorcar came, my father was sick at heart and didn't sleep at night, his occupation was going and anyway, by Christ, he liked the gentry, the style and the smell of them and their haw-haw voices. Dutton here was so fond of animals he'd have kissed the backside of a cow: and once, they say, at the salmon-weir in Galway he lepped in naked to swim upstream with the salmon, to find out how they felt about it: but Dobbs over there rode horses until they fell, and killed as many gamefowl as men were killed at the battle of the Somme from which he escaped with his life and one arm: and the rooks crow over him now like Arabs and niggers in London flying home to roost at the end of the long day: and, Jasus Christ son, get glasses and a bottle, a lady and a gentleman to see Dobbs and we haven't asked them yet if they have a mouth between them, and Dobbs dead and damned and the rooks serenading him. Only the rooks left to lament Dutton and Dobbs, and this big house is as you see it and the other one is worse, the china and furniture went to fancy auction rooms, and the pictures and the jewellery: the woods are going, the government now has its own forests, and well-paid factory workers will live here in new houses. When the parish priest, I recall, saw the gloom on my father he asked what the trouble was and my father threw his hammer on the floor and told him and the priest said, John, do not worry we will have our own gentry, home-cured like Limerick ham. Pour, son, with a strong and steady hand and keep the water for washing. My father picked up the hammer and struck the anvil twice to mark his words and said: Mark my words, father, we will have our own shite.

—A blunt man, even in the presence of the priest, but he passed with the gentry and his trade passed with him and I took to the motor trade, cars and tractors. And good health then, if you can't stay longer, and peace to the dead even if we're better off without them: the whiskey and Edward will guide you past the dogs for it would be God's own pity if friends or acquaintances of Dobbs were eaten by the sons and daughters of the pampered brutes that Dutton left behind him. Godspeed and a good end to your journey.

On the gravel before the house: well, somewhere deep down there is, or was, gravel, but now feet go muffled and awkwardly on a carpet of ragged grass and weeds, and on that carpet six or seven dogs are silent in a semicircle, mongrels, puppies, whelps and hounds and curs of low degree: but playful when the young man approaches, who kneels to talk to them, and as he kneels she rests her hand in a motherly fashion on the crown of his head, and asks him his age. Which he tells her. Nor does he seem in the least surprised but, rising, he pats her gently on the buttocks and kisses her goodbye, a long kiss, and Mervyn notices, almost with a twinge of jealousy and not for the first time, how shapely she still is.

He tells her a story: An African walked into a hospital in Johannesburg carrying his severed right hand in his left and, after an eight-hour operation, surgeons stitched the severed hand back on the wrist. The African, identified only as Jacob, arrived at the huge Baragwanath Hospital in Soweto and told emergency-ward staff: The Tsotsis (township thugs) got me.

A doctor said it appeared he had been the victim of some horrifying form of punishment and his hand had been chopped off, Arab-style, with a neat amputation at the wrist by a razor-sharp panga.

A surgeon said about the stitching: It looks as if it has taken. Within six months Jacob should be able to feel with it.

—That's a hell of a story to tell to a girl approaching like a princess to an enchanted tower.

—But the hands are the hands of Esau. It's a fairy tale for our time. Doctors do now what magic women did long ago, princes into toads and toads back into princes, children into swans. Swans into geriatrics. Did you ever look at your hands and realise that you were looking at the hands of an aging man?

—Or woman.

—The hands may be the first part of you that show the signs of age.

—Is that so?

—Once again, you're no lady. Although I know that it doesn't rise the way it used to.

—You're no gentleman. I implied nothing of the sort. For your age you're as well as could be expected. You'll last for another four years.

—My father before he died, quite happy, at the age of eighty-six, had brown spots on the backs of his hands.

—Why be morbid? If he was happy. To hell with the colour of the spots. To hell with the spots. Freckles are brown spots.

It was the grey spots on the walls of the tower had reminded him of the brown spots on the backs of his father's hands: and seen close up the tower is not the average square Norman tower to be seen here and there all over the country, but a most remarkable nineteenth-century imitation, built from a smooth well-cut brownstone, displaying not the wear and tear of old age but a special sort of desolation: a pampered youth left unable to cope when doting parents are suddenly swept away: a rich man's folly, fallen all too soon on evil days: and a rich man, too, who in his happy times was grateful to God for whatever it was that God had given him, and built this tower to prove his gratitude: and an ancestor of that Dutton who surrounded himself with dogs, kissed the backsides of cows, and swam upstream naked to find out what it was like to be a salmon.

The tower is before us, fifty feet or so in height and, wonder of wonders, carved on the stone the simple word: Hallelujah: and the date of the aedification of the tower, A.D. 1859: and more and more wonders, for round and round the tower, in Latin that is less than classical, the man who paid for the building of the tower had asked the stonecutters to carve pious and improving maxims: NISI QUIA DOMINUS. OMNE BONUM DEI DONUM. SI DEUS QUIS CONTRA. QUALES VITA FINIS ITA. LUX VENIT AB ALTO.

The door at the foot of the winding stairway swings desolately open to the wind. We climb the stairs, solid, clean-cut: and carved on every step the name of a man who worked at the building of the tower, a whole generation, in this locality, of masons and stonecutters and men who carried the hod: step by step, treading on man after man, life after life, all the way up to the well-balustraded platform on the top of the tower.

Were they proud of their names cut in stone? Did they come here on quiet Sundays to display them to wives or lovers or children? On a tower built to praise the Lord: children's voices calling, echoing up and down the stairway, only the sound of the wind now, the echo of our slow steps.

Then Lux venits ab alto and the sun is out over the ragged woods and the prowling dogs, down, very far down, because the tower is built on a high place. The horseshoe lake glistens. The cloud of rooks rises and falls over the church in the deep cleft. The platform on which they stand is a suntrap, a sun-warmed crow's nest. Even the falling house they have just left mellows in the brightness and seems at peace, like Dutton himself and the rooks chanting over him.

—Describe your wife?

—A sort of Creole woman. Mysterious, she seemed at first.

—We all do. I've heard it said.

—She thought that water was the best drink. She dressed well.

—You didn't marry her for money.

—No. She told me that if I slept with her I might be disappointed. I was curious.

—Were you?

—Curious?

—No, disappointed?

—No.

—What then happened?

—We drifted apart. As in two little girls in blue.

—Other women?

—A few.

—Blackguard.

—You should talk. What's your motto? Nothing should last longer than four years.

—But while it lasts it should be real. And exclusive.

—And so it was with me, fair dame. More or less.

—More or less isn't good enough. My third man I might have married. But I didn't. Because he drank. Those men around that bed on the night of the party. That red-faced hunk down there roaring in greed and squalor. They were all drunk. That left a mark on me, that horny thorny finger . . .

—Christ's sake, what was that you said?

—. . . and when I thought I'd try marriage, try anything once, even if it was against my principles and better judgment, I picked a man, that fellow, Mandrake, because he didn't drink.

On the rutted narrow roadway far below, and past the church on the cleft, and round the hillock with the tower on top, and past the falling house, and pursued by a pack of snarling snapping dogs, and vanishing under the ragged trees, and reappearing at the gateway of what was once a demesne, and going away up the straight street of the small town: a red car, her red baby.

—What was that you said?

And they went on wandering after that, all through Ireland, hiding from Fionn in every place, sleeping under cromlechs or with no shelter at all, and there was no place they would dare to remain in.

—What's that you said about the hunk in the hollow?

—I told you he follows me.

—It's Mandrake who follows you. Not the hunk in the hollow.

And wherever they went Fionn would follow them for he knew by his divination where they were. But one time he made out they were on a mountain for he saw them with heather under

them: and it was beside the sea they were, asleep on heather that
Diarmuid had brought down from the hills for their bed: and so
he went searching the hills and could not find them.

—What was that you said about the red-faced hunk in the
hollow?

Tempted by the sun in a sheltered brownstone corner they are
going through the motions: and free of beds and blankets and the
posture of death are, for a moment, feeling young.

—If Mandrake has Fionn's gift of divination he'll swear to
God, Deborah, that we sleep on beds of stone.

—What was what I said? That red-faced hunk in the hollow?
You'd never have guessed who he was. He could have been my
first. That young man who kissed me on the forehead could have
been my son. That's why I asked his age. It clicks. The blast I
didn't get was stored away for the missus after the ball was over.
Chances of life: and today he didn't know me, I've changed more
than he has, only one part of me did he ever study intently and it
wasn't on show today, not to him.

—Hallelujah. And praise the Lord. Omne bonum dei donum.
Qualis vita finis ita. Finis ita. My knees are murdered on the hard
cold stone.

—Never before have I been prayed over. And in Latin.

—Raped, you almost were, by the new Ireland.

—So call me Mother Ireland.

From the house below, the son walks, the father hobbles on an
elbow crutch to a car that's parked in among the goats. They
drive away. Silently the dogs watch them go.

—That, Deborah, is how the gentry end. That's what happens
when they go away. His father, the blacksmith, was quite correct:
we'll have our own . . .

—Mind your manners ladies present.

On the top of the tower they bow to each other.

—But I'm talking rot. The hunk is a crude exception.

—My friend and myself sneaked into a service in that church.
We weren't supposed to. We were Catholics. A tall thin lady
played the harmonium and went up and down with the music.
We giggled. Nobody noticed. Nobody minded. Except that boor
when he heard of it. He flogged my friend. Not so much for the
giggling as for going into a Protestant church. He couldn't flog

me. I wasn't his to flog. But he lectured me. That was two years before the night of the famous party.

—He had better plans for you, for God's sake. Than flogging, I mean.

—After that night I never wanted to see that friend again.

—You might have been mother to her baby brother.

—But that day, giggling in the church at the thin lady rising and falling with the music, we were very happy: and the church that day was like a garden, the Protestants and the English are great people for gardens.

—It was God's haggard, Deborah, and the rooks cawing over the stubble.

They see no dogs as they drive away.

—But the English, Merlin, gardens or no gardens, were always a brutal people, paratroopers in Derry city, only the infiltration of Irish Catholics can save them.

—You're a helluvan Irish Catholic.

—Speak for yourself and mind your manners. You were there too. In bright daylight on the top of a tower like two young ones let loose for the day.

—More power to us. That young American couple could do no better.

The picture of that pair seldom leaves his mind, Peeping Tom, Mexican spitfire, tall blond young man who could like a roaring bull play football: and more besides.

The great ironwork gate is not padlocked but it is bolted and the bolt is rusty. The drawing of the bolt and the snapping home again, the pushing out and back again of a rusty, stiff-hinged, wooden sidegate, leaves him sweaty and breathless: next time you're out on the top of a tower be more circumspect, hoard what's left, keep a few shots in the bag and hold them for the best, when you see the whites of their eyes, a virgin may yet wander into the minotaur's maze.

She sits in the car and laughs at my efforts and seems content.

On the reception desk a black cat with green eyes: on the floor an Afghan hound and a gnawed bone: a parakeet twitters, a late lark from the quiet sky, from a circular cage swinging from the ceiling: a tiger skin, head and tail and all fixed to one wall. The bath in their shared room, no singles are available, is big and black and round and beautiful: come in Merlin and join me in this one, this is really with it, mirror mirror on the wall and porpoises at play: and after a good dinner and much wine, a sodden sleep and nightmares when the long trick's over. Until the phone rings at two in the morning because in Manhattan it is nine in the evening and the place is beginning to swing. She is drunk. In the background the pub noises are uproarious.

—We're in the Lion's Head in Sheridan Square. All your friends are enquiring after you.

—Give them my love.

—They are saying, dear, how is the mean baldy old bastard.

—Repeat that.

She repeats it very slowly.

—She says, Deborah, that she is in the Lion's Head in Sheridan Square. She says they're having a hell of a time. She's spending my money. She says that all my friends are asking for me.

He speaks it all quite clearly into the telephone. Oh, weary, hopeless world.

—Give me the phone, Merlin.

Her chin and nose are parallel. Deborah is a witch. Deborah was a prophetess.

But the phone has gone dead, cutting off the noises from the basement bar close to which Phil Sheridan from Cavan, Ireland, rides on forever to burn the Shenandoah Valley.

—Up from the South, Deborah, at break of day bringing to Winchester fresh dismay. The affrighted air . . . what's after that?

—You're asking the right woman.

—Was it with a shudder or like a shudder bore, like a herald in haste to the chieftain's door, the terrible grumble and rumble and roar . . .

—Rhymes with whore.

—. . . telling the battle was on once more and Sheridan so many miles away. Deborah, how many miles away was Sheridan?

—Don't know, Merlin. Don't care, Merlin. Think yourself a hawk. Think yourself a tiger. Think yourself a snake. Wasn't that what the old fellow with the beard used to say to young Arthur in the film about Richard Harris from Limerick? Merlin was his name. The old man with the beard.

In the dark she reaches out and scratches his chin.

—Sleep, Merlin. We've had a long busy day. Think yourself a bull. Think yourself a ram. Think yourself a buckgoat. Not now but early in the morning. We must be fresh for the wedding.

While we sleep we continue our journey. Downwards. Freewheeling downhill. Life's a treadmill. The odd thing is that the wearier you get the faster the treadmill turns. All night long our whirring wheels sing their song as we speed without need down the hills: and the road descends not to the bridge by the creamery, on which three friends danced, but to the bottomless nameless pit.

—That's the old book you bought in the junkshop in Limerick. Just the place to find such a book. Like a rusted dangerous box that shouldn't be opened. All about death and signs before death and signs after death. Thought it was fun at first. Ghost stories and superstitions. And children going to bed frightened and delighted to be frightened. But no, I opened it . . .

—You opened a book.

—. . . last night when you slept like a log or a hog. And no, no it's not a lucky book. It's a rusty box.

It is a good book, though, to read from when Deborah is driving, the world's worst driver.

The sun is on the road and the fields beside it. Death can only be a little and a distant thing. So he reads: Joan, the relict of Gabriel Constant, late of Durmant in the county of Armagh, gent., deposeth and saith that she oft heard the rebels, Owen Farren, Patrick O'Conellan and divers others of the rebels at Durmant, earnestly say, protest and tell one another that the blood of some of those that were knocked on the head and afterwards drowned at Portnedown bridge still remained on the bridge and would not be washed away . . .

—Portnedown?

—Portadown. This was in 1641.

—. . . and that often there appeared visions or apparitions, sometimes of men, sometimes of women, breast-high above the water, which did most extremely and fearfully screech and cry out for vengeance against the Irish that had murdered their bodies there . . .

—All lies. All English lies.

—. . . Elizabeth, the wife of Captain Richard Price of Armagh deposeth and saith that she and other women, hearing of divers apparitions and visions that were seen near Portnedown bridge, since the drowning of her children and the rest of the Protestants there, went unto the aforesaid bridge about twilight in the evening: then there appeared unto them, upon a sudden, a vision or spirit in the shape of a woman standing upright in the water, naked, with elevated and closed hands, her hair hanging down very white, her eyes seeming to smoulder and her skin as white as snow: which spirit often repeated the word: revenge, revenge, revenge. . . .

They are entering a small village. Deborah swings wide on a sharp bend, hits the kerb of an incipient sidewalk, rises in the air and by a miracle of God regains the roadway: no witnesses to witness, no passing Gárda to step forward and boldly apprehend: and, mercifully, no playing children to be summarily slaughtered.

—Pull up at the nearest pub till I draw my breath and have a drink and get my darling, Deborah, far away from that there wheel.

—You knocked me off my balance. Reading rubbish. I'm breathless too. My girdle's killing me. There must be better stories than that in the old green book. All that rot about the Irish drowning Protestants at Portadown. Politics in everything. Even in ghost stories. From this out read to me from some book about Diarmuid and the golden girl, whatever her name was, and Fionn hiding in the bushes to catch up on them, peep on them, Fionn was a peeper: all love and a yard wide is what we want in the world, Merlin, not snow-white women, leprosy, with blood-shot eyes, rising naked up out of black rivers and crying out for revenge, revenge. Too much of that, Merlin, in the world we're living in and in the land we're going to: and put that book away forever or it'll bring bad luck to the wedding.

At the far end of a cluster of houses they come so quietly to the bank of the big river; or the river, broad, sleek, full, sly, gurgling, creeps up on them out of bogland and deep meadows. No ghosts rise up out of this water. No battle, as far as has been recorded, ever happened at this crossing. On the near bank, a few brightly painted houses, two of them pubs, one a grocery, one a shop for selling fishing tackle. Gardens in front and, in a splendid effort to defy the climate and be as gallant as France, little green tables topped by multicoloured umbrellas. Boats moored all along each bank. From across the water and from a long low wooden shed, the rhythmical lulling sound of saw and hammer. Beyond the shed the street of a village sloping upward and away, and not a dog to be seen.

—This is peace, Merlin, heavenly peace. Think you're a dove. Think you're going tiptoe through the tulips.

Long oblong beds of flowers, but no tulips, on a lawn by the river's edge and the cabin cruisers.

—An ideal place for a small hotel. Exclusive. Rich elderly couples. The better-class English would love it, the river lulling them to sleep at night. Worked in a place once like this in England, on the Tyne away inland from Newcastle, close to the Roman wall, lovely gardens by the river and an aviary with all sorts of pheasants in it, things that you simply would not believe were pheasants, all sizes and colours, the pheasant's a most peculiar bird and not as easy to cook as some people think. Just give me capital and what a place I'd build here.

—In Devon, he assures her, lived a man who experimented in dousing and other devilment. He found by means of the dousing pendulum that some seashore stones he tested responded to the vibration tests for anger. He concluded that once upon a time those stones had been used for war and murder.

—Crap a brick, as my father used to say. What rot is that?

—Deborah, I don't quite follow it myself. Yet places where grim things have happened must have memories. That old ruin there on the hill beyond the village.

On the skyline beyond that upward-sloping street of brightly painted houses, the dark solid remains of a medieval abbey: on the wall inside that ruin, and among many other things of a like nature, a grim effigy of a knight in armour that has one thing distinctive or peculiar about it: that it represents William de Burgo, Burke to you, known as Liam Garbh or William the Rough, not because of his language or complexion, but because of his ways, which you might, for want of a better word, call uncouth. For when a sister of his killed in a quarrel his infant son, he punished her by sitting and binding her straddled on a wild horse, with weights tied to her legs, and keeping her there until her body split in two. The most original rape-incest in Irish or any history.

A little of this he mentions.

—History. Merlin, you move among monsters. You love meditating on them. Are all men who write histories like you? Is history nothing but horror?

From the wooden shed on the far bank comes the whine of a power saw. Stops suddenly.

—Apart from Burns and myself, Merlin, do you know any human beings? Or the girl to whose wedding we're going? Or her sisters and father and mother?

—Over there in that shed there's a friend of mine who builds boats and sings ballads. Boats and ballads are big business nowadays. But he did them both for love. Long before they were big business.

—He sounds normal. But has he two heads or something? We do all for love, don't we? Over we go and see him, so.

—In there, in that pub, there's a kind, pious, praying woman. Another friend of mine. For thirty years. Praying for me all that time.

—Much good it did you. Yet no fault to her prayers.

Laughing, she takes from his hands the old green book of dreams of death, handling it gently, not opening it, not fluttering the pages. She is a superstitious woman. It could be a magic box.

—Go in and see her, Deborah. Introduce yourself. Tidy your hair and spend a penny. I'll walk to the boatshed. And meditate on the good old days of the ducking-stool and the bouncing back of a wild horse. Red Indian husbands in Virginia, where I was, used to truss scolding wives near a greenwood fire to cure their ill-temper. But that was long before my time in Virginia.

He is for the present weary of the company of women, a woman, any woman, and round the corner came the sun and the need of a world of men for me: yet the world of men he wishes to walk in has brought Gráinne, the golden, the beautiful, down lower than the roughest of fishwives, or the last of the old-fashioned hoors who had honesty about her and the antique times, and the clap as well, and all for half a crown.

He hums as he walks: The Dean of St. Patrick's Cathedral

flung open his old-fashioned doors, and the ghost of Dean Swift toddled forth in his shift with the last of the old-fashioned hoors.

Not so any more: her untrammelled mane of hair has become a tremendous sexual turn-on: it is bushy, wild, unfettered, magnificently free-flowing, cascading, spun of gold: and it drives men crazy (it certainly should), as does also her slinky, five-foot six-and-a-half-inch, one hundred-and-twelve-pound frame.

Were they weighing her for the drop as would have been any one of the three dependable Pierrepoints, or even Ellis who cut his own throat?

She has an untamed catlike beauty that captivates men, and a sleek body. She walks like a tigress: and is respectably married or about to be respectably divorced, and has sold or been sold on ten million posters at two dollars the poster, to promote Mercury Cougar, Noxzema shaving cream and conditioning shampoo: and the Bishop of Thasos made forbidding faces at an old man returning from Lourdes, for he knew that his pump was worn to a stump by the last of the old-fashioned hoors: and Diarmuid looked around him, and he saw a little boat at hand in the shelter of the harbour, and he and Gráinne went into it, and there was a man before them in the boat having beautiful clothes on him, and a wide, embroidered, golden-yellow cloak over his shoulders, and they knew it was Aengus of the Birds, the god of youth from the green mound by the river Boyne, who had come again to help them in their love-flight from the jealousy of Fionn. . . .

Yesterday it was that Deborah surprisingly had read aloud from a glossy magazine all that stuff about Farrah Fawcett-Majors and her untamed catlike beauty.

The deep sleek seagoing water sweeps the vision away from him where he leans against the parapet. Aengus of the Birds takes Deborah and himself upstream through reedy lakes, under high mountains, against gravelly rapids to where, in the Land of Youth, in a saucer of deep meadow and bogland, the great river rises mysteriously from a deep pool overhung by whitethorn: and Carmincross is on the other side of those mountains: and woman, she says, is a circle and man is a straight line: and there is no sound of saw or hammer as he approaches the boatshed.

Here he is knee-deep in shavings and no friend to be seen. Through another open doorway he looks up the village street. A half-made boat, prow soaring, is balanced on blocks. He calls but there is no answer. A calendar on the wall catches his eye. There's a picture of a girl on it, not Farrah Fawcett-Majors selling shaving soap but a tall, dark-haired, suntanned young beauty in white sweater and tight blue denims: O mons, O fons. She stands at the doorway of an antique shop in a place he knows in Dublin city, an ancient brass kettle in her hands, a red-plush Victorian chair on one side of the door, a wooden rocking chair on the other. The shop is in a short narrow laneway, opening out through an archway to the Liffey quayside: Merchants Arch: and he thinks of sailing men with Spanish boots swaggering through that archway, and he sees the beauty with the eyes of a young sailor, newly landed, all set for hellery. Does she work in that antique shop? Will he go there go find out when he gets to Dublin after the wedding in Carmincross? The sun shines through the archway adding beauty to beauty. He stares at the picture and forgets for a while about Deborah, no longer so young, on the far side of the river, then feels ashamed of himself, and hears the rustle of feet in the shavings and a voice saying: That's a fine filly, isn't it?

This is mildly embarrassing. A man has come in through the other doorway. It is not his friend. It is a tall thin man, a long nose, a black, pinstriped suit, out of fashion, out of style for the place and the time of the day, well-worn but well-cared for, a thin black moustache drooping at the ends, a black wide-brimmed hat.

The first impulse is to roar with laughter. How could she, even allowing for that moment in girlhood, tipsy and prostrate on a bed and ringed around by drunkards, have, even in the wildest reaction, picked on Mandrake? He doesn't need to see the red car to know who the man is. But he checks the laughter. This is confrontation. Fionn has caught up with Diarmuid. Except that the absurdity of the comparison almost again provokes laughter. Will we fight it out here in the shed, splattering the shavings with our blood? Never was in a position like this before, and then only almost: with the sea-divided wife of a merchant seaman who kept open house while her husband was away: and there was I, one cosy morning, when a knock came to the suburban door and the voice of the next-door neighbour said: Your husband is here.

What to do now? My mother never told me there'd be moments like this. Out the window? A long drop to the garden. Hide behind a screen as in a French farce? Never saw a French farce. No screen. Into the wardrobe? Even then, and long before the great physical expansion began, the wardrobe would not have contained me. That new furniture. Certain, too, to leave my socks right in the middle of the carpet. Sailors home from the sea to find a cuckoo in the nest have been known to do dreadful things. Sweat. Muffled curses. Why did I ever suggest leaving her home from the pub? Then back into the bedroom she comes and not a feather out of place. Her husband has just docked in Liverpool and, since she has no telephone in the house, he has called the next-door neighbour to say that he is safely ashore and will be in Dublin the night after next. Then, in her blue silk dressing gown and curlers, sure as God, curlers, over the garden fence she goes to the neighbour's phone to whisper welcome to Odysseus all the way across the Irish Sea, while her guest relaxes and looks forward, ultimately, to breakfast. She is known to be a good cook.

But that was another story and this is a real visible husband, a poor sort of husband yet one with rights and the right to feel offended, rustling toward me through the pleasant-scented shavings left behind by my friend, the singer of ballads and builder of boats. But Mandrake is lighter than I am and not as tall and shorter in the reach. Brace yourself. He could also be a karate killer. Turn and run. Across the deep water to the bosom of Deborah and the prayers of a good woman. He halts at a distance of four paces. The whites of their eyes. He says: How about a drink, professor?

So I tell him that's a good idea. Booze is better than battle.

—But I was looking for a man, the man who runs this place.

—He was here. He went away in a van. There's a boy about somewhere.

No boy is to be seen. They walk fifty yards up the village street to a modernised bar with a jukebox and pictures of near-nudes, not running horses, on the walls. He drinks whiskey. Mandrake drinks grapefruit juice. He makes odd sucking noises after every sip. Silence. The barboy activates the jukebox. Dolly Parton tells them that love is like a butterfly, as soft and gentle as a sigh.

Deborah is beyond the water listening to the kind talk of a woman who prays for me.

Mandrake says that from his own experience love in no way resembles a butterfly. And adds: Tits on her like pigs' bladders that one.

Merlin knows who Dolly Parton is. He has been to Nashville, primarily to Vanderbilt, only on the side to the Grand Ole Opry. He suggests politely that pigs' bladders may be a harsh analogy. Then Olivia Newton-John tells them that she thinks that maybe she hangs around here a little more than she should.

So much Merlin can interpret. Later he asks Mandrake where she is, who she is, and what she's saying.

—Play a forty-five at thirty-three and you may find out. Some night she'll shake her flaming head off, that one. Long blonde hair swinging like horses' tails.

Politely he again asks Mandrake who that one may be. Their dialogue has not yet leaped off into any heaven, desolate or otherwise. Topics seem limited.

—She's half New Zealand. Maori or something. Makes noises like a bushman, a crazy singer if you could call it singing, Arabic singing, Jimmy Kennedy calls it. Saw her on the telly one night with a daft drag act from Australia and Gloria Swanson. Gloria Swanson looked as if she had a bad smell up her nose. Like Queen Victoria finding herself by accident in a hoorhouse.

—Some accident.

—Sic transit Gloria Swanson. That's what a newspaper headline said once when she sailed out of Southampton water for the U.S.A. I had a job in Southampton then. A fine town. To do with the liners. My job. She was a lady, Gloria Swanson.

This is an odd fellow, an odd conversation. Clearly getting us nowhere. Although it does prove that Mandrake has special interests and may be an Authority.

—Do you know that she calls you Mandrake?

Might as well bring matters to a head. He's on his second grapefruit, I on my second whiskey. He'll do himself damage with that grey fluid. Deborah said he was miserly, yet he insists on paying. He laughs. But it is a lugubrious laugh.

—She always did call me that. You remember the cartoon? In the old *Evening Mail*. Mandrake the Magician. He stopped the

whole street with one wave of his hand. Except that I don't have
a tall hat or a cloak. Or a long cane. A wand. Perhaps I should
have had a wand. Hit me with your rhythm stick. The chap who
sings that song has one leg shorter than the other.

To my horror there is a tear clearly visible in the corner of his
left eye, none in the right. Olivia Newton-John has made her
statement and gone away and the jukebox is silent: and the barboy must love only rich-bosomed Dolly who sings that love is like
a butterfly and wild-haired Olivia who cries out that she hangs
around somewhere a little more than she should. There's a sob in
the silence. Slyly the barboy peeps sideways to see what we're up
to. Jesus. Why did I ever halt in this place? Through the side
window of the pub the red car is visible.

—You might do me a favour.

The magician is making an appeal to me. To me. Mandrake to
Merlin. Thank Christ he isn't a real magician. No more than
myself. For if he were he might strike bunions on my bollicks.

—You're a good friend of hers, professor.

—Just friends.

—She used to talk a lot about you. I know you're just old
friends.

—We met a long time ago.

—She has strong ideas. She's a strong woman.

When will he tell to me what can the favour be? He insists on
buying me a third whiskey. Wisely he stays with his second grapefruit.

—A good woman, Mandrake says. But as hard as nails. We
could have been happy. She doesn't believe in matrimony.

—Is that so?

I could have said: No shid.

What's the point in going all the way to the Blue Ridge mountains if you can't pick up a phrase or two?

—Perhaps you might. Maybe you could. Put in a word for me.
Peacemaker.

The barboy and the jukebox have struck again. Dreadful
screaming noises. Arabic music. Does the builder of boats and
singer of old ballads have to listen to this if he comes in here for a
pint? To make myself heard I must shout. Better like that. Cush-
ioned by quiet this conversation might be even more painful.

Love is like a butterfly. Dolly Parton, you may say that again.

—Be glad to. Do my best.

—Put in a word. A word from an old friend.

—Be delighted to. Do my level best.

Shake hands and get away. God Almighty, what next? Mandrake sendeth Merlin on a mission. A cold hand holds on to mine. It may be a trick, he may stab with the other, or shoot, everybody nowadays has a gun except myself. Squeeze his hand heartily, then break the grip while he's still gasping.

We walk to the red car, her red baby. He drives away along the ascending village street and into the romantic west. But it is to be assumed that we will see him again.

Then Diarmuid and Gráinne went along the right bank of the Shannon westward till they came to the rough river of the men of Fionn. And Diarmuid killed a salmon on the brink of the river and put it to the fire on a spit. Then he himself and Gráinne went across the stream to eat it, and then they went westward to sleep. Odour of leaping salmon in the hero's bed.

The boy is in the boatshed planing a plank. Merlin's friend has gone away for the day.

—And I came all the way from America to see him.

—He'll be sorry to miss you. I know who you are. He talks about you.

On an impulse Merlin tears the page and the tall dark beauty from the calendar. That page is the map of a romantic country, far back upstream, where he has been a long time ago. He says to the boy: This lassie I must visit when I get to Dublin.

The boy is most interested: Do you really know her? She's a beauty.

—Her grandfather I might have known. You don't mind losing her?

—Not when she's only a picture on the wall. She'd be going anyway at the end of the month. And I have two right strappers here, live ones. We've a swinging disco.

He gives the boy, he's a bright boy, a ten-dollar bill. He is the returned American, the man with the golden tooth. He says: Have a drink with them for me. The two of them. But don't get your lines crossed. That ruined many's the good setup.

He walks toward the bridge, stops to lean on the lever of a lockgate where a small navigational canal returns to the river. The lock is brimming full and foaming and very deep. Did the two men from Mesopotamia lean here where I now lean before they stepped, drunk and singing, onto the catwalk? Two men, long ago, returning from all the dangers of war, comrades rejoicing, crossing the water to those white cottages over there in the beech trees where before they went to war they had married two women. They would, for sure, have been drunk and singing, soldiers from the war returning, now to home again we come the long and weary strife of battle over, we are at home, we are at home, and down they went into the lock to be found the next time a barge passed through and the water level was lowered. Every place has its memories. What emotions would a dowser record here, holding his pendulum or willow wand over the black water? She may be right: that book may be evil, all those miasmic stories bringing bad luck to the wedding.

She is leaning beside him on the lever, the book in her hand, looking down with him into the lock water. He will not tell her the story about the singing drunkards home, or almost home from Mesopotamia. For all I know or anyone knows they might have fallen in, cursing and fighting. Send for the dowser to probe the heart. God alone, they used to say, knows the heart but Dolly Parton knows that love is like a butterfly.

—Did you see your friend?

—I had a drink with him.

He sees the boatshed again, boats and ballads, smells the fragrance of crisp, curled wood shavings: some woods smell good enough to eat: both doors wide open, the shavings rustling in a little wind: a happy world still in which a man can drive off for the day and leave his work open to the wind and a careless boy.

—The age of this book, Merlin. More than a hundred years.

On the faded green cover there are, against backgrounds of black panels, parallel lines of golden stars. Superimposed on all that a drawing of a closed, tightly clasped black book as big, seemingly, as a family Bible, the leaves gilt edged. One word, FATE, written in white on that black cover.

She ruffles the leaves of the green book. Like the black book it had been fitted with a clasp so as, perhaps, to hoard its secrets more securely. The marks are still to be seen but the clasp is gone. She holds it out over the water. She says that that would be the best place for it, down in the darkness with all nightmares and omens.

—Let the snow-white leper women with the bloodshot eyes go back where they belong.

—But what about the story here of Ninon de Lenclos who had all the lovers?

—What about her? How many lovers?

—Uncountable. She was hammering away and being hammered and she over ninety.

He takes the book carefully from her hands. He tells her that it is an evil thing to destroy any book: the word is sacred.

—Did your friend sing a ballad for you?

—He sang me a love song.

—I never knew he felt that way.

—He said that love was like a butterfly.

They walk back across the bridge. The evening sunshine is bright on the water, on the moored boats rocking in a strengthening wind coming up from the southwest, on the beds of flowers and the painted houses. He tells her that one evening in the pub to which they are walking his friend was singing a ballad, a long one about the beauties of a place called Sheemore. Somewhere about the twentieth verse his memory failed him and, try as he might, he could not recapture the elusive words. Then in fury he stamped his feet on the flagged floor and said that if he were standing on his own land he would never forget the words of any song.

—Deborah, you see what he meant?

—Merlin, the magician, I do see what he meant. He had to be up to his knees in mud.

—The stone flags came between himself and the earth from which all virtue flows. From which we come. To which we return.

—Compliments of the season to you. Is that what you tell the American college girls? I know where I came from and it wasn't the earth. I know where I'm going. But I can do without being reminded that I'll end up in a hole in the ground. If I'm lucky. These days.

—He meant that he was another man when his feet were on his own land.

—Wasn't the flagged floor part of the earth?

They are at the door of the pub.

—This, Deborah, was always a great house for old songs.

—Hold on to your ass, so, wise man from the west. Be ready for a shock. The flagged floor is gone. A sort of plastic thing in its place. And a combo in the corner where your friend used to sit on his three-legged stool and chant his three times thirty-three verses about Sheemore. Where in the name of Jesus is Sheemore? As the pope said about Knocknagoshel.

Two grey-headed newspapermen, both now dead, had first brought him into this place. They had been drinking their way back from Sligo to Dublin. One of the grey-headed men, whose name, as a matter of curiosity, was Shakespeare, said: The next pub on the road is a port of call for all gentlemen of the press, cameramen, reporters, even advertising and circulation reps who put up to be gentlemen, even the men who drive the truckloads of newspapers like mad or Ben Hur through the country and bomb the doors of shops in the early mornings with bundles of newspapers, and once, in the County Limerick, the truckdriver's assistant missed the shop and sent a bundle of newspapers over a bridge and into the deepest pool of a river: and they all stop here at this pub. She's a lovely, kindly woman, always pregnant, well perhaps not always, but only when we call.

She was a lovely kindly woman and she was pregnant. She welcomed them with a soft western voice and with a drink on the house. Her husband, a quiet man, came and went. There was a farm as well as a public house: a plain country pub, flagged floor, wooden benches. The boat builder and ballad singer was there that day and sang a long ballad about the murder of the fourth earl of Leitrim on the shores of Mulroy bay in Donegal in 1878: when Leitrim's lord fell like a dog not far from Glenswillee.

Nothing so capable of cheering you up as a song that is silly sooth and dallies with the prevalence of murder like the old time.

With two commercial travellers on the way to Sligo they joined in a fierce argument about the nature of Lord Leitrim: his coffin was to be seen in the vaults of St. Michan's in Dublin, his blood-boultered ghost still sat by the table in talks on Irish politics.

Had he been any worse than others of his class and time?

Had he not, perhaps, been a bit better?

Once he seized a church for nonpayment of rates.

We need more of his kind in the country today.

Was there much wrong with him except that he was sunstruck from India?

And that he was overfond of the women?

Who isn't? Who wasn't? Who won't be?

Including, perhaps preferring, the fresh, bouncing daughters of his tenants. Didn't the wife of a bold tenant farmer say, when she found the lord bestriding her daughter in the haggard: Bend up your backside, Maggie, and keep his lordship's bag out of the clabber?

They had all by that time had a little too much to drink. Or they would have remembered that there was a gentle prayerful lady behind the bar. She didn't reproach them. She crossed herself quietly. She said that it might not be a good thing to mock at the past or the poor. And: I'll pray for you all. I'll make a novena for you.

She was always pregnant. She was always making novenas.

At the door, with the cool evening breeze coming up from the river, she said to the other grey-headed man who was not Shakespeare but Sullivan: Drive carefully and I'll pray to your guardian angel.

That was thirty years ago. Also for him the house became a port of call: friendship and prayer never did anyone any harm. Her husband lost a leg in an accident and died lingeringly, sitting at times on a small table in the bar, not saying much, explaining now and again that the stump of his right leg was more comfortable on the table than it could be in a chair; saying: I'm not worth my fother now. I'm not worth my fother.

Fother was fodder.

Prayer couldn't do much that you'd notice for a lost leg.

The years brought changes. What else? The husband died. The pregnancies ceased. The cabin cruisers came to the big river. And the Dutch and Germans. Boats became big business. The ballad singer built his boatshed and every time Merlin passed that way he crossed the bridge to talk with the boat builder and hear him sing among the scented shavings: May peace and plenty reign supreme along Lough Swilly shore, may discord never enter our Irish homes no more.

Or: Oh rise up, Willy Reilly, and come along with me, I mean for to go with you and to leave this counteree, to leave my father's dwelling, his houses and free land. And away goes Willy Reilly and his dear Cooleen Bawn.

—After Diarmuid and Gráinne, he tells Deborah, that was the most notable elopement in Irish history.

And in among the shavings the boat builder sang about lovely sweet Sheemore.

And where in the name of Jesus is Sheemore?

So hand in hand they enter his friend's house: hand in hand, this is a sort of honeymoon, isn't it, astray with a woman on the roads of Ireland and with her sixty and six hundred secrets?

Ten years ago he came in here at dusk with an American friend: the week of a boat rally, foreign voices at the bar, music and singing from the lighted boats, flags and bunting everywhere.

Now, as they enter, a small child with a baby billiard cue in its left hand sips or pretends to sip out of a glass in which there has been sherry. The gleaming instruments the combo will use in the evening are piled on a stage in one corner. The child's father, a tall, dark-haired young man, reaches his hand across the counter to welcome Merlin: the child's grandfather had once sat there, where the smiling instruments wait, and said that he wasn't worth his fother: the child's grandmother is making tea in the private part of the house and they will join her there.

Deborah asks him: Is he building you a boat?

—To sail upstream to the Land of Youth.

—Tell me about Ninon who made love till she was ninety.

—Later, later, as the sailor said about the stale preliminaries.

They whisper as they walk through the long hallway between the bar and the house. The green book of death, rescued from drowning where the drunken soldiers drowned, is safely in his pocket. Family portraits on the wall do not stare down on them as family portraits are supposed to do in novels, but look off into infinity: a bewhiskered man standing as stiff as a post, two long-skirted women seated, one to his right, one to his left, a wide white margin separating all three from the transiencies of this life. On a sideboard cluttered with glistening knickknacks there's a photograph of the husband resting his one leg, or the stump of the other, on the table in the bar, and whispering to Merlin as they pass: No man who hasn't all his legs is worth his fother, fother, fother, fother: and the whisper dies away into a sinister rustling as of a rat among rubbish and dead leaves that always remind Deborah of love: and a woman's kindly voice calls to them from a parlour that with knickknacks and portraits is the hallway all over again, only more so: and the tea is steaming.

On that dusky evening of the boat rally the milking is going on in the byre fifty yards from the back of the house: where he leaves his American friend, a big man from Manhattan, in the company of the cows, the woman of the house, and one servant girl: and goes back to the boats to drink with the boat builder and the other singing people: for the Manhattan islander is of Irish origins and will find something to touch his simple ancestral heart in the odour of byres and the swish of milk passing into the pail.

Then, later, the good woman, the Manhattan islander, the boat builder and himself say goodbye by the edge of the river. From a big cabin cruiser, bright and burning as Cleopatra's barge, comes the sound of riotous singing: a hundred swaying lights are reflected in the water. When they shake hands she grips hard and whispers: He's a lovely man, God bless him, is he happily married?

—Monuar, no. He's going through his second divorce.

—Oh Sacred Heart of Jesus, but 'tis the way of the world and they say it's worse in America. I'll make a novena for him to St. Joseph, the patron of the happy home and a happy and holy death. And that other friend of yours that I see and hear on the television, the writer, is he happily married?

—For the third time, I'm glad to be able to tell you.

—And the other two wives? Dead? It would be a dreadful tragedy to lose two.

—No, alive and well and happily married to other men.

—Sweet Fount of Love and Mercy, I'll put him in the novena as well.

Then after a pause. The singing on the water is louder. She says: And while I'm at it I'll put you in the novena.

Over Lapsang Souchong, she has always been particular about her tea, they laugh at the memory, and how the man from Manhattan had, a few months later, written to thank her for her prayers, and St. Joseph for his attentive ear, and to say that his second divorce had been a great success: and gently they remember the dead and the way he used to say: I'm sitting here not worth my fother. Like a child, she says, like a child, sure God help us most men are children and know not what they do: and for once Deborah has nothing to say, nothing to argue about.

In all journeys a visit to the house of a good woman should bring healing and peace: or a visit to the cell or hermitage of a holy man. Yet the nightmares return, although the telephone calls no longer follow him, and Mandrake driving her red car seems to have vanished into the lonely west. Nobody, not even Mr. Burns, knows for a few days where they are to be found: and the sun shines all the day long, and the isolation and anonymity return them to youth as nothing else could. The poet in Tír-na-nÓg was happy doing nothing, vain gaiety, vain battle, vain repose, alone with a girl and her secret, faraway for a while from his own hometown and his warrior companions shouting bullshit around the campfire, and now and then demanding that he sing them a song or tell them a story.

—But then, Deborah, every hundred years the poet grew homesick and the lovely girl had to vary the entertainment. A hundred years of love and dancing. A hundred years of battle. A hundred years of rest.

—Four years is long enough for anything. Your Tír-na-nÓg's like a party I was at once. In a house in the suburb of Stillorgan: oddly enough. There were three rooms at the party: one for drinking, one for fighting, and one for you know what.

—Which did you favour?

—I left early.

—And when the poet got homesick for the third time she

granted him a trip home. Where he stumbled on old age and death.

—Tell me about Ninon de Whatevershewas.

—All our legends end in blood and death. Christ on the cross.

—Cheer me up for the sake of the sweet mother of our divine redeemer. Tell me about Ninon who made love until she was ninety. Christ rose again, for Christ's sake.

—Jesus Christ was crucified and between two thieves he died as the earth it shook and rocks were rent asunder: and his scoffers fell in fright as the noon became the night while the Roman soldiers watched in awe and wonder. But in three short days he rose, all triumphant o'er his foes: and redeemed us all from death and desolation. Now we're safe from Satan's wrath, on the straight and narrow path that will lead us home to heaven and our salvation.

—We're two little lambs that have gone astray, baa, baa, baa. You should have been a preacher. You must have been a beautiful altar boy. When you had your hair. And your own teeth.

—Never in my life, Deborah, was I an altar boy. But I was a boy scout.

—Did Ninon make love to boy scouts? Dirty old dame.

—The altar boys wore red soutanes and white surplices. An elite class. From sipping at the altar wine they took early to drink.

—Did Ninon make love to altar boys?

—In my capacity as a boy scout I went one year to a summer camp in the hills near Bundoran. A dreadful experience. Rain most of the time hammering on canvas. Sitting round a campfire, a red-hot stove, I can smell it yet, in an L-shaped hut that even the army had discarded. Like Fionn and his companions, Oisín the poet, Diarmuid that all women loved . . .

—Only if they were lucky enough to see his lovespot. So you told me.

She sings: There's a pretty spot in Ireland, in my own dear native sireland . . .

—One sunny day, one of the few, I escaped to a meadow with a country girl. Wrestled with her till the shadows fell. She would not give. Bit my hand once when I was advancing my testudo. Bit me badly too. She liked me a lot. She told me so. But she would not give.

—It was only the taste of you she liked. Tell me what's a testudo? But no, don't tell me, I think I can guess.

—The mark was on my hand for a long time. Love bite. I used to show it like a war wound. Or the stigmata. A fellow I knew used to expose himself at parties to show his chancre. His party piece.

—He must have been welcome in all the best houses, an addition to any polite company.

—And I was drummed out of the Boy Scouts for being AWOL. And all for nothing but a bite on the hand.

—Ninon?

—Oh, Ninon. Like yourself she didn't think highly of marriage. Never really committed it. But made love. And more of it. And then some more. And only with the best. And kept her beauty to the end. And one day in 1633, when she was eighteen, a strange old man came to call on her. Small. Grey-headed. Ugly. Evil-looking.

—Not in the least like you. Tall. Bald. Handsome. Caucasian. Two hundred pounds. Did she make love with her caller?

—He wore no sword which meant he was no gentleman. On his head a calotte.

—A what? A growth?

—Which is French for a small leather cap that just covers the tonsure. A large black patch on his forehead. Glittering eyes. In his left hand a light cane like a wand.

—Mandrake. Wand and all.

Mervyn is momentarily startled. But no, the red car is nowhere to be seen.

They have crossed a high moorland ridge. The road ahead serpentines easily down to woods and deep, high-hedged pastures. Rising above it all, to the east, a bulky hogbacked ugly monster of a mountain. No traffic to be seen. No red car. Nothing.

—So this odd fellow makes an offer to Ninon.

—A testudo?

—Not quite. A spiritual offer. She has a choice. If she signs her name in a black book with red edges she can have either supreme honour, immense riches, or eternal beauty.

—Eternal beauty it was, Merlin. How did I guess?

—Sheer genius, Deborah. And the eternal woman stirring in

you. Eternal beauty it was. And the old fellow tells her that in all his years in the bidnis only four women made that choice. Semiramis. Helen of Troy. Cleopatra. Diane de Poitiers.

—Two of them I never met. What about Olivia Newton-John?

Once again he is startled. Could she have been spying on him in the pub?

—And in the end, the old man came back when she lay down to die. She shrieked when she saw him. Died within three days. Beautiful to her last breath. And that there is the mountain where Diarmuid and Gráinne settled and had four sons and one daughter.

An emerald-green slope rises steep and glittering to a sheer rockface gaping with round black holes. Like the head or bow or whatever it might be of the river lamprey. The famous caves. Bones of bears, bones of wolves to be seen in the museum. A sinister mountain.

—And Diarmuid grew rich and Gráinne discontented. A woman may be jealous or afraid of a man's friends. But the red beauty went one worse. Suggested to him, she did, to make peace. With his sworn enemies. The high king, her father and Diarmuid's father-in-law or out-of-law. And Fionn, the furious cuckold. Peace with a father-in-law with whom he had already quarrelled: I bloody well ask you. And cuckolds never forget.

—Mandrake's father was a decent man.

—Up there on the mountain they had a feast and a hooley that went on for a year.

—Managed by Burns at his best.

—That's the story. Although Mr. Burns is nowhere mentioned. And one night at the end of the year when the feast was over and the guests gone home, Diarmuid heard through his sleep the cry of hounds at the hunt. A sound no hunter can resist. And left Gráinne in the scratcher . . .

—Anyway by then they were well weary of each other. All that moving from house to house. Any excuse was good enough to leave her and join the lads.

—. . . and followed the sound of the hounds to the top of Ben Bulben which is over there beyond Sligo town. To find Fionn there. Alone. And waiting for Diarmuid. Fionn, fair enough, warned him against a wild boar, a brute of ill omen for Diarmuid. And the boar ripped Diarmuid open and Diarmuid dashed out the brains of the boar, and there was blood and brains and guts on the mountain heather, and as I told you, young woman . . .

—Yes, professor man. Do ah look lak a suhthen belle?

—. . . and as I told you all our legends end in blood and death.

They park the car and walk a byway toward the mountain: sand and loose pebbles underfoot, the path rising, the high hedges diminishing to end in stone walls.

—And in the 1920s in the civil war, neighbour murdered neighbour on Ben Bulben mountain.

She cries: Enough.

She says that, one way or another, neighbours are always murdering neighbours.

She says that the two of them are on a sort of honeymoon, and on their way over the mountains to a young and happy wedding.

She says that the sun is shining, the green grass all around them, the mountain high above them, the sky blue and the birds singing . . .

—A harper played on the mountain for a people who may have been gods. He played so well that the gods gave him all the rich land you see below you.

—. . . and food and wine and a bouncing bed waiting for them in a fine hotel by the Garavogue River in Sligo town: and that he should not, because he is no longer receiving Indian lovecalls over the long line from Manhattan, allow himself to sink into old age and melancholy: that what's done is done: that every four years a new life begins: and if a harper ever played on that mountain then look up at the mountain and listen to his music. No mountain is evil. Anyway Diarmuid didn't die on that mountain. The runaway couple were happy there for a while. They enjoyed their four years.

The place has inspired her. She has heard the harp. She has become the wise woman. As perhaps she always was, seeing love in dead leaves or dead leaves in love, aware of impermanence, prowling around hotels and peering, without seeming to peer, into every corner for dust, into every till for dishonesty: yet still conscious of and capable of joy: Deborah, the prophetess, who sat under a palm tree that was called by her name and grew by the

way between Rama and Bethel in Mount Ephraim, and the children of Israel came up to her for all judgement. And arise, arise,
O Deborah, arise, arise, and utter a canticle.

—This strange place, he says, has gotten into you. And let me
tell you that it is a strange place. Once, here, at this gateway, I
heard voices and singing. A crowd of people.

—What's odd about that?

—There was nobody in the world to be seen except myself and
a black bullock.

—You were drunk. You were dreaming.

—No. Let me tell you. There were four of us. Burns. The
American friend of mine that the good woman prayed for. And a
man you'll meet at the wedding.

—You said there was nobody to be seen.

—Let me tell you. Just here where we stand. By this leaning,
five-barred iron gate. Hawthorn bushes for gateposts. The same
bushes and the same gate, and that was twenty-five years ago.
Sense of tradition. Here, just here I sat reading a book. Over there
was the black bullock.

They look that way. But the bullock has long gone to bovril
and been replaced by six or seven heavy Friesian cattle.

—Burns and the Yank and A.N. Other had gone up that green
slope, steep as a house, a faery enchanted slope. Green bright
ground under a spink of rock. Country people used to call such
places Gentle Ground. Sacred to the Good People. Stranger visions now on television. Up they scrambled, the three of them, to
see the caves. I did not go with them.

—Lazy.

—Forty times I'd seen the caves. Or more. And that was more
than enough. They always depressed me. Deep mud and animal
dung and stench. Not the sandy caves of Cornwall, pirates and
treasure and all, we used to read about in books for boys.

—We? Professor.

—So here I sat on a flat stone. Here it is. The same stone.
Doesn't look a day older. And read a book.

He sits on the flat stone. She sits beside him.

—Up they go and into the caves and I think how bloody funny
it would be if a few ancient Irish bears had been marooned there.
To see the boys come out in a scatterment like Keystone cops.

—You love your friends.

—So I read my book and might have dozed a bit as the Kerry-man said in the confessional when the priest asked him had he slept with the girl. And awoke. If I wasn't awake all the time. To hear voices and music and singing, and nobody to be seen in the world except the black bullock and myself.

—Drunk and dreaming.

—In Sligo town I will admit we had a good lunch. But not more I'll swear than five bottles between four of us.

—Three of you. Burns doesn't bottle.

—Say three then. A bottle and a vulgar fraction each. What's that between friends?

—It could be a very vulgar fraction. Enough to put you asleep on a June day so as to hear voices and music and singing.

—No question but I heard them. Now I will admit that I was aware . . .

—You mean you knew.

—. . . that I was sitting . . .

—Where we are now sitting.

—. . . in a place in which for untold centuries . . .

—Or a very long time.

—. . . our ancestors had met in a festival whose origins, and damn it woman don't interrupt again, went back into pagan times in honour of the god Lugh, a sort of Irish Apollo . . .

—The image of yourself.

—. . . and it is possible that my imagination was affected by what I know of such things . . .

—And by good wine, good food, and sleeping in the sun.

On the flat stone that may have been there when the god Lugh was honoured and on the green beside it they fall to laughing and other matters. The Friesian cattle, a phlegmatic crowd from flat fields that never knew a mountain, pay no attention. Black active Kerry cows might have mobbed us.

Afterwards they do not lie side by side as couples used to do in those daring fictions that were tiptoeing toward the great or golden age of pornography. No, they simply drive on toward Carmincross and the wedding of the young and beautiful. He tells her, as they go, how when the three men came out of the cave, the American was transformed: That man is so easy-going he would call a cab to take him to the bathroom. Yet that day he climbed a mountain and entered a cave and came out, as the poet almost said, ready like a roe to bound over the mountains. Irish ancestors. In his heart he heard the voices, the music, and the singing.

—The same food, the same amount of wine.

—This was the road we followed. On into the Valley of the Dead. Don't interrupt. Wait and see.

The road is a dust road, very narrow, banked high like the lanes of Devon, hedges higher still. Another car or a farm cart coming to meet them could be one hell of a problem. But no car, no farm cart appears. Thatched cottages shove their shoulders so intimately out into the road that they feel they are driving through the homes and lives of people they will never know. Farmyard fowl take flight like wild birds. Dogs run barking after the car for longer than dogs would anywhere else. From one narrow road they go to another, to another, to yet another: all roads rising. Houses and high hedges fall away: stone walls, bare fields, and a long mountain pass. The ridges of the slopes rising on both sides are battlemented with conical piles of stones.

—Ancient tombs. There are more of them in this valley than anywhere else in Ireland. But not a skeleton to be seen, not a bone. They cremated them. To end in fire and rise like the phoenix, but in Valhalla. Today a lot of us end in fire with little hope of any resurrection anywhere. I know a man who was caught by night in this valley, walking from West Cork to Leitrim along the march of the great O'Sullivan that the patriot was orating about the other day. Spent the night in one of those tombs and said he never slept better in his life. Dry and comfortable. And that day we climbed up there. To the highest of them all. And Burns gave us a talk on how our ancestors had carried up the corpses, cremated them on the summit and given the ashes urn-burial. And the American. His frenzy had passed and he was limping badly. Said couldn't they have buried them below and carried up the ashes.

So, laughing, they cross the ridge out of the Valley of the Dead: and see bright lakes and then woods rising to a blue ridge. Beyond that ridge is Carmincross.

* * *

Yet the nightmares return as the strange man who called himself Nightwalker returned to the deathbed of Ninon the Beautiful. Nightmares by night and nightmares by day: if that makes sense. From the contortions of the night you awake to the radio news and the morning papers. Now I lay me down to sleep: but hear through sleep more than the cry of the hounds, see more by day than blood on the native neighbouring mountains. Pray to God my soul to keep and if I die before I wake. . . .

In Ardoyne in Belfast a thirty-nine-year-old woman arrives at the army post at Flax Street. She is in a disturbed condition. She has reason. She is accompanied by her husband: but that's not the reason. She tells the troops that she has been beaten by an armed band. Who, or which, burst into her house and accused her of spying: Missus dear, you're a fuckan spy and a stool pigeon and a hoor as well.

A group of masked women put a hood over her head and drove her to a house for questioning.

Classical stuff here. Orpheus and Eurydice: as Jean Cocteau might have seen it if he had been born in Belfast.

Her hair is cut off. She is tied to a lampost. Tar is poured over her. Later she is beaten by the gallant armed band who, or which, tell, or tells, her to get out of the area: and in ancient Celtic times a lady, wearing gems rich and rare, walked the length and breadth of Ireland, although what her purpose was in walking all those roads, and so oddly clad, has never, by legend or poet, been satisfactorily explained. Perhaps she was looking for a man. If so, she didn't find one. For neither her gems nor the bright gold ring she wore on her wand were tampered with: and blest was she, the poet said, who forever relied upon Erin's honour and Erin's pride.

But come on now, fair's fair and faint heart never won fair lady: and take a look at it from the other side of the house.

Peter Loughrey, a twenty-year-old mechanic, is peacefully at home when he hears shouting and screaming outside his house. He looks out of the sitting room window, foolish boy to look out or show interest. A British soldier sees him and shouts: Get that bastard in there.

—They break in the door and grab me. They run me to a Saracen and kick me on the floor.

There's rhythm and a beat in that, almost poetry: And I shall wonder, until I am dead, how it ever came into the Saracen's head.

In the barracks he is put up against the wall, arms and legs outstretched in the search position. Two belts of the butt of a rifle in the ribs. From behind, three kicks between the legs, surprise, surprise, surprise. He collapses, writhing on the floor. He is asked are They sore enough. He does not find it necessary to enquire, even if he had the breath, who They are. More thumps in the groin, lest he forget, lest he forget.

He is taken by helicopter to Bessbrook, a quaint place, a catchy name. He is made to stand on a pallet five feet from the wall, made to stretch out his arms until his fingers touch the wall. He collapses. He is forced up again. Two men who have been similarly made welcome to Bessbrook collapse beside him. Later a doctor notes injuries in his arms, legs, nose, and testicles.

Oh, most observant doctor. Oh, most just judge.

That is the first time Peter has ever been lifted.

And well and truly lifted.

He belongs to no political organisation.

Frequently from nightmares a man may waken up laughing, never to know what he was laughing about. It may be time now for such a meaningless laugh.

Two ten-year-old Belfast schoolboys think of mitching for a day from school.

I had a comrade, Barelegged Joe, and we went mitching long, long ago . . .

They leave their two briefcases, full of books, in the bushes near the city hall.

. . . he came trotting a yard after me, for I was a big chap and Barelegs wee. Down in the turnhole lived a big trout . . .

When they come back the army has the area sealed off and the traffic of the whole centre-city is at a standstill.

. . . and God be with the good days, long, long ago, when I went mitching with Barelegged Joe.

From tumult and the world's alarms nothing is sacred any-more.

* * *

Dancing in and out and around with all the other phantasms comes a dream of fair women in faraway Japan, fair women dancing naked on a white mountain: or, perhaps, just one fair woman, pretty lady, Koko, Victorian fantasy, Oriental flesh, Alice in Wonderland, the smartest little geisha in Japan: and fourteen members of the Japanese Red Army condemned and abandoned by their colleagues are left to freeze to death on the high Alps, a death to music, tinkling music, when icicles hang, a pure death but slow: and here is Koko, gravely dancing, wearing perhaps an acromegalic mask, Hiroko Nagata for it is she, a student of pharmacy and at twenty-eight and in these times still a virgin, yet a member, on virgin snow, of that Red Army and the proud teacher of a doctrine called Sokatsu: and that is an obscure Japanese word meaning the bringing together of isolated facts to form a shining transcendent principle.

Is that what my nightmares are now doing?

But, by Sokatsu, Hiroko Nagata, pale primrose, fearful to behold bright Phoebus in his strength, can, even on the virgin snow, dance her way only to murder most foul, so much a part of the world we murder in, the great reality of our time, says a French Algerian who seldom saw snow: they're all at it, as a wise friend of my boyhood used to say with wonder about fornication: and, once the dance of Sokatsu has commenced, the maiden cries that only death awaits.

She is sexually unbalanced, the doctors say. What else is new?

Up and out on the bright and snowy slopes she devotes herself, excluding all others, to the four females among the victims: she shaves their heads to cure their bourgeois weaknesses for painting the mouth and lying with men.

She has exophthalmic goitre, the doctors say, and that makes her eyes bulge abnormally.

She has buck teeth, as all can see, and that worries her so much that she has them treated by a dentist even at a time when all the policemen in Japan are racing round and round in frantic search for Rollee Pollee Nan.

It has been said (by the doctors) that her pop eyes have more to do with her murders than her (if any) ideology.

On the bright snow she dances to the slow deaths of fourteen former friends: a formal ritual dance.

But a song, a song, give us a bar of a song, sing me the songs my mother sang, sing me an old Irish song: One, two, three.

Sunday morning, went for a drive, took along my Colt forty-five, hey hey what a beautiful day. Went to Derry on a hunch, knew I'd get a Teig before lunch, hey hey it's a beautiful day.

On the fourteenth of August we took a little trip up along Bombay Street and burned out all the shit. We took a little petrol and took a little gun and we fought the bloody Fenians till we had them on the run.

Armoured cars and tanks and guns came to take away our sons, but every man will stand behind the men behind the wire.

We have bombs, we have guns, we have Fenians on the run: and the ones that we killed were all bastards everyone.

All together now and sing along with me: We have bombs we have guns came to take way our sons, we took a little petrol and burned out all the shit, and soldiers are we whose lives are pledged to save our gracious queen. We had joy, we had fun, we had slaughter in the sun: and only, only, the man said, grant to me to write the ballads of a nation, and hey hey it's a beautiful day.

No, the day has not yet dawned. This is the night and its nightmares and here, in a room so bright that it hurts, my bed is surrounded by phantasms: Lust that wrinkled care derides and murder waving human hides, kneecap neighbours as you go on the light fantastic toe. Once, years ago, I awoke in a room as brightly lighted as this: having, three hours previously, rolled in from a jovial Dublin party: and thought, as I awoke, that I was still at a party, even a better party than the one I had left. For although I was alone in my bed, the lighted room was crowded, all my friends, everybody I had ever liked from Bonn and Belfast, Oregon and Omagh, Porlock and Punchestown, Sauchiehall Street and Saffron Walden, London and Limerick, every and any place you care to think of, all merry, all laughing, singing, talking, drinking. For a long time and very happily I lay and looked at them and said nothing: when it seemed odd to me that I should lie at my ease on a bed in a lighted room and a party of my friends going on all around me. Is this how the lonely dead look back from somewhere on the world they have left? So I rolled and slithered quietly to the edge of the bed, tiptoed to the light switch beside the door, switched on the light, and was again alone.

To see rats and pink elephants is bad and very bad. To see all your friends, all laughing and happy and paying no attention to you, may be a damned sight worse.

But here and now it may be as it was then: That I lie in a dark room and the visions parade through a lighted mind tormented by the horrors of everyday happenings.

Outside the window the rush of the waters of the Garravogue from Loch Gill to Sligo Bay: I will arise and go now.

Deborah, in the next and linking room, sleeps the sleep of the satiated: I was about to say. But how do I know that she does or doesn't, and isn't every bed, in light or in darkness, surrounded by its own phantasms?

How happy any child might be to be snug in a caravan and off with the raggle-taggle gypsies, oh: And here is Carrie Allen, all of three years of age and sleeping beside her mother, Margaret Ann, in their caravan home near Middletown in the county of Armagh. It's my own Irish home, no matter where I roam, my heart is at home in old Ireland in the county of Armagh. Carrie clutches in her arms her favourite toy, perhaps, after her mother, her favourite person: a woolly long-legged creature that might by its maker have been meant to resemble Kermit the Frog. Hard to be positive about that now, for here I have nothing to go on but a newsprint picture: and Kermit, whoever he was or was meant to be, is a little the worse for wear and bullet wounds. Which he bears without a murmur: his life goes on and he may, oddly enough, become even more dear to little Carrie. He may be the dearest thing she, at this moment, has left: for round her caravan come creeping in the quiet autumn night a gallant band of the boys of the County Armagh about whom, or about some of them, there is a rousing song. Beside your caravan the campfire's bright, no that's a different song and so is at night when you're asleep, into your tent I'll creep: and the creeping boys shoot bang, bang, bang, through a thin partition that does their bounds divide, and behind which the little girl is sleeping: and kill the mother and wound the toy. Afterwards they say (issue a statement claiming responsibility) that for anyone else to say that they have been shooting at the child is a complete distortion of the facts: the mother, because of her involvement with the British war machine as a part-time member of the Ulster Defence Regiment, was the sole target, not the little girl, not even Kermit the Frog: as through that thin partition they blasted blind.

Meditate on the facts. Do not distort.

Kermit, merely wounded, may feel that he is a very lucky man. Could he also have been a part of the British war machine?

And here on a street in West Belfast lies a sixteen-year-old boy, shot in both elbows and both knees and resting now, and not without reason, in a pool of blood. No bullets have been wasted: for, a short time previously, the staff and customers in a hair-dresser's shop, saloon or salon, heard four shots, one, two, three, four, accounting for two knees and two elbows. No man is a centipede. In the hospital it is said that it is too soon yet to say if the boy will lose his arms or legs or suffer permanent damage: which might reasonably include losing both arms and legs. The parsimonious shooters of the four shots, waste not want not, say that the boy was punished for repeatedly ignoring warnings about his antisocial behaviour. Without elbows and knees it is difficult to be antisocial: difficult even to be social. Those four-shot shooters may have a certain sense of humour and of the fitness of things: and they or their colleagues have also a nervous solicitude for the welfare of the young. For in a publication described as the *Republican News* they have printed this notice:

I.R.A. warns publicians. . . .

Publicians is a misprint. A good one, though. Statement from First Battalion, Belfast Brigade.

To all public bars and off-licences within our area.

We have in the past given warnings to those selling drink to people under age, either through (a) direct selling or (b) the Undereighteens getting an adult to buy drink for them and leaving the owners of bars/off-licences with the impression of selling to adults. . . .

From now on we will give no more warnings. Those who buy or

sell drink to those under age will be dealt with as crimes against the people and will face the consequences. . . .

Certain difficulties arise immediately from that text.

How do you buy or sell drink to?

Is selling drink to Undereighteens a social or antisocial behaviour?

Is Ireland sober really and truly Ireland free?

What will happen to the vintner who does not take the *Republican News* and so goes unwittingly on in the error of his ways? Or who sells drink to an adult and does not know that the adult is reselling it to an Undereighteen?

Will there be drink at the wedding in Carmincross? As at Cana?

Should a wedding be held, sanctified, solemnised, celebrated, consummated in a place that breeds such parodies on Caliban: who even had his pitiable half-human moments?

Is Sycorax another name for the Poor Old Woman?

And the making of a martyr like the patriots of old: he had no gun when the soldiers got him and he said you've got me cold.

And a woman who lived in the street that is called Joy, in Belfast of the builders of ships and the weavers of linen, stands in the shadows and says that they have taken away the body and I know not where they have lain him: and the soldiers walk back down the street and she hears them joking and laughing and one of them says we got the fucking bastard anyway, hot or cold: and she picks up ten spent cartridges, which she knows have been fired by one soldier: and it is known that the dead man has, for his hero record, the shooting from ambush of two soldiers. Age shall not wither him nor the years condemn, the generations shall remember him and call him blessed.

Now I lay me down to sleep I pray to God my soul to keep, and oft in the stilly night the same phrase or line of a poem or, at times, an entire paragraph repeats and repeats and repeats itself in the numbed and/or half-drunken brain. Like the prayer of a good man, the father of thirteen, who prayed: May our Lord, Jesus Christ, be with me that He may defend me, be within me that He may preserve me, precede me that He may guide me, follow me that He may guard me, be over me that He may bless me. . . .

More things are wrought by prayer than this world dreams on, and St. Patrick, apostle of the Gael, prayed that Christ be before him, after him, in the eye of every man who looked on him, on the tongue of every man who spoke to him, in the mind and heart of every man who thought on him. But that was all of two thousand years ago: and when they find that good man, the father of thirteen, after the four butchers from the Shankill Road in Belfast have finished with him, his brother can identify him only by the colour of his eyes: thirteen major lacerations, made by a razor-sharp knife, crisscross on a face that has been beaten to a pulp: six deep gashes on the throat are artistically V-shaped from ear to ear: a fractured skull, teeth torn out, and fingers broken: legs, arms, and torso black and blue and covered with congealed blood and bruises caused by a heavy hammer and hatchet: and in the battered chest under the heart a large stab wound: and, because the butchers may somewhere have heard of Christ, the palm of each hand pierced through, as if by a long, thin knife.

Faraway places with strange-sounding names are far away over the sea, and where on earth else would they be: and sweating or screaming from that last nightmare my soul flies over the ocean, rising higher and higher, and to show that one touch of something makes the whole world kin, looks down into the Land of Silver to see Angle or, perhaps, Angel Benochea happy in a luxury apartment, surrounded by pistols, rifles, light and heavy machine-guns, hand grenades, bazookas, homemade bombs in pipes, tincans, and rockets. Sharing the luxury with him are four young people. All together they form a guerrilla group. They have not yet picked on a name. The pop groups may have used up all the names. But, let myself stop myself muttering in my sleep, what's in a name. While happy in the making of bombs for some as yet undefined purpose, the five nameless ones blow up themselves and a seven-storey building, and go, untitled, to the moon.

Glimmering on the ceiling above me, letters of silver on a sullen background, I read the last will and testament of Angle, or is it Angel, non Angli sed Angeli, Benochea, a letter left as a happy memory for his widow: I know that we cannot achieve a just society unless we achieve what is human by inhuman ways. That means battle. It is a battle in which we must dehumanise ourselves, in the hills and the cities, in order to build a happy society. We dehumanise ourselves so that, by being inhuman, we can achieve what is human.

Angels that around us hover, guard us till the close of day and, after that, until the dawn: and one of my own simple recurrent nightmares is that somewhere in my bedroom sits a silent, motionless, dark figure: there is the customary hopeless struggle to rise, to run, to cry out: Who are you? Who are you?

With agonised emphasis on the middle word.

Then a sweating awakening.

Year follows year.

Some night or day my cry may well be answered.

Come along come, the boat lies low, she lies high and dry on the Ohio: a favourite song with Deborah, yet not so much a favourite song as a few phrases she hums even in the middle of the most serious conversation as if her mind were all the time on something else, not the subject of conversation, not even on the Ohio: Come along come, won't you come along with me and I'll take you down to Tennessee: and several times she has asked me have I seen the Ohio, and each time I have answered that I have not but that in Nashville, Tenn., the Athens of the South, I have leaned on a bridge and looked down at the sullen, muddy Cumberland, very deep, bearing big boats, which flows into the Ohio, which flows into the Mississippi: and also in Nashville, Tenn., home of the noises that are neither country nor western, I have in the morning lectured in the halls of Vanderbilt and, in the evening, listened in the Grand Ole Opry to the clarinet of Boots Carmichael. An achievement that impresses her: Merlin, you're almost human: and sets her again humming that the boat lies low and lies high and dry on the Ohio: and in the state of Ohio a man goes fishing where the boat lies low, because his family tells him that he should go fishing to lift his mind from brooding, come away come, on the whereabouts of his six-year-old son who has vanished. God be with the good days long long ago when I went a-fishing with Barelegged Joe: and the man in Ohio speaks to me and says: I been casting there two or three weeks, ain't hookin' anythin' 'ceppin some tree stumps . . .

No way, I think, to lift the mind from anything. Fishing is for patient and contented men. All the secrets that water hides.

—. . . and when I fust hook-on I have this feeling, rightaway, oh God what have I got: and I pull him up and see his face, blood on it, and I get to screaming and run for help. . . .

Father, behold thy son.

Walking on the green banks of the pleasant river Lea, then ten miles from London, Izaak Walton wondered what would a blind man not give to see the pleasant rivers and meadows and fountains: and prayed that God deliver us from pinching poverty and, also, from the cares that are the keys that often hang so heavily at the rich man's girdle that they clog him with weary days and restless nights: we see but the outside of the rich man's happiness: few consider him to be like the silkworm that, when she seems to play, is, at the very same time, spinning her own bowels and consuming herself. Few indeed, and Deborah says she, sure as God, is not one of them.

Oh happy, happy fisherman, oh good old Izaak casting fly over or dropping maggot into the limpid Lea: whom God spared from any vision of horror in crystal water: to whom God granted in Fleet Street the competency of a haberdashery and the friendship of Mr. Donne, and who thanked his generous God for health and that competency and a quiet conscience: and how Izaak would have loved this water that, all nightmares forgotten in the bright day, races down toward the wedding at Carmincross, sweet Thames run softly till I end my song.

—There's a river, Deborah, in the mountainy far northwest of the United States and it seems to me that it does everything that a good river should do. It's called the Little Mackenzie. It rises in a glacier. I've seen it do so.

—Travelled man. Clever boy. Up early to see the little river rising and putting on its clothes.

On a sunny morning and approaching the end of a journey, blonde hair pulled back to a perfect bun, face plump and almost pink, she is, if you didn't know it all, the image of matronly content.

—Above the glacier there's a monster of a mountain called Three Fingered Jack.

—That fellow I know well.

—With three peaks white with snow. And free of the glacier the young river comes down in waterfall after waterfall, cold as the glacier, white as the snow on the mountain. To form a lake shaped like a pear, dark and still beyond belief, tall pines standing all around it.

—We'll go there on our honeymoon. We'll shuffle off to Buffalo.

—This is our honeymoon. And haste to the wedding, and haste to the wedding.

And he accelerates. And slows up again. This road does not allow for speed and, anyway, they are happy and in no hurry to go down into the world and mingle with other people: his sister and brother-in-law, the bride and her four sisters, his aged, long-widowed mother, Killoran and Jeremiah and Killoran's wife, whatever she may be, Mr. Burns, and the third man from the long-ago dancing bridge, and guests at the wedding, the entire cosmos of Carmincross, the day she said to me we'll wed next June in Carmincross, next June in Carmincross, the Mexican spitfire and her tall, blond, polite husband.

Coming home to his own people he realises with a more painful intensity what he is always conscious of: his oddity, the *éan corr*, the one bird that slipped out of the nest. Community and family are not for him.

She is singing: For young Lanty Reddin's come over the mountain, and I've got a man with a house of his own. . . .

She is saying: Your thoughts?

—Far away in Oregon. From that deep, dark, pine-shaded, pear-shaped lake the river goes on down. . . .

—As rivers are inclined to do.

—Through forests. Taking other waters with it.

—Like the brook. I learned that at school. By heart. From listening to the teacher.

—Growing. Widening. Steadying. Breeding fish. Escaping from the forests. Into flat green land and a valley of fruit farms. Passing through a township called Sweet Home.

—Mid pleasures and palaces.

—The men who crossed those mountains on the Oregon Trail first called it that. Daresay if you'd crossed those mountains on foot and horse and covered wagon, that valley would have seemed like home or heaven. The windfalls from the fruit trees go on with the water. That's my dream of a river. What life should be.

—The good old river of life. The priests used to be always preaching about it. I thought they meant the Liffey, stinking to the heavens. Funny thing I never thought they meant the Dodder, small and twisty and with parks and woods along it. Where I did my early loving. Now, the priests are always on about divorce and contraception. They should have a song about contraception. Like the one about Constantinople.

—The tune would have to be changed.

Together and to various melodies they make vain attempts to sing: Contraception.

On a high moorland the narrow, winding dust road comes to a stone bridge. He pulls to the right and parks on a semicircle of wind-flattened grass.

—But my own river, Deborah. Here, and in a more limited landscape, it does its best to please me.

On the parapet of the bridge they lean, holding hands, by the Lord, like young lovers: a young stream, life beginning. They look down into a red turbulent pool, and watch the course of the water as it goes down, leap after leap, swirling pools, here and there a mountain ash: Degged with dew, dappled with dew are the groins of the brae that the brook treads through: and an odd image (she agrees when he quotes and explains it to her) to be in the mind of a sworn celibate and a Jesuit at that.

—But never did I go back up there behind us to find the source of the stream. That never seemed necessary. I knew without going. Your own river is your mother.

They listen to the quiet of the moorland. She leans her head on his shoulder: two aging people playing a parody in an unspoiled garden. But there are no longer any unspoiled gardens, and on the green half-circle she stamps in anger at the marks left by a picnic fire, and a smashed milk bottle and a plastic bag. People are everywhere: the mark in the wilderness of the most dangerous of all beasts. What age, she wonders, were Adam and Eve when they were booted out of the garden? But whatever age they were, he assures her, they had a stirring future before them and a considerable family: and he squires her back to the car to follow the road toward the gate of the garden, by fifty curves and elbow bends, the growing river curvetting to their right, advancing on them, retreating, disappearing under ash and hazel, surfacing again to stand at ease for a while and form its first lake. Green shores and a white house, a small hotel, in the distance.

Across the road from that hotel by the lake shore, trees grow on a narrow lawn and boats are moored under drooping branches. Ducks are happy among the thin reeds. The trout are lively. A wall of mountain stands up across the water. The girl in the hotel bar says that the trout taste better now than they did early in the year: that, although this place is close to the border and guards in cars and soldiers in lorries coming and going all the time, things, thank God, are quiet, in these parts and far away from Belfast and the like and that brutal thing that happened the other day, brutal things are happening every day: that there was a nervous class of a man once who came here on a holiday to fish and recover from some class of a breakdown, that one morning early he went down the river to the lower lake where there isn't even a house to be seen, but was back here to the hotel before noon. It was so quiet down there he got frightened and raced back up here for the company. He couldn't stand the peace. He was hard to please in times like these.

Hard to please in times like these: and they come to the second lake, where the nervous man was frightened by peace: where a sleeper could lie dreaming where the water laps the shore and his sleep be filled with music by the master of the world. The wind in the heather and mountain grass, the cry of a drifting bird, the soft movement of the water, the splashing of trout. The two of them and the trout and the sheep and the birds possess the place. So he tells her that the great gates of the mountain could fling open once again and the sound of song and dancing fall upon the ears of men: that from here they might walk backward into the Land of Youth and find it flushed with rainbow light and mirth: that an old enchantment lingers in the honey heart of earth.

It is such a heavenly day and she feels so happy that she tolerates all this poetic piffle from a big baldish fat man with false

teeth: and a semi-shattered sort of life on the other side of the Atlantic. No dead leaves here to remind her of first love.

Then they come to the gate of the garden and see a red car,
halted there for a cross-border inspection, and just at that moment passed and released and waved on and driven away before
them.

Over the telephone the third man has described for me the types
I'll meet at Checkpoint Billy: as he calls it in heavy irony, in honour of William of Orange. The third man, in his youth, has been
an old-style I.R.A. man of the period of Hugh McAteer, say the
Forties into the Fifties, the Hitler war, England's difficulty is Ireland's opportunity.

High on a platform a soldier stands, wicked weapon aimed, as
far as I can reckon, at Deborah's cleavage. By the side of the road
six or seven men in various uniforms. Look out first for the British
army. Not the way they used to be, the third man says. The first
thing you notice is the gun, carried at an angle, pointing upward.

But that gun on the platform is not pointing upward.

—Sergeant, Deborah says and quite sharply, does that boy
have to point that thing at me.

The sergeant shouts aloft. The boy above relaxes. Points the
gun at the sky, but holding it back as if it might rocket and take
him with it. There is a little bawdy laughter, not ill-natured.

Black boots, the third man says, rubber-soled, moving like cats
round corners and along alleys: in the old days you could hear the
rattle of the nailed boots from one end of Omagh town to the
other. Tops of boots nowadays stuffed with trouser bottoms.
Trousers all a motley. Camouflage green. Forty shades of green
all over. Odd. The green above the red as the old patriotic song
used to wish for. Combat jacket, four pockets, six or seven buttons
plus a long zip. No panache, not like the old-style jacket and the
shining brass badges and buttons. No grandeur. No shirt even,
unless you could call shirt to a round-necked green thing like an
undervest, and subsidised or complemented by a green necktie or
scarf or something. Bulletproof vest over all, like a lifesaving belt,
tied down back and front. Black beret, no tin hats, never no more.
Crown and harp on beret. England, Ireland, royalty, music, and
wild harp of Erin, God help us all. Polite boys mostly, getting

the lousy day in, getting the night in, no girls talking with them, joking with them in the streets any more. But they still wink hopefully.

The sergeant has just winked at Deborah. Who blows him a kiss. She's a girl for sergeants. Funny that never occurred to me before.

Some of his mates, says the third man, carry a thick-barrelled, snub-nosed Sten gun, which they finger fondly, seemingly to assure themselves that it's there, groping for the loved one in the dark: it's said that it can cut through brick walls. A few days ago I watched a group of them sitting on the back of a jeep at the beginning of the No Man's Land at Rossville Street in Derry city. Long-haired, flatfooted, featherweight youths darted from alleys and threw stones at them. Which they ducked as best they could but did not reply to. A pathetic scene. The boys wanted them to play the game, give chase. And then you have a bloody Sunday. And then you have a bloody Friday: and Ireland is Ireland, as your mother used to sing, through joy and through tears, hope never dies through the long weary years, each age has seen countless brave hearts pass away but their spirit still lives on in the men of today.

So there now, Deborah, from the instructions of the third man, and from my own observations here at the gate that opens out of the lonely garden, I know exactly what a British soldier in combat dress looks like in these graceless times. That tender, now roaring up, has come from the direction of Carmincross. Four soldiers leaping out onto the road. God, those sullen wicked guns. All this activity. Who, Deborah, could they have been expecting today? Ah, but this is only the changing of the guard, yet not performed on this lonely Irish road as they'd do it at the Palace: the royal standard in the breeze will tell you if their majesties are there to watch the changing of the guard.

The sentry being relieved climbs down from his box, a monkey on a stick. Another one climbs up. The sun picks out, in the drab uniforms, the yellow from the green. Let's step out, girl, and stretch our legs and show your style to the soldiers. Get out of the ditches, ye randy young bitches, and let the poor soldiers go home, go home. No offence, Deborah. That was the refrain to a

song the third man used to sing to the rousing air of The Camp-
bells Are Coming: he sang it once at a party in a polite house and
near provoked a riot.

But these words now might better please you: Tell me, ye merchants' daughters, did ye see so fair a creature in your town before.

For Deborah does look fetching today. Red becomes her, tights
and all, and red excites the soldiers, they wore it once themselves
and looked splendid in it but were, alas, too discernible from a
distance and thus too easily shot. So they changed to dirty brown
and then to dirtier greens, and that's the way our world goes. One
of the soldiers, here and now distracted, goes on one knee and
stares at her, quite unashamedly open-mouthed, his dreadful gun
half out of control and wavering more or less in my direction.
Deborah is chatting to the sergeant, not noticing my peril. What
to do? Raise my arms in mock panic: and the young fellow
straightens up and laughs and pretends to look into the opened
trunk (or boot) of the car. The sergeant speaks an English I do not
grasp. One soldier is as black as my boot: but now that I think of
it my boot is dark brown, not black, haven't worn a black boot in
years, and even that soldier is, perhaps, as much brown as black.
The sergeant shakes hands with Deborah, closes the boot (or
trunk) and hands me back my papers; and waves us on. The
tender, showing-off and scattering gravel, roars away ahead of us
with the men whose stint is over.

Calme was the day and through the trembling air sweet-
breathing Zephyrus did softly play.

—And as we go, Deborah, let me tell you the tale of the two
tailors who lived in a tiny white house at a wartime checkpoint in
the town in which Burns and myself and the third man went to
school. They were two brothers, twins or damn near it, neatly
tailored and why not, always in brown, even to small identical
brown moustaches. There was this long row of tiny white houses,
all exactly alike, rising up a slope of road at the very edge of the
town. In each house two rooms, that is a small kitchen and a bedroom much smaller. One storey: and the ceiling and roof so low
that when, in the summer, the brothers hung up a flypaper they
chopped it into lengths of not more than three inches so that it
wouldn't stick to their noses and moustaches. Then Hitler struck

and the panic began and the young conscripts from the big cities of north England would go route marching up the sloping road singing that there would always be an England: and blushing almost if a stranger, or was it a native, looked at them. Unlike the Irish they weren't skilled in, or accustomed to, the singing of doleful patriotic ballads: We are the boys of Wexford who fought with heart and hand and when Ireland was broken and bleeding, and oh may the blood from my bosom you drew in your veins turn to poison if you turn untrue. . . .

—Merlin. Please. Restrain yourself.

—Merlin was the devil's son, some said. And some said he knew a trick more than the devil. And across the road from the two tailors the massive concrete blockhouse was built to halt Hitler if he ever got that far or had ever heard of the place. And all through that horrendous hot summer the two tailors stood at their door, one leaning on each doorpost, identical matching ornaments, and studied the palatial blockhouse and chatted to the guardian soldiers: and one evening proposed to an inspecting major that when all the war was ended the blockhouse should be left there so that they could move across and in and, as a new experience, hang up a full-length flypaper: and once there were similar rows of such tiny houses at the end of every town in these islands. Falstaff's begging veterans.

—Another pop group?

—Left to beg at the town's end. Tiny cells in which to confine the poor. Most of them long gone: the houses not the poor. Fallen down. Wiped away. Garden suburbs. Bloody awful blocks of flats. The world is smaller, more crowded. There may have been more room in the little houses. Tom Campbell, the fiddler, was so small that he fitted easily into the cottage beside the one that housed the two tailors. A first-class traditional fiddler. Much loved by his neighbours. Even if they made jokes about the way he didn't get married until he was man-high. He didn't take up much space in his own cottage or anywhere else in the world. Anyway, when at home he was most of the time sitting down: a Chaucerian small fowl making melody. Which the neighbours and passers-by delighted in. For except in the wildest nights of winter the door was open to the world. He lived by agricultural labour. That was to live sparsely. He had little to do with paper money until an uncle or something died in Australia and left him, it was said, five hundred pounds. And brought trouble down on him. And Jenny Doyle. A girl well-known to the fusiliers. She may never have heard of traditional music until she heard of the Australian money. But thereafter she was to be found sitting on a low stool or squatting on the floor while Tom made the music. She cooked for him. She cleaned the house. She did his laundry and his shopping. For a month or two, until she married him, she gave up the fusiliers. Another two months: and the little man, tears in his eyes, said to my father. In my hearing. One day we were passing into the town. He said before I married her I couldn't keep her outa the house, now I can't keep her in the house. And the Australian gold was diminishing. Worse still she took to bringing the soldiers home with her. Three or four at a time.

—The little house?

—Wouldn't fit more than four. Or she might have brought the regiment. To drink and smoke Tom's money in the most relaxed ˙ fashion. For some time no music was heard. Except when the soldiers sang. And Jenny called the tune.

—Get out of the ditches and let the poor soldiers go home, go home.

—Until a relative of mine who lived in the town. One of those quiet grey-eyed men who never lose their temper. Men to fear. Went hat in hand and stooping one evening into the cottage. And said: Boys, I've been talking to the colonel. You're severely out of bounds.

—So they belted and buckled and buttoned up and left. Soldiers dressed properly in those days. And the grey-eyed man said: Jenny, you may as well go with your friends. They couldn't get on without you.

—-Just like that?

—Just like that. Only instance of drumhead divorce I ever heard of. The colonel was a Scotsman and a great man for the traditional music.

The river runs again beside the road. The road descends gradually, a high heathery bank, almost a cliff, to the left. To the right and beyond the river, a good valley and the colours of late autumn: and the glint of the arm of yet another lake. At the far foot of the slope an oblong building, schoolhouse or chapel, shining white.

—For a man on the far side of ten to know all about that was to start wondering. In those days of innocence. So I started wondering.

—You were still curious when I met you.

—Why had wee Tom so imperilled his peace and his music?

—You found out.

—To some extent. Bit by bit. A shameful process. There was a girl in Connemara with calico drawers. A most disconcerting experience.

—Someday you must tell me the whole sad story.

—How from small beginnings I advanced to where I am now. Laughter.

They stop the car for a while and fumble. Once again the world is empty all around them.

—Forgive my memories of things long gone. That checkpoint set me off. An angel with a flaming sword ushered Adam and Eve out of Eden.

They drive on.

—The checkpoint was the gate out of our lonely garden. There was once a maid in a lonely garden.

—That's a beautiful old song.

—But also a gate into the garden of my boyhood. So many things here I want to show you. Tell you about.

—The next one, Merlin, would seem to be a very large policeman.

They have come to the white building that might have been a schoolhouse or a chapel. It is neither. It is an Orange hall. On the high, pointed gable wall a large medallion, red, white, and blue: white warhorse, William of Orange up, and all in red, rides across a blue river Boyne: striking folk art. The rim of the medallion is barred in red, white, and blue by the hand, obviously, of a careful and devoted painter. But on the concrete wall surrounding the building a rougher hand has daubed in white paint: UVF RULE OK.

And another hand, every bit as rough and using a tarbrush, has answered: BRITS OUT WHAT NEXT EIRE NUA IRA RULE OK.

Great minds have been in conflict here. Green and pleasant land all around. River and lake shining at a distance. What hides in the hedges? The daubers, no doubts in their heads, do not condescend to question marks.

The constable, hand raised, has stepped out around the corner of the building. A cute double-check, like the customs man who lingers by the last door when you think you're safely through with the undeclared bottles of continental booze. But no, he steps forward easily, unsuspiciously. He raises his cap. He is alone, a tall, thin, grey man as old as or older than myself. No hostility here, unless he has a platoon of soldiers behind the wall or hiding in the hedge. The police uniform, unlike the uniform of the soldiers, has improved over the years: smart, blackish green, a harp and crown badge on the peaked cap. The tunic opens at the front, officer style. A pale greenish shirt, a dark green tie. Cap in hand, he salutes the lady. He says he has had a breakdown and would be glad of a lift a few miles down the road.

So Deborah nimbly hops out, and in again to the back seat, and jokes him about the length of his legs: and merrily they drive on, King William waving his sword behind them, the wall around him festooned with conflicting slogans.

—And yes indeed, sir, the hotel on Knocknagon hill is still functioning if you were, as you say, thinking of stopping there, yourself and the good lady, for lunch. Still functioning. In spite of the effort the bombers made to put it out of business. They said they planted the bomb there, the only bomb we've had so far in Carmincross, you might not have heard of it, seeing you were faraway in the U.S.A., but they say they planted the bomb there because army personnel used the bar and the dining room, but the real reason was as old and simple as your money or your life, and the owner of the place was brave enough or foolish enough to refuse to pay black rent. Fellows in Belfast now, on both sides of the fence, making big money out of black rent and all kinds of rackets. So they planted the bomb in the entrance hall and three soldiers who were in the bar raced for it and one of them got it outside the door before it went off and killed them: And the unfortunate bloke who was carrying it, there were bits of him up a beech tree at the edge of the lawn, I saw them myself and knew the bloke. From Sheffield. Bits of him up in a beech tree.

—Strange fruit, sergeant.

—Strange fruit, indeed, Mr. Kavanagh.

—You know me. Who have I here?

—You used to call yourself Nestroake. It was a nickname you made up for yourself. Out of some old story. You were hell for the old stories. It's not fair of me, Vin. I had the drop on you. I knew you were coming for the wedding. And you haven't seen me in forty years.

—Where was it? Give me a hint.

—In the town. Football. The Cow Commons.

He parks the car. They stand out and look at each other. She steps out with them, looks at them with curiosity, they were virgin boys together, dirty little boys most likely, what other sort of boys are there: and looks beyond them to a green metal dome rising above trees on a hilltop: the river curving and shining far below.

—A lot coming and going played football on the Cow Commons. Let me guess now.

This sort of foolery is high among the joys of coming home.

—John McBride I can eliminate right away. Unless you grew out of all order over forty years.

To the lady the sergeant explains: McBride was so small we called him Tall John.

To Mervyn: He's long dead. It didn't take much of a coffin to hold him.

—There was another John McBride. He had a fine singing voice. I saw from the beach as the morning was shining.

—A barque o'er the waters move gloriously on. No, not him. He's a civil servant now in London. He rose very high.

—There was Jerry McGrath. Very quick on his feet. Born to be a footballer.

—A major in the fusiliers. Retired now. Living in Shepton Mallet in Somerset.

—There was Ray Cassidy from Ederney. Played Gaelic football for the county.

—He lived in Chicago for ten years. Then he owned a pub in Trillick. All full of ticking clocks. He collected them. He died six weeks ago.

—Ticking clocks. And Mick Leonard and Jim McVeigh, one from Garrison, one from Ederney, both county footballers.

—Living and well. A teacher and a big man in business.

—And Burns. And Fox, the third man. But I know where they are.

—You were close to Burns and Fox. Fox was taller than me. I saw him in Belfast six months ago. I'd swear to God he's still growing. Burns was a genius of a trick-cyclist.

She says: He still is.

—And Charley Snifter Mulligan.

To Deborah he says: We called him Snifter because–

—I can guess. Not cocaine. Just a runny nose.

—Killed at Anzio beachhead, the sergeant says. A hero.

He knows who the sergeant is, and the sergeant knows that he knows. But this Ulyssean game is too good to relinquish easily: and the memory of the Cow Commons on sunlit evenings. Further to the south of the country the place would have been called the fairgreen. But the breath of Scotland was strong enough to make itself felt as far as the town in which we went to secondary school. Once a month that hillside was crowded with cattle. They overflowed into a few lesser streets at the edge of the town: through a gateless gateway between a corrugated-iron hut known splendidly as the Labour Hall and a malodorous brick blockhouse known even more splendidly as the Old Closet. Socialism to one hand and the assembling of trade unions: excretion to the other. Rural Ireland for that one day in possession of the place, strong farmers slapping hands to clinch bargains, moaning frightened cattle, drovers with wattles and red neckerchiefs, and everywhere dung to the knees, the smell of it battling with the fumes of stout and whiskey: back for one day in the month to the epic, back to the shadows when the only wealth was cattle and the only strength the strength to steal and keep them.

The other and more ancient name of the place was Gallowshill. In better-ordered times every town had its own hill for hanging, every lord and baron bold had his gallows on his lawn or bawn so that he could delight in the different styles of the dancing of the last minuet.

On the day after the fair, when rural Ireland had receded and the dung been washed from the pavements or absorbed by the earth, and the dusty slope of the Commons left bare except for tufts of grass and chickweed, the children of that part of the town and the footballers resumed their rights of commonage, the pitch-and-toss school returned to the balmy vicinage of the Old Closet, where a poor boy who was a chronic masturbator used to put on a performance for the delectation of his contemporaries: mysterious life.

—The Reverend Wright, the sergeant says, used to join us at the football.

The sergeant is remembering other aspects of the multiple life of the Cow Commons.

Saturday nights, out of the darkness of the lampless place, came the voice of a woman singing: relict of a soldier who went away and never came back and nobody, not even the army, could say whether he was living or dead. Saturday night, she drank and, remembering the friendly slums of Dublin, sang her way home: Mellow the moonlight to shine is beginning, close by the window young Eily is spinning . . .

Moon or no moon, always the same song.

—Sprightly and brightly and airily ringing, trills the sweet voice of the young maiden singing. . . .

She whored a little in a casual sort of way: it was also known that other fornicators made use by night of the quiet slope by the hedge that separated the Commons from the Second Presbyterian Church: and Sunday mornings at the back of the Labour Hall an accumulation of empty bottles discarded by the town's winos, black bottles, white labels that made no grander claims than: Finest Old Red Wine.

Yes, the Reverend Wright used to join the boys at the football, indeed the boy who was to become the sergeant was one of his congregation, and his father before him, also a sergeant, with a tall handsome wife and fine tall handsome daughters and that one blond boy. Later the father was transferred to Belcoo on the border, not all that far from Carmincross: and the family prospered, fur coats for all the ladies, six fur coats in one house and matching accessories, all on the strength of bribes from the smugglers of pigs and flour, sugar, butter, cigarettes, whiskey, silk stockings. Belcoo was beautiful.

Now there in the lovely evening light of memory goes the Reverend Wright, grey hat in hand, light-grey hair flying, grey ends of pants tucked into grey socks, quicker on his feet than any of us, deadly accurate shot at goal by the Presbyterian hedge where by night the fornicators flourish, he (as they) enjoying every moment, bringing happiness with him, an earnest Presbyterian beloved by all. Then one twelfth day of July he is, fatally, asked to deliver the main address to the Orange hosting on the same Cow Commons: and in tones as resonant as Gabriel, and audible all over that end of the town, he advises Catholic and Protestant and Jew and Presbyterian to fear God and love the neighbour.

Not the word of God as his Orange listeners heard or read it, and the happy footballer and orator is banished across the border to a village on the Donegal coast where he can wonder what are the wild waves saying, and do no harm. Where years later I see him wandering the bleak shore alone, tossing a coloured rubber ball into the waves for the exercise and amusement of a Labrador dog as big as himself: I came when the sun o'er that beach was declining, the bark was still there but the waters were gone.

—Cecil Morrow, he says, I declare to you and God and the lady here that the Cow Commons was a little world. Every corner is a world. Every day is a little life and our whole life is but a day repeated.

—Sergeant, she says, he's off again.

—Whence it is that old Jacob numbers his life by days. And Moses desires to be taught this point of holy arithmetic, to number not his years but his days.

She tells the sergeant that Mervyn is a class of a professor and so may be excused. The sergeant says that even as a boy Vin Kavanagh could preach as well as any reverend.

—But Vin, he says, the Cow Commons is gone now. All built over the place where we played football. No room even for pitch and toss. The old Labour Hall rusted and fell. The Old Closet was knocked down.

—No room even for our ghosts, Cecil Morrow.

—Goodmorrow, goodmorrow, good Mervyn she says. So you have found each other. After all these years. Tell me sometime about the Cow Commons. After lunch, dear boys, after lunch.

* * *

From the slope beyond the beech tree that flowered and fruited with the fragments of a British soldier they can look down through a gap in more beech trees on a bend of the river and one portion of the main street of Carmincross.

—That there, Deborah, is the eighteenth-century church. Rooks and doves always around it. A lot of white doves. There always seem to be two or three of them walking the street at their ease. And a few collie dogs asleep in the sun. Nothing much has ever happened here.

—Except the odd soldier blown into the bushes. I'm an Irish republican myself, Sergeant. But I draw the line.

—Oh, nothing much does happen here, madam. That bomb was the dreadful exception. And more white doves than ever. They breed well in this place. But the big town's in a bad way, Vin. You'll want to go to see it. But the sight won't do you good. And fair enough, Vin, the queen doesn't need me for the next few hours, and I'd be glad to have a drink and lunch with you. Old times, Vin, and the Reverend Wright and the Old Closet and the Cow Commons and mellow the moonlight to shine is beginning. And I'll help you with the bags. For the good lady and yourself will be making Knocknagon your home for the duration. The bride's home will be packed with young people.

To come all that way to a wedding and to be taken over, you might say, by a member of the Royal Ulster Constabulary. Who is also a friend of my boyhood and youth even if he never was as close to me as Burns and the third man. The Morrows, as far as I know, were never members of the Orange order: I neither knew nor cared. Anyway he's dead on the ball. Knocknagon is the best, perhaps the only place to stay in Carmincross. That scarlet woman, there across the table from me, and myself could scarcely cohabit in my sister's house in the middle of all the happy preparations for the deflowering of my sister's child.

Ye learned sisters which have oftentimes been to me aiding others to adorn.

Nor will this be the first night that I have slept in Knocknagon. For this is the house that James built. James was a boy from a far-away place who came to the local big town. Came, it was said, with no shoes on his feet but the owner, by God, of a small ass and cart and a courage that never lay down. For James was a boy who worked morning and night and made him a mint in the end. He traded in birds, not small ones that sang but big ones to eat and, bugger the dictation of rhyme, turkeys and geese and the eggs that they laid, and chickens by the thousand, and the happier ducks, and gamebirds of every known kind. James had a shop and a store to go with it and, in Stockwell in Glasgow, a place twice the size. James, it was said, when Christmas came round, sent turkeys, the white ones, all the way to the king.

Thinking like the later Melville gone mad is putting me off my lunch. . . .

Anyway James did not actually build this house. But when he had his fortune solidly established he bought and restored it: a triumphant symbol. Thick walls of grey stone and a green dome like a mosque. In the main hall, on the stairways, and even in the servants' rooms the sort of wood panelling that reminded you that the world was once a better place. High from the green dome James could look one way over Carmincross and the widening river to the barren mountains he came from: mountain streams where the moorcocks crow, and little else. The other way down the broad high road to the town he had conquered, and Glasgow and greyhounds, and even the Waterloo cup. Three times a dog that he owned and named after that street in Glasgow almost won the Waterloo cup: almost to win it three times may be as good as to win it once, but not as good as to win it three times as the greatest of all greyhounds did, and had a statue put up to him in the County Waterford and a song written about him: Lord Lurgan stepped forward and he said gentlemen, is there any among you has money to spend. For your great English greyhounds I don't care a straw, here's a thousand to one upon Master McGrath.

Three times the dog that almost won went round the town in torchlight procession: high on a wooden platform on the back of a lorry and posing for admiration. The people, Orange and Green, who had been prudent enough to back him for a place, cheered and sang together. Could a victorious running dog have led my people to unity? Here in Knocknagon James kept two hundred hounds and so ensured that the place would live up to its ancient name: the Hill of the Hounds. So that my father who followed the hounds and was knowledgeable about them was never out of the place. Spent nights of hospitality here, and his son with him: the wind in the ancient beech trees that never knew then that one day one of them would blossom and fruit with the fragments of the body of a young man from Shepton Mallet or Porlock or Kettering camp or Scarborough or Ecclefechan or Stornoway or Dolgelly. A tree grew in a garden in Carmincross. Mother, behold thy son.

The sergeant is telling Deborah that the Americans were here during the war. The master and mistress of the house, James of the Greyhounds and his beloved wife, were then long dead. The family grown up and gone. As were the greyhounds and their continuous yapping, and brandy and beef, better fed, housed, bedded, and cleaned out than many Christians: all gone to be replaced by roaring, randy young men riding all round them, saving your presence, Deborah, for by this time it is very much Deborah and Cecil: and be my guest, she says: and the girls of the town and district went wild, he says, you'd swear to God they'd been hoarding something up for years, a learned man like Mervyn there may persuade me that war and killing have that effect as what he would call a fringe benefit, although I don't see much of it around me, here in the North at the moment, but two girls luring three soldiers into a room in Belfast to be trapped and murdered and, God Christ, the lowest hoor wouldn't do it. And saving my presence again, she says, but I can't say, Cecil, as how I don't agree with you. And settled romances, he says, were wrecked when the boys in blue came in, except that they weren't in blue: and demure spinsters, even of the upper-middle class, did things that we can only mercifully hope they had not even been thinking about up to that moment. We had our own share of black babies without even buying them as Mervyn and all the little papishes used to do to get money for the African missions: buy a black baby the wee girl with the collection box says to the drunk staggering home and wee girl, he says, I couldn't buy a black pudden. And one night in Fintona there was a fight between black soldiers and white soldiers that was worse than the war: and one night in Newry there was a free-for-all, anybody

black or white or striped or spotted was at liberty and even welcome to join, that extended over the border into the Free State,
they hadn't room to finish it here in Ulster: and up in Dublin,
where Mervyn was studying at the time, the government thought
an invasion was on and the Free State army was on the standby
to drive into Ulster, or the Six Counties as Mervyn says, as far as
the petrol ration would take them and then stand and fight. Before D-day there just wasn't room for any more soldiers. A lot of
the girls got husbands, stars in their eyes, thinking they were getting Robert Taylor or Cary Grant with the accent and all, and
penthouses on Sunset Boulevard, and then found themselves in
the slums of New York or in board hutments on the Natchez
Trace, wherever and whatever that is, or in the swamps of Florida
and not a white face to be seen for twenty miles. Instead of the
yapping of the greyhounds we had then, around Knocknagon,
the screeching of the jeeps and the wheels tearing on, and scattering like hailstones, the golden gravel that Big James had brought
all the way from the Donegal shore. There was a soldier in jail
once in the Crumlin Road in Belfast, your friend Fox told me,
because he was in at the same time for batin' the police like the
bold Thady Quill in the song, and this soldier was in for selling
jeeps to the Japs, the whole business caught up on him when he
thought he was safely back in Ireland: and we all know the old
story about the black soldier who thought a jeep was a female
Jap: and Deborah says that she has, indeed, heard that story
more times that she cares to remember: and the night before D-
day, the sergeant says, the hullaballoo here was unbelievable:
and elsewhere, I heard tell, Mervyn says: and in the morning they
were gone like snow off a ditch and this lovely old house left to
the dust and the ghosts. . . .

And Deborah asks what ghosts.

—Well, for one or two, Monty and Eisenhower met in the big
oak room across the hall here from the dining room: but the
tightarsed people in the war office wouldn't say aye, yes, or no
when the present owner asked them about it, he wanted to use it
on a publicity brochure but perhaps, and considering the bloody
and murderous things that are happening around us, it may be
just as well that he never did: not but that they bombed him anyway for he's a dogged boy from Ballymoney and no man to pay

black rent, not, by God, to Beelzebub himself: and spent a lot of money on the restoration of this place, sold a farm and a business he had in Antrim, fell in love with Knocknagon house, timber-work and all. Soldiers don't leave a place in the best condition, even though it was mostly officers here in Knocknagon: and one incident Cecil particularly remembers out of that time, it happened outside Broderick's pub in the big town, a young American soldier, eyes turned in his head with drink and in the none-too-gentle grip of two of their military police, about to load him into a jeep when a British corporal comes along and says I know that bloke, I'll look after him if it's all the same to you, and the MPs say He's all yours, brother, and hand him over, and the corporal arms him gently away like a lost-and-found younger brother: and Jesus, Mervyn, it's a sore thing to think that in that same pub a few weeks ago, one of us, a detective unarmed at the time, was gunned down by three of them, black masks and machine-guns, a decent man too, Mervyn there must have known his father who was a constable in the town in Mervyn's time, a West of Ireland man.

And Mervyn had, indeed, known the murdered man's father.

—And even the night, Mervyn, the Germans came over and bombed Pennyburn in Derry city, and bombed Belfast, we knew it was them up there and us, all together, down here: and the fire brigades raced from Dublin to help quench the burning of Belfast: and that poor crazy Republican woman who was murdered in her hospital bed by one crowd swore that her crowd would take Belfast apart brick by brick: and Belfast was her own city: and London during the blitz was a happier town than Belfast this sad day: no denying, nevertheless, Deborah, as Mervyn points out, that the first constable shot was shot by an Orangeman, Constable Arbuckle, on October eleven, 1969, a day for us all to remember, on the barricades on the Shankill Road in Belfast, Conway Street, North Howard Street, Malvern Street, when neither the constables nor the specials could push the crowd back: and a platoon of soldiers fired CS gas, and a detachment of constables moved in line down Townsend Street and a shot was fired and Victor Arbuckle fell dead and two others injured: and Holy God, but nobody would believe it, the crowd were demonstrating, against, of all things, the disarming of the constables under the Hunt Report: Mervyn there now is a learned man, or so they say in America, but let him, if he can, work out the logic of that: or of Billy Hull of the Loyalist Association of Workers saying that the age of the rubber bullet is over and that it would be lead bullets from now on: and we are, says Billy Hull, British to the core but we won't hesitate to take on even the British if they attempt to sell our country down the river. Now listen to that, Deborah, and tell me if you're on your head or your heels, or sitting there and having lunch on Knocknagon or, as Mervyn calls it, the Hill of the Hounds: and what hounds those hounds were, God only knows, for the place had the name long before Big James here fed two hundred greyhounds on brandy and beef: and Deborah, daughter, let me tell you another story, this time about special duty in Dungiven on the day the loyalists said they would march through the town and teach the Fenians a lesson: and there was I and many others and the army lined across the street: and the loyal men stopped and stood and sang the Queen, I never heard it sung better: and the soldiers, as was only right and proper, when they recognised the tune and knew it wasn't something by the Beatles, stood to attention: and then someone right in the middle of happy and glorious, someone in the rear rank of the loyalists, Mervyn always called them or us Orangemen, threw a half-brick and caught one of the soldiers on the side of the head a most unmerciful bang: his face I'll never forget, not so much hurt as astounded that anyone who sang the Queen with a heart and a half should clobber on the head with the half of a brick a serving soldier of the Queen: and the English, Mervyn says, will never understand the Irish: and there are the three of us laughing at the plight of the puzzled soldier when who should dance in but Jeremiah Gilsenan, all the way from Dublin town. Who wears a white linen suit and a red festive necktie, and waves in his hand a Western wide-brimmed straw hat: and flaunts, already, a virgin-white gardenia, a rare bloom in Carmincross.

And who cries: This time is holy, do you write it down, and bonfires build all night and dance about them and about them sing: and far from us prevent all doleful tears, lamenting cries and hidden fears, deluding dreams and dreadful sights, burning houses, evil sprites, pookas, goblins, witches' charms, ravens, vultures, lightning's harms: and crown the god Bacchus with a

Coronal and Hymen also crown with wreaths of vine: and lay her in lilies and in violets and silken curtains over her display.

He kisses Deborah. And twice. And thrice.

And hard behind him tread Killoran and Killoran's lady, and the Mexican spitfire and her tall young man, and five lovely sisters and their mother proud: and bringing up the rear another tall young singing man who is the groom, about to be.

Are sisters, a German pedant asks, so mysteriously alike that they show it in their sleep, though no likeness in the bright day displays itself in their features? But their voices are alike. Their ages may and do differ. That's obvious. They're not quintuplets. They move in separate ways. But the same father begot them unto the same mother and they are one in their origin . . . obvious again old chap, and he is a brave young man who would marry one of five sisters. . . .

And Deborah is dancing with Jeremiah. And his brother-in-law is saying something he heard somebody say about Earl Mountbatten. And there at the door are Burns and the Third Man and all the memories of boyhood. And the relevant niece is introducing him to the tall singing young man who does actually sing for a living, and who owns a band: and for the wedding the bandsmen will be all assembled that all the woods may answer and their echoes ring.

# THREE
## *The Wedding*

THE SHRILL BELL brings him out of his nightmare to hear her voice. She tells him that she is in the Algonquin.

—It pleases me to hear that you frequent the best places. Your oil scavenger must look a little odd there. No round table wit, he.

—He isn't with me. He's gone. I told you.

—Off to the Caribbean. With his bundle on his shoulder.

—A letter I wrote to you. Has it overtaken you?

—Not yet. What did you write?

—You'll know when you see it. Will you answer it?

—I'll know when I see it.

—Allen Rees, a colleague of yours in the South . . .

—What about him?

—I ran into him on Broadway.

—An unusual place for running into people.

—No, really. On Broadway. Just walking along. He said that they had had some trouble down South. One of the professors and the freshmen. It seems that he had a stable. Good grades for cooperation. And one of them talked. The honour system.

—Can honour mend a . . .

—Quotations. Quotations. Your colleague also told me that one of the waitresses in the local Howard Johnson's asked him was it the Irish professor in trouble in the college. He said no, that they were recalling you by Air Force One to restore the moral order. And they all laughed. All the waitresses, all the professors. Big joke.

—They're a happy people. What has all this to do with me?

—Was he the man who called his double bed *mon plage*? Or was that you, and you attributed the bon mot to him? What one of you was at, you were all at.

—That's not an American turn of phrase.

—Need it be? Contagion spreads. And phrases. The waitress in HoJo's said that all the waitresses loved the Irish professor. That's what your colleague said. Like all the servant maids loved John McCormack telling them that Irish eyes were smiling.

—Including three of my aunts.

—How is Mother Machree?

—She's dead.

—Oh.

He makes use of the following silence to put down the phone gently. She doesn't call again. It is ten in the morning in Dublin and five in the Algonquin and it is to be assumed that she is calling from the couch. The last time she called she had mentioned that same matter of the cooperative freshmen. But mentioned it with a drunken hysterical effort to be more offensive: Rumours follow you, sordid stories from the sunny South, lions from the jungle, black and brown men pursuing the postimperial English back to London, 'twas the green eye of the little yellow god.

And more of the same.

That last call had come to Knocknagon, quite audibly in the middle of all the confusion. The line she was on must have been the only one functioning, at that woeful moment, in the best part of half a county. He looks again at the letter he wrote her before the smoke had settled down. If the smoke ever would settle down. He had not mailed the letter. If he had mailed it he would not now be able to read it:

*Dearly beloved:* Christofano Allori (1577–1642) painted his mistress as Judith, and he himself as the head of Holofernes in her hand. Greetings from Holofernes, the severed and talking head.

Hopping this finds you well as it leaves me at present. As the domestic servants used to write home to rural Ireland on every Thursday in the G.P.O., in Dublin.

For what if your latest love story has finally ended. Do not re-
pine. The world is aflutter with wings, and Dolly Parton has frequently assured me that love is like a butterfly; and a lesser if
more ancient authority, Marcus Antoninus, has held that whatever happens is as common and well known as a rose in the spring
or an apple in the autumn, that everywhere up and down, ages
and histories, towns and families are full of the same stories. As
for instance: across the water in the other island there is a man
who loves his love in the morning and loves his love at noon: but
she is so fat she can find no clothes to fit her and cannot go out of
the house. So he walks alone because to tell you the truth he is
lonely: and becomes bitter because everywhere on the streets he
sees bright, slim, young women stepping along, a dream of ladies
sweeping by, bright virgins, a little colony of hens, robed and
bare of bonnet (see John Crowe Ransom), and fishing in the dark
of his mind he finds a means of revenge: to spray the sprightly
fillies with paint and motor oil, destroying clothes and even
underclothes in sixteen separate attacks, and all for love that had
to her mighty power, perforce, subdued his fat wife's captive
heart.

*Newsflash:* shopkeepers in Kabul who refused to close their
shops in protest against Karmal's communist regime had their
heads cut off and displayed in their own shop windows.

But as I was saying before I was so rudely interrupted: I mean
to sing the praises of love's name and his, or her, victorious con-
quests to Areed: and in another part of these fortunate islands a
young man had the privilege to be fallen for by a happy girl of
seventeen whose only fault was that, like the wife who couldn't
come out of the house, she was overweight, weighing, alas, almost
a stone or fourteen pounds or six to seven kilogrammes or six
thousand to seven thousand grammes (E.E.C.) for every year of
her age. She smiled on him: where'er he walked cool breezes
fanned the glade, and she was there before him. His gentlemanly
friends were first to congratulate him with happy youthful cries
of Where is Moby Dick today, and Where is your elephant, where
is she that all the swains commend her. So that the loved one, on
one tender encounter, began by petting the good-natured girl, she
was ever thus, then killed her with a rock and a rope, and said:
She was on my back all the time, she would not leave me alone,

something snapped, and they called her the gentle maiden wherever she took her way.

But from across the narrow seas and gallant France, and all the way from Sicily comes, as you might expect, a story with more style: of a duke who, in his castle, rings out wild bells to the wild sky every time, or just after every time, he makes love to his young mistress. Oh, happy man. Oh tintinnabulation of the bells. Repeat bells. Ring out the old, ring in the new: for the duchess who lives estranged in another part of the castle says that the bell ringing by night and day is a public nuisance and even the villagers think that three carillons a night may be overmuch: but the duke says that since his people a thousand years ago arrived with the Normans at the place where they now are, they have been constantly ringing bells, bells, bells, bells, bells,

*Newsflash:* five men last night in Strabane, County Tyrone, shaved the head of a seventeen-year-old Catholic girl and then poured green paint over her. It is understood that the girl was accused by her attackers of being a soldier lover. Many a maiden fair is waiting here to greet her truant soldier lover. The green bald girl was taken to Altnagevlin Hospital, Derry, where her condition is described as satisfactory: If I had you, lovely Martha, away down in Inishowen or in some lonely valley in the wild woods of Tyrone, I would do my whole endeavour and try to work my plan for to gain my prize and feast my eyes on the Flower of Sweet Strabane.

*Item:* Two men and two women were stoned to death in the southern Iranian city of Kerman after being sentenced by an Islamic revolutionary court on charges that included rape, homosexual and heterosexual prostitution, and adultery.

Is there a Koranic order of precedence?

One report says that the four had been suitably (and I daresay, forcibly) dressed in white funeral shrouds, buried in earth up to their necks, and then stoned for fifteen minutes. Sitting ducks. And small stones only. Wimbledon rules.

Another report says that they were simply tied to trees and stoned. Bigger targets. Bigger stones.

According to the Koran (it was explained), execution for adultery can be carried out by stoning, by the arrow, or by pushing the guilty man or woman over a cliff or from any high place. Re-

The Wedding ❧ 183

mind me, and yourself, to keep away from the Koran. And the Empire State. And the Cliffs of Moher.

By way of contrast: Alpha Androstenal, a sympathetic version of a human chemical found in underarm perspiration, is shortly to come on the market. Production costs may be as high as forty-four thousand dollars a pound. The president of a famous perfume house has claimed that AA is the very essence of the attraction of one human being for another. Cor ad cor loquitur. That it is capable of triggering a staggering sexual reaction, and that his firm may have documented human pheromones. AA, mixed with other ingredients to form a cologne, will transmit attractant signals to any males within sensory range with a message so powerful, so exciting, there can be only one response. Stampede? The thundering herd? To be dealt with afterward in the criminal courts.

The mixture does not smell like sweat.

Up to this happy moment pheromones have interested only scientists studying sex attractants in the world of insects or, perhaps, sect attractants in the world of insex. The chemical elements have been used in traps to control weevils and Japanese beetles: and farmers have used pheromone sprays in order to encourage pigs to mate.

Then over there in Memphis, Tenn., a soul singer who sold twenty million discs in four years sat happy in his bath when a lady slapped him in the back with a panful of soul food: sizzling hot grits, which in the morning in Memphis you maun eat whether you like them or not. Alas, poor soul, having slapped the soul singer with a panful of the food his soul desired, as the hart panteth after water, grit burns on arms, back, and belly, she wrote a note and shot herself, singing her sad swan song: The more I trust you the more you let me down. You don't know how deep my love is for you, and you turned your back on me without knowing the facts.

Grits. To the sweet, farewell. Hot hominy grits.

Then down in Epping Forest, Essex, something stirs: and a taxi driver out walking comes on a woman whose body has been much marked by love: Great God of Might that reignest in the mind, and all the body to thy Hest doest frame, Victor of Gods, subduer of mankynd, that doest the Lions and fell Tigers tame, making their cruell rage thy scornefull game, and in their roring taking great delight: who can express the glorie of thy might?

Who can, indeed? And this dear lady was, woe to tell, sound asleep in three separate plastic bags, and on her wedding-ring finger she wore a Claddagh (Galway) love ring, and on her left arm written in tattoo the names of Carol, Liz, and Pat, and Melanie and Kath: and also, I LOVE JAN, and ROCK FOLLIES, 1972, and IN MEMORY OF MAM AND DAD and DEATH BEFORE DISHONOUR: and entwined hearts and a swallow on the wing and, over all, the cross of Christ: and on the right another cross, another swallow, a rose, and the names of Terri, John, and Sue: on her right hand the name of Gill and on her left the name of Love. Or who alive can perfectly declare the wondrous cradle of thine infancie, when thy great mother, Venus, first thee bore, begot of Plentie and of Penurie.

Conflicting news flashes from here, there, and everywhere: Appearance of a nude woman on a highway just outside of Comas, on the outskirts of Lima, caused an hour-long blackout in the homes of one hundred thousand residents. . . .

Farmer Tom Trumpington thought it was a load of bull when Morris dancers in Derbyshire offered to perform an ancient fertility rite on one of his fields. . . .

A car turned over when its driver sought to avoid striking the nude woman: and crashed into an electric light post, knocking down high-tension wires, which shorted and caused the blackout. . . .

But Farmer Tom was desperate to grow crops in the barren field known locally as Paradise. So he asked the dancers to go ahead. Just to be on the safe side he kept his wife, Milly, well out of the way of the dancing Morris men. But everyone forgot about Fred, the dozy bull in the next field. . . .

Franny Fortune agreed to share her husband with his lover, Betty Baron, one evening a week in an attempt to save her marriage. . . .

But after the fertility dance Fred the bull suddenly developed a crush on cows. . . .

Three passengers in the car that turned over were slightly injured. They reported that the nude woman disppeared into the woods on the side of that Peruvian highway. . . .

But a fortuneteller told Franny Fortune that such tolerance was not a good idea: and off with her to the home of Betty Baron where, through a window open to the south, she spotted her husband exceeding the ration and in a fit, a fit, a triple fit of fury took love's revenge on an inanimate machine by marking the bodywork of Betty Baron's Buick, by ripping off the wiper blades and wing mirrors, by smashing the rear lights and snapping off the aerial, pouring tar into the engine and over roof, bonnet, and into and over the boot: then hurled a garden spade through the lounge window, followed by plants in pots. Later she was reconciled with her husband, who agreed to cancel the affair.

Chicken! Or did Betty Baron think, like Dolly Parton, that love was like a butterfly: and twitched her mantle blue and on the morrow fled to more quiet gardens and fresh fields and pastures new?

One question: Did Franny Fortune come provided with her own flowing tar?

But back to the bull in Derbyshire because, in most tales of love and particularly in the story of Europa, the prime mover always was the bull: and, inspired by the leaping Morris dancers, Fred, the Derbyshire dozer, awoke, looked over a hedge and spotted a heifer, desirable but underage, burst through the hedge and, with his bull head, broke down a wall and bulled the heifer: who now, her parents say, must have an abortion, disapproved of by the Pope of Rome.

Nor ever did any grass grow in the field called Paradise.

For having yet, in his deducted spright, some sparkes remaining of that heavenly fyre, he is enlumined with that goodly light, unto like goodly semblant to aspyre: therefore in choice of love he doth desyre that seemes on earth most heavenly to embrace, that same is Beautie, borne of heavenly race. . . .

*Item:* A fourteen-year-old County Derry Catholic schoolgirl was taken to hospital yesterday afternoon and later discharged: following an attack by two masked girls and a man. Her attackers cut the letters U.D.A. (Ulster Defence Army or Association) on her right forearm, and said they would let her go if she sang "God Save the Queen."

Which I hope she was able to do.

The things a girl should know.

God Save the Queen!

Ah well, as Barbara Streisand sings so touchingly, I stumble and fall with my ass to the wall, but I gave you it all.

And, in due course, I'll call: Your Everloving and Unsinkable Buoy.

The nightmare from which she aroused him is now a recurrent attraction ever since the third man told him the story and told him about a day he had spent with an archaeologist in the town of Carrickfergus: Two odd things happened on that day. In the morning we went round the town with the archaeologist who was doing a great job on the place, ancient castle, old houses, seawall and all. Then we had lunch in a small hotel, a good lunch and everybody pleasant and civil. We? Oh, the other member of the party was a Belfastman, name of Foster Wilson, you don't know him, a scholar with a red beard, teaching now in Canada, home on holidays. Then after lunch the archaeologist had to meet a party from some learned society to show them what he was up to in the place, and to talk about history as he saw it. So we started to do the rounds all over again. But you know the way it is or the way it can be. We got tired and felt like a drink. At any rate I felt like a drink. Wilson felt like reading a book and sat down, for the sake of peace, in the great hall of the old castle and I crossed the street to a pub. Went into the gents first and said as I went in, to the girl behind the bar: Double Black Bush and ice and a baby soda.

—Perhaps not an original remark.

—But when I emerged there was my double Bush, etcetera, and the barmaid would take no money and wouldn't say why. Great giggling going on between her and three well-dressed ladies sitting in a corner of the lounge and hard at the vodka and tonic and, finally, one of the three says: Guess who bought you the big Bush.

—Then the three of them stood up before me like soldiers on inspection parade. Or the judgement of Paris. All of them women of about your or my age. Fine armfuls any one of them, yet. And all in the best of good humour. Damned if I could guess which of them bought me the drink. The three fine faces, all together and side by side utterly confused me. Damned if they would tell me which of them bought me the drink, or why. So I bought a round of vodkas and stuff and another Bush, and kissed them all and the barmaid for good value, and left the place, still wondering and childishly happy.

—That, says I to myself, is the acceptable face of my Ulster that I love, the friendly people of the Nine Counties: and I thought of the lovely places they live in, the lonely Sperrin mountains, the Nine Glens of Antrim and the Antrim coast road, the Strule valley, the Clogher valley with the high hedges and the deep grass: and I thought, too, of a pub in Galway long ago with a merry group of Orangemen and women from Larne singing all gay and merry each in his chair, down in the wee room underneath the stair. They were all there for the Galway races where not so many of them would be nowadays to be found, and singing also of the Glens of Antrim and the hills of Donegal: and Ulster, I thought, yesterday, today, and the same forever.

Wilson was out on the street, sober and satiated with reading. The ass was frozen off him from sitting in the old cold castle. So I offered to buy the learned man a drink, and back with us into the little hotel where we had the good friendly lunch: and into the public bar. But all was changed, changed utterly, and it was no terrible beauty was born. The barman who earlier on had been so civil scarcely threw us a word. Five young men in a corner fell silent when we came in and gave us the benefit of five long stares. One of them stood up, came to the counter, reached across in front of me to lift a pint that the barman had pulled. He didn't say excuse me. Wilson was visibly sweating and wouldn't sit down and would scarcely speak except to say that we shouldn't wait for a second drink, and said to me when we were out and well away that that was the pub from which a Protestant tartan gang had abducted a Catholic whiskey salesman and afterward murdered him. . . .

Murdered him: after they drank his samples.

The nightmare scene is a public park on a headland from which there is a splendid view of the Irish Sea. In a public park in Atlanta, Georgia, he had once seen policemen sending dogs, in the early morning, under a bandstand to root out ragged bums. So in this nightmare and in this Irish park, his Buster Keaton figure is a ragged bum, running pointlessly from here to there, whispering to this person and that person, a crazy trotter in a crazy ballet, no other person moving or speaking or whispering or anything just standing under trees or sitting on benches, all dressed in black, all wearing odd headgear and black masks, but nobody moving or doing a damned thing except that one ragged bum. Those dark motionless people stand or sit, each one alone, paying not the least attention to the gesturing and whispering of that one moving person. But far away back stage or at the other end of the park there is one group of five people gathered at the foot of an obelisk surmounted by a golden cross, but the cross is draped in heavy purple cloth as, on Good Fridays, the statues and crucifixes in the churches used to be draped. But if the cross is draped in purple cloth then how can I know that it is a golden cross? Answer: the ragged running bum has told me in a whisper. Four of the five are standing and drinking out of golden bottles that sparkle so brightly that the light is reflected, dancing, on the distant and quite motionless sea. The fifth is kneeling, arms extended. He cries: Ah, no boys. Sabacthani.

The trotting whispering bum can do nothing about it and the curious ballet goes on and on, and repeats itself, and nothing happens, and the bum whispers to me that he is looking for children because the four men will not fill in the fifth man until all the children are out of the park, because they do not like to fill in a fella if children are looking on, because children should not be allowed to see or hear anything unpleasant, because in the city a little girl fainted when she first heard gunfire, and fainted again later on when she heard a car backfire, and again when somebody slammed a door: and another little girl had an epileptic fit when she saw a crowd put a building to the torch, and then another when she saw a crowd coming out of a football match, and yet another when the fire was lighted in her own house and she heard at the same time the bell of a fire-engine passing on the street: and suffer the little children, the bum whispers, and runs away toward the sea: and pulls the whole park after him like a carpet: and then little girls in white are rehearsing for the wedding in the garden in Carmincross, and church bells are ringing, and firebells are ringing, and hell's bells are ringing for me and Deborah, my gal, but it is only the phone in this bedroom in this hotel on the southern fringe of Dublin city, and she is talking from the Algonquin to tell him, as he and we already know, that a letter is pursuing him and that her lover has left her, and that far away in the blossomy sunny South some teacher of languages is playing paddywhack with the young women.

The night porter on his way off duty, an affable man made more so by being well-tipped for his willingness and ability to carry drink late at night, brings him his morning mail. This visit, this return may degenerate into a lonely orgy. The letter has not yet overtaken him.

The third man had told him that, afterward, he had found that Foster Wilson had been in error and that the bar in Carrickfergus was not the bar from which the man had been abducted: but from a bar in the Shankill Road in Belfast.

—Not that it makes a damned bit of difference, he said, in these happy times.

—And afterward in a dream, just as in the Bible, I found out who bought me the big Bush. That day in Carrickfergus was not the first time I'd kissed her. She was the blonde one of the three, a bit faded but still blonde. She had been one of four sisters from the town we went to school in. You may or may not have known them. Fine Presbyterian family with biblical names. Deborah, like your friend. Ruth . . .

—Jezebel? Bathsheba?

—No, Judith was her name. On the way home from Belfast in the bus I fell asleep, and woke up suddenly, and saw her face, when she was seventeen, as clearly as I now see you. Four sisters and three brothers, two of the brothers killed in the war, and the father a blacksmith and an honest man.

—Two faces of our Ulster, Mervyn, hapless, hopeless province or country or six counties, or nine counties, or U.K., or unrecovered Ireland, or whatever in hell or out of it you like to call it.

So the girl in reception calls him a cab and he goes from the hotel to the hospital which is away to the north on the far end of the city. But he abandons the cab outside the Shelbourne Hotel to make what has always been for him, and many another, a favourite walk through the city centre. In the golden age before 1939 a gentleman used to dismiss a taxi. Not any more. Not in

Dublin. Perhaps not anywhere. My Jehu will decide if I may or
may not smoke, may compel me to listen to pop music. Old story
once about eminent London-Irish King's counsel who had con-
nections in Donegal, hails taxi in the Haymarket, says: Killybegs.

—Where, Guv?

—Killybegs, Donegal.

Eminent counsel is drunk and in evening dress.

—Donegal is in Ireland, Guv?

—Quite correct. No Donegal has yet been discovered anywhere else.

—'Op in, Guv.

And, long before the day of the car-ferry, drives him all the
way to Killybegs on the edge of the far Atlantic, had the taxi
hoisted and all at Holyhead.

He tries out that story in the Horseshoe Bar, where he is still
remembered. He is in no hurry to get to the hospital. The patient
is restive and most unreconciled, and, up to the moment, has allowed him to feel all the guilt. He listens to a few more stories, has
five drinks in all, three of them bought for him, one by an acquaintance out of the past, two by men he has never met before.
But all the way down Grafton Street and through College Green
and over the Liffey nobody speaks to him, recognises him, stops
him, buttonholes him. Can a man become a ghost in a town he
has known and in which he has been known for so long? The
people have grown younger. The young wash less. The girls wear
dungarees and cut the oddest figures, some stout, some thin, some
hirplin on like cripples with their toes turned in.

Here at this place, and inside there in the post office, the Irish
Republic was solemnly declared in the name of God and of the
dead generations who may or may not have been listening: and
the news mailed out to the world. Up there somewhere at a point
no longer defined or definable, and as late as the 1960s, Nelson
stood on his pillar and according to a poet in the 1940s, who was
there looking up at him, engaged himself in watching his world
collapse. The maimed republic is still with us and the fantasies
that crippledom can breed. Nelson has gone, leaving his world
behind him like a salted snail: Join the navy and see sheepshit on
the Falklands, join the army and see Unity Flats on the Falls

Road in Belfast, or drop by helicopter with the groceries into
Crossmaglen where the dalin' men put whiskey in me tay and up
the ructions rose, and I stood up like a hero and slaughtered
friends and foes.

Faraway in Oregon I was, on a hoarse Trinacrian shore along
which Drake had sailed, when Nelson took his leave of Dublin
town. Work of experts, said the papers. When some ruffian, by
the devil's grace, gets away with something, the papers say: So-
phisticated work of experts.

The top half of the pillar they blew and Nelson with it, and
didn't break a window in the street. Not a word about a teenage
dance going on at the time, the early morning, in the old Metro-
pole ballroom, now no longer with us. If the teenagers had
debouched at the wrong time Nelson would have gone, not un-
accompanied, to the stars. But they didn't. Will of God? Evidence of expert planning by the New Irelanders? Then came the
army to remove the ponderous plinth and that which was left of
the shaft: and broke every window in the street. So: army experts
not as expert as subversive, destabilising experts at blowing up
statues and knocking down pillars.

To me in Oregon came a letter from a Dublin friend. Must call
to see him before I go back to the Algonquin. This he wrote: You
will be interested to hear that Nelson had two heads. Your friend,
Butty Sugrue, the strong man or Sampson from Killorglin,
County Kerry, claims to possess one. A student in Trinity College, the other. Phrenologists may be called in. Two heads. One
eye. One arm. One prick that was found in Madame Nora's
boutique.

Ah well, ah well, Dublin wit and humour.

And thus the New Irelanders declared their intentions where
Pearse and company had bombinated about God and the dead
generations. Let the living generations beware, for the intentions
of this time are to put the torch to the old Ireland, the one we
were trying to live in, blow up the whole fucking joblot and
everybody in it, Catholic and Protestant and Jew and Presbyterian, there is yet no animosity no matter what persuasion: as at
the sporting races of Galway.

Those five drinks in the Shelbourne have made him just the

littlest bit dizzy. Drinking too much since all this happened. And not so well able to take it. So sit in the Gresham and drink black coffee, and let the hospital wait and the woman in it.

There was a Spanish poet who was a friend of mine who wrote: Bebamos amigos, let us drink my friends, death does not exist, the wheat will have its crop and the woman will wait.

He wrote it all in Spanish in Barcelona.

Let us drink black coffee. Death does exist.

Was it my fault? She came with me of her own free will.

This paper here reports the most recent battle of Crossmaglen. To the extreme detriment of the local people the armed struggle against the British empire, which is no longer there, continues. Ten mortar bombs have been fired at a British security post and from the back of a stolen lorry. What unfortunate hoor owned the lorry? May he expect due compensation from the New Ireland?

Only three of the ten bombs got as far as the perimeter fence. One soldier had a slight arm injury from a flying fragment. So the paper says. Woeful waste of perfectly good mortar bombs. But the real damage was elsewhere, when twelve bold heroes in big black masks invaded in the morning the neighbouring housing estate, hammered from door to door, shouted Out, Out, Abandon homes all ye who inhabit here, on the double or perish, and up the republic, and bugger your homes that all these years you kept your hearts in: and one teenage girl who stayed asleep, sweet dreams, in bed, woke up in a shower of splintered glass, and one long-suffering housewife has this to say: I didn't know the attack was on until I heard three or four big bangs and all my front windows have been blown in three times in two years.

The hunt rides by and in the roadway the wife of the peasant counts the dead geese.

In the name of Jasus and the living and suffering generations I'll have a brandy in this final cup of coffee, no brandy alexander here; and sip it, and read with delight about Samantha Barnfield, aged fifteen, who has been appointed official flag raiser for the parish church of Swindon village near Cheltenham. On royal birthdays and other occasions of state she will be privileged to run up the Union Jack. To hoist that is, and my love, and the best of British luck, to Samantha.

This England never did and never shall. . . .
On my way.

Charles Stewart Parnell he salutes where he stands at the foot of his three-cornered pillar, until somebody or something blows him up, and points a hand to a nearby pub and says that no man has a right to fix a boundary to the march of a nation: then he, not Parnell, boards a northbound bus for the rest of the journey. Helps two old ladies to mount the bus. Awkward crates these, designed less for comfort than for combat training. Already known as the Castro Cars because, it is said, they were made for Cuba but the Cubans wouldn't have them. Helps the old ladies also to mount the steep step to the seat. Does everything but bloody well tuck them in. Then sits facing another woman, a young one, he with his back to the south, she with the south in her eyes. She wears a wedding ring, she wears many rings, heavy rings. She is not unlike Deborah was when first we met. But she has purple eyelids. And shopping bags. Studiously she avoids my eyes and stares out at the passing scene. But our knees are not a little in the way of each other as knees on legs of any length maun be in these accursed Castro Crates: working the knee we used to call it when I was an aspiring schoolboy. Her face has not, though, the strength nor boldness of Deborah's bones. What will she look like in twenty-eight years? Flabby? Shapeless? Even with the hint of supplementary chins, Deborah has never been flabby. But that, at the moment, does not matter.

Brakes scream to the empyrean as they always do in Dublin buses. We disentangle or disengage our knees. She quirks her lips in what might be the beginning of a smile. Oh, lady of the purple eyelids, forever fare thee well. She disembarks. The bus is slow in starting again because the conductor has to help those two old ladies to clamber down, and to help aloft an old gentleman who is armed with a shining surgical stick. While the bus throbs and waits the lady of the rings and the eyelids opens a gate and steps into a suburban garden. The name of the house on the plate on the gate is Majorca. She looks back quickly and smiles and waves. At him, or at somebody else in the bus? He will never know. The door closes behind her. She is in another world. Will her knees remember me? Oh Majorca, Majorca!

\* \* \*

It might never have happened if she had not burned the book. Going to bed with Jeremiah on the last, sad night in Knocknagon was not all that important. No young and ripening loves were quenched, no vows of everlasting loyalty were broken: no butterfly survives as long as two days, let alone four years. To bed with Killoran might have been more dignified than to bed with Jeremiah who had degenerated into a sort of performing ape: but then Killoran's wife was present in that fatal place, and Killoran's son, the young priest, and between them they might have constituted an impediment.

—This evil book, she said, has caused it all.

And threw it on the fire in the pub, an open hearth fire as it so happened, a pyramid of peat sods burning, glowing with the colour of the garb of angels, and tall men go by and their clothes the colour of burning sods, burning with the heat of a blast furnace so not a hope in hell, how apt, of rescuing the book. A hateful thing to see a book burn: any book. All those stories consumed to ash, no smoke even to take them up the chimney, all those stories that I had wanted for a special study, hadn't even commenced to make my notes. All of a sudden she acted with no warning nor hint of warning. Picked the book up from where I had left it on the counter when I shook hands with the auditor who played the accordion. She riffled the leaves then opened it and read out the story of the woman who, a few days before her death, dreamed that she was dead and that her soul had ascended to one of the stars where she found several persons she had known in life: who told her that while they were glad to see her they hoped she wouldn't stay too long as that star was a sort of purgatory, that all the stars were for the reception of different kinds of souls, a different star for each different vice, a horrible notion, so that every man and woman must look until purged on the image of his or her own peculiar sin.

But the musical auditor said that if all the lechers were all together on the one star then a good time might be had by all.

But all the murderers? And all the thieves? And all the molesters of children with no children to molest?

—But where do the good go, she cried. And where this woeful day is Smiling Blue Peter?

And read out how a Scottish Lord Lovat had affirmed that at the instant of his birth a number of swords hanging in the hall of the Lovat mansion leaped unaided out of their scabbards: an omen of doom and violent death.

—You and your evil book, Mervyn, she said. Swords then. Bombs now.

She had been drinking pernod. She, it may be, had, unknown to herself and myself, been under shock.

—This evil book, she said, has caused it all.

And tossed it into the fire.

Not too often nowadays, you see a hearth fire, genuine Irish old-style, in a pub. But this was a strange old-style pub. Blackened low rafters. And curved dark oaken wings coming out from the hearth to form a sort of snug or sanctum. Big rough men at the counter, rough but friendly, a sort of blackavised, tinker style about them and a resemblance running through them, half-brothers or cousins, a local clan. Because the name above the door was Kavanagh, and my name was Kavanagh, the woman behind the bar gave me a warm welcome: and at least three of the big rough men were also Kavanagh. Embarrassed they were, when she burned the book. They thought, perhaps, we were husband and wife having a fight and that that was our way of showing it. If there was a tinker strain in them they most likely thought that a welting with a wattle would do her no harm: Irish tinkers have, or used to have, a touch of the Turk in them.

A good place and a good moment to tell the stories of the greatest of the Kavanaghs, so as to keep my own temper and to distract their attention from the odd annoying behaviour of this woman. So here goes:

—There was Bryan Nestroake whose real name was Kavanagh. Called Nestroake because of his valour and the blows he struck for King James at the battles of Aughrim and the Boyne. Or, perhaps, because of a scar on his face.

—Why Nestroake?

The speaker had no Irish.

—Bryan of the blows. Or the strokes. Or the scar. When I was a schoolboy I was a good fighter and for a while they called me that for a nickname.

But I remember and do not say that the name did not stick.

Not because I was beaten in battle. But because no effort to give me a nickname ever succeeded. Is there something odd, even sinister, about a young fellow who cannot keep a nickname?

—Where, she said. On what star? Where is Smiling Blue Peter? He was a warrior far from home.

She is woebegone, her makeup tawdry and awry, her eyes staring beyond us.

On the accordion the auditor drew out a long strain to sound like a distant bugle.

—Wailing from sad shires, he said.

He was a most unusual and accomplished auditor. He was the only auditor I ever met who played the accordion in a pub. He had been in the office behind the bar when we came in. More a living room than an office. He had been doing the books of the pub and grocery and small hotel. Because of my surname and the assumption by the lady of the house that Deborah shared my name, we had been asked into the office as guests of honour to meet the auditor, drink tea against the rain and wind outside, and whiskey and pernod on the house. The accordion just happened to be there. For jokes, the auditor strapped it on and marched bravado back into the bar playing it. He played it well. There was laughter and a grand hurrah. He was a big, sandy, jovial man. Very popular. Several times she told him that he was like Blue Peter except that he had no tattoo. He did not understand. How could he? And I was too glad to be in from the ill day outside to realise that she was acting distrait.

—He had, later on in history, a relative called Morgan Prussia Kavanagh.

—Who had?

—Nestroake.

—They went in for rare names. Couldn't they be content with Kavanagh?

—Nicknames. They were wandering men. And wandering once on the mainland of Europe, Morgan was grabbed by the Prussians for the emperor Frederick's regiment of tall men. It was said at the time that he was the tallest man in Europe.

—Frederick?

—Morgan.

Solemnly, and on the deepest notes the bloody box could muster, and with considerable comic effect, the auditor played the music of the Hitlerian lyric about marching against England.

—Yes. Morgan it was. Morgan Prussia Kavanagh, for it was he. And no fancy in the world whatever had he for conditions of service in the Prussian army. So, cute enough, he had the word passed around that if he had furlough to go for a while to Ireland he would go, and return bringing with him four brothers who were bigger and better men than himself. Thackeray knew the story.

—Blue Peter, she said. Tattoo. Thackeray.

The auditor played a few bars about coming back to Erin.

—And back to Erin came Morgan Kavanagh. And stayed. And ever after and once a year and on the birthday of the king of Prussia he would climb to the top of Brandon hill above the river Barrow, and turn his back to Berlin and fart three times to wish the king a happy birthday.

Laughter, prolonged and coarse.

—Oh, there's a lot more about Morgan.

But as it happened I am never to get around to telling it.

—Blue Peter, she said, is dead. And all you can do, Mervyn, is tell stories that all of you think are funny.

—You all, he said.

Trying to make light of the embarrassing situation.

—Who, said one of the Kavanaghs, is Smiling Blue Peter.

—Not is. Was, she said. Blue Peter smiled at me. Blue Peter is no more.

She walked quietly out of the pub by a dark doorway at the far end of the counter, and we all thought as one would think that she was bound for the powder room. The front door blew open. A blast of rain swept in. Another of the Kavanaghs with considerable physical effort closed the door.

—Tell us, he said, about Smiling Blue Peter.

We had passed a burned-out red, once red, telephone box to the side of the rural roadway. Just outside a pelting village with a pub wiremeshed as if for siege. The old man or ancient mariner to whom we had given a lift said: The pubs today are not what they use to be. That pub now, no Catholic would be served in it. Sojers go in there. There's dark suspicion everywhere. British officer fellow thought he was a Catholic and make friends in Crossmaglen and they let him think it and led him on and not a hair on his head ever found, and one side worse than the other, and Christ save us they say they fed him to the pigs. How could pubs be the same when you might get a pint one minit and a bomb the next? Still I have a brother in Belfast and do you know he lost a leg sitting in a pub. The pub he was used to all his life. The bomb was in a schoolbag, a cub's schoolbag that somebody tossed in through the door the way you'd do when you were young and coming home from school. And it lay on the floor for a while and all looking at it like a hissing snake and then up it went and what was left of his left leg had to be amputated.

We were at that moment an hour away from the shambles of Carmincross and headed a little south of east. Deborah was very quiet. Had been so for two days.

A sharp bump over a ramp on the road close to a bridge over a small stream, and nobody anywhere to be seen.

—Still he goes back to the same pub, my brother that I mentioned. He'd be lost without the pint and the bit of crack. And where is there to go? He says with a sort of a laugh that the city changes every time you duck your head. They have sayings now that they never had before. He says that they'll soon have to invent a new language, that English has run out of words: and Micky Minnis the busker, he used to entertain the theatre queues with his melodium, he's gone, blown up when he was playing, not to a queue, no queues now, just playing for a few ha'pence on a miserable bit of a street, and gone like that and others with him, he didn't even get a farewell picture in the paper, gone melodium, music, and all, and God Christ what are we coming to the brother says, name of Timoney like myself, my elder brother. . . .

Deborah is biting her lip and silently weeping.

—A wee place like that now would be very suspicious, barbed wire round the pub, and look at the telephone box that was put there for the convenience of the people and ringing loved ones far away. None of the phones work any more. In Carmincross the phones didn't work to take the warnings, no phones worked.

Deborah said: We know.

But Mervyn knew that one phone had worked, although to no particular purpose.

—As suspicious as ferrets in a wee place like that. If you'd say to a Catholic when did you have the last bomb here he'd tell you to enquire from the sojers in the barracks and if you say to a Protestant where the parish priest lives he says he wouldn't know. People have closed up like crabs.

So we come to the checkpoint that will release us back into the one-legged Irish republic. Fumbling for papers. Sullen search of the boot of the car.

—But look at him, she said, take a look at him.

And suddenly her face seemed to brighten.

A tall, redheaded, smiling young soldier. Eyes roaming the skies, happy in some faraway world, dancing over the fields and hedges, coming home to rest with appreciation on Deborah. She reminded him, I'd swear to God, of something or somewhere or somebody. Their eyes did a tango. Both his arms were tattooed up to the elbows, which was as far as we could see, with the British crown and naval pennants. The open neck of his shirt showed similar ornamentations.

—Look at him, she said. He's like an art gallery. He must have a Blue Peter on his backside. Or a Blue Peter somewhere.

Almost laughing, she took a step or two toward him. Laughing like a young fellow meeting his love he took a step toward her. And suddenly sang: I'm leaning on a lampost at the corner of the street . . .

Then something happened. Mervyn has no recollection of hearing anything. But the soldiers must have trained ears, and with bloody good reason. They moved, they knelt, they ducked, they dived, they watched, they waited, but they fired no shots: only Mervyn and Deborah and an officer chap stood up like sticks in the middle of the road. The ancient mariner was out of sight in the back of the car. That was the first time Mervyn had ever seen a man shot dead. Afterward he heard that Blue Peter had got it in the groin. But Mervyn saw no sign, no stain of blood, he heard no cry. For a few fleeting seconds Blue Peter looked around him, surprised, yet not displeased, like a lad who had just detected a friend trying out some harmless practical joke. What was he doing here far from home? Where was his home? Where was this place? Then he sat down on the roadway with his back to the radiator of the red car. He said: Captain Myers, sir.

—Robinson, the Captain said.

Or something like that. But before the officer chap could turn around Blue Peter rolled over on the roadway and was dead.

And suddenly soldiers here and soldiers there and soldiers everywhere and c'est la guerre, and soldiers running stooping across a meadow and firing shots: and Mike Connolly from Boston who marched with Patch's eleventh army from Marseilles, which they wrecked when landing, and up through France, told me once about being under German fire on a long straight flat French road: and Mike and all his men behind poplar trees, not much use for cover, or flat on their bellies, and a French general, a long thin fellow, Le Clerc or something, up like the fucking Eiffel tower in the middle of the road, and not a bloody bother on him, and reading a map, they're so well used to it, the fucking French. Ah Marseilles, Marseilles, Mike Connolly used to sing, you were one fine town until we got you down.

Deborah didn't scream. Not that Mervyn heard. But he saw her run and kneel beside Blue Peter. He heard her say: Sacred Heart of Jesus have mercy on his soul.

He saw her touch the cross of a set of rosary beads to the forehead of Blue Peter.

The captain stood above them like the fucking Nelson column and looked toward a distant hilltop circle of beech trees from which the shot might have come that ended the simple song of Smiling Blue Peter.

Ten miles further on the ancient mariner says that the elder brother in Belfast saw a sojer falling under a hail of bullets in Andersonstown in 1972: Dozens of weans, childher ma'am, egging on the gunmen to finish him off, and when the bleeding corpse had been carted away a wee cub twirled the sojer's helmet on a stick and then did a wardance with the helmet on his head.

—Death, she said, has followed us from Carmincross.

After that the rain came on and we came to the pub and the house of the Kavanaghs where the ancient mariner thanked us many times over and went his own way. To visit some relatives in the neighbourhood. But in the porch of the pub he held me with his skinny hand, and thanked me for the transport and hoped that my lady would be well and not brood too much about what she had seen: these were terrible times. And told me two stories, to make me laugh, he said: There was this Protestant man, you see, over by Forkhill and he was missing for a long time: and the wife, you see, wanted to find a corpse and prove death and claim the insurance. So all the neighbours helped and found a corpse in a ditch, only you see it had Roman Catholic rosary beads twined and tangled in what was left of its fingers. And that worried everybody for a bit until one man worked it out the way the I.R.A. always buried a man decent. Catholic or Protestant all one to them. Except the man they fed to the pigs.

He stepped out into the rain, stepped back again, and gave my hand a final clasp: If ever you come this road again I'll tell you where to find me on the far side of what they call the Border.

In great detail he told me: And I've a long garden there that I'd like to show the pair of you, with all due respect. Flowers and plants from as far away as China, and the ground rising and falling like the lone prairie, and travelling on all the way down to the Lough shore. And this evening last June, I'm out there plowtering about, and quite content in Tyrone among the bushes as the song says, when I hear a rustle, and there before me is a black nigger in British uniform and he says to me: Man, what you doing here.

—And me in my own long garden.

—So I says to him, man o' dear, whoever you are and wherever you come from and however you got the rigout, but that's a curious question. The Timoneys, you may never have heard of them, but I'm one of them and we're here since a bit before the time that Hugh O'Neill of Dungannon had the spot of trouble with Queen Elizabeth of England, not the present nice wee cutty that I saw once in Derry city on a visit, no the other Elizabeth long ago that cut the head of many's the man, and the Timoneys were here then and have been here since, and we know where we came from before that, and what I would ask you, man o' dear, is another question and that is what in the name of the merciful Jasus are you doing here?

—A pungent question, Mervyn said.

—A good one, indeed. And goodbye and good luck to herself

and yourself, and thanks for the lift and, no, I won't join you inside, but with the help of God we'll meet again, don't know
where, don't know when. . . .

And what in the name of the merciful Jasus are we doing here?
Or anywhere else?

He is, at this moment, on the steps of the main entrance to the
hospital and looking back over the way he has ascended. Suburbia below him, semidetached houses, a new parish church, and,
bosomed high in and glimmering out of tufted trees, the great
glass houses of the botanical gardens. My heart's in the tropics,
my heart is not here. Visiting her in hospital has not proved to be
his favourite occupation. Cut and run now and heigh-ho for New
York and the Algonquin. Out of the fire and back to the frying
pan. After all: she had betrayed him with Jeremiah. That for a
laugh. After all: he had not compelled her to make the golden
journey to Carmincross. In the ambulance before the sedation
had knocked her out, she had said: Bad luck follows you. And
everything connected with you.

No, that statement did not stand up to detailed rational examination. He might admit a bit here and a bit there, a misunderstanding there, a mishap here: and he stands with his back to the
hospital and looks down the slope, and suburbia fades away, and
the new church and the glimmer of the glass houses. The life we
have lived fades away like that when we look back and down.
What, oh dear Christ, was it all about? What were we doing here?

Because of that downpour outside, the great hearth fire had been
most welcome when we came into the pub: and the storm was
still on when she walked out, as we thought, to the powder room.
Although powder room is a description I never want to hear
again after my reading of one frivolous footnote to what happened in Carmincross.

She was a long time gone but what with the talk and the wine
or whatever and the intermittent music nobody passed any comment. Nor with the heigh-ho of the wind and the rain did we hear
the sound of the car starting. Nor bother our heads about a
bloody thing until the door of the wind burst open and a young

fellow in kneeboots and yellow oilskins and a black sou'wester ran in and shouted something to two of the Kavanaghs. Then we were all out on the road and running in the rain and running in the rain and so on: all the way to a right-angled bend with a high hill to the right hand where a ditch drain had swollen up into a brown torrent that crossed the road almost with a roar. Into which she had driven smack and gone with it down a slow slope and through a gateway where, praise Jesus, there was no gate, and into a sodden meadow. There was the red car like an upset, exotic insect, on its back with the wheels still buzzing. But the Kavanaghs, by God, lifted the thing clean off the ground and set it back on its feet. Ankle-deep I stood and watched and no more belonged to that place than I did to the mountains of the moon. She had been driving west of north. Back toward the place where Blue Peter smiled and sang and was killed in the groin. Did she wish to commune with the ghost of Blue Peter? Or was she heading that way for no reason under heaven or on God's earth as people used to call them?

They carried her back on the back seat taken out of the car. She was conscious and vaguely smiling. They propped her in an armchair before the hearth fire although the auditor felt that the heat might be too much for her and that she should lie flat. She sipped a sip of brandy. Then she tumbled forward. Not quite the way Blue Peter did. They carried her into a couch in the living room or office. She didn't seem to know that I was there. The auditor called the ambulance. The woman of the house said that that was a foolish thing to do, ma'am, but sure when the drink is in the wit is out. And looked at me with pity and poured me a brandy which I drank. And thanked her.

There is a hand laid on his left shoulder. He turns around but does not right away recognise the man who has intruded on his reverie, or his mental and physical paralysis. And for why does he not right away recognise him? Because the man has shaved off his moustache. Mandrake has shaved off his moustache. So he is no longer Mandrake. But more than ever he looks like de Valera. And he wears a black beret. Jesus, why? Black berets and dark glasses are the regimental badges of the Bombomb Yahoos. But it is Mandrake and none other. It is his voice, melancholy, apologetic. Is he coming or going? Going, he says. And God be thanked for that. It would be too much to sit by her bitter bedside in the company of this sad, poor fellow.

Mandrake tells Mervyn that she is much better today, that she is much more reconciled.

—I am very glad to hear that.

He sees Mandrake as he was the last time he saw him, sitting in what was left of the police station with Cecil Morrow and two younger constables: and Cecil doing his best to act like a real formal policeman on television or something.

—He says, madam, that he is your husband.

—That is true.

She is not, at that moment, overjoyed to admit it.

—He says, madam, that he was going to a wedding.

—He was at one wedding too many.

—Can you vouch for him? You see he's a stranger here.

—We're all strangers here.

Cecil says: Except Mr. Kavanagh. And myself. And the rest of us that are left.

And wearily raises a hand in salute.

She says: It all depends on which of his many good qualities you wish me to vouch for

—Please, madam.

Mervyn vouches for him.

—Oh, do let him go, she says. He has nothing to do with anything.

That was the last time she had really sounded like herself. From then on in, the strain began to tell. Perhaps all the edifice needed was that final little touch of farce, Mandrake a suspect, Deborah springing him, Mandrake departing and so glad to be departing that he went without the little red car, which was just as well, for the car that Mervyn had hired for the journey had been hijacked from somewhere by the Bombomb Yahoos. Or, in the end, had it been just as well? Perhaps she might never have driven away from the pub in the tempest in that unfamiliar hired automobile. The little red car was to her a symbol of something recognisable. It has survived very well. He stands on the steps and watches Mandrake drive it away. With tears in his eyes Mandrake has thanked him for bringing them together again. Ah well, the Lord and Merlin move in mysterious ways, and one magician would do well to stand up for another.

Some have a honeymoon, he thinks to himself as he walks up the perilously polished stairway.

Never use an elevator in a hospital. Walk, even if the steps and floors are slippery. Tread carefully, slowly, short firm steps. See all the sights. Fine young nurses trotting this way and that. Old ladies in moving if not musical chairs. Trolleys with recumbent figures going to or coming from operations. Behan once made to me one of his mock phone calls, six o'clock in the morning, mimicking the quavery querulous voice of a grand old lady: I am Madame O'Regan Carew. You have a friend who is a lawyer. Go to him this instant. I am being held against my will by the Blue Nuns. They say I am insane merely because I poisoned my grandson's wife. But I am not insane. Excuse me one moment. There is a trolleyload of corpses passing and I must find my perfumed handkerchief. . . .

Echoes of long-ago laughter. Saddest of all echoes. Fading away. Then mouths opening silently. Ghosts do not laugh.

Some, he thinks to himself, some have a honeymoon with a husband too soon, some have a honeymoon with a husband soon enough.

Good old Gertrude. What in hell did she mean?

There is a storeroom to his left full of all sorts of metal things, the door open, a nurse on tiptoe on steps reaching up to a shelf, red hair flaming through the tail of her veil. A bedpan is a bedpan is a bedpan. She overreaches, totters, and he is there like a flash to grasp and steady her. Laughter and blushes and thanks and the odour of good, clean linen. Empty the bottle and drink free brandy and here before him is a shelf of white, enamelled, blue-rimmed bottles as yet untouched by human anything. What hell good is compensation? A northern accent: and names are exchanged and the names of places of origins, Carmincross, Dromintee and Newry town, and Carmincross and were you there when, God save us all? Carpe diem and a telephone number, complete with extension, and the old dog isn't dead yet: but here is room twenty-seven, and with one hand on the doorknob and the other raised to rap, he pauses to think he should turn and walk away and never return. After that transatlantic flight with the legless symbol from Peoria should he have taken the next plane back to New York and burnt sacrifices to Viator, the god of journeys, and started all over again? Meet a redheaded woman on the way to market and turn back, preferably with the redheaded woman. Meet a legless man on the way to a wedding. . . .

But the very first thing she says to him when he steps into the room is: Mervyn, you are welcome. What was the name of that man you mentioned in the ambulance?

—What man?

—Just before I passed out.

—You have me puzzled.

She is propped up at an angle of forty-five, her hair, more blonde than ever, also propped up in a topknot, her good shoulders gracefully draped in a multicoloured shawl. On the coverlet there's a package wrapped in the wrapping paper of a city bookshop. Is she buying books? Or having them bought for her?

—When I said that if I must go to hospital let it be a Dublin hospital, you laughed and said a name.

—Oh, Laçenaire.

—Trying to remember it ever since. A lovely name. Who or what was he?

He shrinks away from the unlovely topic. Too much recently about that matter. But she insists.

—Oh, he was a Parisian. A paid assassin.

The word murderer is nowadays too commonplace.

—Away back in the nineteenth century. They caught up with him in the country. In the provinces. His big worry was that he might be guillotined in the country and not in Paris. First things first.

—He didn't want to die among the country caubogues.

—Something like that. He had his proper pride. His wish was granted.

Suddenly she laughs. This is the first time he has heard her laugh since Carmincross. She says: I did remember the name. I was testing your memory, Merlin.

Nor has she used the enchanter's name since that first night in Knocknagon. She reaches him the bookseller's package. She says that she owes him a long, long apology: Yesterday in the morning, in God's blessed morning, a change came over me. It brought

me back to my senses. Prayer, I think. I feel that I was in a daze
for a long, long time.

—The world's in a daze.

—There are two books there. One for you. To make up for the
book I burnt. How stupid could I get? And you value books so
much. This one here for me. But you must write your name in it.
Even if you didn't write the book you did read bits of it to me.

The package opened, he looks at the story of Laçenaire and the
story of Diarmuid and Gráinne: odd company.

—And your own books you must send to me when you get back
to the States. I'd better get used to reading. And I really can read.
I practised all my life on the racing pages. And the form books.
AP means always prominent. And at school I was always tops in
history, AP, dates and all, England's villainy and Ireland's
wrongs. . . .

He writes his name and some gentle matters on the flyleaf of
the story of Diarmuid and Gráinne. She writes her name and
some things similar on the flyleaf of the story of the Parisian assassin. Is it possible that he and this woman did, in warm dark
moments of frenzy, make passing references to love?

—Timothy got those books for me. He knows all the book-
shops. He reads a lot himself. He's a very good messenger.

It has never occurred to him that Mandrake has another name.

—We met at the door.

—He's better without that moustache. I always wanted him to
get rid of it. And he finally did it. To please me.

—A decent man.

—Oh, you really don't know him. You only met him that one
awful time.

Then, after an awkward pause: I've begun to see things as they
are.

—How are they?

—He can push a wheelchair. He's not fit for much else. He'll
do what I tell him. He'll run and fetch.

And suddenly he sees her walking in Carmincross. The storm
that had struck them at the beginning of their northward journey
had prematurely brought down hordes of leaves, yellow and
black and pale and hectic red, as Percy said, and more besides.
Dead leaves had always reminded her of love. Love may always

and equally well remind him of dead leaves. He sees her walking with two of his five nieces from the church gateway of the white doves to the lawn and the pathway by the swollen river's edge: a walk that for several reasons she is most unlikely ever to take again. The trees by the church gateway bow their heads like druids and acknowledge the parade of the laughing, coloured women. The sun is shining. The river now and again spits silver into the air. It is a pretty picture, sir, and he is most reluctant to turn his eyes from it all and to look at her sitting there before him in a hospital bed. But, looking at her bravely, he thinks, perhaps, that he might have loved her all the time. For the moment, her mercantile brittleness is gone. She is soft and gentle and, God help us, repentant and, to his excessive embarrassment, she says: Was I punished, Merlin, because I was unfaithful to you. Perhaps the only real thing in the world is fidelity. Like my father and mother. Faithful until death. They never could have thought of being any other way. Death had no terrors for them, no regrets.

He suggests that he is not, on the readily available evidence, the greatest living authority: and thinks that he may always have been afraid of love, or of affection, with her or anybody else, or thought that love could be only sweet and simple like his niece, now dead, and her singing young man, or wild and exotic, like the Mexican spitfire and her handsome Americano: or of the other side of love, dark, violent, or bitter, vengeful, mean: and he remembers and talks to her about a picture or a memory out of the days of his boyhood:

—There was this little couple really this little couple, two tiny people who came together in love or something. A matching pair from an old-fashioned mantelpiece. Or perhaps it was just their good humour brought them together. They were laughing little people. His name was Davy Nixon. He had a big moustache. It looked bigger because it was growing on such a small man. He wore a threadbare navy-blue jacket and corduroy trousers and hobnailed boots, and never a necktie, and a cloth cap, and smoked a big pipe. Like the moustache, the pipe probably looked bigger than it was. She was like a little round bottle with a pert, girlish currant-bun sort of a face. They got married modestly in the evening of a September day. In a good-natured way the people made great fun at the wedding, a bonfire outside the house and melodeons playing. They had a little house that fitted them, or they fitted it, in a side street and with a tiny garden before it, and she had green fingers, and every morning she was in there among the blossoms like a porcelain figurine except that she moved and breathed, and planted the flowers that grew better than flowers in any other garden in the big town, even sunflowers that, sure as God or the sun himself, smiled down on her: and he was a cobbler and tick-tack-tick his hammer went, like the hammer of the leprechaun in the song, though not on a moonlit night but all day long, nor on a weeny shoe but on boots and shoes that he could himself have hidden in. And three years passed and to the wonder of the world they had a son, a baby as big as the mother, and she had it without a bother. And seven years passed and ten and twelve, and the boy grew up as tall and handsome as if he had been the son of a beauty queen and a grenadier guard, and smiling and well-spoken: and fourteen years passed and he sickened and died of meningitis, and I heard it said that it was God's mercy he died because if he had gone on living he would have been some sort of an imbecile: and they went on living, cobbling and growing flowers. They became quiet little people not laughing little people. They never told anybody what their hopes had been. They went on living until they died. At a ripe old age. The little house is gone now, and the flowers.

For the house of the two little people was the first place he went to search for when he revisited the big town.

—If you had told me, Vin, what you had in mind, Cecil Morrow said, I could have told you it was no longer there.

—Change and decay in all things round I see. But it happens much quicker nowadays.

—Always the good man for the bit of poetry. But it was better maybe to let you find out for yourself. They tell me that Americans are all like that, see it for yourself, do it for yourself. And I daresay by now you're as much an American as you are anything else. I knew an Anzac fellow in London at the end of the war. A tall man. One of the tallest men I ever met. Like the Kavanagh fellow that long ago you used to tell the stories about. If he wasn't the tallest man in Europe, this Anzac, he sure as God must have been the tallest man who ever came out of New Zealand. He said it was no bloody joke being the tallest man in a landing craft and I'd be well inclined to believe him. He was so tall he could look down on me and that's saying something. He told me he was in Fiji when the Yanks got there. Tough men, and they'd take no advice. They insisted on making their own mistakes. Although by that time, he said, he and the other men from Down Under knew all about all the mistakes. But the Yanks wouldn't listen. Go ahead, right on, bang, bang, bang.

Where the little house had been, not too far from the riverbank, there was now a parking lot. Not only that little house but the whole narrow street was gone, part of it blown up because there had been a garage there in which a man and a few boys in oily dungarees mended cars and supported the British empire by refusing to pay black rent to the Provos.

—I'm due to go shortly, Cecil said. Retire I mean.

He laughed at his own macabre joke. A slip of the tongue or the mind.

—The wife died ten years ago, Vin. The children grown up and gone and living their own lives. Nothing to hold me any longer in this part of the world.

He is in plainclothes for the day. He had said: Less chance maybe, we'll be shot at if I'm in mufti. Although we have no guarantee, as my mother used to say. She meant about the hour of our death.

He has a daughter married in Wiltshire and doing well: and a son, likewise, in Carlisle: and another daughter in London and the civil service and single.

—But that Anzac said he'd see me settled out there and I'd like to try it for a few years. They say it's the best country in the world. Lovely mountains. Super fishing. That Anzac had a woman friend and she owned ninety thousand sheep.

—She walks, the lady of my delight, a shepherdess of sheep . . . Job had seven thousand.

—Come again, Vin. Anyway I'd like to meet the man again before I die. He was one square man.

—A man so tall couldn't be square or he'd block the street.

Simple schoolboy laughter: how little over the years old Cecil had changed.

—He was so tall, Vin. Would you believe it? He went on a spe-cial visit to Dublin to see President de Valera. He was a major, high up, over in London on rehabilitation. That was getting the Enzees out of the pubs and getting them home more-or-less sober, and when he went to meet de Valera he couldn't wear his big bush hat or he'd have made de Valera look like a pygmy, and the length of de Valera.

So we walk the town where we once played football on the fairgreen. The great river flows north. Down memory lane we go as Cecil puts it, not too originally, nor accurately. For an easy target that town was, close to the border, an easy target for the makers of the new Ireland, Eire Nua. There's a firm in Dublin that with no humorous intention in the world had the misfortune to call itself Demolition, Ireland.

—He has a job for me out there. We kept in touch, over the years. Meeting old friends is good. Like yourself, Vin. Never thought I'd meet you that day crossing the border.

Old friends walk here in no mellow September with red and golden apples dropping dancing to the ground. On a wall by the big river an old man greets Cecil and, after an effort, remembers Mervyn as the youth who set fire to the burning bush. For the old man had long ago been nicknamed Moses and one day, when Moses was fishing the river, Mervyn and a few bright spirits set a bonfire going around a scrawny old boortree so that they could with pride tell the town that they had seen Moses and the burn-ing bush. And Moses laughs about the past and mourns for the present: No fishing visitors now. They'd have nowhere to lodge. The two hotels were burned out. What have they got against hotels? People would be afeard to come here to fish.

What had been the grander of the two hotels, named after a bloody belted earl, has now been well-torched, a fine adjective derived from the sport of hotel burning, one of the favourite minor diversions of the Bombomb Yahoos who are great men for coining new words: and is now a blackened eyeless ruin out of which no happy visitor will ever again look with joy on the morning waters and look forward to the day ahead. On the streets of Boston a white woman has been burned black; the town hall here has likewise been torched: and the town clerk says that the labour exchange, where labour is seldom or never exchanged, is busier than the bank, almost always has been in a town with the highest unemployment rate in Western Europe and all it needed to put the tinhat on it forever was the busy-as-bees bombers: and we have the highest birth rate and the most broken marriages, and the most bombs, in inverse proportion, per head of population, and the highest drug consumption, the country's only growth industry.

—But a lot of that, Cecil says, is bloody statistical nonsense.

And the town clerk, halted in his stride, is half inclined to agree: We do not deny that we are an unfortunate community. But, Mr. Kavanagh, there are uneasy marriages everywhere.

Mr. Kavanagh must admit that that is so.

And Bowling Green Square, says Cecil, look at it now, like a set abandoned after a war film. And do you remember the open markets here? Pat McAlister, the veteran boxer with the cauliflower ear, selling a medicine or a dose, something white in a bottle that he said he got the recipe from an Indian witch doctor. And old Sproule, the hardware man that they used to shout at and say sell us a glass hammer. And Andy Glass with the hole in his ass who sold shoelaces and never had a seat in his trousers: and across the Green, there, is the police barracks, we never called it the police station, with barbed wire now and sandbags and reinforced concrete. The architecture of alienation, a lady architect called it: nothing in the world more dangerous than windows, you can be seen through them or shot through them, they let in light and armalite bullets, they splinter and slash.

A tall building, grey, quiet, sinister, it hunches a thorny back against the sad remnant of a marketplace where voices meet and mingle.

One voice: I walk my greyhounds. The dole makes you lazy. The British government doesn't care if we rot here. It's the best thing they can think of in the way of policy.

Another voice: Five years on the dole. Always the same here. We used to emigrate to get work. I was a pearl-diver in London: dishwashing. I slept in every kip in Scotland. I remember the bothy fire in Kirkintilloch. Now there's nowhere to go. Nobody wants you. They generate their own homemade unemployment.

And another: Bill Craig and the Orangemen and Paisley himself were too thick and ignorant about the one man one vote, and
the Royal fucking Irish constabulary, no offence to you, Cecil.

Cecil takes no offence. He is an easy tolerant man.

—Bludgeoned us out of the bloody streets they did. And the
civil rights marchers up in Glenshane pass. That began it all. And
the brutal attack on the marchers up at Burntollet bridge. Maybe
it was a wrong thing for us to take to the streets. But we had no
choice. You can't forever keep the lid on a boiling pot. Wilson,
and that Callaghan, a fake-English Irishman if ever there was
one, up in an air force plane over the Mediterranean, and they
had to ask a RAFman for an atlas to find out where Ulster was,
Ulster me arse. Well they know now as the Lord in his mercy said
to the sinners in the flames of hell.

The sun picks out the yellow in the battledress of a patrol. The
men move warily down the street, bereted heads alert like the
heads of lizards for hostile movement. Wounded walls are harshly
exposed to that slanting light. The great river moves silently toward the North. He drifts with it, and dozes in the chair, and
awakens in the hospital, and Deborah there half-lying, half-sit-
ting in the bed before his tired eyes.

—And the compliment of all time it is for a former lover to fall
asleep beside my bed of pain.

—Honest Cecil, he says, who had for so long wanted to be a
community policeman without benefit of guns, will now never see
the mountains of New Zealand.

—Do not remind me, Merlin. Read to me about love. And to
keep yourself awake.

—There's a doctor here in Dublin who can give you a new hip.
The bony part of it, I mean. The part you work and walk on. For
two thousand pounds. His hip is famous all over Europe. Not his
hip. But the hips that he gives to other people.

—Two thousand pounds worth of hip. My hip will be famous
all over Europe.

They are again laughing together. He says: I'd love to pay for
your hip. With Timothy's permission. In dollars.

—An American hip. We don't need poor Timothy's permission. Anyway you're entitled to pay. You had more fun out of

that hip than Timothy ever had. But they're slow here to give me a straight answer. Lying here with my legs apart for the longest time ever in my life. Will I or won't I walk again?

—Give them time. You'll walk again. On a European hip.

—In the Common Market. Anyway, and whether or no, Burns will have me. Even on a whirly chair, as the song says. Like Ironside. Ironbackside. Anything Burr can do I can do better.

She tells him that once, by night, in the lane at the back of Clery's big store in Dublin's fair city where the girls are so pretty, she saw a one-legged prostitute and an old fellow performing on a wide windowsill.

—What were you doing in the lane behind Clery's?

—Shortcutting to a thirty bus to go to Dollymount Strand to meet a fella.

There are no dead leaves on Dollymount Strand because there are no trees on Dollymount Strand, only the purity of sand and bent grass and salt seawater. A wise god would have placed Eden on Dollymount Strand.

—But that was a brave girl, Merlin. Nothing would daunt her. Today she'd be in the Olympics. Why should I worry?

And: Read to me, Merlin. Read me asleep. I'm suddenly tired.

So he reads that after a while, and after the death of Diarmuid, Fionn went, secretly and unknown to the Fianna, to the place where Gráinne was: and he got to see her in spite of her high talk: and he spoke gently to her. And she would not listen to him but bade him to get out of her sight, and whatever hard thing her tongue could say, she said it . . .

—I'm listening, Merlin. No more hard words.

—. . . but all the same he went on giving her gentle talk and loving words, till in the end he brought her to his own will.

The redheaded nurse comes in, administers tablets, fiddles with pillows and bedclothes, takes a tray from the bedside locker, and goes away smiling. She walks well.

And he reads to Deborah how Fionn brought Gráinne back to the seven battalions of the Fianna and when the soldiers saw him coming, and Gráinne with him like any new wife with her husband, they gave a great shout of laughter and mockery, and Gráinne bowed down her head with shame: and Oisín, the poet,

said: By my word, Fionn, you will keep a good watch on Gráinne
from this out. . . .

—That was no way for a boy to talk to his father.

And he reads how some said that the change had come on
Gráinne because the mind of a woman changes like the water of a
running stream. . . .

The reading matter might have been better chosen. But fortunately, and aided by those tablets, she is already somnolent and
she has heard little more than the droning of his voice.

—Happy ever after, she says, happy ever after. . . .

There are tears on her cheeks. He closes the book.

—That, he says to no one in particular, was the first love story
that ever impressed me.

She murmurs about Romeo and Juliet.

—No. The story of the two little laughing people with the lovely son.

But she is asleep. So he kisses her forehead and goes. Forever?

In the company of two other letters, the letter from the Algonquin has overtaken him and is waiting for him in his hotel. It has
been much redirected. It has come to him by way of Knocknagon
where it seems to him miraculous that they should still bother to
forward letters or to do anything but, as Jesus said, gather up the
fragments ne pereant. Also: the letter is not from the Algonquin
but from the Edison. A matter of mere detail. Has she no home
to go to? She explains that the Algonquin has become too expensive. Also: too crowded with people she does not wish to meet or
talk to. She explains that the apartment is too lonely. That it has
unhappy associations. Does she mean memories of Mervyn? Or
that her Oil King has flown, or folded his tent like the Arab
and slipped and slithered away, easy, greasy, it's a long way
to slide. She writes: Frankly he has left me, never would have
tolerated him anyway except for anger against you, and this is
a terrible city and this is a desolate world, and I feel I am sinking and I need help and support and buoyancy, and you did
once say you would be my buoy, and I'm raw and sliced inside,
and perhaps you are happy there in Ireland and could take me
over. . . .

He is almost moved. He puts the letter aside. It will need a long and careful answer.

The second letter is more than a letter. It is contained, whatever it is, in a thick quarto-sized envelope. It has been following him for a long time. It has even like himself been to America and back. It is a parish publication from Carmincross, news from nowhere and about nothing which is the only good news, old group photographs of old friends, articles, by retired schoolmasters, about local history and antiquities, more recent group photographs, which he inspects with a searching eye for the faces of children and grandchildren of people he has known. Then on one page, ornamentally framed and presented, he reads, under a headline that might have been written by himself: And Nothing ever Happens round Carmin:

It is now sixteen months since the first volume of this magazine, which we have called An Tearmann, hit the parish. So it is surely fitting at this stage to look back briefly at what has occurred locally during this time.

The January of this year saw the county convention of the Gaelic Athletic Association take place in the Social Centre, Loughmacrory.

The first Sunday in February was the day on which the parishioners of Termonmaguirk signed a petition protesting against harassment by members of the security forces.

The week of the drama festival began on the last day of March and what a week it proved to be. Drama galore. See last item.

In May a number of pupils from the secondary school paid a visit to the Isle of Man, a trip that was the forerunner of further ventures: the parish pilgrimage to Lourdes and the Youth pilgrimage to the shrine of the apparition of Our Lady of Knock, Co. Mayo.

On the second Sunday in May the Youth Club raised £2,500 for the Cancer Scanner Fund as the result of a highly successful sponsored walk.

The following Tuesday was the day of the first sporting event in the new Fr. Macgilligan park, a primary schools football tournament won by St. Columbcille's, Carmincross. Six days later the Loughmacrory handballers broke the world handball endurance record.

Sunday, the tenth day of June, marked the re-emergence of what

*used to be a great occasion: Knocknagon sports day. A great time
was had by all.*

*During the week 25th–29th June, Miss Mary Moloney, our
local librarian, staged a local history exhibition in the secondary
school.*

*On Sunday, August 26th, our footballers did Carmincross proud
when they chalked up the club's first-ever three in a row.*

*Sunday, the second day of December, marked the reopening of the
parish hall, and what a week followed, a week culminating in a
massive bazaar and draw for the big prize money.*

*On Thursday the 21st February of this year Jim Scully won for
the Carmincross Holy Family boxing club its first Ulster senior title
when he topped on points in the middleweight division.*

*Then this year's drama festival, a success as usual, began on Sat-
urday, 22nd March.*

*Finally, the most recent achievement was that of our cycling club
in a ride round Ireland in honour of our Holy Father the Pope.*

*And who says nothing ever happens round Carmincross?*

*But holy heavens above, I was almost forgetting there was That
Day. Der Tag, the Germans would call it. When activities on our
main street subsequently made the media and all the headlines.
With pride we call it Panorama Day. 'Nuff said.*

With considerable pride, indeed, his brother-in-law, father of
five beautiful daughters now reduced to four, had told him about
Panorama Day.

—Carmincross here is Gaelic country, he had said. It always
was Gaelic country. Every bit as much as Crossmaglen ever was.

—Is that what Crossmaglen is? Not cowboy country? The
dalin' men from Crossmaglen put whiskey in me tay.

—Indian country! Bandit country! That's what the gutter
press of Fleet Street, London, says. Mervyn, boy, you have been
too long and too far away from your roots.

—Praises be to Jasus, what you are talking about, never had
the least thing to do with my roots.

—Now listen to me. Great patriots came from this village. Men
that were close friends and comrades of de Valera.

—Until they became enemies of de Valera. Was de Valera ever
comrade to anybody?

—It was our great tragedy as a nation, and because of the wiles of the hereditary foe, that in the heat of the struggle for nation-hood, brother was turned against brother.

The echo of the voice of Fionn in the valley of a million sheep. Ancient Ireland is marked by bronze men who speak forever in the same gonglike tones.

—We had a brotherly reputation for that when the Brits were ornamenting themselves with woad.

—No, Merv, you've got it wrong. According to the poet. We ranked high as poets and statesmen and sages when the Britons ran naked and wild o'er the hills. They hadn't a woad to call their own.

His brother-in-law at moments, but not too often, shows signs of a sense of humour.

—So it seems to me that for one day at any rate the lads had the right to take over the village and run it as if all Ireland were free.

—Then heaven help us when it is.

It hadn't been much of an event to celebrate, when compared with the achievement of that member of the Holy Family boxing club. But by Carmincross standards it had, it seemed, been a sort of a happening. There was at that time no police barracks or sta-tion in happy Carmincross. That had never been considered nec-essary. So it could safely be reckoned that no thick-witted coppers, no gormless British soldiers trying to work out where they were or what it was all about, would interfere: and twenty-five patriots, heads modestly veiled in black bags, took over the place for the day. A propaganda exercise. The press were notified. The press were there. Even the television cameras. Panorama or piss your trousers. How galling it must be to wear a black bag and not have your fine heroic features revealed for stardom. General Staff ordered all shops closed as a mark of solidarity with the hunger-strikers in Long Kesh who may not have needed shops but could have done with some solidarity. One greasy-tiller who did not shut up shop had his windows broken, his body beaten, and green paint and red paint poured over his only daughter.

—What could he expect, Mervyn?

—He talked to me yesterday. He jests not at scars. Nor green nor red paint.

—What could he expect? The lads were only doing their duty.

—Stern daughter of the voice of God. What this country needs is firm provisional government. Jews out.

The white doves walked as usual by the gateway into the old churchyard. What to them were black bags with eyeholes any more or less than pink-white faces with eyeholes: or even the sallow faces, with eyeholes, of the dealers in the temple who trafficked in the doves of peace.

—And Carmincross, poor Cecil said, had moved into what we may call the war zone. Fuck me, Carmincross. Where nothing louder was ever heard than the farts of Brannigan, the butcher, with the greasy apron. A windy man. Vin, do you remember Brannigan?

More echoes of lost laughter, our echoes roll from soul to soul, etcetera, etcetera.

—And what the lovely girl, what was her name, said about Brannigan's blue apron with the white stripes. Do you remember?

—Cecil, there were so many lovely girls.

—Maybe for you, Vin. There was only one for me and she's dead.

A silence.

—But now that you mention it, Cecil, I do remember.

That lovely girl he had once, at the request of her parents, grounded in school Latin in a house surrounded by apple orchards and once, by God, written to her or about her a whole poem: Young men with your worlds settled round you, with each mouse and each man in its place, have you walked where the trees were on fire, and the world was a frame for one face.

That sort of a poem. Deborah would sure admire to hear that one. But there would be no point in quoting it to Cecil who, after his moment of sad silence, is back again to Brannigan, the butcher: as comically monstrous as Chaucer's miller and who had that apron, not often laundered, to which adhered so many raw fragments of the corpses of edible animals that, when meat rationing came in during the Hitler war, the lovely girl said that if the worst came to the worst we could always eat Brannigan's apron.

—And, the brother-in-law said, we never wanted a police barracks in this neighborhood. We don't need one. We can govern ourselves.

—The lads, as you call them, provoked it.

—That old abandoned rectory, Mervyn. It should have been left to the ghost of your old friend. The mildewed poetess. That you'd give her a penny if you met her on the road. There will be trouble yet about putting the police into that old rectory.

And the third letter comes also from New York and is so easy to answer that he is able to deal with it right away. It is from his agent, a good lady who says that a publisher has suggested to her that she should suggest to Mervyn Kavanagh that Mervyn Kavanagh might compose a coffee-table history, lavishly illustrated, of Ireland. The publisher thinks that Ireland is once again in an interesting situation.

Interesting situation?

Pregnant with what?

Mother Ireland may be about to give birth to something.

Like a black pig. A black pig once gave birth to Ireland.

In the 1950s a veteran London publisher had said to him that the Irish situation or the Irish problem was no longer of interest to anybody. By which the publisher meant himself and the people who bought the books he published. At the time the veteran's words had offended Kavanagh but later he came to see the point. Nor does he now think that matters have much changed since the 1950s. Many countries today have much worse and, therefore, more interesting situations than Ireland. Even our wild men, and God help them and us who reared them, are only small-time thugs or blaggers: as an odd new word now has it in England. Only one small part of the thuggery and blaggery that flourishes all over the world in this year of Jesus our Saviour. Whose sad face on the cross sees only this after the passion of two thousand years. Just important enough they are further to disfigure the already misgoverned fifth of one small, one-legged, hunchbacked island. Just of enough interest to set every Tom, Dick, and Harry writing books about Ireland. Yet if they wish me to do a coffee-table book about Ireland, I'll do it and welcome: anything to oblige and the money's good. I'll send them my plan here and now. Begin with the latest atrocity. Even since Carmincross there has been another good one. Carmincross is fading back into our half-remembered, misinterpreted history. To join Patrick Pearse and the Fenians and the men of 1848 and the boys of Wexford and the Whiteboys and the Irish Brigade who lie, all for Ireland, on far foreign fields from Dunkirk to Belgrade. Carmincross will soon be forgotten. No, the last notable patriotic bombing, a disco or something and a man in flames rushing madly out, his arms extended, a highland or deep southern fiery cross, and dying like that. And a witness said: One man came out with his arms out. He was on fire from head to toe. He died like that. The way he stood. In the shape of a cross.

That would make a striking large-format dustcover to see on coffee-tables from Maine to Los Angeles, from Coos Bay to the Okefenokee Swamp, with the old Irish saw happily printed underneath: Health and long life to you, land without rent at you, the woman of your choice at you, and death in Ireland.

That last being the greatest of all possible blessings that an Irishman can bestow on another Irishman or on any variety of a man anywhere.

At the same disco, or after the destruction of the same disco, there was a crippled girl so badly burned that her nearest and dearest could guess who she was only by the metal frame on her artificial leg. But, no, she would not be so photogenic, would not so illuminate a coloured dustcover as the burning man in the shape of the fiery cross.

There then, he writes, my history would begin with a detailed account of that episode in the age-long armed struggle against English tyranny. No Irish republicans, an Irish republican leader has just said, should ask another Irish republican to rejoice at the unauthorised car-bomb, so described, that the other day scattered death like hailstones over a London street. But may we modestly ask at what do Irish republicans ask Irish republicans to rejoice? At an Irishman suddenly transformed into a flaming Christian symbol? For Appendix One to his coffee-table book he promises a Provisional Gaudeamus.

Then from the splendid symbol of the Burning Man he will work his way back, dead generation after dead generation, to find out how God's chosen sons of St. Patrick, with the indispensable help of the neighbours, have advanced as far as that disco.

But a title, a title! Let me test some possible titles by putting them down now, to judge them by sight, in block capitals.

A Backward Glance at Ireland
The Island Recedes
The Monster on the Sea
To Market, to Market to Buy a Black Pig
An Arsewise Aspect of Ireland
The Binoculars of Jeremiah Gilsenan

The phone rings. It is inevitably Jeremiah. He says: Where have you been?

He continues, reading, or reciting, more likely, from a prepared script: So, I have set thee this day over the nations, and over kingdoms, to root up and to pull down, and to waste and destroy. And thus the Lord spoke to his prophet, Jeremias Gelignite Gilsenan, and said: For behold I will call together all the families of the kingdoms of the North, and from the North shall an evil break forth, and I see a rod watching, I see a boiling cauldron, and the face thereof from the face of the North. Behold my wrath and my indignation is enkindled against this place, upon men and upon beasts and the trees of the field, and the wise men are confounded for they have cast away the word of the Lord, therefore I will give their women to strangers, for behold I will send among you serpents, basilisks against which there is no charm. Behold I will feed this people with wormwood and give them water of gall to drink, and will visit upon everyone that hath the foreskin circumcised, and all that have the hair polled round, that dwell in the desert.

—I am bald, Jeremiah. My foreskin is all present and correct.

—We must meet, Merlin. We must have lunch.

Nothing can halt this lunatic. Yet we have something in common, have travelled, well not exactly together, in realms of gold.

—I am preparing for you, Merlin, the first handmade copy of Jeremiah Gilsenan's Revised Irish Minstrelsy.

They arrange to have lunch.

And Jeremiah warns him: Beware the touchers, panhandlers to you, in this town. They won't leave you with a penny piece. In your day the expected contribution was a pound. Now with inflation they ask for a fiver and expect twice that: I have met them all times of the day, coming with livid faces, from counter or snug, between ramshackle, falling-down houses. I have passed without nodding my head, ignoring the wink and the touch from the loafer demanding some bread and the pensioner up on his crutch. Effing-well knowing that they never worked since the day they were born. Why should they expect me to pay for their booze or their horses or horn. . . .

Gently he puts down the phone while Jeremiah is still orating.

Yet there is no reason why he should not meet Jeremiah for lunch.

So early the next morning he begins the long letter. He does not superscribe it to anyone in particular. He will post it to the Edison.

As I write to you now, he writes, the wedding is over. It happened in Dublin, not in Carmincross. Nothing happens in Carmincross. Not even weddings.

John Butler Yeats, the father, once wrote that in New York anything may happen, in Dublin nothing ever happens except the occasional insolvency. So in 1916 they wrecked the town to prove him wrong. And *Ulysses* was happening at the time he wrote of. But then nothing happens in *Ulysses*.

This wedding happened in Dublin. Quietly in University Church in Stephen's Green. Where Newman preached. But not at the wedding. And said. . . . But then I have often quoted to you what that unfortunate man, Newman, said in that place. I enclose three copies of the announcement of the wedding, one from each of the Dublin morning papers. Since you do not know my people, nor ever showed any wish to know them, you will not be aware that the groom has married the sister of the deceased bride-to-be. Who was blown to pieces in Carmincross as she was walking across the street to post (mail) a few final wedding invitations. At a red pillarbox that had still engraven on it the letters V.R. and the Crown of England, the light of other days, which may, perhaps, have been what the bombers wished to destroy. To marry one of the four surviving sisters out of a set of five seemed to the aspiring groom, and to almost everybody else, to be the best or only way to attempt to heal a wound that may or may not be subject to healing. There may be some sort of precedent for it in Irish history. When Michael Collins was murdered in the course of the making of the then new Ireland, his bride-to-be married a young man who had hero-worshipped Collins: and they were quite happy together. The people were saying no two were ere wed but one had a sorrow that never was said. There is no rooftree that does not shelter one ghost, or more, ghosts of the living, ghosts of the dead.

And there was just yesterday in the town of Portadown, where in 1641 the wraiths of the slaughtered rose from the slow river, a worse, perhaps, intrusion on a wedding. The young bride, she is just eighteen, is even at this moment lying in hospital after a bomb blast that injured her and fifty-one other people who hastened to her wedding. The roof of the Yachtsman Inn collapsed as the bomb, containing three to five pounds of commercial explosives, went off without warning. The inn is owned by Protestants but frequented mostly by Catholics. It stands, or what's left of it stands, on a line dividing a Catholic ghetto from a Protestant ghetto. So anyone who cares to may try to work out the complex theological motivation and implications of that wedding gift. Which was cunningly concealed in the attic directly above the wedding guests and placed, it is said, so as to kill or maim as many as possible: and the bridegroom's door is open wide, the bomb is placed within, the guests are met, the feast is set, dost hear the merry din. . . .

All this I write down to show you that you may be as happy in the Edison or even in the Algonquin, or even in our own apartment, as in Ireland, Ireland, although you are over the sea, Erin, my country, at nighttime I'm dreaming of thee, dear little isle of the West, sweet spot by memory blest, land of the bard and the shamrock . . . and on and on.

He continues: Her name was Stephanie. She was my favourite niece. Somebody said to me when I was on the way North to the wedding that it was not a proper thing to pick a favourite out of one family, least of all one niece out of a set of five. But I never actually did that. It was merely that there were things about her that one remembered more readily than anything about any of the others. Casual, trivial things. Like once some years ago when I visited the convent secondary school she was then attending. The reverend mother had invited me to look at a play or a pageant, or something between a play and a pageant, that the young ladies were performing. About Blessed Martin de Porres, of all people. Blessed Martin de Porres has this lesson for us, it is no longer impossible for a mulatto to become a beato. That clerihew I owe to a poet who is a friend of mine. He points out, though, that it is not historically accurate. There are still poets in Ireland. Although you might not think so from listening to the morning news.

Anyway: after the performance I am talking to the reverend mother, two other nuns and one priest, when a young mulatto girl runs up to me and embraces me in a way that is obviously not quite approved of by the reverend mother. For a moment I think the old dog's not done yet, and sweet it was in Aves to hear the landward breeze, aswing with good tobacco in a net beneath the trees, with a negro lass to fan you while you listened to the roar of the breakers on the reef outside that never touched the shore.

But it was merely Stephanie fresh from the play or pageant and saying *fáilte* to her favourite and only uncle. A trivial thing, indeed, to remember about somebody whose flesh was roasted and shredded while asking some late-remembered guests to her wedding.

She ran a boutique in the neighbouring big town and ran it well. She had a flair for that sort of thing. She dressed well on every occasion. At that fatal moment of her final wedding tryst she was, I am told, wearing, she was auburn-haired, a black leather skirt, white, cotton-knit sweater, a wide studded leather belt. About the boots or shoes in which she walked to death, I have not been informed.

Nor had she been, previously, unacquainted with bombs. I quote from the local newspaper of a year or so ago: A sleeping bomb and an absent-minded diner in a restaurant caused terrorist scares in the High Street and Market Street of our town yesterday. The bomb was spotted by staff in a boutique owned by Stephanie Curran in the High Street. It was a cassette-type incendiary. It was believed to have been in the shop since last Thursday when two teenage girls used a pram with two babies in it to ferry more than ten firebombs around the town. . . .

Day's work, week's work as we go up and down, there are many firebombs all around the town.

Here I must intrude on myself and, perhaps, on your patience, to tell you about Cossack or Hendry Cowan.

There were two families, Cowans and Mulgrews. They lived in the one house. They were all cousins through other. Which is which, as Jack Jones said. Mostly the Mulgrews were dark-haired and the Cowans flaming red. They were Protestants and of Scottish origin, not very remote. In my memory the two most notable of the multitude were Sammy Mulgrew and Henry (pr. Hendry) Cowan, nicknamed Cossack because his mountain of burning red hair had reminded some wit of the headgear of Cossack horsemen seen hard-riding by in the Star Kinema. Sammy was quiet and dark. They were devoted cousins: and devoted also to the transport to remote arenas and secret fields of fighting and illegal gamecocks. For which purpose they used two double-decker perambulators, with infant cousins, cherubic, and two at a time, visible and smiling and gurgling and burping on the upper deck: and two spurred and vicious gamecocks concealed in the holds in airholed and separate compartments. It was a sight to see the loading and unloading of those unusual trucks. Gamecocks, then, in that age of innocence. And bombs today, and how are the darling twins today, and how are their teeth progressing, and boom, boom, boom, and rockabye baby on the treetop.

But the bomb thus delivered, and still sleeping like a baby, was detected in the boutique and the area around was sealed off until the army experts came. Then there were two other objects, thought to be bombs, in two other shops. One in the shape of a cassette, in a sports shop, turned out to be, in all truth, merely a cassette: and when tested played merry tunes. The other, in a restaurant, was taken away and destroyed by army sharpshooters but turned out to be boots in a box left behind by an absentminded diner.

So never any more, not even on Broadway, trust a smiling baby in a pram or a manger and, when in Bloomingdale's, handle with feather-fingers the most delicate of fabrics.

The bomb in Queen Victoria's red pillarbox was not asleep but only dreaming and may have been fully aroused, hark, murder

like a lion wakes and roars to the resounding plain, by the light
and airy touch of a few descending wedding invitations.

There was, and this may interest you, a young American couple
present on that happy occasion: and one of them, the man, was a
witness to the passing of Stephanie not, like Pippa, singing. They
met me, or I met them, in the first hotel I stayed in after I left
Shannon Airport: under the management of, the hotel that is, my
old school friend Burns, whom I must often have described to
you. The young man's ancestors had some connection with Carmincross, and the couple were, I am happy to say, already headed
in that direction when they met me. Happy to say because I cannot reproach myself with being the sole cause of their presence in
that place. Which brought them no luck.

The young man, tall, blond, handsome, straightforward, enthusiastic about life, love, and even about Ireland, had been
reading Thomas Davis. Perhaps I may have mentioned him and
you may not have been listening but that was a moderate, Protestant, cultural nationalist of the 1840s. The young man, when I
met him again in Carmincross, kept talking like this: This country will be rich, prosperous, powerful, and proud. Perchance 'tis a
fanciful thing, yet in the misfortunes of Ireland, in her laurelled
martyrs, in those who died, persecuted men of a persecuted country, in the necessity she was under of bearing the palms to deck
her best on the scaffold and the lost battlefield, she has seemed to
me chosen for some great future.

And asking me, the young American man, that is, not Thomas
Davis, should he learn Irish.

And saying: We Americans are a crowd of Canutes. Merely
because we elect a man president, we expect him to be perfect.

Then the young wife told him he was stoned.

Which he, at that moment, admitted. But said to us all: But
think of it. Now with my living eyes I look at last on Carmincross.

And with his living eyes he was reading in, and occasionally
looking out of, the first-floor bay window of the lesser of the two
hotels, Riverview, which is in the main street of the village. He
actually saw the girl who parked the car, dropped the package
into the letter box, left the car parked and walked away and

murdered Stephanie. That may be the last thing he'll see, for the window came in fragments around his face and eyes: something for which the reading of Thomas Davis on the future of Ireland had not in the least prepared him. He took it well though. He is a fine courageous American boy. He was to 'Nam and back, unscathed. He asked me not to blame myself for their being in Carmincross. He said they were going there anyway, that his people way back came from somewhere near Carmincross. The closer he got to Carmincross the vaguer he became about where somewhere near was: good Scots-Irish stock, they had emigrated to somewhere near Grandfather Mountain about the time that Arthur Young was wandering in Ireland looking for turnips. His name is Gene Perry. They have Highland games at Grandfather Mountain. His mother came from the Lebanon. He was, he said, almost with a laugh, in quest of his roots and he had found them or they had found him: and I was merely the first person he had met, in Ireland or anywhere else, who had ever heard of Carmincross. His wife, he said, loved the name of the place. They both loved my description of it. Plastic surgery, he says, can work wonders. His eyesight may be permanently affected. But he is very grateful that he was in the window and not his wife. She is very beautiful. He said that there seemed to be a long awful silence before the actual explosion, and referrred me to a passage in Proust. Our French friend has written of the eternal tragic instant of unconscious expectancy and calm torpor which, in retrospect, seems always to have preceded the explosion of a bomb or the first flicker of a fire.

Always? Remind me sometime to look the matter up. How many bombs had Marcel heard? How many fires spied by night in populous cities? Some veteran of La Débâcle told him. No car bombs on the Guermantes Way: as a young journalist said to me when later on I met him after the harrowing of Carmincross, and who had been much about in Belfast and who assured me that many people do not realise that after an explosion there is, as well as the dreadful sight of dismembered bodies, a lingering smell of scattered intestines, sweet and sickly: and he had, with his own living eyes, seen, on a sidewalk in East Belfast, a dislodged eye, a source of fascination for schoolchildren after its previous owner and his three companions had been scraped off the pavement:

their bomb was away too soon. And a young man writhing in a pool of flame when the nitro-benzine he had been making into a bomb caught fire: and a woman wandering around the scattered remains of her husband asking everyone where he was. Nor had anybody the courage to say to her:

Away for his tea.

Or: Nutled.

Or: Tatey Bread.

—One can count the dead, the young man said to me, but not the lost humanity.

And the ghost of Thomas Davis said: There are two ways of success for the Irish: arms and persuasion. They have chosen the latter. They have resolved to win their rights by moral force.

For some reason that he could not satisfactorily explain the young journalist was wearing a brown shoe on the left and on the right a white. For luck? Out of haste? Eyesight? Eccentricity? He could not say.

If Stephanie on her way to post those last invitations had but gone a little out of her way to walk with the white doves at the churchyard gate, could the shredding and burning have been averted? For sent by the hand of Love a turtle flies and lays delicious food before her wondering eyes. That was the luck of wandering Psyche: and, cheered by the favouring omen, softer tears relieve her bosom from its cruel weight, she blames the sad despondence of her fears when still protected by a power so great . . .

Amor, you see, is, in spite of her wicked mother-in-law who was also into doves, still thinking of her.

. . . and, as she went, behold with hovering flight the dove preceded still her doubtful way. Its spotless plumage of the purest white which shone resplendent in the blaze of day, could even in darkest gloom a light display, of heavenly birth when first to mortals given, named Innocence. . . .

But these are meagre days for Innocence, black days for white doves. Even Psyche's white dove, all that long ago, could not stand the pace, and all too short its stay, for by ravenous wild birds it fearfully was driven back to live for aye with Love who, according to the legend, is a permanent resident of heaven.

What happened in Carmincross was much more spectacular.

A flash there was indeed, a man told me, and from no heavenly car parked opposite the churchyard gate, a flash, a light far whiter than daylight, which shone resplendent to the sky of day. The white doves rose in a flock. Then three fell back, dead, to the ground. The brightness of the flash made the gloom of the following smoke cloud more intense. The doves who did not fall have never returned: and at that particular flashpoint a young woman of the travelling people, tinkers, begging from door to door, wandering Psyche perhaps, had her head squashed, a boy had his leg blown off, another boy, Cupid, had a piece of wood rammed into his chest, a middle-aged woman, Venus, had her hands blown off. The man told me that he could see the bones of her fingers.

Also, the Mayarunas in the remote Amazon basin have at times in the past killed their young girls so as to ensure tribal balance among the sexes. At the moment, because of the intrusion of diseases caught from the white man, their numbers are down from four thousand to five hundred. Slaughtering the little girls may also have had something to do with that decline. Which was the state of affairs when I last heard from them. And now, in despair, they are killing all the children, male and female. Not too hot on logic, the old Mayarunas. Yet in the remote 1950s they did seem to have a little more sense: when they killed many rubber tappers and lumbermen and abducted their women: and were the scourge of the Javari-Caruca valley.

In my sister's house, now a sad sister and a sad house, there are many mansions. But for various reasons I thought it better not to stretch my bones in any of them. So I spent my nights in a hilltop hotel at a place called Knocknagon. Perhaps I should say my brother-in-law's house, for he bought it and restored it on hard-earned English money. In the building trade in Britain. Beginning right down at the bottom, shovelling muck. MacAlpine's fusiliers and all that. But over in the States few people ever heard of that elite regiment. And the English gaffer would say to the man with the pick: Swipe into it, Paddy. It ain't your own bleeding country.

And the only thing that could be said for the English gaffer was that he wasn't as bad as the gaffer when the gaffer was Irish. But my brother-in-law graduated to gafferdom and, from what I hear, wasn't a bad fellow to his own people, and went into patriotism toward which he always had strong leanings: and in the 1930s in Birmingham, England, was up on an explosives charge (dismissed), because some daring fellows who would capsize the stars, and he never told me whether or not he was one of them, endeavoured to blow up a powerhouse in a street of warehouses, and blew up everything in the street except the powerhouse. The explosive patriots of the Seventies are much better at the job: Practice makes Perfect. Although they still do manage now and again to hoist themselves which, to the unprejudiced onlooker, seems only fair: and just yesterday a common slave, you know him well by sight, held up his left hand which did flame and burn like twenty torches joined, and yet his hand, not sensible of fire, remained untouched. No, that was not what I was thinking of: but a boy from Benraw Road in Belfast ran screaming down the train that runs from Belfast to Ballymena (Was he running back toward Belfast or forward to Ballymena?), and screaming, Help me, I'm on fire, because the bomb he was carrying to plant in Ballymena went off too soon like a honeymoon in Gertrude Stein, and killed a schoolboy and a black man from Nigeria who had nothing to do with anything: and a third man who was helping the roaring, self-commiserating, help-seeking runner to carry the bomb went up with the bomb he carried: and round about the moment that Stephanie was murdered a barman in the Riverview Hotel heard a bang and then the screams, and burst open the door of the powder room in which, aptly enough, the bang had banged: and out came smoke and he saw, as he afterward with some sense of style testified, two girls like torches: and who, guess, should it be but the couple who had, on a happier day for themselves, perambulated all day up and down and all around the town, with incendiary cassettes. Oh dear, what can the matter be, two young lassies ablaze in the lavatory, nobody's fault but their own. Both eighteen years of age: and one caught fire from her own cassette, and the other caught fire while trying to extinguish her comrade. They came from a place called Glockamorra Gardens: and are still seriously ill in hospital and unable to face charges, which may be that they had an incendiary device in their possession and under their control. Not quite.

This world is wild as an old wives' tale and crowded now with ardent girls, and strange the plain things are, and bronze beauties rich with all the perfumes of Arabia carry bombs and breasts in their bras, and the earth is enough and the air is enough for our wonder and our war, but our rest is as far as the firedrake swings, and a Lebanese Arab girl in the airport in Rome was discovered to have two pistols strapped to her underthighs. Then there were the miniskirted terrorists led by Evelyn Barges, blonde, highly attractive teacher of English in the Paris suburbs: joined a group of saboteurs who faced, for an outlet, to the Orient and with plans to blow up tourist hotels in Israel: and with her went, as walking bombs, Nadia and Marlene, two richly left dames from Casablanca, play it again Sam, with explosives in bras and girdles, lipsticks, Tampax, hollowed heels of shoes, and the linings of their long and modiste coats were impregnated with explosive fluid. Evelyn herself carried, in what container I do not know, a chemical product that when linked with those impregnated linings could produce a napalm effect. Those girls, sure as God, were dynamite. Those girls were no suitable near neighbours for a compulsive pincher or groper: give me a feeler and I'll lift the world. And how about the two Arabs, lamps in the desert by Ethel M. Dell, tonight I live, tonight you die, at night when you're asleep into your tent I'll creep, who gave as a farewell present to a beloved English girl, the houri of one or both of them, a bomb disguised as a taperecorder. On an El Al flight to Lod. How did they ever kiss goodbye? Take the flower and turn the hour and kiss your love again. And, as the plane levitated, or was assumed, they turned their faces toward Lod with, perhaps, upon lips that had just kissed, the fervent prayer of that tormented flying angel Lelia Khaled: Oh, Palestine, I am ready to die and I shall live by dying for thee! Oh, my homeland! My love, my only love! I shall revolt against thine enemies, all enemies. I shall make bombs from the atoms of my body and weave a new Palestine from the fabric of my soul. With all my power and the power of my sisters we shall convert our existence into bombs to redeem the land, the coast, the mountain. . . .

Later on in the Forties the brother-in-law was more successful at, and made money by, the knocking-down of air-raid shelters when the empire no longer needed them, and never looked back, and came back to Erin a rich man. But the demolition incident he speaks of with most laughter, for he is, although a patriot, by no means devoid of a sense of humour, happened on a night in London when he gave shelter to a homeless Irish poet. One room he had in Kilburn and two chairs and a table and a cooker and a cupboard and a double bed and a dartboard: and a pair of hob-nailed boots as big as barges to steady his feet on the job: and in the room or apartment above him three gentle gentlemen who, when the mood was on them, whipped each other and danced and sang, and sometimes squealed, and the poet, unable to sleep, caught a hobnail by the laces and swung it like the sling of David and let fly at the ceiling and, because of the shaken and insecure state of the ceilings of London at the time, brought down on himself and his host in the double bed every square inch of ceiling plaster. That night, he tells me, in the heat and the dust and the laughter and the coughs and curses of the smothering poet, he knew he was going to be rich. And would buy and live in the best house in Carmincross. All of which came to pass.

And in the walled garden behind that house the children, pages and handmaidens, rehearsed for the wedding.

That house and walled garden I remember from sunny days in my boyhood when the place was the property of a kindly wid-owed lady. For whom I used to do odd jobs and run messages. Or scythe the grass on the long lawn that sloped down to the river. The house, long and white, is high on a headland. And has often seemed to me the sort of house I'd admire to live out my life in. You know, or do you, the sort of house you, in passing, see from a country road, there's a lot of country in the U.S.A., and a house that seems to sing to you of security and content and happy fami-lies and settled ways? But think, then, of having such a house only for a lifetime and of the added agony of having to leave it in the end. A man who lives in this or that apartment, hotel room, college quarters, faculty row, and among people who will not be with him always, has so much less to lose. In lowly homes old age sleeps easily. Green valleys seldom feel the stroke of thunder. Or Seneca for sexagenarians.

That walled garden slopes gently toward the south, as every good garden should, and presents a noble prospect of Carmincross: the square tower of the Protestant church with a loyal Union Jack fluttering from every corner, the grey block of the convent building that was once the palace of a Protestant arch-bishop, and half a mile away along the riverbank the white-washed Catholic church. Built there about 1829 after the Catholic emancipation act: and thus far out of the village be-cause the Protestant landowner of the time wouldn't give a site within the village to the Papists. And he was the ancestor of the gracious old lady for whom I ran messages and mowed grass.

But that garden was, in my boyhood, Andrew Marvell coun-try. And still would be were it not for the ghost of a girl who loved that garden. You'll know what I mean. You've struggled with Marvell in college. Struggled even more with Donne. But Mar-vell and that garden, green thoughts in a green shade, ripe apples, the curious peach, th'ensnaring grass, even to the sun-dial where the milder sun does through a fragrant zodiac run. A most eloquent sun-dial. Speaking out of the Book of Proverbs noble thoughts: Why is the diamond counted precious? What charms does it disclose? Say does its beauty so refresh us as the bursting summer rose?

When I last walked in that garden, a silent broken sister by my side, what the sun-dial said to me was: How is the gold become dim, the finest colour is changed, the stones of the sanctuary are scattered in every street.

That, as you know, is from the prophet Jeremias, who also died by violence, stoned to death, a bloody raving ranting symbol of the Christ to come.

Could it be that even on the three streets of Carmincross where nothing ever happened, Christ has at last come into his own?

Which reminds me that on the way to the wedding I met an odd fellow called Jeremias or Jeremiah Gilsenan whom I will de-scribe in detail when I meet you in the Algonquin or the Edison or the El Quixote or the Lion's Head by Phil Sheridan on his horse: if all or any of those places are still there when I close my eyes on my last glimpse of Erin. Or perhaps even in our own apartment, which was, for a while, a sort of home.

He writes: More to follow.
He signs the letter: Merlin.

He closes and addresses the envelope.

He will issue forth and walk along the Liffey quays and amuse himself by searching in Merchant's Arch for the black-haired beauty from the page torn from the calendar in the boatshed by the big river. Who will not, as a matter of course, be there. He takes the page of the calendar from the folder where he had carefully placed it with the notes, now rewritten, of his journey to the wedding. There she still stands, white sweater, long legs in the blue jeans, O mons, O fons. She is still holding up like a chalice, a life-giving cup, the same shining brass kettle. In her hands it does not seem to be a shabby antique. She is still smiling subtly at the camera, at the cameraman, at Merlin, at the world of men. And glimpsed beyond her beauty is the shadowy archway through which drunken sailors had staggered in search of a beauty that would last for a night, or a short time, or as long as any beauty lasts anywhere. How to keep—is there any any, is there none such, nowhere known some . . . lace, latch or catch or key to keep back beauty, keep it, beauty, beauty, beauty, . . . from vanishing away, wrote the scrupulous English Jesuit who, in his time in Dublin, must certainly have walked through that archway and across the narrow pedestrian bridge that was once a toll-bridge. Where another poet, when young, was once halted because he had not the halfpenny to pay his way across. How to keep is there any? The camera can? And the modish painter. And the wishful imagination. He studies her as carefully as if she were alive and really there, and she is the image of Stephanie, even if her hair is black and not auburn, who was blown to bits on the eve of her delight. How to keep is there any, is there nowhere known some? He folds the page and the picture into six sections and puts it into his wallet. What joy if she were there and he could unfold the picture and tell her that, old as he may be, he had walked all the way to see if she were still standing at the dark door of the antique shop.

But as he walks the quays and lingers in the last surviving bookshop he finds that he is back again in the old house and the walled garden.

The oldest part of the house, a grey tower at one corner, dates from 1697. How long the family of that widowed lady had been in the place I never did know. Her half-sister, the poetess, lived in smoke, jackdaws in the chimney, if not exactly in squalor, in the old rectory. From the drawing room of the white house on the headland great windows do genuinely open to the south. Old prints, good books, family portraits once told of careful, cultivated generations. Cases of British military medals long ago to be seen. And a huge battlescape of the storming of Seringapatam. And the watercolours of William Burgess, talented amateur, also of the Bengal engineers. Painted Highland cattle true to life. Died in India 1861. Burgess was the family name.

So my patriotic brother-in-law, who has by the Provos been so well repaid for his patriotism, fancied that property even when he didn't have an arse in his trousers. Or, as they say around Carmincross, a seat in his arse. Tells me he used to dream about owning it. Every man has a house in his heart. Except Merlin, who had a cave, or something, down at the far end of Cornwall.

Being able to purchase that property, and with money hard earned in England, did in a way intensify his patriotism. As if he single-handed had possessed himself of a portion of the empire. Which he still thinks is there, for he would be lost without it. Wasn't there a Paddy long ago, he argues, who nearly pinched the Punjab. George Thomas from Tipperary who jumped ship at Madras in 1781, got well in with an Arab lady who was a Begum, and might have ruled all round him but that a glic Frenchman beat him, not in battle but in the Begum's bed. Never trust the French. As Theobald Wolfe Tone found out. And the ragged bloody Irish rebels left hanging on every bush from Granard to Killala after Humbert threw them to the English wolves at the battle of Ballinamuck, the place of the eternal pig.

He is a good simple-minded man, my brother-in-law. Renowned for his honesty. A good Catholic. A fine Irishman. His word is his bond. To be related to him, even by affinity, is almost to become respectable.

He wakes up from his drowsing in that quayside bookshop. He has been sitting in a basket-chair in a sunny corner, leafing through an 1838 edition of Corinne or Italy by Guess Who, translated by Isabel Hill and with metrical versions of the odes by L. E. Landon, and a memoir of the authoress. To the two men who run the place and are old friends of his, and who have seated him in that chair and corner, he reads: Another life! Another life! That is my hope! But still such force hath this we bear, that we demand in heaven the same rebellious band of passions that, here, caused our strife. The Northern zealots paint the Shade, still hunting, with his hound and horse, the phantom stag through shady glade. Yet dare we call such shapes unreal? Naught here is sure save that Distress, whose power all suffer who can feel, keeps her unpitying promises. . . .

—That bloody North, he says, follows me into the oddest places.

—They say, one of the men says, that you can do damn all about the vowel sounds. Short of a major operation.

They make a great comic play of helping him up out of the chair. They chant: Old age has laid his hand upon him, cold as a fire of ashy coal. . . .

He caps the rhyme: but where is the lovely Spanish lady who looked so neat about the sole.

He shakes hands and says farewell to his friends. For the last time? They are two brothers. A long time ago he met the younger of the two in a convalescent home. How long ago was that? They wonder about the years. It being low tide, the weary Liffey outside the door falls down to the sea. Even the dirtiest river winds somewhere safe. The river of life. By no means the tiny Dodder. They shake hands again, and again, and refuse to take any money for Corinne, and walk him to the door. He steps out and turns left, upstream. The Corinne under his oxter is aged about a century and a half. But where is the lovely Spanish lady who looked so neat about the sole? Should have asked the brothers about the reality, or otherwise, of the enchantress of Merchant's Arch, the dark lady of the dusty archway. He faces west. Ireland, or what is left of her, is away out there. Eire Nua is yet to come.

The archway is empty. The bird has flown. The shop is closed for the day. She has gone with another and forsaken me. . . . And left behind the smell of old stone and dust, and something worse, much worse. But not quite empty, the archway. A wretched fellow in a dirty raincoat, long blond beard, matted blond hair, well, call it blond with accretions and variegations, plays the fiddle and, oddly enough, to the tune to which you can sing Carmincross or Skibbereen or any one of twenty or thirty other ballads. Drop a fifty-pee piece into the cap on the ground at his feet and pass on to fresher air. The music stops. A voice says: Jasus, Mervyn Kavanagh.

In my days in Dublin I was mildly renowned for the wideness of my acquaintance.

So he says: Jasus, Mervyn and Joseph.

And: Whom, have I here? As the sentry said in the Local Defence Force in Glenties.

—You wouldn't remember me, Mervyn. Well, you might remember me. But you wouldn't recognise me. Big changes in the world today.

He names a name. But the name means nothing. Pretend that the name clicks. Shake his hand. He complimented me, by remembering who I was.

—You were a hard man, Mervyn, in those days.

Hard man means gay dog. No, not any more it doesn't mean gay dog. Shall we say: boisterous, merry fellow. Drink and women. Even horses. But which days? The old days, it is to be presumed. The accent is not northern. So: the days not as old as those days. He tries to remember how hard he may ever have been. And when.

—You remember poor Larry.

There is no reason why he should not pretend to remember poor Larry.

—You heard about it. Gone. Just like that. Three nights ago. And I had a pint with him on the Tuesday. When I saw you coming up the steps like I thought you were coming to see the place. Like to write a bit about him for the papers.

So: the old newspaper days.

—Poor old Larry. Wasn't the worst. The nuns in Donnybrook gave him a dinner a day. Every day, wet or shine. Slipped in here for a quiet crap. Three nights ago, as you know. It's a quiet corner this. The way the young ones are these nights no place is that quiet. Died like that where he was squatting. Just where you're standing this minit. The very spot. They found him like that. Hunched up like.

It would be undignified to hop suddenly to another spot. Or even to shuffle the feet. The spot looks spotless. Because the litterer, so to speak, had died in the act even the cleansing depart-

ment of the city corporation has had to take cognisance of the
fact. Is this the spot on which Beauty stood? Can't very well con-
sult the picture to find out. A moment of silent memory for poor
Larry.

—Many's the night I drove you home, Mervyn. In right condition. Mawgalore. Singing and talking. And quotations for further
orders. And those behind cried forward and those in front cried
back.

He can only say: Those were good days.

—Good. You can say that. Never the like again. I lost my taxi.
Lost the licence. Lost the wife. Lost fuck everything.

There is nothing for it but to cross to the pub and sit in the corner and buy the man a drink and slip him a fiver. And the Lord
of Lamentations may listen if he likes to Jeremiah's cautionary
verses. A fiver is little enough nowadays for a man who has lost
fuck everything. Faintly his face and his voice come to me out of
the past.

It's pretty obvious that the barman would prefer if the fiddler
were elsewhere. So, buy him another drink.

—That tune you were playing. There were words to it.

—Skibbereen.

—I was thinking of Carmincross.

He recites the words. They are much appreciated. In the
walled garden the white-clad children dance in wedding re-
hearsal: There in a meadow by the river's side, a flocke of
nymphes I chauncéd to espy. . . .

The fiddler hums: The day she said to me we'll wed, next June
in Carmincross.

The barman says: No singing.

—Carmincross had a bomb, Mervyn.

—It had. And more besides.

—Bombs away. Everywhere. Bomber Harris was only an amateur. That's a good song.

—I'll write the words down and post them to you.

Into Mervyn's notebook the fiddler writes his name and address. He lives in the Morning Star. A charitable hostel. In stella
matutina where the morning star sings for glory and the sons of
God shout for joy.

—We'll keep in touch, Sammy.

—You're a good man to meet, Mervyn.

To annoy the bollicks off the boor of a barman he buys Sammy another large whiskey and leaves him there to finish it and walks on to say hello to Thomas Davis.

Who are you? Who are you? What forms do you take? Like a thief in the night? You wouldn't even let poor Larry finish his crap. Dutch Schultz also died on the throne. But somebody, Kid Twist Reles or somebody, shot him while he was sitting there.

Who are you? Who are you? I will go with my father a-sowing to the red field by the sea. And in Methven, Perthshire, a four-year-old boy walks out with his father who is doing a routine check of grain-drying equipment on a large farm. Except the grain falling to the ground die: and not to go near the hopper, which holds five tons of barley, the boy is warned, but the father turns his head to see the boy's head vanishing in the barley to be sucked to the bottom before the machinery can be stopped: and I will sing to the striding sowers, with the finch on the greening sloe, and my father will sing the seed-song that only the wisemen know: and buried down in the barley is the lovely innocent boy. Who are you? Who are you?

He buys an evening paper.

And here is Bloom's Hotel, a new addition to the town, where for a moment I may rest: and in the basket-lounge of the other hotel that was here before Bloom walked this way, and for a long time after that, a lady I knew told me an odd story of how You walked once into a young woman's bedroom in Donnybrook. It happened in Donnybrook a long time ago and on the fringe of that public park that Berryman, the poet, who leaped into Your icy arms from a high bridge over a mighty river, described as the most beautiful park since Bombay. And all on an April evening when, in the park, April airs were abroad, and the magnolia and cherry, loveliest of trees, abloom: the sheep with their little lambs passed me by on the road, all in the April evening I thought of the lamb of God.

—Oh yes, the lady told me, on a lovely evening in early April I got so worried I sent for a man and had him break down the door of her apartment.

Now, the way it was, this lady who lived alone, had had, more for company than for money, a large house, once filled by a numerous family, broken up into quite costly apartments. This quiet young woman lived in one of those apartments. Always, she went, expensively, yet plainly dressed. No cosmetics. A little French and faint perfume. No boyfriends. No drink. No parties. No wild life. A little classical music on a hi-fi.

So the quiet girl goes off for her Easter holidays: or so she says. Stays away for two weeks. But one day passing the door the Chatelaine smells the smell that says You have arrived. Behind the broken door the musical maiden two weeks dead on pills and gin, and cosmetised like Cleopatra, and in a negligée worth nuggets and most revealing. With only one lover had she ever lain. Who are You? Who are You?

They burned the bedclothes and scraped the paper off the walls to banish your body odour but they never found your name.

From the feature pages of the evening paper the face of my favourite niece, Stephanie, smiles out at me from somewhere far beyond Carmincross. Some sentimental, or is it ghoulish, journalist has assembled a gallery of young people for whose violent passing various odd organisations have admitted, or is it claimed, responsibility. Along with the photographs go brief pen-portraits of the murdered and some details about the way in which they were unwittingly compelled to meet You.

The faces in the photographs are, mostly, happily smiling, gazing, glancing, staring at me out of some other happy occasion before the evil will that is in the world and the man going round taking names, Your Agent, brought them all together. Sweet smiling faces passing to and fro. Oh, we know all about the bridge of San Luis Rey and Katherine Anne Porter's ship of fools: and Arthur G. Hailey's hotel and airport, God help us, and the blazing movie about the bloody big hotel that went all on fire, and all in together in that most unfrosty weather, and about John Ford's jolly old whipcrackaway stagecoach, and about Chaucer on the road to Canterbury. People meet, the mountains never, the old Irish proverb says. The mountains are wise: and I am here in the hotel called after Leopold Bloom who in one day in Dublin met a lot of people: and I am looking at the pictures of fifteen people, young and murdered, pictures taken long before You were, by the impulses of clods, invited to come and take them delighted to be photographed, not knowing, how could they, that those photographs would ever come together. Not one of the fifteen had ever met another. How may it feel to look in the newspapers at the smiling faces of people you have murdered and never even known: for here on another page, and also smiling, are the faces of three young people who have been not murdered but out and about, murdering. A boy of eighteen, a boy of nineteen, a girl of twenty-two who has said to the police that while she and one of the boys were driving away from Carmincross there was an awful bang and I just died when the bomb went off, I just wanted to get out, I was never so cowardly in my life, I want to see Ireland free but I said to myself, Jesus Christ, if you do it this way how is all the wee folk to grow up.

She may never have met Stephanie or bought anything in her boutique.

And how is all the wee folk to grow up? And that's a good question and neatly put by a girl who is herself little more than wee folk. Even if she has already gone out on a dubious mission. Lelia Khaled says that she loves children because they are not guilty. Everybody else in the world, except herself and her pals, seems to be. When in the course of her aerial activities she saw that she might be risking the lives of children she eased her gentle heart by the thought of what Arab children had already suffered. We will the youth of the Arab nation to search for death so that life is given to them. Jesus, where are you? How are you? Baking bread for guerrillas, Lelia sees herself as a revolutionary Jesus blessing the fishes and feeding the multitude: and how now about a bomb in the Belfast bap or the barmbrack, and my Aunt Jane she took me in, she gave me tay outa her wee tin, half a bap with sugar on the top and three brown bombs outa her wee shop.

Ayatollah Ghilani, a religious judge in Tehran, holds on the other hand that a nine-year-old girl, having arrived at puberty, may by Islamic law be executed. A delicate issue and a moot point among Islamic divinity scholars.

Why, anyway, should mass murderers feel so touchy about the welfare of children? Mr. Reginald Halliday Christie was kind to cats. Somewhere in every one of us there is a little child lost, a lost childhood: and after riots in Belfast, and in Watts and Harlem, children in school playgrounds build barricades, organise armies, and throw rocks: and a psychiatrist I met somewhere talked to me about that most dangerous of fauna, the child guerrilla, who graduates from sticks and stones which can only break your bones to the higher productivity of petrol-bombs and gelignite: and to give a nod to a member of another gang may be friendly but to wave the tip of your scarf may provoke a degree of fury that has to be seen to be believed. A fig for you, a Spanish fico, and do you bite your thumb at me?

And, after the Californian earthquake, some children thought the world was sliding into the sea. Others thought that the whole world was on fire. Different temperaments? Or did they simply live in different parts of California?

And in Aberfan in Wales, after the slagheaps from the pitheads moved and swallowed up the schoolhouse, children who had lost brothers and sisters had sleeping difficulties, nervousness, the jumps, bed wetting, abnormal fears of a change in the weather: and one boy developed encopresis, or faecal incontinence, on the evening after the landslide or slagslide. He recovered. But the disease recurred when, on a winter's night, he was awakened by snow sliding off a roof.

Look for me, sang Francis Thompson, in the nurseries of heaven.

And here we are.

Black blazers, green skirts, black bowlers, sixty of each on sixty little girls, three young nuns, dainty as dolls, in control, and all ring o' ring o' rosy around the feet of Thomas Davis. Who stands up, black and solemn and forty feet high as Ned Delaney, the sculptor, saw him: and looks over the head and shoulders of Henry Grattan at Edmund Burke and Oliver Goldsmith and Trinity College. What a lovely gathering. All those noble men. All those eager little twittering girls. All those dainty little nuns. What are they all doing here? Forty feet high Davis stands above a plashing fount and dominates College Green as he never did in his thirty-one years of innocence. Behind one of those little windows at the top of the college I once, at a students' party, drank porter out of a po with Pope O'Mahony and Florry O'Donoughue, a merry token drink from a virgin po and all the assembly singing in the words of Richard Brinsley Sheridan: Let the toast pass, drink to the lass, I'll warrant she'll prove an excuse for the glass.

That was after an inaugural meeting of the ancient and august Trinity historical society. At which I had taken the chair for a debate on the origins and implications of the partition of Ireland, and how the problem should, and when it would, be solved. That was back in the days of innocence and, perhaps, hope. Ancient ghosts all around us in those old buildings. Even to the ghost of Goldsmith slipping out at night to wander the lanes by the Liffey and haunt the shebeens and hang around the Smock Alley theatre to hear his anonymous ballads bewailed by the beggarmen. Or so the story went. And the ghost of noble and innocent Davis lecturing to that same society: The history of a nation is the birthright of her sons. When Grattan paced the garden or Burns trod his hillside were they less students than the print-dizzy denizens of a library? No, that pale form of the Irish regenerator, the mighty and most eloquent Henry Grattan, is trembling with the rush of ideas, and the murmuring stream and the gently rich landscape and the fresh winds converse with him through keen interesting senses. . . .

Grattan has not the least intention of trembling. He hasn't even turned his head to look around at Davis. Is he listening at all? He is extending his arm over or out to something. To the risen Irish nation he may be saying: Esto perpetua.

Burke and Goldsmith are off over in London and don't give a damn.

William of Orange was here once, on a horse, where Davis now stands. But somebody blew William up. And the horse. George III was up in Stephen's Green, on a horse. But somebody blew him up. And his horse. A Dublin humorous magazine of the time said King George III left Dublin by air, early this morning. And in the Phoenix Park somebody blew up Lord Gough. And his handsome horse. Blowing up statues used to be the best of fun. The sky above this town is mottled with the fragments of kings and lords and horses.

But hark and hear how thin and clear and thinner clearer farther going, for Davis is still speaking loud and clear: I do not fear that any of you will be found among Ireland's foes. . . .

About the nuns and little girls he could well be dead on the ball. The nuns have hushed the children and straightened up their ranks. As efficient, by God, as sergeant majors.

—To Ireland every energy should be consecrated. Were she prosperous she would have many to serve her, though their hearts were cold in her cause. But it is because her people lieth down in misery and riseth to suffer, it is, therefore, you should be more deeply devoted. She has no foreign friend. Beyond the limits of green Erin there is none to aid her. She may gain by the feuds of the stranger. She cannot hope for his peaceful help, be he distant, be he near. Her trust is in her sons . . .

But who is this bloody miserable woman? Have I met her? And where? And when? And the voice that is speaking is not the voice of Thomas Davis. How, anyway, would I know? I never heard his voice. Like Molly Malone who was a fishmonger, and sure 'twas no wonder, he died of a faver. And in the year 1845. And in the prime of his manhood. No, by God, this voice I know. Do I sleep, do I dream, do I wonder or doubt, are things what they seem or is visions about? For this vox clamantis in foro, and the nuns and the little girls regarding it, is the voice of Jeremiah Gilsenan. He is standing on the far side of the plinth. He is as yet to me invisible. He is preaching patriotism to the little girls and the guardian nuns. He is telling them that Davis was the son of an Irish mother and an Englishman of Welsh extraction who was a surgeon in the Royal Artillery, that he, the son, became more Irish than the Irish themselves, that at school in Dublin he learned to know and, knowing, to love his fellow countrymen.

Quite a crowd gathering. The little girls are rapt. Push sideways through the people so that I can get a look at Jeremiah Gelignite Gilsenan in this most unfamiliar role. Scratch every Irishman deeply enough and you will find a windy patriot. You Irish, as he himself would say, constantly amuse me. Or: Contemplate the fearful hazards of being more Irish than the Irish themselves.

And there he is, in a good dark suit and gold-rimmed spectacles, and a stout green book in his royal Irish fist. He reads: And now, Englishmen, listen to us: Though you were to equalise Presbyterian, Catholic and Episcopalian, though you were to give us the amplest representation in your Senate, though you were to restore our absentees, disencumber us of your debt and redress every one of our fiscal wrongs, and though, in addition to all this, you plundered the treasures of the world to lay gold at our feet, and exhausted the resources of your genius to do us worship and honour, still we tell you, we tell you in the name of liberty and country, we tell you in the name of enthusiastic hearts, thoughtful souls and fearless spirits, we tell you by the past, the present and the future, we would spurn your gifts, if the condition were that Ireland should remain a province. We tell you, in the name of Ireland, that Ireland shall be a nation. . . .

Since six of them, or thereabouts, are giggling, the little girls seem to be delighted at the information.

Jeremiah is now reciting poetry: Oh, brave young men, my love, my pride, my promise, 'tis on you my hopes are set, in manliness, in kindness, in virtue to make Erin a nation yet, self-respecting, self-relying, self-advancing, in union or in severance free or strong. And if God grant this, then, under God to Thomas Davis let the greater praise belong.

Jeremiah is away in the head.

Jeremiah is singing.

But, with one of the nuns conducting, the little girls are singing with him: When boyhood's fire was in my blood I read of ancient freemen, for Greece and Rome who bravely stood, three hundred men and three men. And then I thought I yet might see our fetters rent in twain, and Ireland, long a province, be a nation once again.

Here in College Green and under the bulbous eyes of Jeremiah Gilsenan has not the Irish nation been born again?

Dixit Jeremiah.

Jeremiah is shaking hands with the nuns. He kisses one of them on the cheek. He chats to the children and even pats a few of them on the head. Is he running for Lord Mayor? One of the nuns marshalls or sergeant majors the little girls two deep, then leads them away. The other two nuns follow. The arched gateway of the ancient college swallows the crocodile. The crowd disperses.

—Well, what would you have me do, Merlin? One of those holy nuns is me bloody second cousin twice removed. She asked me.

He has not even bothered to turn around to face me. As you might expect he has eyes, not bulbous but sharp as the eyes of a ferret, in the back of his turnip-shaped head.

—Davis, when you think of it, he says, was mighty hard to please. If the English had wiped his virtuous Protestant arse, he still wouldn't have given them an inch. Or am I mixing my metaphors?

—And what, he says, had the poor bastard got against provinces? And in the end to get nothing but a good name, and the pure love and sad memory of a virgin girl, and death from scarlet fever at the age of thirty-one, and he a doctor's son. Although, unlike Gandhi, he died in his bed.

Jeremiah, while speaking, has turned around slowly without, it would almost seem, moving his feet: as if he were on a turntable. In utter contrast to his words he is smiling welcome, relaxing somewhat the tight rubbery outline of his face. He says: You have caught me at a melting moment. I have been but briefly the voice of Ireland. My virginal second cousin would not be denied. And off they go now to see the Book of Kells, the word of God.

—Illuminated by holy men who had a hand in heaven. As the poet said. Mr. Austin Clarke to you.

—Merlin, we've come a long way since the Book of Kells. Look now upon this statue. You all did know the great surgeon Dolan.

—In fact, I did.

Long ago and not so far away, and in hospital, and some time spent on a sun balcony, and a rich young boy, tubercular kidney, pale and dying in the bed beside me. Over the boy's bed the great surgeon bends, kind and comforting. But not all his skill and kindness can save that boy. You were there to claim him.

—Well, if you knew the great surgeon Dolan you will know that the man up there isn't Thomas Davis at all. Delaney foxed us all. That man up there is Surgeon Dolan.

Careful consideration and standing back and looking up and walking all around. That man could be Dolan, not Davis. But then we have never seen Thomas Davis. He may in his time have been the living double of the great surgeon who was yet to be.

—Then Merlin, cast thy wizard eye upon this sparkling fountain. Read out to me that inscription.

—A nation once again.

—Then recall for what relaxing and releasing operation the great Dolan was famous.

—The prostate gland.

—And there you have it. Urination once again.

O God, O Venus, O Mercury, patron of thieves, O Dublin, Dublin.

The bulbous eyes transfix me with a long, unsmiling, maniacal stare.

—It's talk like that, Jeremiah Gilsenan, has Ireland the way it is.

So we are not alone, there is a third man here, yet not that third man who, away back in the morning of the world, danced with Burns and myself on a bridge in West Tyrone. An Ulster accent: even if it echoes again the tone of the voice of Fionn in the Munster valley of a million sheep. Not Fionn himself, but it might be the son of Fionn. Or nephew. For the son of Fionn was a poet and this man does not look like a poet. What should a poet look like? This man is blond and burly, smiling, well-dressed in warm tweeds, bronzed in the face as if he had felt the sun in warm places. Or could it have been in the Land of Youth?

—Oh, Pat Loughran is it you, Jeremiah says. Did the Arabs let you out?

Then: Merlin, this ill-shapen college friend of mine finds oil in the Persian Gulf. Or in the neighbourhood of. Since he grew up in Newry he finds the gulf a welcome change.

—Newry, the big man says, is by no means what it was. It has changed since Hugh O'Neill rode through it with Mabel Bagenal. To make her his bride.

He smiles all the time but he is, quite clearly, a very serious man.

—Loughran, your friends, the Provos, have I hear tell, added no end to the urban amenities of Newry.

—The Brits, Gilsenan. The Brits. Did you ever hear tell, as you put it, of a crowd of Christian brothers called the Third Paras.

—Oh, the Paras and the Provos, Jeremiah sings. Oh, the Martins and the Coys.

Thomas Davis looks down on all of us. He is about to hear about the daring doings of the Third Paras. And his father, and all, in the British army.

—I'll tell you, Gilsenan, what they did at Silverbridge, near Forkhill.

—Where I once saw the most radiant kingfisher I have ever seen.

This does not seem to be a happy college reunion between Loughran and Gilsenan and, perhaps, that scarcely relevant remark of mine may distract, divert them. But there is no distracting or diverting this big blond man whose smile goes no further than his quite handsome face: Erin, the tear and the smile.

—No offence, to you, he says, whoever you are. But the Third Paras are fishers for the Queen, and not all that radiant.

A conceit, i' faith. Not quite successful. But let it pass.

—At Silverbridge they took a young man from his car and thumped him on the neck, below the right jaw, slapped him round the head, pulled him by the hair, pushed the muzzle of a gun into his mouth, and threatened his life.

—Loughran, it is almost impossible to push the muzzle of a gun into a man's mouth without threatening his life.

—Gilsenan, when the boy's girlfriend stepped in to save him one of the Paras said: I cut and butchered women in Aden.

—Perhaps he was but boasting, says the bold Jeremiah. Regimental pride.

Dear God, let me away from here and back to the dear old Edison or anywhere at all from the lakes of Connemara to the hills of Donegal.

—And they took another young fellow that I know into a field and put him down on his mouth and nose in the nettles, and took his sandwiches and ate them, and broke the brakes of his car.

—He should have carried poisoned sandwiches. Semper paratum.

—And burned a house at Drumilly, Beleeks, and burned a hayshed at Carrickovaddy was worth five thousand pounds. And on the Carrickovaddy Road two Paras exposed themselves to an old woman and a young girl.

—Valiantly exposed themselves to enemy fire. As was written about a notable patriot at the General Post Office at Easter, 1916. Must say, though, the Paras didn't show much discrimination. Yet they didn't blow the legs off the old lady and the young girl.

—There's a war on, Gilsenan. War has been declared. What about Dresden? What do you mean by violence? Do you mean republican violence, or loyalist violence, or British violence, or Irish violence. I myself have a definitional problem about violence. I don't know what it means.

Jeremiah says: Jesus, save us. You're a wit. You're a bloody intellectual.

He is, clearly, quite impressed. He says: A car-bomb, Loughran, here and now would have made a right job of all those little girls. Not to mention me cousin the nun.

—That's emotive talk, Gilsenan. Down here in Dublin it's easy to rationalise.

—The bomb would, sure as God, have emoted the little girls. And ourselves. And that young mother. And the child in the go-cart. Crossing the street before our eyes.

That last bit was Mervyn, attempting to pour oil. He must say something or turn and run. There is a silence that seems to affect even the traffic while the young woman wheels the child across the street and turns the corner at the bank and goes on, unscathed, toward the Liffey.

—But what, says the man from Newry and the Persian Gulf, about the murder of Dan McElhone.

—Blood on the meadowgrass in the mountains of Pomeroy. Mervyn has again contributed.

—So you heard about that did you, stranger. Even in distant Dublin.

—A man told me about it. On the phone.

We laugh, for no very good reason. And shake hands. He says that he must catch a train.

—And do you know, Jeremiah Gilsenan, a little bit of jogging with the marine commandos would do your figure all the good in the world. A young fellow I know in Fermanagh. They broke into his house in the middle of the night. Did the jolly old commandos. What Ho! Admirals all, for England's sake. Pulled him out of bed. Terrified his wife and children. Pulled him out of the house. Twisted his arms behind his back. Made him run along a road in the dark. Put a hood over his head and hammered him. Clicked a gun and said they'd shoot him. Nicked him with a knife and said they'd cut his throat. Kept him hours on the road. Asked no questions. Made no charges. Then they threw him over a hedge and left him.

—You have, says Jeremiah, made a certain point.

They shake hands.

Thank God for that.

He says again that he must catch a train.

—To Newry or the Gulf, says Jeremiah.

And: There ain't no buses running from the Bank to Mandalay.

They shake hands again. He goes off smiling, following the path of the young mother and the child.

—Never did I think, says Jeremiah, that I could be outtalked by a man who is even a greater idiot than myself. But let it pass. Free I now am, O Merlin, to walk with you. In that noble college that Father Joe Furlong of Finglas used to call Queen Elizabeth's cesspool, my cousin, the nun, and the little angels will have a lady librarian to lead them through the radiant mazes of the Book of Kells. So let us walk. To the Horseshoe in the Shelbourne to Jim Kelly who will welcome us as a gentleman should. Through history we will walk. Our streets vibrate with history. Oh, happy town. At one and the same moment, Merlin, you have had the privilege of gazing on two different forms of the Irish lunatic, the men on whom God has laid his hand, Loughran and myself. From the Irish State I draw my money and rail against the Irish State. Bold Pat Loughran sucks his sustenance from some multinational, mostly English, and rails forever against the English or what he calls the English presence in Ireland. He tolerates the English in England. And in other places. But noway in Newry. He told me once that his blood boiled when he was touched at a checkpoint by a frisking British soldier. Something, mayhap, sexual there. Virginal Irish. So I told him that under similar circumstances I said to the soldier, do that again, mate, haven't had a thrill like that since I was last in Morocco. He did, the soldier I mean, call me a filthy Fenian fucker, but not only did he smile when he said it, he laughed outright and we jested together like brothers akin. Some local scholar must have introduced him to the word Fenian. Oh happy land, oh happy town. There in that corner building, now an insurance office, once an hotel, did Parnell, the uncrowned king, lie abed with Kitty, the uncrowned queen. Pope O'Mahony once told me that Kitty had halitosis but how he ever found out he never did say. Kitty, I must say it, you have . . . Charles, I have Scope, the new mouthwash. And in that same building did the imagination of George Moore place the comic story of Albert Nobbs and the other fellow who both turned out to be women. And here in this street did James walk with Nora on a June day to be remembered forever by American scholars and assorted drunks. While round that corner Lady Morgan, Glorvina, the wild Irish girl, entertained or was entertained by Paganini, the demon fidddler. Stand, then, here beside me, Merlin of Clan Kavanagh, and look over this wall and through the railings into College Park. Where, as you well know, the great Gogarty, poet, wit, and raconteur, all the Irish, Jesus help us, are raconteurs, where, I resume, the great Oliver St. John Gogarty ran races on a bicycle. Also a surgeon and friend of the great: and our friends go with us where we go, down the long path where Beauty wends, where all we loved foregather, so why should we fear to join our friends. And turn now and look up that high narrow street where Protestant country gentlemen up to the town for the Thursday market day used, when full of wine, to run footraces from the Kildare Street Club to St. Stephen's Green where the notorious Darky Kelly, who tried to add to the gaiety of Dublin by running a brothel, was burnt in full view and for murder in 1764. And down that high and narrow street and coming from her work in the hotel to which we are now going – French polishing was her work, the creation of brightness and beauty – down that street she came, as fine a lady as you ever met and civil even to me, Jeremiah Gilsenan, to be blown to her death just here where we stand: in the company, oddly enough, of a French girl whom she had never met until that moment. A French girl student over here on holiday. And in the company of some other people who were also just walking by, as we are, as James and Nora once were. And across the river in another part of the forest there was a girl in three bits, and two other girls, merely dead, they were all flatmates, and work out the vulgar fractions for yourself: and a woman looking for her husband but failing to recognise him where he lay in the gutter at her feet. And in the Richmond hospital where Gogarty once performed, and on a night in May, the streams of blood running down the slight slope from the stretcher bay, homeport for ambulances, to the operating theatres: So do not shudder at the knife that Death's indifferent hand drives home. You see what happened, Merlin, was that the other boys, the Orangemen, were up on a brief visit from Belfast and for Queen and Ulster as, God help them, they call it, not being willing or able to understand or pronouce the original Irish, well, they wanted their turn, fair's fair, at the blowing of the legs or heads or anything off the bodies of the unfortunate passers-by at any given or ungiven moment. Twenty-six dead and about one hundred and fifty injured while you would wink an eye, and, oh, but we talked at large before those sixteen men were shot, and all the dead men we now have, and women and children, to stir the boiling pot, and converse bone to bone with those new comrades they have found Lord Edward and Wolfe Tone. And in that oblong mansion to the left, where the statesmen of Ireland suffer for a purgatorial time before they go to Europe, was Lord Edward Fitzgerald reared who soldiered in your America, and commanded William Cobbett, and who died for Ireland by the stab of a penknife, if it be long, how long ago, when I begin to think how long. . . .

With the money to buy the first drink there emerges also from my wallet the picture of the girl in the archway which Jeremiah inspects carefully, pronounces that he knows her, by sight, tears the picture slowly to pieces, says: Merlin who once, by deceit and disguise, did enable a king to dishonour and impregnate another king's queen, abandon your craft, you are too old for dreams. I have spread your dreams, not under your feet, for that would be to litter: and Dublin, as you cannot fail to have noticed, is already much belittered: but here on the bar counter where they can easily be swept up and carried away. And now let us, for a while, enjoy ourselves.

Shaving in the morning he mouths the words of an item from Jeremiah Gilsenan's deplorable Revised Irish Minstrelsy: I called on the Judge on a bright sunny morning. I stood at his door, shot him dead without warning. The Brit war machine I was gallantly scorning. But the Judge had no gun said the bold Fenian men.

And: On her bed in the trailer the young girl was sleeping. By her side, her young daughter her dolly is keeping. But we blasted the plyboard and left the child weeping. You're a shower of shits, cried the bold Fenian men.

And: In a school in the Newry an Orangeman is teaching Christian doctrine, they say, and he's good at the preaching. When we shot him. . . .

The telephone rings. But it is only the redheaded nurse reminding him that they are to drive to Roundwood in the Wicklow mountains for lunch and, afterward, to walk in the Devil's Glen or somewhere.

In the bath, after shaving, he thinks of the redhead . . .

This must cease. That rhythm goes with the obscene cackle of Jeremiah. So switch back, and to hell with the bad times, to the songs my mother sang: When I was a maiden, fair and young, on the pleasant banks of Lee, no bird that in the greenwood sung was half so blithe and free. My heart never beat with flying feet, no Love sang me his queen, till down the glen rode Sarsfield's men and they wore the jackets green. . . .

And when William stormed with shot and shell at the walls of Garryowen, in the breach of death my Domhnall fell . . .

Stop there. Here You are again. Wearing a mask like William of Orange. Who are You?

Yet listening to Jeremiah Thersites Gilsenan might turn me into a patriot, if not into a Provo.

Who in hell does Jeremiah think is too old for dreams? Does the heart of the redhead beat with flying feet? After all she did ring me, call me, to remind me. I hear you calling me. Few places in Ireland can, when one is in the proper, or improper, company, be more romantic than the Devil's Glen.

Then after breakfast, to resume the Epistle to the Edison.

My mother, he writes, I found where I knew I was sure to find her: in the church, where she was more at home than she would ever be again anywhere on earth. She lived above a shop in the village, hoarding her loneliness and talking about it a great deal, asking her innumerable visitors why she should have been left alone. She enquired most delicately about your health. Most delicately avoiding any reference to your absence. Her chief companion was my niece, Mary, the one who substituted bravely for the burned and lacerated bride. A physiotherapist. A tall, dark-haired, practical girl, always formal, who calls her uncle, Uncle. Agile, as a physiotherapist should be. Cycles to work in the county infirmary in the neighbouring town. Five days a week. Says she is illiterate and can spell only long medical words: like epidemiology, kwashiorkor, which is also known in Europe as the starch dystrophy, marasmus, amoebiasis, trypanosomiasis, rhodesiense, lymphatic leishmaniasis, pyrimethamine, chloroquime, fansidar, maloprim, and many others. She was not there but away in the infirmary when the second bomb went off, six doors away from the house my mother lived in. It was planted in an outhouse at the back of a pub that had once served drink to some marine commandos passing through on patrol. How exactly do you tell marine commandos: Gentlemen, you are not served on these premises? To begin with they are, I have been informed, by no means gentlemen.

When I drove the old lady back from the church to the village she made tea, offered me a brandy and sang the Wild Rover, which was a favourite song with my father: I'll go back to my parents, confess what I've done, and I'll ask them to pardon the prodigal son. . . .

And being literary I thought of Baudelaire: Dans les plis sinueux des vieilles capitales. . . . Or: In winding folds of ancient capitals where all things have enchantment, even fear, I wait, obeying humours whimsical, to see frail creatures, sweet and singular. These broken souls were women long ago, Laïs or Eponine. . . .

Mean bastard: He himself wasn't all that much to look at. Wrote more begging letters to his mother than he ever wrote poems. Stop there! Unfair to Baudelaire.

What I mean is that my mother was so small and frail that for some time Stephanie had been worried that if her grandmother died, her wedding, Stephanie's wedding, might have to be postponed. My mother had a tiny, tinkling, silvery voice. Long ago it was deeper and more varied. She had been waiting for the bride-to-be to visit her in all her rehearsing finery when the second bomb went off. Stephanie was already dead. All through the time between that and her own passing the old lady kept saying: Is Stephanie there. She was to come and show me her wedding gown.

And the groom, who was very close to the old lady, like herself, or like as she was, he's a singer, he sings in public and for money and does very well out of it, kept repeating: Granny, she's gone on a message. She'll be back in a minute.

The pub that was so unpatriotic as to sell booze to those un-gentlemanly commandos was also a grocery. So the bomb in the outhouse was blanketed with empty cardboard boxes, cases of empty bottles, the customary mounds and pyramids of damaged fruit and rotting vegetables. Which may, perhaps, have deadened somewhat the thrust of the explosion. But sent showers of muck even over the roof of the house and out into the main streeet. And the blast was strong enough to take down the plaster from the ceiling of the old lady's living room. And, since her two windows were open to the warm day, to lift her rocking chair out of its cor-ner and smash it to bits against the far wall. She was not in the chair. She was not in the room. But halfway up the stair from the hallway. Or halfway down. Because when the first bomb went off, the bomb that destroyed Stephanie—it was planted a hun-dred yards away—a friend of mine was walking past my mother's door. By the name of Cecil Morrow. Good old Cecil. A police-man. So he rushed in through the shop and the side door into the long hallway. Because he had heard from a messenger sent by a curate, i.e., assistant in the pub-cum-grocery, that two suspicious characters had been seen on the waste ground at the back of that block. And he suspected and feared a second bomb. Since my mother was the mother of a friend of his, and since my mother was also a friend of his, he was concerned. To get her away to a safer place. Wherever that might be. But she refused to leave her rocking chair.

She said that no bomb nor no blackguards of bombers would drive her out of her own home. So he carried her out like a child in his arms. They were halfway down the stairs when the blast made bits of the rocking chair and took all the plaster off the ceiling. Good old Cecil. We played football together when we were boys. He had hopes, recently expressed to me, to emigrate to New Zealand and spend the rest of his life there. On the day after the bombing, during which he had comported himself like a hero, rescuing and carrying people, or what was left of them, here, there, and everywhere, he was killed by a single bullet. Fired by a boy of seventeen who took off on the pillion of a motorbike. But he and the other rider, and the machine, made violent contact with a humpy old stone bridge two miles away. Both killed. The other fellow was nineteen. Neither of them were natives of Carmincross. They were members of a splinter group calling themselves the Irish Liberation Army. As far as is known, the killing of Cecil who rescued my mother seems to have been their only contribution to any form of liberation.

One crowded hour of glorious life.

Cecil was unarmed at the time. He never did much believe in carrying a gun. He held that if he were attacked he would never get a chance to use it. He wanted to be a community policeman, serving the community. People would bring him their troubles and he would help to solve them. That was his ideal. Some people did, and he did help them. He carried my mother to safety and rest, even if only for a few days, even if Cecil himself were to go on or to be sent on before her. The shock of that day was too much for her, and the destruction of her rocking chair. About which she talked a lot. It had been my father's favourite chair.

She had been a mighty handsome woman even if you would never think it to look at her son. She had never seemed more handsome than in the coffin. But tiny, tiny like a large doll: for many an old woman's bier is little bigger than that of a child: old Baudelaire again. How many different shapes it has to be, the box that takes all creatures' measurement. But tell me, good M. Baudelaire, what shape is the box for the bodies that have to be picked up in bits or hosed or swept off the streets. Baudelaire might have written well about the multiple uses of the plastic bag. Wise death inspires these coffins similar, symbol engaging and unparalleled. Tell me, how wise is Death?

But my mother died peacefully and in one piece. That is not, perhaps, the best way to phrase it. The only screaming cancer death I ever saw was in a Bergman movie. Or ever want to see.

The young man who was to marry Stephanie sang about the wild rover. The old lady was closer to that young man than to anybody else around that bed, or to anybody anywhere else. He sang: And now I'm returning with gold in great store, and I never will play the wild rover no more. I went into an alehouse that I used to frequent, and I told the landlady my money was spent. . . .

Faintly my mother said: The poor welcome the wild rover would get there.

Then with an astonishing effort she pulled herself up on the pillow and sang with him. And reached out toward him. Or toward my father who had in his youth been a bit of a wanderer.

Then she went away from us taking with her all her stories and memories, and her own mother's memories back to the days of that Thomas Davis that I so much mention, a decent man who had great hopes for Ireland. And leaving us with the present and as much future, as she herself might have said, as any of us will see. My sister and my brother-in-law joined in the final song. On the other shore the angels may have taken up the chorus. Their heroic singing, the young man and my sister and her husband, made me feel less than the dust. Stephanie, my favourite, had never returned from that message. No chorus did I join in. Never did I feel more sadly that I was a stranger in that place, the odd bird that slipped out of the nest. All that had made me was now part of the clay. And I was no more than a shadow on the wall.

The muck from the back of the pub-and-grocery showered down, it would seem, for a long time: and even on a dead body left behind by the third bomb. Body of a young Catholic fellow, aged twenty-four, who gave his life to save a Protestant neighbour, elderly lady, who owned a news agent's shop on the far side of the street. He was leaning, elbows on a low wall, and looking into a neighbour's garden and, even in the heart of danger, putting fine talk on the neighbour's handsome daughter, when a shabby motorvan pulled up outside the shop. And then drove on. He heard the crash of breaking glass, and shouted Jasus, and ran like a hare to warn the woman: and was leading her to safety when the bomb went off. He was killed outright. She by the blast was levitated over a ten-foot wall. She is still alive or was when I left the place. Miraculously the neighbour's handsome daughter was unharmed. Some of these details are obscure and difficult to reconcile with other details. It was the fourth bomb that banished the white doves.

This is what life looks like after the bomb, this is the house that. . . .
   Did I say life?
   On the sidewalk a lump of clothes with the blood running out of it. People flat on that sidewalk as if a steamroller had rolled over them. A priest tells of two legs sticking out of a pile of rubble, of shattered bodies, you could see the life going out of them. He anointed what he found there. In this car there was a body, decapitated, but no way of knowing whether it was man or woman. Busy traffic that morning in Carmincross. Friday. Old people picking up pensions. Commercial travellers making calls. So that one distrait bomber could not find a parking place. His objective was a garage. As next best he opted for the home of a lady pensioner, aged eighty, just as she was opening her door to step in with her pension.
   On the morning of that day I am, in a news magazine, reading something about the instinctive poetry of everyday life. Then my phone rings. It is you. Ringing me from wherever you are at five in the morning. Ten o'clock with me and the sun gilding, you might say, the tips of the trees around the hill and hotel of Knocknagon.
   Gabriel the archangel must have made your connection. The angel of the Lord declared unto Merlin. For the phones that day were even worse than what is customary in Ireland. That you were cut off was fortunate because you had nothing pleasant to say. Neither had the voice that briefly came on in your place. A young person's voice, male or female it would be hard to say. Faint and faraway and the line crackled. Although as I was to find out the call came only from the village of Nendrum, ten miles away. It said: The codeword is Crosscarmin.
   A subtle touch.
   It said: We have planted bombs.
   It said: You have thirty minutes to evacuate.
   Which sounded rude.
   Then the line went dead and I heard the bomb that killed Stephanie. Then the churchbell tolled. Heard only once or twice.

There was a funeral that morning. A normal funeral. The barracks I tried to phone and my friend, Cecil. The angel of the Lord was no longer on the alert. Then that voice of the youth, male or female, was in my ear again. It said: Jesus, mister, run. Jesus, mister. . . .

Then no more. So I ran. Spirals of black smoke all over the place as I raced down, jumped down, the steep path, interspersed with steps, from the back of what used to be the stables at Knocknagon. Black spirals come, I have been told, from the vapourisation of black fuel oil. The bombs were mostly what are known in the trade as ANFO. A mixture of ammonium nitrate and fuel oil. Blast effect equals sixty per cent of a similar weight of gelignite. Any clever boy can make one. Life is so easy nowadays. Equal opportunity for all. AN from fertiliser. FO you may buy at any garage. Add a soupçon of root ginger to flavour. Boost with single stick of gelignite. Stir well with fuse and detonator to set the bubbles bubbling. These technical details I pass on to you in case you may ever feel like blowing up somebody or something. There are moments when even the mildest man, or woman, grows tense with some sort of violence. Or so we are told by the poet who no more than myself ever saw a stick of gelignite even if he did write a schoolboyish quatrain about a stick of incense.

So I ran and ran to little purpose, good or bad.

This is an old lady pinned to the ground. This is the lampost that's pinning her down. . . .

Outside a burning garage an old lady, not otherwise injured, was pinned to the ground by a fallen lampost: one of a set of lamposts that were antiques from an earlier, oil-lit age. Carmincross was very proud of them. Two young men were struggling to raise the lampost. With my help they managed. But she died as we raised it. With a wheeze of air like a bursting football.

And here's a small boy with his hair burned away. . . .

Not a bother on him apart from that fiery alteration to his hairstyle. But he may remember it for a long time.

Cars all over the street, thrown by the blast or abandoned in panic. One car with the engine still running. But nobody madly anxious to switch it off. Two petrol pumps blazing. Pillars of fire. A woman's body in shreds and tatters on the ground at an entryway. A hole in the ground still burning. No telling whether she was lying on her face or her back. Across the road a chemist in a white coat, unbelievably white, trying to staunch a wound in a young man's head. The young man flat on his back but his right arm keeps moving up and down. He is still alive, I hear.

The whiteness of the chemist's coat is what I will most remember. And three doors away a good woman walking about and tidying up for the day ahead in a small restaurant run by herself and her husband. A fragment of a disintegrating auto crashes in through the wide window and gets her on the back of the head. Her husband in hysteria kneels by her side, crying out that she is dying. He is wrong. She is dead. The café, apart from the window, is undamaged. The tables are set for the day. She had eight children. Two daughters were there with her. A neighbour took them away.

Not even after hard, retrospective thinking can I say that I felt any intense, Proustian silence before the bombs began. Perhaps that was because you were, even briefly, on the phone. Or does the nature of explosion simply emphasise the natural quiet that precedes it?

But after the bombs there was a strange silence. Not before. After the bombs there was no sound of machines. Even the car engine that was running seemed to make no sound. The petrol pumps that were pillars of fire burned silently. The only sounds came from living people. And crowds suddenly on the street. Crowded as the sidewalks of New York. It was, as I said, a busy day in Carmincross. Yet so many people and all of a sudden seemed beyond reason. As if they had been there all the time and only now began to move.

Human voices wake us and we drown.

Sweet was the sound when oft, at evening's close, up yonder hill the village murmur rose.

In another village on a similarly happy day the whole place had to be evacuated in the pouring rain. But the Lord blessed Carmincross with a calm pet of a mellow Tennysonian day. So that the forty-one badly injured, eight of them children, could be laid out on a green slope by the river that comes down from a lake where the silence is so absolute that it once frightened away a neurotic fisherman. You might have thought that the bodies were sunbathing. Except for missing limbs and some horrifying burns. They stayed there until the ambulances came. From quite a distance.

In the lounge of the Riverview Hotel the windows were broken. But the ornaments, plates and plaques and pictures on the walls, were with one exception undisturbed. As in the lounge in another hotel I visited on my journey, that lounge had a black cat and an Afghan hound. General issue now, perhaps, for the tourist trade. The cat stayed put. The hound vanished and has never returned. How or why or where to? You can't just lose an Afghan hound.

And in silence in the hills somewhere above Carmincross, perhaps by the shore of that quiet lake, water lapping with low sound and all that, the killers mixed their ingredients on the previous night. And their cars were manned in silence and in silence pulled away and in silence every gunner took his post. Among the cars: a battered light-coloured Mini Traveller and an orange Volkswagen Fastback meant to be used as a getaway car. And the van already mentioned. Two other cars were so badly disintegrated that their owners or their mothers or their makers wouldn't know them.

So having spent a prayerful night of vigil watching their armour and mixing their brew, fillet of a fenny snake, eye of newt and toe of frog, wool of bat and tongue of dog, scale of dragon, tooth of wolf, root of hemlock, they descended on the dark tower of Carmincross. With a volley from their broadsides the citadel they shook and they hammered back like heroes all the night. A lady who was watching a television programme called Watch with Mother was the first to hear the heavenly cars descending from the hills. The swishing of their tyres was distinct. She thought it was the army. She called her husband. He looked out the window. He saw the cars. He knew they meant no good.

The phones from Nendrum did not work to give warning because another active service unit of what the local newspaper called, fairly enough, perpetrators had sometime previously blown up an exchange in the neighbourhood. Should one patriotic perpetrator not remember what another patriotic perpetrator has recently perpetrated? Where is their sense of history? Should perpetrators perpetrate murder and maiming on hapless people and then perpetrate another perpetration by phoning the police to say that hapless people may be murdered or maimed? Work it out for yourself over there in the Edison or the Algonquin. Or anywhere else you may happen to be.

Howandever: several young perpetrators were seen in Nendrum, running from one public phone to another. There are three kiosks in the place. From one of the three somebody, male or female, interrupted you and whispered warning in my ear. Too late, too late. Then a young fellow rushed up to a girl who was putting out on the sidewalk a poster telling Nendrum that her shop sold the best ice-cream. He was, she said, in a panic. He asked her to run to the barracks and tell the police that bombs were due to go off in Carmincross. She said she could not leave the shop. She assumed he was a common robber. But when he rushed across the street shouting she changed her mind. She ran to the barracks. She told the police. Who radio-phoned the newly established barracks in Carmincross. Too late.

So are great deeds done or perpetrated in my homeland in these our days. Purity in our hearts, truth on our lips, strength in our arms. For the glory of God and the honour of Ireland: and in the name of God and of the dead generations.

To you there faraway in America, and far away from me and everything that I belong to or that belongs to me, or that, for good or bad, made me the way I am, it may be difficult to explain how or why destruction came to Carmincross.

One reason for blowing up Carmincross may have been that nobody had previously thought of blowing it up. It may have seemed essential to somebody that the people of Carmincross should be made more conscious of their national heritage. It has also been claimed by those who claim, or whatever, responsibility, or whatever, that the military action, or whatever, was one small part of a coordinated campaign to strike at any commercial stability that might underwrite, or support, or prop up, or aid and abet the British war machine. That would allow for the blowing up of huxter shops whose imperialist owners refuse to pay black rent. Fight the Brits, Jeremiah Gilsenan said to me, to the last Catholic shop in the border village of Belleek, renowned throughout the world for rare and delicate china: and no place for bombs.

There was also the matter of the old rectory. Inhabited in the days of my boyhood, and after it had ceased to be a rectory, by an aged patriotic poetess who was stepsister or cousin or something to the lady for whom I clipped grass, and who lived in the great house now inhabited by my sister and her husband. Where the ghost of Stephanie walks in the walled garden. Where the little girls and boys in bloodless white rehearsed for her wedding.

When I was a patriot boy . . . oh, believe it or not, when I was a patriot boy I used to visit the old poetess. Sitting with her memories in a musty, old drawing room, smoky with jackdaws in the chimney, herself wrinkled and begrimed and so well rewarded for a life of poetry and patriotism that the people said that if you met her on the road you'd be inclined to give her a penny. And when she died I wrote in her honour a considerable length of doggerel, never published needless to say and God be praised, but carefully preserved in manuscript by my sister, a wonderful keeper of things and a hoarder of family memories: and here it is for your edification and instruction. It looks and sounds no worse in the shape of prose than it would if cut up, as Percy French would put it, into lengths of poetry, God help us. So over there in Manhattan lift up your voice and sing along with the patriot boy:

> *Let that house be a shrine and the place where she dwelt, who laboured through years to give life to a dream that was bright in her eyes when her countrymen slept in the night.*
>
> *For her eyes caught the first steel-grey gleam of the new dawn astir in the east, and she stood, hands upraised, face alight with the sun's first red beam.*

You must admit that that's a telling bit. The poetess, the prophetess is on fire.

There is more.

> *And to her thus awake, when the knee-bending throng was heavy with slumber, God gave, as he would, to her lips the wild, light, lilting power of song . . .*

The young poet, you see, is well aware of how the Almighty distributes his gifts.

He, the poet, and also, perhaps, God continues.

> . . . *of song that not needed, for beauty or birth, the far misty legends of Greece or of Rome. Her soul wandered not to the lost lands of earth, there was all that she needed of beauty at home. There was strong faith and prayer, and a love for the land that had sorrowed long years in the darkness and gloom, and the glorious dead who were living and grand to the eyes of a girl in a rectory room.*
>
> *How her lips could give life to the dead who had died, to the brave men she loved when they laboured in life: to that strange man of visions, poor Pearse. By his side went the laughing MacDonagh. Apart from the strife, in his wattled hut laboured of music and dreams, was Yeats, the great poet, who half-understood what was meant by the conflict. And yet, in that throng, who was dearer than she who with life to begin gave her white soul to God by the shores of Lough Finn.*

That last reference, to you perhaps obscure, I may annotate when I see you in Manhattan. If, that is, you are in the least interested.

Now sing on . . .

> *Dear shadows, they passed one by one in my mind while she talked in the half-light of that quiet room: an old withered woman.*
>
> *And yet on the wind that was low in the limes we could hear the dull boom of big guns in the city, could see the red flames of the fires, could hear the sharp rattle of rifles, the cries of the men. And high over Dublin, quite clear in the skies, were lettered in gold the unperishing names. . . .*

The first instance in Irish history of aerial advertising. More to follow. Ten point black to end.

> *She had known them and loved them, stood by them in life when the wise of the world had wheeled by in their pride. She had lived when they perished in fighting and strife, to tell to the living why those men had died.*
>
> *Let that house be a shrine then, built high in the hills where the village smoke easily curls in the air: and the winds are alive with*

*the music of rills and the cries of wild birds on the bare sloping hills, and the branch song resounds like a choir at prayer. To this place shall we come on some day yet unborn, to this place of brown uplands and wind-ruffled lakes, when the wind in the trees is the wind of the morn and our glad hearts are telling that Ulster awakes.*

End of young patriot's poem.

Ulster is now awake.

On the like of that we were reared in the North. Some of us. The others had their own fantasies.

In Magilligan prison camp now the Loyalist prisoners in prison for being loyal to the English crown to the point of murdering Catholics are on hunger strike. Following in the footsteps, if that's the word, of Terence MacSwiney, lord-mayor of Cork who was unloyalist to the point of dying of hunger in Brixton prison. The humble petition of the loyalist prisoners is merely to be separated from what are known as republican prisoners. Who outnumber them and who, they fear, may murder them. They know a good deal about murder. So to keep alive they are prepared to starve themselves to death. If they succeed in doing so, do they also die for Ireland? Or for six of the nine counties of Ulster? Or for Queen Elizabeth? Or the Protestant religion to maintain? Or for what? Do they carry their cross for loyalty, Lord? A Protestant cross for a Protestant people.

Anyway, that old house did not by no means become a shrine.

For sometime back a group of fellows with black bags on their heads set up roadblocks around Carmincross and asked all who passed what their names were. Even though they knew their names very well. As the Orange Bashi-Bazouk, the B Specials, used to do in rural places in the long evenings of my youth: so as to terrorise or, at least, bully or annoy Roman Catholics. Except that the Blackbag Boys acted so as to prove to all that they had voluntarily become part of Ireland Gaelic and Ireland free. You are now entering free Ireland. Id est: Carmincross. Where, hitherto, there had been nothing but a ballad and one joke.

And on the day of the liberation roadblocks there was no barracks in Carmincross, either for police or soldiers. The roadblocks annoyed the security forces, as they are sometimes called. So they, in their turn, set up a barracks for police in the old rectory, deserted since the dear old poetess died. Military or constabulary HQ in the old house. Quarters and canteen in the overgrown shrubbery in the grounds.

The blackbird has fled to another retreat where the hazel affords him a screen from the heat.

Wise bloody blackbird.

For this was the Grand Strategy on the day of the harrowing of Carmincross: to launch a mortar attack on the old rectory or the new barracks. To draw attention from that attack by planting bombs in the village.

Von Moltke at the top of his form.

The rectory is a mile from the village.

And eight mortars, each containing forty-five pounds of explosives, were launched from the back of a stolen lorry. One of the mortars soared over the steel security fence, and made mincemeat out of the canteen, and killed one young constable, a Roman Catholic, one of the few in that force, and the father of three young children who will grow up to remember this event. The mortars injured six other constables, one of them seriously. The stolen lorry was left behind. The bombardiers made off in a stolen Toyota. Anything would have served. Even a Rolls Royce. Ford Cortinas are much favoured for quick starting.

The most seriously injured of the police officers was sitting in the passenger seat of a police car when the first of the mortars exploded. He sustained, as the newspapers say, head, arm, and leg wounds. But is by now comfortable. The car was riddled with holes caused by flying shrapnel.

The old rectory where the patriotic poetess lived in the smoke and the memories and with the jackdaws was untouched.

There you have it. You can see that Carmincross was only peripheral to the main action. Only the faint thin line upon the shore. The great tide of war was a mile away. And Stephanie was only peripheral. Incidental. And all the others.

C'est simple, as Balzac said about something else.

And an old woman in a smoky, musty room, and the ghost of a girl in a walled garden, and a policeman who dreamed about the mountains of New Zealand, and Christ knows how many others, and yourself and myself and Jeremiah Gilsenan may all meet together somewhere in some land of shadows.

Dixit Merlin.

He recalls as he seals and addresses the envelope that the aged poetess was once, by some broadcasting men from Belfast, brought into the big town to broadcast some of her poetry from the stage in the town hall. For some royal occasion or other the Union Jack was then over that building, giving itself to the Ulster wind, the black, black wind from the northern hills.

Another patriotic poetess had written: Said Shiela Ní Gara, (meaning poor old mother Erin), 'tis a kind wind and a true, for it rustled oft through Aileach's halls and stirred the hair of Hugh. Then blow, wind, and snow, wind, what matter storms to me, now I know the faery sleep must break and set the sleepers free.

Forever he sits under ancient Aileach, the great Hugh O'Neill, waiting for the moment to come and the hill to open so that he can march out and liberate Ireland: when the Gael shall sweep his foe through the yawning gates of hell.

Hugh is Roman dust.

Arthur is under Cadbury. Waiting for what?

And other heroes under other hills. Or in palaces under lakewater.

But enter the town hall the old poetess would not until the flag was lowered. And lowered it was by one of the broadcasting men. Who, when she was safely inside, ran it up again. And lowered it again when she was coming out.

Nobody was any the wiser. Nobody was the worse off.

# FOUR

## *The Rock*

❧ ❧

BECAUSE OF THE REDHEADED NURSE, the pot of gold at the
end of the rainbow, and because he has compassionate leave he
does not return to New York until a while before Christmas. Mr.
Burns walks him to the plane, right to the steps before the door.
There are no barriers for Mr. Burns. Deborah has not yet walked
nor worked. But will again. She is still in Dublin acquiring her
European hip. For which her insurance will pay.

—You will remember, says Mr. Burns, that we talked of
McGivern who had been a policeman. R.U.C. But who quit to
become an insurance consultant. His advice was of some use to
Deborah. He was murdered a few days ago.

—It seems unfair that an insurance consultant should end so.

—How right you are, dear boy. While briefly revisiting Belfast.
Unarmed. Shot dead. Someone remembered that he had been a
policeman. The Provos admit responsibility. They are not given
to forgiveness.

—We may hope that he was well insured.

—Against being shot? I must look the matter up. Prudential or
Canada Life. Dear boy, as you keep saying, Death is all around
us. Once, when I was a young hotel manager, I took over a new
hotel in a certain suburb. Old house, converted. Great garden at
the back, gone wild. Had it cleared and replanted and in the dig-

ging the workmen found an iron chest. Bones in it. Bones of a child. In a forsaken garden. Swinburne. The ghost of a garden fronts the sea. Nobody ever found out where the bones came from. I mean, whose child. Which reminds me, old boy, that I have composed your epitaph. In the style of the eminent Mr. Yeats whose brother you knew. Meeting you in Dublin and you drinking wine with that lusty redhead inspired me. At the very least I am as a poet the equal of Jeremiah Gilsenan. Oh, listen, for the vale profound: You think it marvellous that lust and drink should dance attendance when I'm on the brink. I was a modest, temperate man when young. So let me have my fling before I stink. Or, perhaps, more Chaucerian: Swink before I stink. You were never a violent man, Mervyn, nor an angry man, except in fits and starts like your father before you. So I offer you those lines to be cut on limestone quarried near the spot. I may assume that they have much limestone and many limestones on what that woeful ballad describes as the shores of Amerikay. It must take a lot of stone to hold the States together. And talking of Yeats and under Ben Bulben and all that, there was a wonderful story Sunday last in an English newspaper. Which I know you have not read. Because last Sunday you were happy on the hills near Dublin pretending to be young.

—Or playing the devil in the Devil's Glen.

—It seems that in a space hollowed under the Rock of Gibraltar the British army have constructed an Ulster village. And last week while the paint was still fresh on what the newspaper called the quaint rows of cottages, the marines in training fought gun battles against the Provos. Deafening, it was said. Under the rock, the echoes of Ulster. The village has a main street and four side-streets. Two more, as I recall, than Carmincross. It has shops. Including Tom's Chippy. Rather more Coronation Street than North Irish, I'd say. A church called St. Malachy's R.C. Church, complete with spire. Now, in the North, without being told, most everybody would know that St. Malachy was an R.C. A cemetery with gravestones.

—Most apt.

—A St. Trinian's School.

—Never was one of those in Carmincross.

—And a woman's toilet.

—Fulfilling a long-felt want.

—There are also parked cars, traffic lights, and a pub called the Hope and Anchor.

—A fine old English inn. Where the bacon's on the rafter and the wine is in the wood. Couldn't they have called it something Irish like Doherty's Den or the Boozer Burns.

—Or Kavanagh's Kip, old boy. But down deep in the belly of an Iberian rock those fine British boys search a car for Irish bombs. And a real-life drunk abandons all Hope and Anchor and staggers out to ask them, in what the newspaper calls a passable Irish accent: What are ye bastards doing over here?

—But a real Irish accent would have said: What in the name o' Jasus. . . .

—He pesters them, the paper says.

—Then they beat him up the balls.

—No, being of their own he is exempt. He is but a pretending Paddy. All they need is a visiting Irish-American. From Noraid.

—And a pig in the parlour.

—Lighting dim, the paper says. The atmosphere under the Rock is cold and damp. The wooden buildings are so realistic that the scene resembles Ulster on a November night.

—I've been there, God help us. But anywhere on a November night? Except, mayhap, Kalgoorlie.

—During one patrol a gunfight breaks out when the marines are fired at by Provos who are digging up arms in a cemetery.

—Arms?

—Weapons. They also find an informer who has been knee-capped. His trousers are smeared with detergent to represent blood.

—No shid? No ketchup?

—The soldiers are from the Duke of Wellington's regiment.

—Who was himself a class of an Irishman. Who had more shots fired at him by his own men than were ever fired at him by the French. Cobbett said.

—I bow, dear boy, I bow. His own men must have been bad shots. Under the Rock, though, blanks are normally used, the paper says. But sometimes the stuff is live. And models are positioned as snipers in the shadow.

—Not also alive, let us hope.

—Who cannot shoot nor snipe.

—Nor fight, fuck, fiddle nor bate the drum.

—The soldiers are taught never never to use their weapons if there is the slightest, slightest, teeny-weeniest danger of innocent bystanders being hit. So the chap says in the newspaper.

—I am much impressed. Tell that to the relations of Dan McElhone.

—Indeed, dear boy. The newpaper says that that solicitude for the innocent bystander represents a reversal of normal war training.

—Normal. How profound. There were no bystanders at the Somme. Nor at Stalingrad. Nor in Coventry. Nor in Dresden.

—Also: as training for life in Ulster, the marines land on the Rock from a submarine called Oracle. And climb the Rock on ropes. And rescue the governor and his wife, played by a captain and a nurse, who are being held by Provos on the top of the Rock.

—Tu es petrus.

—That was all done by night so as not to offend the Spaniards.

—Who can't see in the dark. And I dream of white ships and the king of Spain's daughter. Sir Francis Drake wouldn't have given a fart about the Spaniards.

—But, dear boy, you must see that the Brits are on to something here. The grand design. Even the final solution. An Ulster hamlet under every hill. Crossmaglen, par example, under Carntuathal. Keady under Krakatoa. Belfast under Ben Bulben. Derry under Divis. Armagh under Annapurna. Like Ashton-under-Lyme. It is a thought to take with you over the ocean. Get 'em in and keep 'em down.

—Then shall they begin to say to the mountains: Fall upon us. And to the hills: Cover us up.

—Precisely. You took the words out of my mouth. And what with the big bomb coming, and all, it might not be such a bad idea. They tell me now the end will come from a nuclear submarine. And quite by accident. Nobody to blame, nobody to hang, nobody left to hang 'em, no rope, no timber. . . .

—When Cromwell's General Ludlow marched into the stony Burren in the County Clare. . . .

—Not water to drown a man, nor wood to hang him, nor earth to bury him. But Captain Bush of the submarine Simon Bolivar says to me. . . .

—Oh Bush of the Bolivar says to me as he surfaces out of the nuclear sea. . . .

—Nothing to stop any old bold captain, Henry Morgan, letting fly with an SLBM. And once unloosed it cannot be recalled. Nor disarmed. Nor defused. Keep your eyes peeled as you fly over. A monster from the deep may get you in the end. Captain Ahab, sir.

They shake hands.

—All aboard, Mr. Burns says. Have a good trip. We may dance some day on Brooklyn Bridge. A parting gift, dear boy.

He takes a book from the inside pocket of his raincoat.

—As you frequently say: Seneca for Sexagenarians. Here is a new book about that unfortunate man. To bear with you to the New World. Arise now. Follow St. Brendan.

This is the evening, Brendan, O sailor, stand off the mainland, backwater and glimmer, though kirtles be flittered and flesh be sea-salted. Watch while this Ireland, a mirage, grows dimmer. What have you come for? Why cease from faring through paradise islands and indigo water, through vinland and bloomland and caribbean glory? Follow your chart with the smoky sea monsters. Stay with the bright birds where music is pouring balm for the hurt souls, and Judas, repentant, sits for one day on a rock in the ocean. Turn from the ghostland, O great navigator. Lower the oars for a legend of journeys. Scan tossed, empty horizons from pole to equator, for Ireland, time-foundered, that Ireland has lost.

Odd to think that a friend of mine wrote that and a lot more besides.

He unfastens his safety-belt.

Every morning the sun rises and what we had accepted as the world is never the same as it was the day before.

Speak up to me, Seneca, dear boy: Now rivers diminish and disappear, now the ocean flees the coast, mountains rumble and lofty peaks collapse and fall. But why talk of such small things? The vault of this glorious heaven will of itself suddenly burst into flame. . . .

A slim girl sits beside him. Later he may put talk on her. For the moment he has had enough of women. Erin, my country, though sad and forsaken, in dreams I revisit thy sea-beaten shore. . . .

Everything must die, not as a punishment but in obedience to a law. One day our world will no longer exist.

Why should Carmincross be exempt?

Think how often towns in Asia or in Greece have fallen at a single earth tremor, how many villages in Syria or Macedonia have been engulfed, how often this form of disaster has wrought devastations in Cyprus, how often Paphos has tumbled about itself. Time and again we hear the news of the annihilation of a whole city, and how small a fraction of mankind are we who hear such news thus often. So let us face up to the blows of circumstance and be aware that whatever happens is never as serious as rumour makes it out to be.

But nothing had ever happened in Carmincross. Barring the ballad and the joke and the Holy Family boxing club.

How many nuclear submarines are now nosing about down there below?

The privileged lands that possess them do, we are told, possess, all told, one hundred such monsters. A good round number. Forty or so are at sea or in the sea at any one time.

No band of music at the airport played to me to come back to Erin as in another age the band played at Cobh as the liners went westward-ho. But, alas, in a far foreign land I awaken and sigh for the friends who will greet me no more.

When he falls asleep the girl takes the book from his loosening hands and reads in it until he awakens. So she tells him. She is a history student from Trinity and has good Latin but no Greek. Like everything else, as a famous Dublin councillor said, nothing is perfect. They talk about Seneca, and sight the shores and the towers of Amerikay.

His first hostess in Thomas Wolfe's golden city is the decent daughter of a lawyer from Des Moines and her apartment has just been burgled. She lives in a street inhabited mostly by Puerto Ricans.

—But that is not to say, she says, that my Puerto Ricans had a damn thing to do with the burglary.

Persons unknown had made sawdust out of her door on a third-floor landing. Made love to her sewing machine and all the clothes in her closet, including a huge fur coat that in winter weather had always made the good girl look like a grizzly bear with an oddly attractive face. They left in peace, fortunately not in pieces for they were gentle robbers, her television set, an old-fashioned model too heavy to carry away. They left unruffled her travel brochures. She is planning a trip, part business, part vacation, to the monuments of ancient Egypt.

—My Puerto Ricans, she says, are good neighbours. They talk a lot. They sing. They shout. They crowd the doorsteps in the warm weather. They play stickball.

She has joined them at stickball in the street.

—They have, she says, contributed a new dimension to the food stores in the neighbourhood. Now and again they fight. Among themselves. They may even use knives. That's nature to them. They are good neighbours to me. They are courteous to women.

Her burglars have not touched her larder. She feeds her guests on goose. The snow outside is seasonably deep. Far off and shining the golden city rises in the vision of Thomas Wolfe who died there around the corner. The vision is upborne: and sustained as lightly as a cloud. Yet firm and soaring and full of golden light. There is the murmur of the million-footed throng and all the mystery of earth and time is in that sound.

From sea to shining sea.

The burglars have also spared the elaborate chandelier, which the hostess especially prizes. Under its myriad tinkling lights the guests chew goose, munch salad, drink wine. Things could be worse. The flavour of the goose brings back to him the strong tang of the first goose at whose demolition he had ever assisted: a wild goose. He had watched an uncle of his shoot it over Loch a' Bhradain, Salmon Lake, where high in wild heather Tyrone and Fermanagh, unseen, melt into each other. No man could mark that boundary. Not ten miles from Carmincross.

After dinner he thanks and kisses his hostess, shakes hands with the other two guests: a Welshman with a Danish name who takes pictures for television and a tall, blonde, Jewish New Yorker who writes plays. He stumbles through slush to the bar from which he had set out to Stephanie's wedding. He is welcomed. He drinks a brandy alexander. He drinks another. He steps out again through the slush and, with some difficulty, hails a cab to take him to the Edison.

# Last Post

If it is of any comfort to anyone, the four men who sounded REVEILLE were James Joyce, William Butler Yeats, John Henry Newman and Éamon de Valera.

The earnest student of atrocities will detect anachronisms. Some specimens have been moved about in time. And in place. Does it matter?

The expert observations of Liam Robinson, Kevin Myers, Martin Dillon, Tom McGurk, Joe MacAnthony and Sean J. White have been of great help. The Third Man and Mr. Burns, more or less, have been around for a long time.

The Senecan volume is: *Seneca: the Humanist at the Court of Nero,* by Villy Sørensen, translated by W. Glyn Jones (Canongate: 1984).

The passage on St. Brendan was by the novelist, the late Francis MacManus.

NOTHING HAPPENS IN CARMINCROSS
has been set by American-Stratford Graphic Services, Inc., Brattleboro, Vermont, in Baskerville, a fine transitional typeface designed about 1760 by the English printer John Baskerville. A controversial face which originally found more favor on the Continent than in England, Baskerville did not win popular acceptance until its recutting by the Monotype Corporation in 1923. Since then this widely used face has been adapted to use on the Linotype and for photocomposition. A round, open typeface, it is characterized by thin hairlines, slightly bracketed serifs, and generous proportions.

The book has been printed and bound by Haddon Craftsmen, Scranton, Pennsylvania.